The naked i is a collection of fictions by twenty-five writers who in various ways change or challenge our perceptions of the world. They do this by shattering conventional expectations: about time, about 'character', about appearance and reality, about the boundaries between fact and fantasy, about narrative technique (as regards both form and style). *The naked i* is edited and introduced by Frederick R. Karl and Leo Hamalian, two American authorities on modern fiction.

FICTIONS FOR THE SEVENTIES

the naked i

edited by Frederick R. Karl
and Leo Hamalian

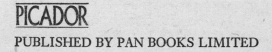

PICADOR
PUBLISHED BY PAN BOOKS LIMITED

First British edition published in Picador by
PAN BOOKS LTD, 33 TOTHILL STREET, LONDON, SW1
© Fawcett Publications, Inc, 1971
Printed in Great Britain by
Cox & Wyman Ltd, London, Reading and Fakenham

ISBN 0 330 23347 5

CONTENTS

ACKNOWLEDGEMENTS AND COPYRIGHT NOTICES

the naked i

Introduction

Today the creative writer himself appears to be reviving the idea that fiction is another form of the lie that disguises reality. And today the serious critic elaborates such morbid theories of fictional crisis that the practising writer who listens to him could well fall into silence. If this is the modern condition, is there any justification, then, for still one more collection of contemporary fiction and still one more critical introduction?

Like the reader who buys this book, the editors will have to take the risk of being burned by their own scepticism. Our purpose here, however, is not to probe relentlessly for a metaphysical order of meaning but simply to map out certain roads that contemporary short fiction appears to be following. Yet, even as we try to simplify, we must note that modern fiction is complex; and modernist complexity, which has achieved the status of historical necessity, cannot be understood except against the backdrop of its historical precedents.

Until very recently, in modern American and European fiction there was still a common public language and, more important, a common mode of perception that almost any writer of fiction could employ with some assurance. Such a language and such a mode assumed that both writer and reader understood certain common symbols and tones. Also, the possible range of fiction was wide, for the behavioural scientists had not yet pre-empted large swaths of human experience from the domain of fiction. The dramatizing and guiding of human sympathies were regarded as something very fundamental to fictional activity – a kind of therapeutic encounter, as it were, for the reader. Nor was fiction pinned down to a few basic epistemological questions; its philosophic reach matched the spectrum of inquiries commonly investigated by philosophy itself.

Such fiction involved the conventions and attitudes principally of a realistic mode, what we still see commonly practised in much 'Third World' fiction. New currents, however, have been forming in the contemporary European and American short story. There is an obsession with linguistic structure rather than with symbolic meanings. Realism of character and even location has been largely abandoned, and, in their place, the hallucinatory theme, the dreamlike setting, and the driven, self-contained narrator have become dominant. Traditional plot and sequence have become less significant than before. Suspended between the choice of pure history and pure fiction, the contemporary writer chooses fiction. With this option, the writer is bound to a more acute awareness of himself in the act of creating. The external becomes diminished, and the writer moves away from objective reality, away from history, away from plot, away from defined character, until the subjective perception of the narrator is the only guaranteed fact in the fiction.

The nature of the world beyond the eye of the observer depends upon his perception of it. There is no way of knowing the nature of Nature, human or otherwise; there is no neutral witness who can be presumed to have truth. And there are no other means of arriving at such a blessed vision, short of a leap into faith. Only the subjective eye can confer value on what is perceived and on how it is perceived. Perhaps that 'subjective eye' is the modern leap into faith.

Most of this is generally comprehensible to a generation raised in the shadow of Heisenberg's Theory of Indeterminacy – or 'Uncertainty Principle' – which implies a breakdown of the law of cause and effect. But the writers in this volume can also be related to certain literary antecedents and understood in those terms, as well. When Dostoevsky wrote, 'If God is not alive, then everything is possible', he was echoing (not approving) Nietzsche's lyrical declaration that 'God is dead'. This insight meant to those who accepted it the end of omniscience – omniscience of any kind, superhuman (religious) or subhuman (scientific). Man stood alone, responsible for his own fate in a universe that was hostile or benign or neither, depending on the eye of the viewer.

With objectivity so challenged on the metaphysical levels, there were bound to be implications for fiction, which has always been a mirror of the metaphysical. For certain writers it meant an end to the omniscient narrator, the third-person teller of tales who either put himself above his characters or merged with them. Soon the narrator became his own man who resented such intrusions. In a novel by Miguel de Unamuno, the Spanish philosopher, the narrator challenged his creator and declared his independence of him. The literary revolution was on.

In place of the all-knowing narrator rooted in a fixed world, there arose the central intelligence of Henry James, Joseph Conrad, and the Melville of *Moby Dick*. There emerged a type of character who acted like a telephone exchange that accepted all messages from the outside world as they came to him and who in turn sent out to the reader only what he could perceive and understand. This central intelligence often coincided with the author himself, so that, as a consequence, the characters did not always appear to have a maximum life of their own. For one, Joyce withdrew from his fiction until he stood completely outside it, like Flaubert coolly paring his fingernails, while the action spun on. A different kind of literary intelligence was at work, and a new kind of fiction was forming.

The first-person narrative returned to popularity, but with a distinction. Previously the 'I' of the story had been either a minor character who would repeat at second hand a narrative he had heard or an observer who merely described the events and people passing before his eyes. He was usually objective, clear-sighted, gifted with a sense of order, and reasonably reliable as a reporter on the world (Huck Finn, Ishmael, for example). Although in such stories as Poe's 'The Tell-Tale Heart' and Dostoevsky's *Notes from Underground* the bizarre, disorganized, and morbid narrator prefigures techniques to come, these works are anomalies and had rather little influence in their time.

But in recent fiction the action, the events, the world itself are reported through the single eye of the narrator, without correction from the objective data of things otherwise perceived and without coercion from the omniscient author. The 'I' is likely to be the central character as well as the narrator. If the 'I' is a drug addict, the world is seen through the sensibility of a drug addict who is his own hero (or villain). Things are perceived as authentically as he would see them, not as a 'straight' narrator would see a drug addict seeing the world. If the 'I' is an imbecile, the world is taken in and described as it might appear to him, without the intervening intelligence of the author. Joyce's success with this technique in the third section of *Ulysses* and Faulkner's in the first section of *The Sound and the Fury* exerted enormous influence on the contemporary short story. As a liberating force, the legacy of Poe, Dostoevsky, Joyce, Faulkner, Conrad, and, in variant form, of Franz Kafka has been so completely absorbed by the modern writer that one might say it is now almost in the process of being liquidated.

The loneliness of man in the existentially styled universe is thus reflected in the fiction of his age. In this sense, one might assert that there is a metaphysical order or meaning behind the historical, sequential development of fiction. It has been argued, however, that the limit of individual experience reduces the story's field of vision and that this reduction does not allow the narrator to tell us what we may want to know about the responses of the other characters in the story. To a degree this is truc. The consequence of a subjective technique is a subjective view that stops short at the wall of the skin. But this technique at its best creates a sense of unity and a felt continuum that other techniques rarely achieve.

This is not to suggest that there is continuity in most of these stories. On the contrary, their forms have evolved from sudden and unexpected turns or twists, from games, parody, self-parody, from artifice of every type. Discontinuity or the disconnected narrative is often, paradoxically, a technique for creating coherence. The failure of the narrator to discover or to create unity out of his experience might actually unify a particular story. As the critic Richard Kostelanetz puts it, 'Formal discontinuity as a perceptual mode duplicates both the omniattention that we experience in our ordinary lives, as well as the marijuana and psychedelic experience that is now more prevalent than a decade ago.' By the same token, if a story does not cohere in linear fashion (as in Plath, Cortázar, LeRoi Jones), that by itself does not mean that the story lacks coherence.

The Swiss-French film director, Jean-Luc Godard, has said, 'Narrative has a beginning, middle, and an end, but not necessarily in that order'; and writers like Donald Barthelme, John Barth, and Jorge Luis Borges illustrate the point. In fact, their fictions, like Kafka's 'A Country Doctor', one of the earliest and best examples of discontinuity with design, must be read several times before they provide pleasure. They challenge us to pick up coherences and juxtapositions that we may have failed to perceive in the first reading – just as we sometimes miss the meaning of a raw experience until we run it backwards through our heads again. Often the reader is confronted with a work the meaning and value of which he must determine by himself, since the very mode of narration prohibits direct interpretation by the author or frequent discursive interpolation.

Even the accumulation of external details and images, or traditional 'symbols', is absent. The reader receives almost no assistance from the author (much as existential man cannot depend upon the support of tradition), and the effect of such independence on the reader accustomed to having the author spell out his purpose can be dizzying. In other words, the contemporary writer assumes we will read unfamiliar fiction with expectations entirely different from those that we have learned from traditional literature. We must, he insists, learn anew not to retreat from the unfamiliar.

The reader should also watch for the effect that content and point of view have upon form itself. For the moment we might define form as the way words are organized in sentences and paragraphs and the way these larger units are organized in a story. To his surprise the reader will find that many of these stories remain traditional and even conservative in form and that they contain little which can be considered 'experimental' in structure. This realism is, as we have indicated, especially true of black and 'Third World' writers, who perhaps have lived with a more traditional literature and a more traditional culture. For them it is tempting to slip into shapes already on hand.

Nevertheless, several of the stories from each world are experimental; their form, clearly, has been modified to accommodate the purely personal flow of perception. Sometimes the writer shatters the syntax, fractures the flow of perception, breaks up the surface in any number of ways in an attempt to reflect accurately the inward state of being or the very process of perception itself. William Burroughs does this in the novel and LeRoi Jones in the short story. Robert Coover also comes close to this technique but uses, so to speak, a wide-angle lens and keeps running the scene through the mind like a film director shooting take after take. His point of view, like those of Dylan Thomas and Jerzy Kosinski, might be called 'third-person subjective'. The effect is of pseudo-omniscience, but in this mode there is no way of knowing what ultimately happened: there is no one in the story who presumes to perceive objectively, without interference from his introjected self.

In many of these stories the content and the form of narration fuse and yield the kind of authenticity of mode that is consistent with the existentialist's demand for 'good faith'. Indeed, sincerity replaces the search for truth, a quest characteristic of an earlier fiction – of Gide, Mann, Camus, Hemingway. It is in this sense that many contemporary writers seem unconcerned with the possibility that their fiction may be another form of lie. They concede that everything in one sense is a lie, for we cannot even be certain that what we are looking at really resembles what we appear to see. It is a matter of whether we will have, let us say, 'honest' lies (deeply felt) or 'dishonest' lies (unfelt).

Perhaps the best the contemporary writer can do is to reduce the magnitude of the lie by rendering the perception of his narrator as precisely and as authentically as possible. Such authenticity is achieved by the author's fidelity to the precise word or phrase, by his avoidance of cliché, and by his attention to the rhythms of common speech. If the reader is persuaded that 'this or that' is the way such and such a person would indeed perceive, then 'this or that' becomes the truth of the situation. God, if He were not dead, might put to the narrator the kind of questions He once put to Job. But today God would have to accept the subjective truth of the narrator's feelings; the truth of religion belongs in church, the truth of science belongs in the laboratory. The truth about human feeling, about the human condition, must be found in man's infinite modes of perception. It is this that the writers for the seventies reveal to us.

Not all authors, however, express fictional ideas through fiction. For this reason, we have included selections from two widely differing writers, Ken Kesey and Norman O. Brown, whose nonfiction here is an attempt to arrive at fictional intensity.

In a sense, they are pursuing the same objectives as many of the other authors in the book, who are themselves attempting to gain intensity of feeling and response through whatever means they can command. Known chiefly as a novelist, Kesey uses his 'Letters to Larry McMurtry', a Texas writer, as a way of trying out creative ideas in a traditionally non-creative form. While we have always thought of the letter as a mode for direct communication, Kesey uses the form to convey a short, ambiguous fiction.

Norman O. Brown, a classicist and philosopher, is seeking the limits or frontiers of Love and Body (in the selection from *Love's Body*). Yet he wishes to use traditional material, that is, relying on the great writers of the past in history, psychology, philosophy, and anthropology. Through a combination of aphorism, quotation, and exegesis, Brown hopes to transform scholarly fields of study into spiritual excursions, to put Love, Soul, Spirit into Intellect. And towards that end, he must find a new method, since fiction by itself lacks historical substance and history by itself lacks creativity.

As we noted above, these two writers are hardly isolated. A majority of the writers in this collection are trying to communicate the un-mentionable and are seeking, as well, to reach beyond frontiers and boundaries in their fiction. We need name only Borges, Cortázar, Bar-thelme, Jones, Plath, Barth, Kosinski, Kafka. In like fashion, many novelists such as William Burroughs, Thomas Pynchon, and John Hawkes, are pursuing the 'naked I' through inventive forms so, perhaps, one day we may see a complete breakdown of the barriers between fiction and nonfiction. We find numerous precedents in our political and social lives for this breakdown and our present literature gives us reason to believe that, in the future, history, certain branches of psychology, anthropology, philosophy, and fiction will merge one with the other in some subjective, apocalyptic vision of man and his universe.

Frederick R. Karl and Leo Hamalian

discontinuity with design
an early example

FRANZ KAFKA was born in Prague in 1883, and he died in 1924. He is known for the intense visionary character of his novels, stories, parables, and sketches, all written in German. Less than one-quarter of his writing consists of completed works. The most famous of his works are the unfinished novels *The Trial*, *The Castle* and *Amerika*, and the short stories collected under the title *The Penal Colony*.

a country doctor

FRANZ KAFKA

I was in great perplexity: I had to start on an urgent journey; a seriously ill patient was waiting for me in a village ten miles off; a thick blizzard of snow filled all the wide spaces between him and me; I had a gig, a light gig with big wheels, exactly right for our country roads; muffled in furs, my bag of instruments in my hand, I was in the courtyard all ready for the journey; but there was no horse to be had, no horse. My own horse had died in the night, worn out by the fatigues of this icy winter; my servant girl was now running round the village trying to borrow a horse; but it was hopeless, I knew it, and I stood there forlornly, with the snow gathering more and more thickly upon me, more and more unable to move. In the gateway the girl appeared, alone, and waved the lantern; of course, who would lend a horse at this time for such a journey? I strode through the courtyard once more; I could see no way out; in my confused distress I kicked at the dilapidated door of the year-long uninhabited pigsty. It flew open and flapped to and fro on its hinges. A steam and smell as of horses came out from it. A dim stable lantern was swinging inside from a rope. A man, crouching on his hams in that low space, showed an open blue-eyed face. 'Shall I yoke up?' he asked, crawling out on all fours. I did not know what to say and merely stooped down to see what else was in the sty. The servant girl was standing beside me. 'You never know what you're going to find in your own house,' she said, and we both laughed. 'Hey there, Brother, hey there, Sister!' called the groom, and two horses, enormous creatures with powerful flanks, one after the other, their legs tucked close to their bodies, each well-shaped head lowered like a camel's, by sheer strength of buttocking squeezed out through the door hole which they filled entirely. But at once they were standing up, their legs long and their bodies steaming thickly. 'Give him a hand,' I said, and the willing girl hurried to help the groom with the harnessing. Yet hardly was she beside him when the groom clipped hold of her and pushed his face against hers. She screamed and fled back to me; on her cheek stood out in red the marks of two rows of teeth. 'You brute,' I yelled in fury, 'do you want a whipping?' but in the same moment reflected that the man was a stranger; that I did not know where he came from, and that of his own free will he was helping me out when everyone else had failed me. As if he knew my thoughts he took no offence at my threat but, still busied with the horses, only turned round once towards me. 'Get in,' he said then, and indeed everything was ready. A magnificent pair of horses, I observed, such as I had never sat behind, and I climbed in happily. 'But I'll drive, you don't know the way,' I said. 'Of course,' said he, 'I'm not coming with you anyway, I'm staying with Rose.' 'No,' shrieked Rose, fleeing into the house with a justified presentiment that her fate was inescapable: I heard the door chain rattle as she put it up; I heard the key turn in the lock; I could see, moreover, how she put out the lights in the entrance hall and in further flight all through the rooms to keep herself from being discovered. 'You're coming with me,' I said to the groom, 'or I won't go, urgent as my journey is. I'm not thinking of paying for it by handing the girl over to you.' 'Gee up!' he said; clapped his hands; the gig whirled off like a log in a freshet; I could just hear the door of my house splitting and bursting as the groom charged at it, and then I was deafened and blinded by a storming rush that steadily buffeted all my senses. But this only for a moment, since, as if my patient's farmyard had opened out just before my courtyard gate, I was already there; the horses had come quietly to a standstill; the blizzard had stopped; moonlight all around; my patient's parents hurried out of the house, his sister behind them; I was almost lifted out of the gig; from their confused ejaculations I gathered not a word; in the sickroom the air was almost unbreathable; the neglected stove was smoking; I wanted to push open a window; but first I had to look at my patient. Gaunt, without any fever, not cold, not warm, with vacant eyes, without a shirt, the youngster heaved himself up from under the feather bedding, threw his arms round my neck, and whispered in my ear: 'Doctor, let me die.' I glanced round the room; no one had heard it; the parents were leaning forward in silence waiting for my verdict; the sister had set a chair for my handbag; I opened the bag and hunted among my instruments; the boy kept clutching at me from his bed to remind me of his entreaty; I picked up a pair of tweezers, examined them in the candlelight and laid them down again. 'Yes,' I thought blasphemously, 'in cases like this the gods are helpful, send the missing horse, add to it a second because of the urgency, and to crown everything bestow even a groom—' And only now did I remember Rose again; what was I to do, how could I rescue her, how could I pull her away from under that groom at ten miles' distance, with a team of horses I couldn't control. These horses, now, they had somehow slipped the reins loose, pushed the windows open from outside, I did not know how; each of them had stuck a head in at a window and, quite unmoved by the startled cries of the family, stood eyeing the patient. 'Better go back at once,' I thought, as if the horses were summoning me to the return journey, yet I permitted the patient's sister, who fancied that I was dazed by the heat, to take my fur coat from me. A glass of rum was poured out for me, the old man clapped me on the shoulder, a familiarity justified by this offer of his treasure. I shook my head; in the narrow confines of the old man's thoughts I felt ill; that was my only reason for refusing the drink. The mother stood by the bedside and cajoled me towards it; I yielded, and while one of the horses whinnied loudly to the ceiling, laid my head to the boy's breast, which shivered under my wet beard. I confirmed what I already knew; the boy was quite sound, something a little wrong with his circulation, saturated with coffee by his solicitous mother, but sound and best turned out of bed with one shove. I am no world reformer and so I let him lie. I was the district doctor and did my duty to the uttermost, to the point where it became almost too much. I was badly paid and yet generous and helpful to the poor. I had still to see that Rose was all right, and then the boy might have his way, and I wanted to die too. What was I doing there in that endless winter! My horse was dead, and not a single person in the village would lend me another. I had to get my team out of the pigsty; if they hadn't chanced to be horses I should have had to travel with swine. That was how it was. And I nodded to the family. They knew nothing about it and, had they known, would not have believed it. To write prescriptions is easy, but to come to an understanding with people is hard. Well, this should be the end of my visit, I had once more been called out needlessly, I was used to that, the whole district made my life a torment with my night bell, but that I should have to sacrifice Rose this time as well, the pretty girl who had lived in my house for years almost without my noticing her – that sacrifice was too much to ask, and I had somehow to get it reasoned out in my head with the help of what craft I could muster, in order not to let fly at this family, which with the best will in the world could not restore Rose to me. But as I shut my bag and put an arm out for my fur coat, the family meanwhile standing together, the father sniffing at the glass of rum in his hand, the mother, apparently disappointed in me – why, what do people expect? – biting her lips with tears in her eyes, the sister fluttering a blood-soaked towel, I was somehow ready to admit conditionally that the boy might be ill after all. I went towards him, he welcomed me smiling as if I were bringing him the most nourishing invalid broth – ah, now both horses were whinnying together; the noise, I suppose, was ordained by heaven to assist my examination of the patient – and this time I discovered that the boy was indeed ill. In his right side, near the hip, was an open wound as big as the palm of my hand. Rose red, in many variations of shade, dark in the hollows, lighter at the edges, softly granulated, with irregular clots of blood, open as a surface mine to the daylight. That was how it looked from a distance. But on a closer inspection there was another complication. I could not help a low whistle of surprise. Worms, as thick and as long as my little finger, themselves rose red and blood-spotted as well, were wriggling from their fastness in the interior of the wound towards the light, with small white heads and many little legs. Poor boy, you were past helping. I had discovered your great wound; this blossom in your side was destroying you. The family was pleased; they saw me busying myself; the sister told the mother, the mother the father, the father told several guests who were coming in, through the moonlight at the open door, walking on tiptoe, keeping their balance with out-stretched arms. 'Will you save me?' whispered the boy with a sob, quite blinded by the life within his wound. That is what people are like in my district. Always expecting the impossible from the doctor. They have lost their ancient beliefs; the parson sits at home and unravels his vest-ments, one after another; but the doctor is supposed to be omnipotent with his merciful surgeon's hand. Well, as it pleases them; I have not thrust my services on them; if they misuse me for sacred ends, I let that happen to me too; what better do I want, old country doctor that I am, bereft of my servant girl! And so they came, the family and the village elders, and stripped my clothes off me; a school choir with the teacher at the head of it stood before the house and sang these words to an utterly simple tune:

> Strip his clothes off, then he'll heal us,
> If he doesn't, kill him dead!
> Only a doctor, only a doctor.

Then my clothes were off and I looked at the people quietly, my fingers in my beard and my head cocked to one side. I was altogether composed and equal to the situation and remained so, although it was no help to me, since they now took me by the head and feet and carried me to the bed. They laid me down in it next to the wall, on the side of the wound. Then they all left the room; the door was shut; the singing stopped; clouds covered the moon; the bedding was warm around me; the horses' heads in the open windows wavered like shadows. 'Do you know,' said a voice in my ear, 'I have very little confidence in you. Why, you were only blown in here, you didn't come on your own feet. Instead of helping me, you're cramping me on my deathbed. What I'd like best is to scratch your eyes out.' 'Right,' I said, 'it is a shame. And yet I am a doctor. What am I to do? Believe me, it is not too easy for me either.' 'Am I supposed to be content with this apology? Oh, I must be, I can't help it. I always have to put up with things. A fine wound is all I brought into the world; that was my sole endowment.' 'My young friend,' said I, 'your mistake is: you have not a wide enough view. I have been in all the sickrooms, far and wide, and I tell you: your wound is not so bad. Done in a tight corner with two strokes of the axe. Many a one proffers his side and can hardly hear the axe in the forest, far less that it is coming nearer to him.' 'Is that really so, or are you deluding me in my fever?' 'It is really so, take the word of honour of an official doctor.' And he took it and lay still. But now it was time for me to think of escaping. The horses were still standing faithfully in their places. My clothes, my fur coat, my bag were quickly collected; I didn't want to waste time dressing; if the horses raced home as they had come, I should only be springing, as it were, out of this bed into my own. Obediently a horse backed away from the window; I threw my bundle into the gig; the fur coat missed its mark and was caught on a hook only by the sleeve. Good enough. I swung myself onto the horse. With the reins loosely trailing, one horse barely fastened to the other, the gig swaying behind, my fur coat last of all in the snow. 'Gee up!' I said, but there was no galloping; slowly, like old men, we crawled through the snowy wastes; a long time echoed behind us the new but faulty song of the children:

> O be joyful, all you patients,
> The doctor's laid in bed beside you!

Never shall I reach home at this rate; my flourishing practice is done for; my successor is robbing me, but in vain, for he cannot take my place; in my house the disgusting groom is raging; Rose is his victim; I do not want to think about it any more. Naked, exposed to the frost of this most unhappy of ages, with an earthly vehicle, unearthly horses, old man that I am, I wander astray. My fur coat is hanging from the back of the gig, but I cannot reach it, and none of my limber pack of patients lifts a finger. Betrayed! Betrayed! A false alarm on the night bell once answered — it cannot be made good, not ever.

an earlier generation

the lottery in babylon

JORGE LUIS BORGES

Like all men in Babylon, I have been proconsul; like all, a slave. I have also known omnipotence, opprobrium, imprisonment. Look: the index finger on my right hand is missing. Look: through the rip in my cape you can see a vermilion tattoo on my stomach. It is the second symbol, Beth. This letter, on nights when the moon is full, gives me power over men whose mark is Gimmel, but it subordinates me to the men of Aleph, who on moonless nights owe obedience to those marked with Gimmel. In the half-light of dawn, in a cellar, I have cut the jugular vein of sacred bulls before a black stone. During a lunar year I have been declared invisible. I shouted and they did not answer me; I stole bread and they did not behead me. I have known what the Greeks do not know, incertitude. In a bronze chamber, before the silent handkerchief of the strangler, hope has been faithful to me, as has panic in the river of pleasure. Heraclides Ponticus tells with amazement that Pythagoras remembered having been Pyrrhus and before that Euphorbus and before that some other mortal. In order to remember similar vicissitudes I do not need to have recourse to death or even to deception.

I owe this almost atrocious variety to an institution which other republics do not know or which operates in them in an imperfect and secret manner: the lottery. I have not looked into its history; I know that the wise men cannot agree. I know of its powerful purposes what a man who is not versed in astrology can know about the moon. I come from a dizzy land where the lottery is the basis of reality. Until today I have thought as little about it as I have about the conduct of indecipherable divinities or about my heart. Now, far from Babylon and its beloved customs, I think with a certain amount of amazement about the lottery and about the blasphemous conjectures which veiled men murmur in the twilight.

My father used to say that formerly – a matter of centuries, of years? – the lottery in Babylon was a game of plebeian character. He recounted (I don't know whether rightly) that barbers sold, in exchange for copper coins, squares of bone or of parchment adorned with symbols. In broad daylight a drawing took place. Those who won received silver coins without any other test of luck. The system was elementary, as you can see.

Naturally these 'lotteries' failed. Their moral virtue was nil. They were not directed at all of man's faculties, but only at hope. In the face of public indifference, the merchants who founded these venal lotteries began to lose money. Someone tried a reform: the interpolation of a few unfavourable tickets in the list of favourable numbers. By means of this reform, the buyers of numbered squares ran the double risk of winning a sum and of paying a fine that could be considerable. This slight danger (for every thirty favourable numbers there was one unlucky one) awoke, as is natural, the interest of the public. The Babylonians threw themselves into the game. Those who did not acquire chances were considered pusillanimous, cowardly. In time, that justified disdain was doubled. Those who did not play were scorned, but also the losers who paid the fine were scorned. The Company (as it came to be known then) had to take care of the winners, who could not cash in their prizes if almost the total amount of the fines was unpaid. It started a lawsuit against the losers. The judge condemned them to pay the original fine and costs or spend several days in jail. All chose jail in order to defraud the Company. The bravado of a few is the source of the omnipotence of the Company and of its metaphysical and ecclesiastical power.

A little while afterwards the lottery lists omitted the amounts of fines and limited themselves to publishing the days of imprisonment that each unfavourable number indicated. That laconic spirit, almost unnoticed at the time, was of capital importance. *It was the first appearance in the lottery of non-monetary elements.* The success was tremendous. Urged by the clientele, the Company was obliged to increase the unfavourable numbers.

Everyone knows that the people of Babylon are fond of logic and even of symmetry. It was illogical for the lucky numbers to be computed in round coins and the unlucky ones in days and nights of imprisonment. Some moralists reasoned that the possession of money does not always determine happiness and that other forms of happiness are perhaps more direct.

Another concern swept the quarters of the poorer classes. The members of the college of priests multiplied their stakes and enjoyed all the vicissitudes of terror and hope; the poor (with reasonable or unavoidable envy) knew that they were excluded from that notoriously delicious rhythm. The just desire that all, rich and poor, should participate equally in the lottery inspired an indignant agitation, the memory of which the years have not erased. Some obstinate people did not understand (or pretended not to understand) that it was a question of a new order, or a necessary historical stage. A slave stole a crimson ticket, which in the drawing credited him with the burning of his tongue. The legal code fixed that same penalty for the one who stole a ticket. Some Babylonians argued that he deserved the burning irons in his status of a thief; others, generously, that the executioner should apply it to him because chance had determined it that way. There were disturbances, there were lamentable drawings of blood, but the masses of Babylon finally imposed their will against the opposition of the rich. The people achieved amply its generous purposes. In the first place, it caused the Company to accept total power. (That unification was necessary, given the vastness and complexity of the new operations.) In the second place, it made the lottery secret, free and general. The mercenary sale of chances was abolished. Once initiated in the mysteries of Baal, every free man automatically participated in the sacred drawings, which took place in the labryinths of the god every sixty nights and which determined his destiny until the next drawing. The consequences were incalculable. A fortunate play could bring about his promotion to the council of wise men or the imprisonment of an enemy (public or private) or finding, in the peaceful darkness of his room, the woman who begins to excite him and whom he never expected to see again. A bad play: mutilation, different kinds of infamy, death. At times one single fact – the vulgar murder of C, the mysterious apotheosis of B – was the happy solution of thirty or forty drawings. To combine the plays was difficult, but one must remember that the individuals of the Company were (and are) omnipotent and astute. In many cases the knowledge that certain happinesses were the simple product of chance would have diminished their virtue. To avoid that obstacle, the agents of the Company made use of the power of suggestion and magic. Their steps, their manoeuvrings, were secret. To find out about the intimate hopes and terrors of each individual, they had astrologists and spies. There were certain stone lions, there was a sacred latrine called Qaphqa, there were fissures in a dusty aqueduct which, according to general opinion, led to the Company; malignant or benevolent persons deposited information in these places. An alphabetical file collected these items of varying truthfulness.

Incredibly, there were complaints. The Company, with its usual discretion, did not answer directly. It preferred to scrawl in the rubbish of a mask factory a brief statement which now figures in the sacred scriptures. This doctrinal item observed that the lottery is an interpolation of chance in the order of the world and that to accept errors is not to contradict chance: it is to corroborate it. It likewise observed that those lions and that sacred receptacle, although not disavowed by the Company (which did not abandon the right to consult them), functioned without official guarantee.

This declaration pacified the public's restlessness. It also produced other effects, perhaps unforeseen by its writer. It deeply modified the spirit and the operations of the Company. I don't have much time left; they tell us that the ship is about to weigh anchor. But I shall try to explain it.

However unlikely it might seem, no one had tried out before then a general theory of chance. Babylonians are not very speculative. They revere the judgements of fate, they deliver to them their lives, their hopes, their panic, but it does not occur to them to investigate fate's labyrinthine laws nor the gyratory spheres which reveal it. Nevertheless, the unofficial declaration that I have mentioned inspired many discussions of judicial-mathematical character. From some one of them the following conjecture was born: If the lottery is an intensification of chance, a periodical infusion of chaos in the cosmos, would it not be right for chance to intervene in all stages of the drawing and not in one alone? Is it not ridiculous for chance to dictate someone's death and have the circumstances of that death — secrecy, publicity, the fixed time of an hour or a century — not subject to chance? These just scruples finally caused a considerable reform, whose complexities (aggravated by centuries' practice) only a few specialists understand, but which I shall try to summarize, at least in a symbolic way.

Let us imagine a first drawing, which decrees the death of a man. For its fulfilment one proceeds to another drawing, which proposes (let us say) nine possible executors. Of these executors, four can initiate a third drawing which will tell the name of the executioner, two can replace the adverse order with a fortunate one (finding a treasure, let us say), another will intensify the death penalty (that is, will make it infamous or enrich it with tortures), others can refuse to fulfil it. This is the symbolic scheme. In reality *the number of drawings is infinite*. No decision is final, all branch into others. Ignorant people suppose that infinite drawings require an infinite time; actually it is sufficient for time to be infinitely subdivisible, as the famous parable of the contest with the tortoise teaches. This infinity harmonizes admirably with the sinuous members of Chance and with the Celestial Archetype of the Lottery, which the Platonists adore. Some warped echo of our rites seems to have resounded on the Tiber: Ellus Lampridius, in the *Life of Antoninus Heliogabalus*, tells that this emperor wrote on shells the lots that were destined for his guests, so that one received ten pounds of gold and another ten flies, ten dormice, ten bears. It is permissible to recall that Heliogabalus was brought up in Asia Minor, among the priests of the eponymous god.

There are also impersonal drawings, with an indefinite purpose. One decrees that a sapphire of Taprobana be thrown into the waters of the Euphrates; another, that a bird be released from the roof of a tower; another, that each century there be withdrawn (or added) a grain of sand from the innumerable ones on the beach. The consequences are, at times, terrible.

Under the beneficent influence of the Company, our customs are saturated with chance. The buyer of a dozen amphoras of Damascene wine will not be surprised if one of them contains a talisman or a snake. The scribe who writes a contract almost never fails to introduce some erroneous information. I myself, in this hasty declaration, have falsified some splendour, some atrocity. Perhaps, also, some mysterious monotony . . . Our historians, who are the most penetrating on the globe, have invented a method to correct chance. It is well known that the operations of this method are (in general) reliable, although naturally, they are not divulged without some portion of deceit. Furthermore, there is nothing so contaminated with fiction as the history of the Company. A paleographic document, exhumed in a temple, can be the result of yesterday's lottery or of an age-old lottery. No book is published without some discrepancy in each one of the copies. Scribes take a secret oath to omit, to interpolate, to change. The indirect lie is also cultivated.

The Company, with divine modesty, avoids all publicity. Its agents, as is natural, are secret. The orders which it issues continually (perhaps incessantly) do not differ from those lavished by impostors. Moreover, who can brag about being a mere impostor? The drunkard who improvises an absurd order, the dreamer who awakens suddenly and strangles the woman who sleeps at his side, do they not execute, perhaps, a secret decision of the Company? That silent functioning, comparable to God's, gives rise to all sorts of conjectures. One abominably insinuates that the Company has not existed for centuries and that the sacred disorder of our lives is purely hereditary, traditional. Another judges it eternal and teaches that it will last until the last night, when the last god annihilates the world. Another declares that the Company is omnipotent, but that it only has influence in tiny things: in a bird's call, in the shadings of rust and of dust, in the half dreams of dawn. Another, in the words of masked heresiarchs, *that it has never existed and will not exist.* Another, no less vile, reasons that it is indifferent to affirm or deny the reality of the shadowy corporation, because Babylon is nothing else than an infinite game of chance.

JULIO CORTÁZAR, an Argentine, was born in Brussels, Belgium, in 1914 and has lived most of his adult life in Paris. In the 1950s he published, in Spanish, several collections of stories, including *Bestario*, *Final del Juego*, and *Las Armas Secretas*. The second of these collections was translated and published in English as *End of the Game, and Other Stories,* from which 'Blow-Up' is taken.

blow-up

JULIO CORTÁZAR

It'll never be known how this has to be told, in the first person or in the second, using the third person plural or continually inventing modes that will serve for nothing. If one might say: I will see the moon rose, or: we hurt me at the back of my eyes, and especially: you the blonde woman was the clouds that race before my your his our yours their faces. What the hell.

Seated ready to tell it, if one might go to drink a bock over there, and the typewriter continue by itself (because I use the machine), that would be perfection. And that's not just a manner of speaking. Perfection, yes, because here is the aperture which must be counted also as a machine (of another sort, a Contax 1.1.2), and it is possible that one machine may know more about another machine than I, you, she – the blonde – and the clouds. But I have the dumb luck to know that if I go this Remington will sit turned to stone on top of the table with the air of being twice as quiet that mobile things have when they are not moving. So, I have to write. One of us all has to write, if this is going to get told. Better that it be me who am dead, for I'm less compromised than the

rest; I who see only the clouds and can think without being distracted,
write without being distracted (there goes another, with a grey edge),
and remember without being distracted, I who am dead (and I'm alive,
I'm not trying to fool anybody, you'll see when we get to the moment,
because I have to begin some way and I've begun with this period, the
last one back, the one at the beginning, which in the end is the best of
the periods when you want to tell something).

All of a sudden I wonder why I have to tell this, but if one begins to
wonder why he does all he does do, if one wonders why he accepts an
invitation to lunch (now a pigeon's flying by and it seems to me a
sparrow), or why when someone has told us a good joke immediately
there starts up something like a tickling in the stomach and we are not
at peace until we've gone into the office across the hall and told the joke
over again; then it feels good immediately, one is fine, happy, and can
get back to work. For I imagine that no one has explained this, that
really the best thing is to put aside all decorum and tell it, because, after
all's done, nobody is ashamed of breathing or of putting on his shoes;
they're things that you do, and when something weird happens, when
you find a spider in your shoe or if you take a breath and feel like a
broken window, then you have to tell what's happening, tell it to the
guys at the office or to the doctor. Oh, doctor, every time I take a breath
. . . Always tell it, always get rid of that tickle in the stomach that
bothers you.

And now that we're finally going to tell it, let's put things a little bit
in order, we'd be walking down the staircase in this house as far as
Sunday, November 7th, just a month back. One goes down five floors
and stands then in the Sunday in the sun one would not have suspected
of Paris in November, with a large appetite to walk around, to see
things, to take photos (because we were photographers, I'm a photographer). I know that the most difficult thing is going to be finding a way to
tell it, and I'm not afraid of repeating myself. It's going to be difficult
because nobody really knows who it is telling it, if I am I or what actually
occurred or what I'm seeing (clouds, and once in a while a pigeon), or
if, simply, I'm telling a truth which is only my truth, and then is the truth
only for my stomach, for this impulse to go running out and to finish
up in some manner with, this, whatever it is.

We're going to tell it slowly, what happens in the middle of what I'm
writing is coming already. If they replace me, if, so soon, I don't know
what to say, if the clouds stop coming and something else starts (because it's impossible that this keep coming, clouds passing continually
and occasionally a pigeon), if something out of all this . . . And after the
'if' what am I going to put if I'm going to close the sentence structure
correctly? But if I begin to ask questions, I'll never tell anything, maybe

to tell would be like an answer, at least for someone who's reading it.

Roberto Michel, French-Chilean, translator and in his spare time an amateur photographer, left number 11, rue Monsieur-le-Prince Sunday, November 7th of the current year (now there're two small ones passing, with silver linings). He had spent three weeks working on the French version of a treatise on challenges and appeals by José Norberto Allende, professor at the University of Santiago. It's rare that there's wind in Paris, and even less seldom a wind like this that swirled around corners and rose up to whip at old wooden venetian blinds behind which astonished ladies commented variously on how unreliable the weather had been these last few years. But the sun was out also, riding the wind and friend of the cats, so there was nothing that would keep me from taking a walk along the docks of the Seine and taking photos of the Conservatoire and Sainte-Chapelle. It was hardly ten o'clock, and I figured that by eleven the light would be good, the best you can get in the fall; to kill some time I detoured around by the Isle Saint-Louis and started to walk along the quai d'Anjou, I stared for a bit at the hôtel de Lauzun, I recited bits from Apollinaire which always get into my head whenever I pass in front of the hôtel de Lauzun (and at that I ought to be remembering the other poet, but Michel is an obstinate beggar), and when the wind stopped all at once and the sun came out at least twice as hard (I mean warmer, but really it's the same thing), I sat down on the parapet and felt terribly happy in the Sunday morning.

One of the many ways of contesting level-zero, and one of the best, is to take photographs, an activity in which one should start becoming an adept very early in life, teach it to children since it requires discipline, aesthetic education, a good eye, and steady fingers. I'm not talking about waylaying the lie like any old reporter, snapping the stupid silhouette of the VIP leaving number 10 Downing Street, but in all ways when one is walking about with a camera, one has almost a duty to be attentive, to not lose that abrupt and happy rebound of sun's rays off an old stone, or the pigtails-flying run of a small girl going home with a loaf of bread or a bottle of milk. Michel knew that the photographer always worked as a permutation of his personal way of seeing the world as other than the camera insidiously imposed upon it (now a large cloud is going by, almost black), but he lacked no confidence in himself, knowing that he had only to go out without the Contax to recover the keynote of distraction, the sight without a frame around it, light without the diaphragm aperture or 1/250 sec. Right now (what a word, *now*, what a dumb lie) I was able to sit quietly on the railing overlooking the river, watching the red and black motorboats passing below without it occurring to me to think photographically of the scenes, nothing more than letting myself go in the letting go of objects, running immobile in the stream of time. And then the wind was not blowing.

After, I wandered down the quai de Bourbon until getting to the end of the isle where the intimate square was (intimate because it was small, not that it was hidden, it offered its whole breast to the river and the sky), I enjoyed it, a lot. Nothing there but a couple and, of course, pigeons; maybe even some of those which are flying past now so that I'm seeing them. A leap up and I settled on the wall, and let myself turn about and be caught and fixed by the sun, giving it my face and ears and hands (I kept my gloves in my pocket). I had no desire to shoot pictures, and lit a cigarette to be doing something; I think it was that moment when the match was about to touch the tobacco that I saw the young boy for the first time.

What I'd thought was a couple seemed much more now a boy with his mother, although at the same time I realized that it was not a kid and his mother, and that it was a couple in the sense that we always allegate to couples when we see them leaning up against the parapets or embracing on the benches in the squares. As I had nothing else to do, I had more than enough time to wonder why the boy was so nervous, like a young colt or a hare, sticking his hands into his pockets, taking them out immediately, one after the other, running his fingers through his hair, changing his stance, and especially why was he afraid, well, you could guess that from every gesture, a fear suffocated by his shyness, an impulse to step backwards which he telegraphed, his body standing as if it were on the edge of flight, holding itself back in a final, pitiful decorum.

All this was so clear, ten feet away — and we were alone against the parapet at the tip of the island — that at the beginning the boy's fright didn't let me see the blonde very well. Now, thinking back on it, I see her much better at that first second when I read her face (she'd turned around suddenly, swinging like a metal weathercock, and the eyes, the eyes were there), when I vaguely understood what might have been occurring to the boy and figured it would be worth the trouble to stay and watch (the wind was blowing their words away and they were speaking in a low murmur). I think that I know how to look, if it's something I know, and also that every looking oozes with mendacity, because it's that which expels us furthest outside ourselves, without the least guarantee, whereas to smell, or (but Michel rambles on to himself easily enough, there's no need to let him harangue on this way). In any case, if the likely inaccuracy can be seen beforehand, it becomes possible again to look; perhaps it suffices to choose between looking and the reality looked at, to strip things of all their unnecessary clothing. And surely all that is difficult besides.

As for the boy I remember the image before his actual body (that will clear itself up later), while now I am sure that I remember the woman's body much better than the image. She was thin and willowy, two unfair words to describe what she was, and was wearing an almost-black fur coat, almost long, almost handsome. All the morning's wind (now it was hardly a breeze and it wasn't cold) had blown through her blonde hair, which pared away her white, bleak face – two unfair words – and put the world at her feet and horribly alone in front of her dark eyes, her eyes fell on things like two eagles, two leaps into nothingness, two puffs of green slime. I'm not describing anything, it's more a matter of trying to understand it. And I said two puffs of green slime.

Let's be fair, the boy was well-enough dressed and was sporting yellow gloves which I would have sworn belonged to his older brother, a student of law or sociology; it was pleasant to see the fingers of the gloves sticking out of his jacket pocket. For a long time I didn't see his face, barely a profile, not stupid – a terrified bird, a Fra Filippo angel, rice pudding with milk – and the back of an adolescent who wants to take up judo and has had a scuffle or two in defence of an idea or his sister. Turning fourteen, perhaps fifteen, one would guess that he was dressed and fed by his parents but without a nickel in his pocket, having to debate with his buddies before making up his mind to buy a coffee, a cognac, a pack of cigarettes. He'd walk through the streets thinking of the girls in his class, about how good it would be to go to the movies and see the latest film, or to buy novels or neckties or bottles of liquor with green and white labels on them. At home (it would be a respectable home, lunch at noon and romantic landscapes on the walls, with a dark entry-way and a mahogany umbrella stand inside the door) there'd be the slow rain of time, for studying, for being mama's hope, for looking like dad, for writing to his aunt in Avignon. So that there was a lot of walking the streets, the whole of the river for him (but without a nickel) and the mysterious city of fifteen-year-olds with its signs in doorways, its terrifying cats, a paper of fried potatoes for thirty francs, the pornographic magazine folded four ways, a solitude like the emptiness of his pockets, the eagerness for so much that was incomprehensible but illumined by a total love, by the availability analogous to the wind and the streets.

This biography was of the boy and of any boy whatsoever, but this particular one now, you could see he was insular, surrounded solely by the blonde's presence as she continued talking with him. (I'm tired of insisting, but two long ragged ones just went by. That morning I don't think I looked at the sky once, because what was happening with the boy and the woman appeared so soon I could do nothing but look at them and wait, look at them and . . .) To cut it short, the boy was agitated and one could guess without too much trouble what had just occurred a few minutes before, at most half an hour. The boy had come onto the tip of the island, seen the woman, and thought her marvellous. The woman was waiting for that because she was there waiting for that, or maybe the boy arrived before her and she saw him from one of the balconies or from a car and got out to meet him, starting the conversation with whatever, from the beginning she was sure that he was going to be afraid and want to run off, and that, naturally, he'd stay, stiff and sullen, pretending experience and the pleasure of the adventure. The rest was easy because it was happening ten feet away from me, and anyone could have gauged the stages of the game, the derisive, competitive fencing; its major attraction was not that it was happening but in foreseeing its denouement. The boy would try to end it by pretending a date, an obligation, whatever, and would go stumbling off disconcerted, wishing he were walking with some assurance, but naked under the mocking glance which would follow him until he was out of sight. Or rather, he would stay there, fascinated or simply incapable of taking the initiative, and the woman would begin to touch his face gently, muss his hair, still talking to him voicelessly, and soon would take him by the arm to lead him off, unless he, with an uneasiness beginning to tinge the edge of desire, even his stake in the adventure, would rouse himself to put his arm around her waist and to kiss her. Any of this could have happened, though it did not, and perversely Michel waited, sitting on the railing, making the settings almost without looking at the camera, ready to take a picturesque shot of a corner of the island with an uncommon couple talking and looking at one another.

Strange how the scene (almost nothing: two figures there mismatched in their youth) was taking on a disquieting aura. I thought it was I imposing it, and that my photo, if I shot it, would reconstitute things in their true stupidity. I would have liked to know what he was thinking, a man in a grey hat sitting at the wheel of a car parked on the dock which led up to the footbridge, and whether he was reading the paper or asleep. I had just discovered him because people inside a parked car have a tendency to disappear, they get lost in that wretched, private cage stripped of the beauty that motion and danger give it. And nevertheless, the car had been there the whole time, forming part (or deforming that part) of the isle. A car: like saying a lighted street-lamp, a park bench. Never like saying wind, sunlight, those elements always new to the skin and the eyes, and also the boy and the woman, unique, put there to change the island, to show it to me in another way. Finally, it may have been that the man with the newspaper also became aware of what was happening and would, like me, feel that malicious sensation of waiting for everything to happen. Now the woman had swung around smoothly, putting the young boy between herself and the wall, I saw them almost in profile, and he was taller, though not much taller, and yet she dominated him, it seemed like she was hovering over him (her laugh, all at once, a whip of feathers), crushing him just by being there, smiling, one hand taking a stroll through the air. Why wait any longer? Aperture at sixteen, a sighting which would not include the horrible black car, but yes, that tree, necessary to break up too much grey space . . .

I raised the camera, pretended to study a focus which did not include them, and waited and watched closely, sure that I would finally catch the revealing expression, one that would sum it all up, life that is rhythmed by movement but which a stiff image destroys, taking time in cross section, if we do not choose the essential imperceptible fraction of it. I did not have to wait long. The woman was getting on with the job of handcuffing the boy smoothly, stripping from him what was left of his freedom a hair at a time, in an incredibly slow and delicious torture. I imagined the possible endings (now a small fluffy cloud appears, almost alone in the sky), I saw their arrival at the house (a basement apartment probably, which she would have filled with large cushions and cats) and conjectured the boy's terror and his desperate decision to play it cool and to be led off pretending there was nothing new in it for him. Closing my eyes, if I did in fact close my eyes, I set the scene: the teasing kisses, the woman mildly repelling the hands which were trying to undress her, like in novels, on a bed that would have a lilac-coloured comforter, on the other hand she taking off his clothes, plainly mother and son under a milky yellow light and everything would end up as usual, perhaps, but maybe everything would go otherwise, and the initiation of the adolescent would not happen, she would not let it happen, after a long prologue wherein the awkwardnesses, the exasperating caresses, the running of hands over bodies would be resolved in who knows what, in a separate and solitary pleasure, in a petulant denial mixed with the art of tiring and disconcerting so much poor innocence. It might go like that, it might very well go like that; that woman was not looking for the boy as a lover, and at the same time she was dominating him towards some end impossible to understand if you do not imagine it as a cruel game, the desire to desire without satisfaction, to excite herself for someone else, someone who in no way could be that kid.

Michel is guilty of making literature, of indulging in fabricated unrealities. Nothing pleases him more than to imagine exceptions to the rule, individuals outside the species, not-always-repugnant monsters. But that woman invited speculation, perhaps giving clues enough for the fantasy to hit the bull's-eye. Before she left, and now that she would fill my imaginings for several days, for I'm given to ruminating, I decided not to lose a moment more. I got it all into the viewfinder (with the tree, the railing, the eleven-o'clock sun) and took the shot. In time to realize that they both had noticed and stood there looking at me, the boy surprised and as though questioning, but she was irritated, her face and body flat-footedly hostile, feeling robbed, ignominiously recorded on a small chemical image.

I might be able to tell it in much greater detail but it's not worth the trouble. The woman said that no one had the right to take a picture without permission, and demanded that I hand her over the film. All this in a dry, clear voice with a good Parisian accent, which rose in colour and tone with every phrase. For my part, it hardly mattered whether she got the roll of film or not, but anyone who knows me will tell you, if you want anything from me, ask nicely. With the result that I restricted myself to formulating the opinion that not only was photography in public places not prohibited, but it was looked upon with decided favour, both private and official. And while that was getting said, I noticed on the sly how the boy was falling back, sort of actively backing up though without moving, and all at once (it seemed almost incredible) he turned and broke into a run, the poor kid, thinking that he was walking off and in fact in full flight, running past the side of the car, disappearing like a gossamer filament of angel spit in the morning air.

But filaments of angel spittle are also called devil spit, and Michel had to endure rather particular curses, to hear himself called meddler and imbecile, taking great pains meanwhile to smile and to abate with simple movements of his head such a hard sell. As I was beginning to get tired, I heard the car door slam. The man in the grey hat was there, looking at us. It was only at that point that I realized he was playing a part in the comedy.

He began to walk towards us, carrying in his hand the paper he had been pretending to read. What I remember best is the grimace that twisted his mouth askew, it covered his face with wrinkles, changed somewhat both in location and shape because his lips trembled and the grimace went from one side of his mouth to the other as though it were on wheels, independent and involuntary. But the rest stayed fixed, a flour-powdered clown or bloodless man, dull dry skin, eyes deep-set, the nostrils black and prominently visible, blacker than the eyebrows or hair or the black necktie. Walking cautiously as though the pavement hurt his feet; I saw patent-leather shoes with such thin soles that he must have felt every roughness in the pavement. I don't know why I got down off the railing, nor very well why I decided to not give them the photo, to refuse that demand in which I guessed at their fear and cowardice. The clown and the woman consulted one another in silence: we made a perfect and unbearable triangle, something I felt compelled to break with a crack of a whip. I laughed in their faces and began to walk off, a little more slowly, I imagine, than the boy. At the level of the first houses, beside the iron footbridge, I turned around to look at them. They were not moving, but the man had dropped his newspaper; it seemed to me that the woman, her back to the parapet, ran her hands over the stone with the classical and absurd gesture of someone pursued looking for a way out.

What happened after that happened here, almost just now, in a room on the fifth floor. Several days went by before Michel developed the photos he'd taken on Sunday; his shots of the Conservatoire and of Sainte-Chapelle were all they should be. Then he found two or three proof-shots he'd forgotten, a poor attempt to catch a cat perched astonishingly on the roof of a rambling public urinal, and also the shot of the blonde and the kid. The negative was so good that he made an enlargement; the enlargement was so good that he made one very much larger, almost the size of a poster. It did not occur to him (now one wonders and wonders) that only the shots of the Conservatoire were worth so much work. Of the whole series, the snapshot of the tip of the island was the only one which interested him; he tacked up the enlargement on one wall of the room, and the first day he spent some time looking at it and remembering, that gloomy operation of comparing the memory with the gone reality; a frozen memory, like any photo, where nothing is missing, not even, and especially, nothingness, the true solidifier of the scene. There was the woman, there was the boy, the tree rigid above their heads, the sky as sharp as the stone of the parapet, clouds and stones melded into a single substance and inseparable (now one with sharp edges is going by, like a thunderhead). The first two days I accepted what I had done, from the photo itself to the enlargement on the wall, and didn't even question that every once in a while I would interrupt my translation of José Norberto Allende's treatise to encounter once more the woman's face, the dark splotches on the railing. I'm such a jerk; it had never occurred to me that when we look at a photo from the front, the eyes reproduce exactly the position and the vision of the lens; it's these things that are taken for granted and it never occurs to anyone to think about them. From my chair, with the typewriter directly in front of me, I looked at the photo ten feet away, and then it occurred to me that I had hung it exactly at the point of view of the lens. It looked very good that way; no doubt, it was the best way to appreciate a photo, though the angle from the diagonal doubtless has its pleasures and might even divulge different aspects. Every few minutes, for example when I was unable to find the way to say in good French what José Norberto Allende was saying in very good Spanish, I raised my eyes and looked at the photo; sometimes the woman would catch my eye, sometimes the boy, sometimes the pavement where a dry leaf had fallen admirably situated to heighten a lateral section. Then I rested a bit from my labours, and I enclosed myself again happily in that morning in which the photo was drenched, I recalled ironically the angry picture of the woman demanding I give her the photograph, the boy's pathetic and ridiculous flight, the entrance on the scene of the man with the white face. Basically, I was satisfied with myself; my part had not been too brilliant, and since the French have been given the gift of the sharp response, I did not see very well why I'd chosen to leave without a complete demonstration of the rights, privileges and prerogatives of citizens. The important thing, the really important thing was having helped the kid to escape in time (this in case my theorizing was correct, which was not sufficiently proven, but the running away itself seemed to show it so). Out of plain meddling, I had given him the opportunity finally to take advantage of his fright to do something useful; now he would be regretting it, feeling his honour impaired, his manhood diminished. That was better than the attentions of a woman capable of looking as she had looked at him on that island. Michel is something of a puritan at times, he believes that one should not seduce someone from a position of strength. In the last analysis, taking that photo had been a good act.

Well, it wasn't because of the good act that I looked at it between paragraphs while I was working. At that moment I didn't know the reason, the reason I had tacked the enlargement onto the wall; maybe all fatal acts happen that way, and that is the condition of their fulfilment. I don't think the almost-furtive trembling of the leaves on the tree alarmed me, I was working on a sentence and rounded it out successfully. Habits are like immense herbariums, in the end an enlargement of 32 × 28 looks like a movie screen, where on the tip of the island, a woman is speaking with a boy and a tree is shaking its dry leaves over their heads.

But her hands were just too much. I had just translated: 'In that case, the second key resides in the intrinsic nature of difficulties which societies . . .' – when I saw the woman's hand beginning to stir slowly, finger by finger. There was nothing left of me, a phrase in French which I would never have to finish, a typewriter on the floor, a chair that squeaked and shook, fog. The kid had ducked his head like boxers do when they've done all they can and are waiting for the final blow to fall; he had turned up the collar of his overcoat and seemed more a prisoner than ever, the perfect victim helping promote the catastrophe. Now the woman was talking into his ear, and her hand opened again to lay itself against his cheekbone, to caress and caress it, burning it, taking her time. The kid was less startled than he was suspicious, once or twice he poked his head over the woman's shoulder and she continued talking, saying something that made him look back every few minutes towards that area where Michel knew the car was parked and the man in the grey hat, carefully eliminated from the photo but present in the boy's eyes (how doubt that now?), in the words of the woman, in the woman's hands, in the vicarious presence of the woman. When I saw the man come up, stop near them, and look at them, his hands in his pockets and a stance somewhere between disgusted and demanding, the master who is about to whistle in his dog after a frolic in the square, I understood, if that was to understand, what had to happen now, what had to have happened then, what would have to happen at that moment, among these people, just where I had poked my nose in to upset an established order, interfering innocently in that which had not happened, but which was now going to happen, now was going to be fulfilled. And what I had imagined earlier was much less horrible than the reality, that woman, who was not there by herself, she was not caressing or propositioning or encouraging for her own pleasure, to lead the angel away with his tousled hair and play the tease with his terror and his eager grace. The real boss was waiting there, smiling petulantly, already certain of the business; he was not the first to send a woman in the vanguard, to bring him the prisoners manacled with flowers. The rest of it would be so simple, the car, some house or another, drinks, stimulating engravings, tardy tears, the awakening in hell. And there was nothing I could do, this time I could do absolutely nothing. My strength had been a photograph, that, there, where they were taking their revenge on me, demonstrating clearly what was going to happen. The photo had been taken, the time had run out, gone; we were so far from one another, the abusive act had certainly already taken place, the tears already shed, and the rest conjecture and sorrow. All at once the order was inverted, they were alive, moving, they were deciding and had decided, they were going to their future; and I on this side, prisoner of another time, in a room on the fifth floor, to not know who they were, that woman, that man, and that boy, to be only the lens of my camera, something fixed, rigid, incapable of intervention. It was horrible, their mocking me, deciding it before my impotent eye, mocking me, for the boy again was looking at the flour-faced clown and I had to accept the fact that he was going to say yes, that the proposition carried money with it or a gimmick and I couldn't yell for him to run, or even open the road to him again with a new photo, a small and almost meek intervention which would ruin the framework of drool and perfume. Everything was going to resolve itself right there, at that moment; there was like an immense silence which had nothing to do with physical silence. It was stretching it out, setting itself up. I think I screamed, I screamed terribly, and that at that exact second I realized that I was beginning to move towards them, four inches, a step, another step, the tree swung its branches rhythmically in the foreground, a place where the railing was tarnished emerged from the frame, the woman's face turned towards me as though surprised, was enlarging, and then I turned a bit, I mean that the camera turned a little, and without losing sight of the woman, I began to close in on the man who was looking at me with the black holes he had in place of eyes, surprised and angered both, he looked, wanting to nail me onto the air, and at that instant I happened to see something like a large bird outside the focus that was flying in a single swoop in front of the picture, and I leaned up against the wall of my room and was happy because the boy had just managed to escape, I saw him running off, in focus again, sprinting with his hair flying in the wind, learning finally to fly across the island, to arrive at the footbridge, return to the city. For the second time he'd escaped them, for the second time I was helping him to escape, returning him to his precarious paradise. Out of breath, I stood in front of them; no need to step closer, the game was played out. Of the woman you could see just maybe a shoulder and a bit of the hair, brutally cut off by the frame of the picture; but the man was directly centre, his mouth half open, you could see a shaking black tongue, and he lifted his hands slowly, bringing them into the foreground, an instant still in perfect focus, and then all of him a lump that blotted out the island, the tree, and I shut my eyes, I didn't want to see any more, and I covered my face and broke into tears like an idiot.

Now there's a big white cloud, as on all these days, all this untellable time. What remains to be said is always a cloud, two clouds, or long hours of a sky perfectly clear, a very clean, clear rectangle tacked up with pins on the wall of my room. That was what I saw when I opened my eyes and dried them with my fingers: the clear sky, and then a cloud that drifted in from the left, passed gracefully and slowly across, and disappeared on the right. And then another, and for a change sometimes, everything gets grey, all one enormous cloud, and suddenly the splotches of rain cracking down, for a long spell you can see it raining over the picture, like a spell of weeping reversed, and little by little, the frame becomes clear, perhaps the sun comes out, and again the clouds begin to come, two at a time, three at a time. And the pigeons once in a while, and a sparrow or two.

RALPH ELLISON, born in Oklahoma in 1914, has written what is generally considered the finest novel of the Negro predicament in America, *Invisible Man*, from which this extract has been taken. In a poll of editors, critics, and authors taken in 1965, this novel was judged to be the 'most distinguished single work' published in America since 1945. Before the publication of *Invisible Man* in 1952, Mr Ellison published several stories, and in 1964 he collected his critical essays in *Shadow and Act*.

from invisible man

RALPH ELLISON

I was sitting in a cold, white rigid chair and a man was looking at me out of a bright third eye that glowed from the centre of his forehead. He reached out, touching my skull gingerly, and said something encouraging, as though I were a child. His fingers went away.

'Take this,' he said. 'It's good for you.' I swallowed. Suddenly my skin itched, all over. I had on new overalls, strange white ones. The taste ran bitter through my mouth. My fingers trembled.

A thin voice with a mirror on the end of it said, 'How is he?'

'I don't think it's anything serious. Merely stunned.'

'Should he be sent home now?'

'No, just to be certain we'll keep him here a few days. Want to keep him under observation. Then he may leave.'

Now I was lying on a cot, the bright eye still burning into mine, although the man was gone. It was quiet and I was numb. I closed my eyes only to be awakened.

'What is your name?' a voice said.

'My head . . .' I said.

'Yes, but your name. Address?'

'My head – that burning eye . . .' I said.

'Eye?'

'Inside,' I said.

'Shoot him up for an X-ray,' another voice said.

'My head . . .'

'Careful!'

Somewhere a machine began to hum and I distrusted the man and woman above me.

They were holding me firm and it was fiery and above it all I kept hearing the opening motif of Beethoven's Fifth – three short and one long buzz, repeated again and again in varying volume, and I was struggling and breaking through, rising up, to find myself lying on my back with two pink-faced men laughing down.

'Be quiet now,' one of them said firmly. 'You'll be all right.' I raised my eyes, seeing two indefinite young women in white, looking down at me. A third, a desert of heat waves away, sat at a panel arrayed with coils and dials. Where was I? From far below me a barber-chair thumping began and I felt myself rise on the tip of the sound from the floor. A face was now level with mine, looking closely and saying something without meaning. A whirring began that snapped and cracked with static, and suddenly I seemed to be crushed between the floor and ceiling. Two forces tore savagely at my stomach and back. A flash of cold-edged heat enclosed me. I was pounded between crushing electrical pressures; pumped between live electrodes like an accordion between a player's hands. My lungs were compressed like a bellows and each time my breath returned I yelled, punctuating the rhymical action of the nodes.

'Hush, goddamit,' one of the faces ordered. 'We're trying to get you started again. Now shut up!'

The voice throbbed with icy authority and I quieted and tried to contain the pain. I discovered now that my head was encircled by a piece of cold metal like the iron cap worn by the occupant of an electric chair. I tried unsuccessfully to struggle, to cry out. But the people were so remote, the pain so immediate. A face moved in and out of the circle of lights, peering for a moment, then disappeared. A freckled, red-haired woman with gold nose-glasses appeared; then a man with a circular mirror attached to his forehead – a doctor. Yes, he was a doctor and the women were nurses; it was coming clear. I was in a hospital. They would care for me. It was all geared towards the easing of pain. I felt thankful.

I tried to remember how I'd gotten here, but nothing came. My mind was blank, as though I had just begun to live. When the next face appeared I saw the eyes behind the thick glasses blinking as though noticing me for the first time.

'You're all right, boy. You're OK. You just be patient,' said the voice, hollow with profound detachment.

I seemed to go away; the lights receded like a tail-light racing down a dark country road. I couldn't follow. A sharp pain stabbed my shoulder. I twisted about on my back, fighting something I couldn't see. Then after a while my vision cleared.

Now a man sitting with his back to me, manipulating dials on a panel. I wanted to call him, but the Fifth Symphony rhythm racked me, and he seemed too serene and too far away. Bright metal bars were between us and when I strained my neck around I discovered that I was not lying *on* an operating table but *in* a kind of glass and nickel box, the lid of which was propped open. Why was I here?

'Doctor! Doctor!' I called.

No answer. Perhaps he hadn't heard, I thought, calling again and feeling the stabbing pulses of the machine again and feeling myself going under and fighting against it and coming up to hear voices carrying on a conversation behind my head. The static sounds became a quiet drone. Strains of music, a Sunday air, drifted from a distance. With closed eyes, barely breathing I warded off the pain. The voices droned harmoniously. Was it a radio I heard – a phonograph? The *vox humana* of a hidden organ? If so, what organ and where? I felt warm. Green hedges, dazzling with red wild roses appeared behind my eyes, stretching with a gentle curving to an infinity empty of objects, a limpid blue space. Scenes of a shaded lawn in summer drifted past; I saw a uniformed military band arrayed decorously in concert, each musician with well-oiled hair, heard a sweet-voiced trumpet rendering *The Holy City* as from an echoing distance, buoyed by a choir of muted horns; and above, the mocking obbligato of a mocking bird. I felt giddy. The air seemed to grow thick with fine white gnats, filling my eyes, boiling so thickly that the dark trumpeter breathed them in and expelled them through the bell of his golden horn, a live white cloud mixing with the tones upon the torpid air.

I came back. The voices still droned above me and I disliked them. Why didn't they go away? Smug ones. Oh, doctor, I thought drowsily, did you ever wade in a brook before breakfast? Ever chew on sugar cane? You know, doc, the same fall day I first saw the hounds chasing black men in stripes and chains my grandmother sat with me and sang with twinkling eyes:

> 'Godamighty made a monkey
> Godamighty made a whale

And Godamighty made a 'gator
With hickeys all over his tail . . .'

Or you, nurse, did you know that when you strolled in pink organdy and
picture hat between the rows of cape jasmine, cooing to your beau in a
drawl as thick as sorghum, we little black boys hidden snug in the
bushes called out so loud that you daren't hear:

'Did you ever see Miss Margaret boil water?
Man, she hisses a wonderful stream,
Seventeen miles and a quarter,
Man, and you can't see her pot for the steam . . .'

But now the music became a distinct wail of female pain. I opened my
eyes. Glass and metal floated above me.
'How are you feeling, boy?' a voice said.
A pair of eyes peered down through lenses as thick as the bottom of a
Coca Cola bottle, eyes protruding, luminous and veined, like an old
biology specimen preserved in alcohol.
'I don't have enough room,' I said angrily.
'Oh, that's a necessary part of the treatment.'
'But I need more room,' I insisted. 'I'm cramped.'
'Don't worry about it, boy. You'll get used to it after a while. How is
your stomach and head?'
'Stomach?'
'Yes, and your head?'
'I don't know,' I said, realizing that I could feel nothing beyond the
pressure around my head and on the tender surface of my body. Yet my
senses seemed to focus sharply.
'I don't feel it,' I cried, alarmed.
'Aha! You see! My little gadget will solve everything!' he exploded.
'I don't know,' another voice said. 'I think I still prefer surgery. And in
this case especially, with this, uh . . . background, I'm not so sure that I
don't believe in the effectiveness of simple prayer.'
'Nonsense, from now on do your praying to my little machine. I'll
deliver the cure.'
'I don't know, but I believe it a mistake to assume that solutions —
cures, that is — that apply in, uh . . . primitive instances, are, uh . . .
equally effective when more advanced conditions are in question. Suppose it were a New Englander with a Harvard background?'
'Now you're arguing politics,' the first voice said banteringly.
'Oh, no, but it is a problem.'
I listened with growing uneasiness to the conversation fuzzing away

to a whisper. Their simplest words seemed to refer to something else, as did many of the notions that unfurled through my head. I wasn't sure whether they were talking about me or someone else. Some of it sounded like a discussion of history . . .

'The machine will produce the results of a prefrontal lobotomy without the negative effects of the knife,' the voice said. 'You see, instead of severing the prefrontal lobe, a single lobe, that is, we apply pressure in the proper degrees to the major centres of nerve control – our concept is Gestalt – and the result is as complete a change of personality as you'll find in your famous fairy-tale cases of criminals transformed into amiable fellows after all that bloody business of a brain operation. And what's more,' the voice went on triumphantly, 'that patient is both physically and neurally whole.'

'But what of his psychology?'

'Absolutely of no importance!' the voice said. 'The patient will live as he has to live, and with absolute integrity. Who could ask more? He'll experience no major conflict of motives, and what is even better, society will suffer no traumata on his account.'

There was a pause. A pen scratched upon paper. Then, 'Why not castration, doctor?' a voice asked waggishly, causing me to start, a pain tearing through me.

'There goes your love of blood again,' the first voice laughed. 'What's that definition of a surgeon, "a butcher with a bad conscience"?'

They laughed.

'It's not so funny. It would be more scientific to try to define the case. It has been developing some three hundred years—'

'Define? Hell, man, we know all that.'

'Then why don't you try more current?'

'You suggest it?'

'I do, why not?'

'But isn't there a danger . . .?' the voice trailed off.

I heard them move away; a chair scraped. The machine droned, and I knew definitely that they were discussing me and steeled myself for the shocks, but was blasted nevertheless. The pulse came swift and staccato, increasing gradually until I fairly danced between the nodes. My teeth chattered. I closed my eyes and bit my lips to smother my screams. Warm blood filled my mouth. Between my lids I saw a circle of hands and faces, dazzling with light. Some were scribbling upon charts.

'Look, he's dancing,' someone called.

'No, really?'

An oily face looked in. 'They really do have rhythm, don't they? Get hot, boy! Get hot!' it said with a laugh.

And suddenly my bewilderment suspended and I wanted to be angry, murderously angry. But somehow the pulse of current smashing through my body prevented me. Something had been disconnected. For though I had seldom used my capacities for anger and indignation, I had no doubt that I possessed them; and, like a man who knows that he must fight, whether angry or not, when called a son of a bitch, I tried to *imagine* myself angry – only to discover a deeper sense of remoteness. I was beyond anger. I was only bewildered. And those above seemed to sense it. There was no avoiding the shock and I rolled with the agitated tide, out into the blackness.

When I emerged, the lights were still there. I lay beneath the slab of glass, feeling deflated. All my limbs seemed amputated. It was very warm. A dim white ceiling stretched far above me. My eyes were swimming with tears. Why, I didn't know. It worried me. I wanted to knock on the glass to attract attention, but I couldn't move. The slightest effort, hardly more than desire, tired me. I lay experiencing the vague processes of my body. I seemed to have lost all sense of proportion. Where did my body and the crystal and white world begin? Thoughts evaded me, hiding in the vast stretch of clinical whiteness to which I seemed connected only by a scale of receding greys. No sounds beyond the sluggish inner roar of the blood. I couldn't open my eyes. I seemed to exist in some other dimension, utterly alone; until after a while a nurse bent down and forced a warm fluid between my lips. I gagged, swallowed, feeling the fluid course slowly to my vague middle. A huge iridescent bubble seemed to enfold me. Gentle hands moved over me, bringing vague impressions of memory. I was laved with warm liquids, felt gentle hands move through the indefinite limits of my flesh. The sterile and weightless texture of a sheet enfolded me. I felt myself bounce, sail off like a ball thrown over the roof into mist, striking a hidden wall beyond a pile of broken machinery and sailing back. How long it took, I didn't know. But now above the movement of the hands I heard a friendly voice, uttering familiar words to which I could assign no meaning. I listened intensely, aware of the form and movement of sentences and grasping the now subtle rhythmical differences between progressions of sound that questioned and those that made a statement. But still their meanings were lost in the vast whiteness in which I myself was lost.

Other voices emerged. Faces hovered above me like inscrutable fish peering myopically through a glass aquarium wall. I saw them suspended motionless above me, then two floating off, first their heads, then the tips of their finlike fingers, moving dreamily from the top of the case. A thoroughly mysterious coming and going, like the surging of torpid tides. I watched the two make furious movements with their mouths. I didn't understand. They tried again, the meaning still escaping me. I felt uneasy. I saw a scribbled card, held over me. All a jumble of alphabets. They consulted heatedly. Somehow I felt responsible. A terrible sense of loneliness came over me; they seemed to enact a mysterious pantomime. And seeing them from this angle was disturbing. They appeared utterly stupid and I didn't like it. It wasn't right. I could see smut in one doctor's nose; a nurse had two flabby chins. Other faces came up, their mouths working with soundless fury. But we are all human, I thought, wondering what I meant.

A man dressed in black appeared, a long-haired fellow, whose piercing eyes looked down upon me out of an intense and friendly face. The others hovered about him, their eyes anxious as he alternately peered at me and consulted my chart. Then he scribbled something on a large card and thrust it before my eyes:

WHAT IS YOUR NAME?

A tremor shook me; it was as though he had suddenly given a name to, had organized the vagueness that drifted through my head, and I was overcome with swift shame. I realized that I no longer knew my own name. I shut my eyes and shook my head with sorrow. Here was the first warm attempt to communicate with me and I was failing. I tried again, plunging into the blackness of my mind. It was no use; I found nothing but pain. I saw the card again and he pointed slowly to each word:

WHAT . . . IS . . . YOUR . . . NAME?

I tried desperately, diving below the blackness until I was limp with fatigue. It was as though a vein had been opened and my energy syphoned away; I could only stare back mutely. But with an irritating burst of activity he gestured for another card and wrote:

WHO . . . ARE . . . YOU?

Something inside me turned with a sluggish excitement. This phrasing of the question seemed to set off a series of weak and distant lights where the other had thrown a spark that failed. Who am I? I asked myself. But it was like trying to identify one particular cell that coursed through the torpid veins of my body. Maybe I was just this blackness and bewilderment and pain, but that seemed less like a suitable answer than something I'd read somewhere.

The card was back again:

WHAT IS YOUR MOTHER'S NAME?

Mother, who *was* my mother? Mother, the one who screams when you suffer — but who? This was stupid, you always knew your mother's name. Who was it that screamed? Mother? But the scream came from the machine. A machine my mother? ... Clearly, I was out of my head.

He shot questions at me: *Where were you born? Try to think of your name.*

I tried, thinking vainly of many names, but none seemed to fit, and yet it was as though I was somehow a part of all of them, had become submerged within them and lost.

You must remember, the placard read. But it was useless. Each time I found myself back in the clinging white mist and my name just beyond my fingertips. I shook my head and watched him disappear for a moment and return with a companion, a short, scholarly-looking man who stared at me with a blank expression. I watched him produce a child's slate and a piece of chalk, writing upon it:

WHO WAS YOUR MOTHER?

I looked at him, feeling a quick dislike and thinking, half in amusement, I don't play the dozens. And how's *your* old lady today?

THINK

I stared, seeing him frown and write a long time. The slate was filled with meaningless names.

I smiled, seeing his eyes blaze with annoyance. Old Friendly Face said something. The new man wrote a question at which I stared in wide-eyed amazement:

WHO WAS BUCKEYE THE RABBIT?

I was filled with turmoil. Why should he think of *that*? He pointed to the question, word by word. I laughed, deep, deep inside me, giddy with the delight of self-discovery and the desire to hide it. Somehow *I* was Buckeye the Rabbit ... or had been, when as children we danced and sang barefoot in the dusty streets:

> Buckeye the Rabbit
> Shake it, shake it
> Buckeye the Rabbit
> Break it, break it ...

Yet, I could not bring myself to admit it, it was too ridiculous – and somehow too dangerous. It was annoying that he had hit upon an old identity and I shook my head, seeing him purse his lips and eye me sharply.

BOY, WHO WAS BRER RABBIT?

He was your mother's back-door man, I thought. Anyone knew they were one and the same: 'Buckeye' when you were very young and hid yourself behind wide innocent eyes; 'Brer', when you were older. But why was he playing around with these childish names? Did they think I was a child? Why didn't they leave me alone? I would remember soon enough when they let me out of the machine ... A palm smacked sharply upon the glass, but I was tired of them. Yet as my eyes focused upon Old Friendly Face he seemed pleased. I couldn't understand it, but there he was, smiling and leaving with the new assistant.

Left alone, I lay fretting over my identity. I suspected that I was really playing a game with myself and that they were taking part. A kind of combat. Actually they knew as well as I, and I for some reason preferred not to face it. It was irritating, and it made me feel sly and alert. I would solve the mystery the next instant. I imagined myself whirling about in my mind like an old man attempting to catch a small boy in some mischief, thinking, Who am I? It was no good. I felt like a clown. Nor was I up to being both criminal and detective – though why criminal I didn't know.

I fell to plotting ways of short-circuiting the machine. Perhaps if I shifted my body about so that the two nodes would come together – no, not only was there no room but it might electrocute me. I shuddered. Whoever else I was, I was no Samson. I had no desire to destroy myself even if it destroyed the machine; I wanted freedom, not destruction. It was exhausting, for no matter what the scheme I conceived, there was one constant flaw – myself. There was no getting around it. I could no more escape than I could think of my identity. Perhaps, I thought, the two things are involved with each other. When I discover who I am, I'll be free.

It was as though my thoughts of escape had alerted them. I looked up to see two agitated physicians and a nurse, and thought, it's too late now, and lay in a veil of sweat watching them manipulate the controls. I was braced for the usual shock, but nothing happened. Instead I saw their hands at the lid, loosening the bolts, and before I could react they had opened the lid and pulled me erect.

'What's happened?' I began, seeing the nurse pause to look at me.

'Well?' she said.

My mouth worked soundlessly.

'Come on, get it out,' she said.

'What hospital is this?' I said.

'It's the factory hospital,' she said. 'Now be quiet.'

They were around me now, inspecting my body, and I watched with growing bewilderment, thinking, what is a *factory* hospital?

I felt a tug at my belly and looked down to see one of the physicians pull the cord which was attached to the stomach node, jerking me forward.

'What is this?' I said.

'Get the shears,' he said.

'Sure,' the other said. 'Let's not waste time.'

I recoiled inwardly as though the cord were part of me. Then they had it free and the nurse clipped through the belly band and removed the heavy node. I opened my mouth to speak but one of the physicians shook his head. They worked swiftly. The nodes off, the nurse went over me with rubbing alcohol. Then I was told to climb out of the case. I looked from face to face, overcome with indecision. For now that it appeared that I was being freed, I dared not believe it. What if they were transferring me to some even more painful machine? I sat there, refusing to move. Should I struggle against them?

'Take his arm,' one of them said.

'I can do it,' I said, climbing fearfully out.

I was told to stand while they went over my body with the stethoscope.

'How's the articulation?' the one with the chart said as the other examined my shoulder.

'Perfect,' he said.

I could feel a tightness there but no pain.

'I'd say he's surprisingly strong, considering,' the other said.

'Shall we call in Drexel? It seems rather unusual for him to be so strong.'

'No, just note it on the chart.'

'All right, nurse, give him his clothes.'

'What are you going to do with me?' I said. She handed me clean underclothing and a pair of white overalls.

'No questions,' she said. 'Just dress as quickly as possible.'

The air outside the machine seemed extremely rare. When I bent over to tie my shoes I thought I would faint, but fought it off. I stood shakily and they looked me up and down.

'Well, boy, it looks as though you're cured,' one of them said. 'You're a new man. You came through fine. Come with us,' he said.

We went slowly out of the room and down a long white corridor into an elevator, then swiftly down three floors to a reception room with rows of chairs. At the front were a number of private offices with frosted glass doors and walls.

'Sit down there,' they said. 'The director will see you shortly.'

I sat, seeing them disappear inside one of the offices for a second and emerge, passing me without a word. I trembled like a leaf. Were they really freeing me? My head spun. I looked at my white overalls. The nurse said that this was the factory hospital . . . Why couldn't I remember what kind of factory it was? And why a *factory* hospital? Yes . . . I did remember some vague factory; perhaps I was being sent back there. Yes, and he'd spoken of the director instead of the head doctor; could they be one and the same? Perhaps I was in the factory already. I listened but could hear no machinery.

Across the room a newspaper lay on a chair, but I was too concerned to get it. Somewhere a fan droned. Then one of the doors with frosted glass was opened and I saw a tall austere-looking man in a white coat, beckoning me with a chart.

'Come,' he said.

I got up and went past him into a large, simply furnished office, thinking, *Now, I'll know. Now.*

'Sit down,' he said.

I eased myself into the chair beside his desk. He watched me with a calm, scientific gaze.

'What is your name? Oh here, I have it,' he said, studying the chart. And it was as though someone inside of me tried to tell him to be silent, but already he had called my name and I heard myself say, 'Oh!' as a pain stabbed through my head and I shot to my feet and looked wildly around me and sat down and got up and down again very fast, remembering. I don't know why I did it, but suddenly I saw him looking at me intently, and I stayed down this time.

He began asking questions and I could hear myself replying fluently, though inside I was reeling with swiftly changing emotional images that shrilled and chattered, like a sound track, reversed at high speed.

'Well, my boy,' he said, 'you're cured. We are going to release you. How does that strike you?'

Suddenly I didn't know. I noticed a company calendar beside a stethoscope and a miniature silver paintbrush. Did he mean from the hospital or from the job? . . .

'Sir?' I said.

'I said, how does that strike you?'

'All right, sir,' I said in an unreal voice. 'I'll be glad to get back to work.'

He looked at the chart, frowning, 'You'll be released, but I'm afraid that you'll be disappointed about the work,' he said.

'What do you mean, sir?'

'You've been through a severe experience,' he said. 'You aren't ready for the rigours of industry. Now I want you to rest, undertake a period of convalescence. You need to become readjusted and get your strength back.'

'But sir—'

'You mustn't try to go too fast. You're glad to be released, are you not?'

'Oh, yes. But how shall I live?'

'Live?' his eyebrows raised and lowered. 'Take another job,' he said. 'Something easier, quieter. Something for which you're better prepared.'

'Prepared?' I looked at him, thinking, is he in on it too? 'I'll take anything sir,' I said.

'That isn't the problem, my boy. You just aren't prepared for work under our industrial conditions. Later, perhaps, but not now. And remember, you'll be adequately compensated for your experience.'

'Compensated, sir?'

'Oh, yes,' he said. 'We follow a policy of enlightened humanitarianism; all our employees are automatically insured. You have only to sign a few papers.'

'What kind of papers, sir?'

'We require an affidavit releasing the company of responsibility,' he said. 'Yours was a difficult case, and a number of specialists had to be called in. But, after all, any new occupation has its hazards. They are part of growing up, of becoming adjusted, as it were. One takes a chance and while some are prepared, others are not.'

I looked at his lined face. Was he doctor, factory official, or both? I couldn't get it; and now he seemed to move back and forth across my field of vision, although he sat perfectly calm in his chair.

It came out of itself: 'Do you know Mr Norton, sir?' I said.

'Norton?' His brows knitted. 'What Norton is this?'

Then it was as though I hadn't asked him; the name sounded strange. I ran my hand over my eyes.

'I'm sorry,' I said. 'It occurred to me that you might. He was just a man I used to know.'

'I see. Well' – he picked up some papers – 'so that's the way it is, my boy. A little later perhaps we'll be able to do something. You may take the papers along if you wish. Just mail them to us. Your cheque will be sent upon their return. Meanwhile, take as much time as you like. You'll find that we are perfectly fair.'

I took the folded papers and looked at him for what seemed to be too long a time. He seemed to waver. Then I heard myself say, 'Do you know him?' my voice rising.

'Who?'

'Mr Norton,' I said. 'Mr Norton!'

'Oh, why, no.'

'No,' I said, 'no one knows anybody and it was too long a time ago.'

He frowned and I laughed. 'They picked poor Robin clean,' I said. 'Do you happen to know Bled?'

He looked at me, his head to one side. 'Are these people friends of yours?'

'Friends? Oh, yes,' I said, 'we're all good friends. Buddies from way back. But I don't suppose we get around in the same circles.'

His eyes widened. 'No,' he said, 'I don't suppose we do. However, good friends are valuable to have.'

I felt light-headed and started to laugh and he seemed to waver again and I thought of asking him about Emerson, but now he was clearing his throat and indicating that he was finished.

I put the folded papers in my overalls and started out. The door beyond the rows of chairs seemed far away.

'Take care of yourself,' he said.

'And you,' I said, thinking, it's time, it's past time.

Turning abruptly, I went weakly back to the desk, seeing him looking up at me with his steady scientific gaze. I was overcome with ceremonial feelings but unable to remember the proper formula. So as I deliberately extended my hand I fought down laughter with a cough.

'It's been quite pleasant, our little palaver, sir,' I said. I listened to myself and to his answer.

'Yes, indeed,' he said.

He shook my hand gravely, without surprise or distaste. I looked down, he was there somewhere behind the lined face and outstretched hand.

'And now our palaver is finished,' I said. 'Goodbye.'

He raised his hand. 'Goodbye,' he said, his voice non-committal.

Leaving him and going out into the paint-fuming air I had the feeling that I had been talking beyond myself, had used words and expressed attitudes not my own, that I was in the grip of some alien personality lodged deep within me. Like the servant about whom I'd read in psychology class who, during a trance, had recited pages of Greek philosophy which she had overheard one day while she worked. It was as though I were acting out a scene from some crazy movie. Or perhaps I was catching up with myself and had put into words feeling which I had hitherto suppressed. Or was it, I thought, starting up the walk, that I was no longer afraid? I stopped, looking at the buildings down the bright street slanting with sun and shade. I *was* no longer afraid. Not of important men, not of trustees and such; for knowing now that there was nothing which I could expect from them, there was no reason to be afraid. Was that it? I felt light-headed, my ears were ringing. I went on.

Along the walk the buildings rose, uniform and close together. It was day's end now and on top of every building the flags were fluttering and diving down, collapsing. And I felt that I would fall, had fallen, moved now as against a current sweeping swiftly against me. Out of the grounds and up the street I found the bridge by which I'd come, but the stairs leading back to the car that crossed the top were too dizzily steep to climb, swim, or fly, and I found a subway instead.

Things whirled too fast around me. My mind went alternately bright and blank in slow, rolling waves. We, he, him -- my mind and I -- were no longer getting around in the same circles. Nor my body either. Across the aisle a young platinum blonde nibbled at a Red Delicious apple as station lights rippled past behind her. The train plunged. I dropped through the roar, giddy and vacuum-minded, sucked under and out into late afternoon Harlem.

a world ends

WOLFGANG HILDESHEIMER

The Marchesa Montetristo's last evening party has impressed itself indelibly on my memory. This is partly due, of course, to its extraordinary conclusion, but in other ways as well the evening was unforgettable.

My acquaintance with the Marchesa – a Waterman by birth, of Little Gidding, Ohio – came about by a coincidence. I had sold her, through the intermediary of my friend, Herr von Perlhuhn (I mean of course the Abraham-a-Santa Clara expert, not the neo-mystic), the bathtub in which Marat was murdered. It is perhaps not generally known that it had been until then in my possession. Gambling debts obliged me to offer it for sale. So it was that I came to the Marchesa, who had long wanted this appliance for her collection of eighteenth-century washing utensils. This was the occasion of my getting to know her. From the bathtub our conversation soon passed to more general aesthetic topics. I noticed that the possession of this collector's piece had given me a certain prestige in her eyes. And I was not surprised when one day I was invited to one of her famous parties in her palazzo on the artificial island of San Amerigo. The Marchesa had had the island thrown up a few miles south-east of Murano on a sudden whim, for she detested the mainland – she said it was hurtful to her spiritual equilibrium, and she could find nothing to suit her in the existing stock of islands. So here she resided, devoting her life to the cult of the antique and forgotten, or as she liked to put it, of the 'true and eternal'.

The invitation card gave the time of the party as eight o'clock, which meant that the guests were expected at ten. So custom ordered it. Further it ordered that the guests come in gondolas. In this fashion, it is true, the crossing lasted nearly two hours and was moreover uncomfortable when the sea was rough, but these were unwritten rules of behaviour at which no one but a barbarian would cavil – and barbarians were not invited. Besides, many of the younger guests, not yet fully sensible of the dignity of the occasion, would hire a *vaporetto* to take them within a hundred yards of the island whence they were ferried over one by one in a gondola which had been brought in tow.

The splendour of the building needs no description from me. For outside it was an exact replica of the Palazzo Vendramin, and inside every period, from the Gothic onward, was represented. But of course they were not intermingled. Each one had its own room. The Marchesa could really not be accused of breaches of style. Nor need the opulence of the catering be referred to her. Anyone who has ever attended a state banquet in a monarchy – and it is to such that I principally addressed myself – knows what it was like. Moreover it would hardly be true to the spirit of the Marchesa and her circle to mention the pleasures of the table, especially here, where I have to describe the last hours on earth of some of the most eminent figures of the age, which I as sole survivor had the privilege to witness.

After exchanging a few civilities with my hostess and stroking the long-haired Pekingese which never stirred from her side, I was introduced to the Dombrowska, a woman doubly famous, first for her contributions to the rhythmic-expressionist dance, a vanishing art form, and secondly as the author of the book *Back to Youth*, which, as the title indicates, argued in favour of a return to youthfulness of style and which, I need hardly remind the reader, has won adherents far and wide. While we were chatting together, an elderly gentleman of upright bearing came up to us. It was Golch. The Golch. (Unnecessary to give further particulars of a man whose share in the enrichment of our intellectual life is so widely known.) The Dombrowska introduced me: 'Herr Sebald, the late owner of Marat's bathtub.' My fame had spread.

'Aha,' said Golch. I inferred, from the inflection he gave to these syllables, that he was weighing my potentialities as a candidate for the cultural elite. I asked him how he had liked the exhibition of contemporary painting in Luxemburg. For one might, indeed, one must, assume that those here assembled had seen, read, and heard everything of any real importance. That was why they were here. Golch raised his eyes as if looking for a word in space and said, 'Passé.' (He used the English accentuation of the word which was then in fashion. The words 'cliché' and 'pastiche' too were pronounced à l'anglaise. I don't know what the current usage is. I am now too much taken up with everyday affairs to concern myself with such matters.) I noticed in any case that I had blundered in thus mentioning the contemporary. I had gone down a step, but I had learned my lesson.

A move was made to the buffet. Here I encountered Signora Sgambati, the astrologer, who had recently made a considerable stir by her theory that not only the fate of individuals but whole trends in the history of ideas could be read in the stars. She was no ordinary phenomenon, this Sgambati, as was at once clear from her appearance. Yet I find it incomprehensible in the circumstances that she did not see in the constellation of the heavens the imminent engulfment of so many substantial members of the intellectual world. She was deep in conversation with Professor Kuntz-Sartori, the politician and royalist, who had been trying for decades to introduce a monarchy in Switzerland. Another notable figure.

After taking some refreshment the company moved to the Silver Room for what was to be the climax of the evening's entertainment, a performance of a special kind – the world première of two flute sonatas by Antonio Giambattista Bloch, a contemporary and friend of Rameau, who had been discovered by the musicologist Weltli. He too, of course, was there. They were played by the flautist Béranger (yes, a descendant) and accompanied by the Marchesa herself, on the self-same harpsichord on which Célestine Rameau had initiated her son into the fundamental principles of counterpoint, and which had been sent for from Paris. The flute too had a history, but I have forgotten it. The two performers had put on rococo costume for the occasion, and the little ensemble looked – they had purposely so arranged themselves – like a picture by Watteau. The performance of course took place by the dimmest of candlelight. There was not a person there who would have found electric light for such an occasion anything but intolerable. By a further sensitive whim of the Marchesa the guests were required after the first sonata (D major) to move over from the Silver Room (Baroque) to the Golden Room (early Rococo), there to enjoy the second sonata. For the Silver Room had a major resonance, the Golden, it could not be disputed, a minor.

At this point I must remark that the tedious elegance which clings to the flute sonatas of second-rank, and more particularly of newly discovered, masters of this period was in the present case to be explained by the fact that no such person as Giambattista Bloch had ever lived.

The works here performed had in reality been composed by the musicologist Weltli. Although this circumstance did not become known till later, I cannot, in retrospect, help feeling it a humiliation for the Marchesa that she should have employed her last moments in the interpretation, however masterly, of a forgery.

During the second movement of the F minor sonata I saw a rat creeping along the wall. I was astonished. At first I thought it might have been lured from its hole by the sound of the flute – such things do happen, they say – but it was creeping in the opposite direction. It was followed by another rat. I looked at the guests. They had not noticed anything, and indeed most of them were keeping their eyes closed in order to be able to abandon themselves to the harmonies of Weltli's forgery. I now heard a dull reverberation, like very distant thunder. The floor began to vibrate. Again I looked at the guests. If they had heard anything – and something they must be hearing – it was at any rate not discernible from their hunched-up postures. I however was made uneasy by these strange symptoms.

A manservant entered. This is barely the place to remark that in the unusual costume worn by the Marchesa's domestic staff he looked like a character out of *Tosca*. He went up to the performers and whispered something in the Marchesa's ear. I saw her turn pale. How well it suited her in the dim candlelight! But she controlled herself and without interruption played the *andante* calmly to the end. Then she nodded to the flautist, stood up, and addressed the company.

'Ladies and gentlemen,' she said. 'I have just learnt that the foundations of the island and those of the palace with them are breaking up. The Office of Submarine Works has been informed. The right thing, I think we shall all agree, is to go on with the music.'

She sat down again, gave the sign to Monsieur Béranger, and they played the *allegro con brio*, the last movement, which did seem to me at the time, though I had yet no inkling that it was a forgery, little suited to the uniqueness of the situation.

On the polished floor small puddles were forming. The reverberation had grown louder and sounded nearer. Most of the guests were now sitting upright, their faces ashen in the candlelight, and looking as if they were long dead already. I stood up and said, 'I'm going,' not so loud as to give offence to the musicians, but loud enough to intimate to the other guests that I had the courage to admit my fear. The floor was now almost evenly covered with water. Although I walked on tiptoe, I could not help splashing an evening dress or two as I passed. But, in view of what was soon to come, the damage I did must be reckoned inconsiderable. Few of the guests thought me worthy of a glance, but I did not care. As I opened the door to the passage a wave of water poured into the room and caused Lady Fitzjones (the preserver of Celtic customs) to draw her fur wrap more closely about her – no doubt a reflex movement, for it could not be of any use. Before shutting the door behind me I saw Herr von Perlhuhn (the neo-mystic, not the Abraham-a-Santa Clara expert) casting a half-contemptuous, half-melancholy glance in my direction. He too was now sitting in water almost to his knees. So was the Marchesa, who could no longer use the pedals. I do not as a matter of fact know how essential they are on the harpsichord. I remember thinking that if the piece had been a cello sonata, they would perforce have had to break it off here, since the instrument would not sound in water. Strange what irrelevant thoughts occur to one in such moments.

In the entrance hall it was suddenly as quiet as in a grotto, only in the distance a sound of rushing water was to be heard. I divested myself of my tail-coat and was soon swimming through the sinking palace towards the portals. My splashes echoed mysteriously from the walls and columns. Not a soul was to be seen. Evidently the servants had all fled. And why should they not? They had no obligation to the true and eternal culture, and those assembled here had no further need of their services.

Outside the moon shone as if nothing were amiss, and yet a world, no less, was here sinking beneath the ocean. As if at a great distance I could still hear the high notes of Monsieur Béranger's flute. He had a wonderful *embouchure*, that one must allow him.

I unhitched the last gondola which the escaping servants had left behind and pushed out to sea. Through the windows past which I paddled the water was now flooding into the palace. I saw that the guests had risen from their seats. The sonata must be at an end, for they were clapping, their hands held high over their heads, since the water was now up to their chins. With dignity the Marchesa and Monsieur Béranger were acknowledging the applause, though in the circumstances they could not bow.

The water had now reached the candles. Slowly they were extinguished, and as the darkness grew, it became quiet; the applause was silenced. Suddenly I heard the crash and roar of a building in collapse. The Palazzo was falling. I steered the gondola seaward so as not to be hit by plaster fragments.

After paddling some hundreds of yards across the lagoon in the direction of the island of San Giorgio, I turned round once more. The sea lay dead calm in the moonlight as if no island had ever stood there. A pity about the bathtub, I thought, for that was a loss which could never be made good. The thought was perhaps rather heartless, but experience teaches us that we need a certain distance from such events in order to appreciate their full scope.

VLADIMIR NABOKOV was born in 1899 in St Petersburg, Russia, and at present lives with his wife in Switzerland. His reputation as the major émigré Russian writer of our time is based on the novels *Pnin*, *Pale Fire*, *Lolita*, and *Ada* and on a collection of short stories, *Nabokov's Dozen*.

'that in aleppo once . . .'

VLADIMIR NABOKOV

Dear V – Among other things, this is to tell you that at last I am here, in the country whither so many sunsets have led. One of the first persons I saw was our good old Gleb Alexandrovich Gekko gloomily crossing Columbus Avenue in quest of the *petit café du coin* which none of us three will ever visit again. He seemed to think that somehow or other you were betraying our national literature, and he gave me your address with a deprecatory shake of his grey head, as if you did not deserve the treat of hearing from me.

I have a story for you. Which reminds me – I mean putting it like this reminds me – of the days when we wrote our first udder-warm bubbling verse, and all things, a rose, a puddle, a lighted window, cried out to us: 'I'm a rhyme!' Yes, this is a most useful universe. We play, we die, *ig-rhyme, umi-rhyme*. And the sonorous souls of Russian verbs lend a meaning to the wild gesticulation of trees or to some discarded newspaper sliding and pausing, and shuffling again, with abortive flaps and apterous jerks along an endless windswept embankment. But just now I am not a poet. I come to you like that gushing lady in Chekhov who was dying to be described.

I married, let me see, about a month after you left France and a few weeks before the gentle Germans roared into Paris. Although I can produce documentary proofs of matrimony, I am positive now that my wife never existed. You may know her name from some other source, but that does not matter: it is the name of an illusion. Therefore, I am able to speak of her with as much detachment as I would of a character in a story (one of your stories, to be precise).

It was love at first touch rather than at first sight, for I had met her several times before without experiencing any special emotions; but one night, as I was seeing her home, something quaint she had said made me stoop with a laugh and lightly kiss her on the hair – and of course we all know of that blinding blast which is caused by merely picking up a small doll from the floor of a carefully abandoned house: the soldier involved hears nothing; for him it is but an ecstatic soundless and boundless expansion of what had been during his life a pinpoint of light in the dark centre of his being. And really, the reason we think of death in celestial terms is that the visible firmament, especially at night (above our blacked-out Paris with the gaunt arches of its Boulevard Exelmans and the ceaseless Alpine gurgle of desolate latrines), is the most adequate and ever-present symbol of that vast silent explosion.

But I cannot discern her. She remains as nebulous as my best poem – the one you made such gruesome fun of in the *Literaturnïe Zapiski*. When I want to imagine her, I have to cling mentally to a tiny brown birthmark on her downy forearm, as one concentrates upon a punctuation mark in an illegible sentence. Perhaps, had she used a greater amount of make-up or used it more constantly, I might have visualized her face today, or at least the delicate transverse furrows of dry, hot, rouged lips; but I fail, I fail – although I still feel their elusive touch now and then in the blindman's buff of my senses, in that sobbing sort of dream when she and I clumsily clutch at each other through a heart-breaking mist and I cannot see the colour of her eyes for the blank lustre of brimming tears drowning their irises.

She was much younger than I – not as much younger as was Nathalie of the lovely bare shoulders and long earrings in relation to swarthy Pushkin; but still there was a sufficient margin for that kind of retrospective romanticism which finds pleasure in imitating the destiny of a unique genius (down to the jealousy, down to the filth, down to the stab of seeing her almond-shaped eyes turn to her blond Cassio behind her peacock-feathered fan), even if one cannot imitate his verse. She liked mine though, and would scarcely have yawned as the other was wont to do every time her husband's poem happened to exceed the length of a sonnet. If she has remained a phantom to me, I may have been one to her: I suppose she had been solely attracted by the obscurity of my poetry; then tore a hole through its veil and saw a stranger's unlovable face.

As you know, I had been for some time planning to follow the example of your fortunate flight. She described to me an uncle of hers who lived, she said, in New York: he had taught riding at a Southern college and had wound up by marrying a wealthy American woman; they had a little daughter born deaf. She said she had lost their address long ago, but a few days later it miraculously turned up, and we wrote a dramatic letter to which we never received any reply. This did not much matter, as I had already obtained a sound affidavit from Professor Lomchenko of Chicago; but little else had been done in the way of getting the necessary papers when the invasion began, whereas I foresaw that if we stayed on in Paris some helpful compatriot of mine would sooner or later point out to the interested party sundry passages in one of my books where I argued that, with all her many black sins, Germany was still bound to remain forever and ever the laughing-stock of the world.

So we started upon our disastrous honeymoon. Crushed and jolted amid the apocalyptic exodus, waiting for unscheduled trains that were bound for unknown destinations, walking through the stale stage setting of abstract towns, living in a permanent twilight of physical exhaustion, we fled; and the farther we fled, the clearer it became that what was driving us on was something more than a booted and buckled fool with his assortment of variously propelled junk – something of which he was a mere symbol, something monstrous and impalpable, a timeless and faceless mass of immemorial horror that still keeps coming at me from behind even here, in the green vacuum of Central Park.

Oh, she bore it gamely enough – with a kind of dazed cheerfulness. Once, however, quite suddenly she started to sob in a sympathetic railway carriage. 'The dog,' she said, 'the dog we left. I cannot forget the poor dog.' The honesty of her grief shocked me, as we had never had any dog. 'I know,' she said. 'But I tried to imagine we had actually bought that setter. And just think, he would be now whining behind a locked door.' There had never been any talk of buying a setter.

I should also not like to forget a certain stretch of highroad and the sight of a family of refugees (two women, a child) whose old father, or grandfather, had died on the way. The sky was a chaos of black and flesh-coloured clouds with an ugly sunburst beyond a hooded hill, and the dead man was lying on his back under a dusty plane tree. With a stick and their hands the women had tried to dig a roadside grave, but the soil was too hard; they had given it up and were sitting side by side, among the anaemic poppies, a little apart from the corpse and its upturned beard. But the little boy was still scratching and scraping and tugging until he tumbled a flat stone and forgot the object of his solemn exertions as he crouched on his haunches, his thin, eloquent neck showing all its vertebrae to the headsman, and watched with surprise and delight thousands of minute brown ants seething, zigzagging, dispersing, heading for places of safety in the Gard, and the Aude, and the Drome, and the Var, and the Basses-Pyrénées – we two paused only in Pau.

Spain proved too difficult and we decided to move on to Nice. At a place called Faugères (a ten-minute stop) I squeezed out of the train to buy some food. When a couple of minutes later I came back, the train was gone, and the muddled old man responsible for the atrocious void that faced me (coal dust glittering in the heat between naked indifferent rails, and a lone piece of orange peel) brutally told me that, anyway, I had had no right to get out.

In a better world I could have had my wife located and told what to do (I had both tickets and most of the money); as it was, my nightmare struggle with the telephone proved futile, so I dismissed the whole series of diminutive voices barking at me from afar, sent two or three telegrams which are probably on their way only now, and late in the evening took the next local to Montpellier, farther than which her train would not stumble. Not finding her there, I had to choose between two alternatives: going on because she might have boarded the Marseilles train which I had just missed, or going back because she might have returned to Faugères. I forget now what tangle of reasoning led me to Marseilles and Nice.

Beyond such routine action as forwarding false data to a few unlikely places, the police did nothing to help: one man bellowed at me for being a nuisance; another sidetracked the question by doubting the authenticity of my marriage certificate because it was stamped on what he contended to be the wrong side; a third, a fat *commissaire* with liquid brown eyes, confessed that he wrote poetry in his spare time. I looked up various acquaintances among the numerous Russians domiciled or stranded in Nice. I heard those among them who chanced to have Jewish blood talk of their doomed kinsmen crammed into hell-bound trains; and my own plight, by contrast, acquired a commonplace air of irreality while I sat in some crowded café with the milky blue sea in front of me and a shell-hollow murmur behind telling and retelling the tale of massacre and misery, and the grey paradise beyond the ocean, the ways and whims of harsh consuls.

A week after my arrival an indolent plain-clothes man called upon me and took me down a crooked and smelly street to a black-stained house with the word 'hotel' almost erased by dirt and time; there, he said, my wife had been found. The girl he produced was an absolute stranger, of course; but my friend Holmes kept on trying for some time to make her and me confess we were married, while her taciturn and muscular bed-fellow stood by and listened, his bare arms crossed on his striped chest.

When at length I got rid of those people and had wandered back to my neighbourhood, I happened to pass by a compact queue waiting at the entrance of a food store; and there, at the very end, was my wife, straining on tiptoe to catch a glimpse of what exactly was being sold. I think the first thing she said to me was that she hoped it was oranges.

Her tale seemed a trifle hazy, but perfectly banal. She had returned to Faugères and gone straight to the Commissariat instead of making inquiries at the station, where I had left a message for her. A party of refugees suggested that she join them; she spent the night in a bicycle shop with no bicycles, on the floor, together with the three elderly women who lay, she said, like three logs in a row. Next day she realized that she had not enough money to reach Nice. Eventually she borrowed some from one of the log-women. She got into the wrong train, however, and travelled to a town the name of which she could not remember. She had arrived at Nice two days ago and had found some friends at the Russian church. They had told her I was somewhere around, looking for her, and would surely turn up soon.

Some time later, as I sat on the edge of the only chair in my garret and held her by her slender young hips (she was combing her soft hair and tossing her head back with every stroke), her dim smile changed all at once into an odd quiver and she placed one hand on my shoulder, staring down at me as if I were a reflection in a pool, which she had noticed for the first time.

'I've been lying to you, dear,' she said. '*Ya lgunia.* I stayed for several nights in Montpellier with a brute of a man I met on the train. I did not want it at all. He sold hair lotions.'

The time, the place, the torture. Her fan, her gloves, her mask. I spent that night and many others getting it out of her bit by bit, but not getting it all. I was under the strange delusion that first I must find out every detail, reconstruct every minute, and only then decide whether I could bear it. But the limit of desired knowledge was unattainable, nor could I ever foretell the approximate point after which I might imagine myself satiated, because of course the denominator of every fraction of knowledge was potentially as infinite as the number of intervals between the fractions themselves.

Oh, the first time she had been too tired to mind, and the next had not minded because she was sure I had deserted her; and she apparently considered that such explanations ought to be a kind of consolation prize for me instead of the nonsense and agony they really were. It went on like that for aeons, she breaking down every now and then, but soon rallying again, answering my unprintable questions in a breathless whisper or trying with a pitiful smile to wriggle into the semi-security of irrelevant commentaries, and I crushing and crushing the mad molar till my jaw almost burst with pain, a flaming pain which seemed somehow preferable to the dull, humming ache of humble endurance.

And mark, in between the periods of this inquest, we were trying to get from reluctant authorities certain papers which in their turn would make it lawful to apply for a third kind which would serve as a stepping-stone towards a permit enabling the holder to apply for yet other papers which might or might not give him the means of discovering how and why it had happened. For even if I could imagine the accursed recurrent scene, I failed to link up its sharp-angled grotesque shadows with the dim limbs of my wife as she shook and rattled and dissolved in my violent grasp.

So nothing remained but to torture each other, to wait for hours on end in the Prefecture, filling forms, conferring with friends who had already probed the innermost viscera of all visas, pleading with secretaries, and filling forms again, with the result that her lusty and versatile travelling salesman became blended in a ghastly mix-up with rat-whiskered snarling officials, rotting bundles of obsolete records, the reek of violet ink, bribes slipped under gangrenous blotting paper, fat flies tickling moist necks with their rapid cold padded feet, new-laid clumsy concave photographs of your six subhuman doubles, the tragic eyes and patient politeness of petitioners born in Slutzk, Starodub, or Bobruisk, the funnels and pulleys of the Holy Inquisition, the awful smile of the bald man with the glasses, who had been told that his passport could not be found.

I confess that one evening, after a particularly abominable day, I sank down on a stone bench weeping and cursing a mock world where millions of lives were being juggled by the clammy hands of consuls and *commissaires*. I noticed she was crying too, and then I told her that nothing would really have mattered the way it mattered now, had she not gone and done what she did.

'You will think me crazy,' she said with a vehemence that, for a second, almost made a real person of her, 'but I didn't – I swear that I didn't. Perhaps I live several lives at once. Perhaps I wanted to test you. Perhaps this bench is a dream and we are in Saratov or on some star.'

It would be tedious to niggle the different stages through which I passed before accepting finally the first version of her delay. I did not talk to her and was a good deal alone. She would glimmer and fade, and reappear with some trifle she thought I would appreciate – a handful of cherries, three precious cigarettes or the like – treating me with the unruffled mute sweetness of a nurse that trips from and to a gruff convalescent. I ceased visiting most of our mutual friends because they had lost all interest in my passport affairs and seemed to have turned vaguely inimical. I composed several poems. I drank all the wine I could get. I clasped her one day to my groaning breast, and we went for a week to Caboule and lay on the round pink pebbles of the narrow beach. Strange to say, the happier our new relations seemed, the stronger I felt an undercurrent of poignant sadness, but I kept telling myself that this was an intrinsic feature of all true bliss.

In the meantime, something had shifted in the moving pattern of our fates and at last I emerged from a dark and hot office with a couple of plump *visas de sortie* cupped in my trembling hands. Into these the USA serum was duly injected, and I dashed to Marseilles and managed to get tickets for the very next boat. I returned and tramped up the stairs. I saw a rose in a glass on the table – the sugar pink of its obvious beauty, the parasitic air bubbles clinging to its stem. Her two spare dresses were gone, her comb was gone, her checkered coat was gone, and so was the mauve hairband with a mauve bow that had been her hat. There was no note pinned to the pillow, nothing at all in the room to enlighten me, for of course the rose was merely what French rhymsters call *une cheville*.

I went to the Veretennikovs, who could tell me nothing; to the Hellmans, who refused to say anything; and to the Elagins, who were not sure whether to tell me or not. Finally the old lady – and you know what Anna Vladimirovna is like at crucial moments – asked for her rubber-tipped cane, heavily but energetically dislodged her bulk from her favourite armchair, and took me into the garden. There she informed me that, being twice my age, she had the right to say I was a bully and a cad.

You must imagine the scene: the tiny gravelled garden with its blue Arabian Nights jar and solitary cypress; the cracked terrace where the old lady's father had dozed with a rug on his knees when he retired from his Novgorod governorship to spend a few last evenings in Nice; the pale-green sky; a whiff of vanilla in the deepening dusk; the crickets emitting their metallic trill pitched at two octaves above middle C; and Anna Vladimirovna, the folds of her cheeks jerkily dangling as she flung at me a motherly but quite undeserved insult.

During several preceding weeks, my dear V, every time she had visited by herself the three or four families we both knew, my ghostly wife had filled the eager ears of all those kind people with an extraordinary story. To wit: that she had madly fallen in love with a young Frenchman who could give her a turreted home and a crested name; that she had implored me for a divorce and I had refused; that in fact I had said I would rather shoot her and myself than sail to New York alone; that she had said her father in a similar case had acted like a gentleman; that I had answered I did not give a hoot for her *cocu de père*.

There were loads of other preposterous details of the kind – but they all hung together in such a remarkable fashion that no wonder the old lady made me swear I would not seek to pursue the lovers with a cocked pistol. They had gone, she said, to a château in Lozère. I inquired whether she had ever set eyes upon the man. No, but she had been shown his picture. As I was about to leave, Anna Vladimirovna, who had slightly relaxed and had even given me her five fingers to kiss, suddenly flared up again, struck the gravel with her cane, and said in her deep strong voice: 'But one thing I shall never forgive you – her dog, that poor beast which you hanged with your own hands before leaving Paris.'

Whether the gentleman of leisure had changed into a travelling salesman, or whether the metamorphosis had been reversed, or whether again he was neither the one nor the other, but the nondescript Russian who had courted her before our marriage – all this was absolutely inessential. She had gone. That was the end. I should have been a fool had I begun the nightmare business of searching and waiting for her all over again.

On the fourth morning of a long and dismal sea voyage, I met on the deck a solemn but pleasant old doctor with whom I had played chess in Paris. He asked me whether my wife was very much incommoded by the rough seas. I answered that I had sailed alone; whereupon he looked taken aback and then said he had seen her a couple of days before going on board, namely in Marseilles, walking, rather aimlessly he thought, along the embankment. She said that I would presently join her with bag and tickets.

This is, I gather, the point of the whole story – although if you write it, you had better not make him a doctor, as that kind of thing has been overdone. It was at that moment that I suddenly knew for certain that she had never existed at all. I shall tell you another thing. When I arrived I hastened to satisfy a certain morbid curiosity: I went to the address she had given me once; it proved to be an anonymous gap between two office buildings; I looked for her uncle's name in the directory; it was not there; I made some inquiries, and Gekko, who knows everything, informed me that the man and his horsey wife existed all right, but had moved to San Francisco after their deaf little girl had died.

Viewing the past graphically, I see our mangled romance engulfed in a deep valley of mist between the crags of two matter-of-fact mountains: life has been real before, life will be real from now on, I hope. Not tomorrow, though. Perhaps after tomorrow. You, happy mortal, with your lovely family (how is Ines? how are the twins?) and your diversified work (how are the lichens?), can hardly be expected to puzzle out my misfortune in terms of human communion, but you may clarify things for me through the prism of your art.

Yet the pity of it. Curse your art, I am hideously unhappy. She keeps on walking to and fro where the brown nets are spread to dry on the hot stone slabs and the dappled light of the water plays on the side of a moored fishing boat. Somewhere, somehow, I have made some fatal mistake. There are tiny pale bits of broken fish scales glistening here and there in the brown meshes. It may all end in *Aleppo* if I am not careful. Spare me, V: you would load your dice with an unbearable implication if you took that for a title.

DYLAN THOMAS was born in 1914 in Wales. During his brief career (he died in 1953) he was acclaimed as a poet, but he also wrote some remarkable stories and essays unmatched in their lyrical power and surrealistic suggestiveness. This prose appears in *Portrait of the Artist as a Young Dog, Adventures in the Skin Trade, Quite Early One Morning,* and *A Prospect of the Sea.*

one warm saturday

DYLAN THOMAS

The young man in a sailor's jersey, sitting near the summer huts to see the brown-and-white women coming out and the groups of pretty-faced girls with pale vees and scorched backs who picked their way delicately on ugly, red-toed feet over the sharp stones to the sea, drew on the sand a large, indented woman's figure; and a naked child, just out of the sea, ran over it and shook water, marking on the figure two wide wet eyes and a hole in the footprinted middle. He rubbed the woman away and drew a paunched man: the child ran over it, tossing her hair, and shook a row of buttons down its belly and a line of drops, like piddle in a child's drawing, between the long legs stuck with shells.

In a huddle of picnicking women and their children, stretched out limp and damp in the sweltering sun or fussing over paper carriers or building castles that were at once destroyed by the tattered march of other picnickers to different pieces of the beach, among the ice-cream cries, the angrily happy shouts of boys playing ball, and the screams of girls as the sea rose to their waists, the young man sat alone with the shadows of his failure at his side. Some silent husbands, with rolled-up trousers and suspenders dangling, paddled slowly on the border of the sea, paddling women, in thick, black picnic dresses, laughed at their own legs, dogs chased stones, and one proud boy rode the water on a rubber seal. The young man, in his wilderness, saw the holiday Saturday set down before him, false and pretty, as a flat picture under the vulgar sun; the disporting families with paper bags, buckets and spades, parasols and bottles, the happy, hot, and aching girls with sunburn liniments in their bags, the bronzed young men with chests, and the envious, white young men in waistcoats, the thin, pale, hairy, pathetic legs of the husbands silently walking through the water, the plump and curly, shaven-headed and bowed-backed children up to no sense with unrepeatable delight in the dirty sand, moved him, he thought dramatically in his isolation, to an old shame and pity; outside all holiday, like a young man doomed forever to the company of his maggots, beyond the high and ordinary, sweating, sun-awakened power and stupidity of the summer flesh on a day and a world out, he caught the ball that a small boy had whacked into the air with a tiny tray, and rose to throw it back.

The boy invited him to play. A friendly family stood waiting some way off, the tousled women with their dresses tucked in their knickers, the barefooted men in shirtsleeves, a number of children in slips and cut-down underwear. He bowed bitterly to a father standing with a tray before a wicket of hats. 'The lone wolf playing ball,' he said to himself as the tray whirled. Chasing the ball towards the sea, passing undressing women with a rush and a wink, tripping over a castle into a coil of wet girls lying like snakes, soaking his shoes as he grabbed the ball off a wave, he felt his happiness return in a boast of the body, and, 'Look out, Duckworth, here's a fast one coming,' he cried to the mother behind the hats. The ball bounced on a boy's head. In and out of the scattered families, among the sandwiches and clothes, uncles and mothers fielded the bouncing ball. A bald man, with his shirt hanging out, returned it in the wrong direction, and a collie carried it into the sea. Now it was mother's turn with the tray. Tray and ball together flew over her head. An uncle in a panama smacked the ball to the dog, who swam with it out of reach. They offered the young man egg-and-cress sandwiches and warm stout, and he and an uncle and a father sat down on the *Evening Post* until the sea touched their feet.

Alone again, hot and unhappy, for the boasting minute when he ran among the unknown people lying and running loudly at peace was struck away, like a ball, he said, into the sea, he walked to a space on the beach where a hellfire preacher on a box marked 'Mr Matthews' was talking to a congregation of expressionless women. Boys with peashooters sat quietly near him. A ragged man collected nothing in a cap.

Mr Matthews shook his cold hands, stormed at the holiday, and cursed the summer from his shivering box. He cried for a new warmth. The strong sun shone into his bones, and he buttoned his coat collar. Valley children, with sunken, impudent eyes, quick tongues, and singing voices, chests thin as shells, gathered round the Punch and Judy and the Stop Me tricycles, and he denied them all. He contradicted the girls in their underclothes combing and powdering, and the modest girls cleverly dressing under tents of towels.

As Mr Matthews cast down the scarlet town, drove out the bare-bellied boys who danced around the ice-cream man, and wound the girls' sunburnt thighs about with his black overcoat – 'Down! down!' he cried, 'the night is upon us' – the young man in dejection stood, with a shadow at his shoulder, and thought of Porthcawl's Coney Beach, where his friends were rocking with girls on the Giant Racer or tearing in the Ghost Train down the skeletons' tunnel. Leslie Bird would have his arms full of coconuts. Brenda was with Herbert at the rifle range. Gil Morris was buying Molly a cocktail with a cherry at the 'Esplanade'. Here he stood, listening to Mr Matthews, the retired drinker, crying darkness on the evening sands, with money hot in his pocket and Saturday burning away.

In his loneliness he had refused their invitations. Herbert, in his low, red sports car, GB at the back, a sea-blown nymph on the radiator, called at his father's house, but he said: 'I'm not in the mood, old man. I'm going to spend a quiet day. Enjoy yourselves. Don't take too much pop.' Only waiting for the sun to set, he stood in the sad circle with the pleasureless women who were staring at a point in the sky behind their prophet, and wished the morning back. Oh, boy! to be wasting his money now on the rings and ranges of the fair, to be sitting in the chromium lounge with a short worth one and six and a Turkish ciga-rette, telling the latest one to the girls, seeing the sun, through the palms in the lounge window, sink over the promenade, over the Bath chairs, the cripples and widows, the beach-trousered, kerchiefed, week-end wives, the smart, kiss-curled girls with plain and spectacled girl-friends, the innocent, swaggering, loud bad boys, and the poms at the ankles, and the cycling sweetmen. Ronald had sailed to Ilfracombe on the *Lady Moira*, and, in the thick saloon, with a party from Brynhyfryd, he'd be knocking back nips without a thought that on the sands at home his friend was alone and pussyfoot at six o'clock, and the evening dull as a chapel. All his friends had vanished into their pleasures.

He thought: poets live and walk with their poems; a man with visions needs no other company; Saturday is a crude day; I must go home and sit in my bedroom by the boiler. But he was not a poet living and walking, he was a young man in a sea town on a warm Bank Holiday, with two pounds to spend; he had no visions, only two pounds and a small body with its feet on the littered sand; serenity was for old men; and he moved away, over the railway points, on to the tramlined road.

He snarled at the flower clock in Victoria Gardens.

'And what shall a prig do now?' he said aloud, causing a young woman on a bench opposite the white-tiled urinal to smile and put her novel down.

She had chestnut hair arranged high on her head in an old-fashioned way, in loose coils and a bun, and a Woolworth's white rose grew out of it and drooped to touch her ear. She wore a white frock with a red paper flower pinned on the breast, and rings and bracelets that came from a fun-fair stall. Her eyes were small and quite green.

He marked, carefully and coldly in one glance, all the unusual details of her appearance; it was the calm, unstartled certainty of her bearing before his glance from head to foot, the innocent knowledge, in her smile and the set of her head, that she was defended by her gentleness and accessible strangeness against all rude encounters and picking looks, that made his fingers tremble. Though her frock was long and the collar high, she could as well be naked there on the blistered bench. Her smile confessed her body bare and spotless and willing and warm under the cotton, and she waited without guilt.

How beautiful she is, he thought, with his mind on words and his eyes on her hair and red-and-white skin, how beautifully she waits for me, though she does not know she is waiting and I can never tell her.

He had stopped and was staring. Like a confident girl before a camera, she sat smiling, her hands folded, her head slightly to one side so that the rose brushed her neck. She accepted his admiration. The girl in a million took his long look to herself, and cherished his stupid love.

Midges flew into his mouth. He hurried on shamefully. At the gates of the Gardens he turned to see her for the last time on earth. She had lost her calm with his abrupt and awkward going, and stared in confusion after him. One hand was raised as though to beckon him back. If he waited, she would call him. He walked round the corner and heard her voice, a hundred voices, and all hers, calling his name, and a hundred names that were all his, over the bushy walls.

And what shall the terrified prig of a love-mad young man do next? he asked his reflection silently in the distorting mirror of the empty 'Victoria' saloon. His apelike, hanging face, with 'Bass' across the forehead, gave back a cracked sneer.

If Venus came in on a plate, said the two red, melon-slice lips, I would ask for vinegar to put on her.

She could drive my guilt out; she could smooth away my shame; why didn't I stop to talk to her? he asked.

You saw a queer tart in a park, his reflection answered, she was a child of nature, oh my ! oh my! Did you see the dewdrops in her hair? Stop talking to the mirror like a man in a magazine, I know you too well.

A new head, swollen and low-jawed, wagged behind his shoulder. He spun round, to hear the barman say:

'Has the one and only let you down? You look like death warmed up. Have this one on the house. Free beer today. Free X's.' He pulled the beer handle. 'Only the best served here. Straight from the rust. You do look queer,' he said, 'the only one saved from the wreck and the only wreck saved. Here's looking at you!' He drank the beer he had drawn.

'May I have a glass of beer, please?'

'What do you think this is, a public house?'

On the polished table in the middle of the saloon the young man drew, with a finger dipped in strong, the round head of a girl and piled a yellow froth of hair upon it.

'Ah! dirty, dirty!' said the barman, running round from behind the counter and rubbing the head away with a dry cloth.

Shielding the dirtiness with his hat, the young man wrote his name on the edge of the table and watched the letters dry and fade.

Through the open bay window, across the useless railway covered with sand, he saw the black dots of bathers, the stunted huts, the jumping dwarfs round the Punch and Judy, and the tiny religious circle. Since he had walked and played down there in the crowded wilderness, excusing his despair, searching for company though he refused it, he had found his own true happiness and lost her all in one bewildering and clumsy half a minute by the 'Gentlemen' and the flower clock. Older and wiser and no better, he would have looked in the mirror to see if his discovery and loss had marked themselves upon his face in shadows under the eyes or lines about the mouth, were it not for the answer he knew he would receive from the distorted reflection.

The barman came to sit near him, and said in a false voice: 'Now you tell me all about it, I'm a regular storehouse of secrets.'

'There isn't anything to tell. I saw a girl in Victoria Gardens and I was too shy to speak to her. She was a piece of God-help-us all right.'

Ashamed of his wish to be companionable, even in the depth of love and distress, with her calm face before his eyes and her smile reproving and forgiving him as he spoke, the young man defiled his girl on the bench, dragged her down into the spit and sawdust and dolled her up to make the barman say:

'I like them big myself. Once round Bessy, once round the gasworks. I missed the chance of a lifetime, too. Fifty lovelies in the rude and I'd left my Bunsen burner home.'

'Give me the same, please.'

'You mean similar.'

The barman drew a glass of beer, drank it, and drew another.

'I always have one with the customers,' he said, 'it puts us on even terms. Now we're just two heartbroken bachelors together.' He sat down again.

'You can't tell me anything I don't know,' he said. 'I've seen over twenty chorines from the Empire in this bar, drunk as printers. Oh, les girls! les limbs!'

'Will they be in tonight?'

'There's only a fellow sawing a woman in half this week.'

'Keep a half for me.'

A drunk man walked in on an invisible white line, and the barman, reeling in sympathy across the room, served him with a pint. 'Free beer today,' he said. 'Free Xs. You've been out in the sun.'

'I've been out in the sun all day,' said the man.

'I thought you looked sunburnt.'

'That's drink,' said the man. 'I've been drinking.'

'The holiday is drawing to an end,' the young man whispered into his glass. Bye-bye blackbird, the moment is lost, he thought, examining, with an interest he could not forgive, the comic coloured postcards of mountain-buttocked women on the beach and henpecked, pin-legged men with telescopes, pasted on the wall beneath the picture of a terrier drinking stout; and now, with a jolly barman and a drunk in a crushed cap, he was mopping the failing day down. He tipped his hat over his forehead, and a lock of hair that fell below the hat tickled his eyelid. He saw, with a stranger's darting eye that missed no single subtlety of the wry grin or the faintest gesture drawing the shape of his death on the air, an unruly-haired young man who coughed into his hand in the corner of a rotting room and puffed the smoke of his doped Weight.

But as the drunk man weaved towards him on wilful feet, carrying his dignity as a man might carry a full glass around a quaking ship, as the barman behind the counter clattered and whistled and dipped to drink, he shook off the truthless, secret tragedy with a sneer and a blush, straightened his melancholy hat into a hard-brimmed trilby, dismissed the affected stranger. In the safe centre of his own identity, the familiar world about him like another flesh, he sat sad and content in the plain room of the undistinguished hotel at the sea-end of the shabby, spreading town where everything was happening. He had no need of the dark interior world when Tawe pressed in upon him and the eccentric ordinary people came bursting and crawling, with noise and colours, out of their houses, out of the graceless buildings, the factories and avenues, the shining shops and blaspheming chapels, the terminuses and the meeting halls, the falling alleys and brick lanes, from the arches and shelters and holes behind the hoardings, out of the common, wild intelligence of the town.

At last the drunk man had reached him. 'Put your hand here,' he said, and turned about and tapped himself on the bottom.

The barman whistled and rose from his drink to see the young man touch the drunk man on the seat of the trousers.

'What can you feel there?'

'Nothing.'

'That's right. Nothing. Nothing. There's nothing there to feel.'

'How can you sit down then?' asked the barman.

'I just sit down on what the doctor left,' the man said angrily. 'I had as good a bottom as you've got once. I was working underground in Dowlais, and the end of the world came down on me. Do you know what I got for losing my bottom? Four and three! Two and three ha'pence a cheek. That's cheaper than a pig.'

The girl from Victoria Gardens came into the bar with two friends: a blonde young girl almost as beautiful as she was, and a middle-aged woman dressed and made up to look young. The three of them sat at the table. The girl he loved ordered three ports and gins.

'Isn't it delicious weather?' said the middle-aged woman.

The barman said: 'Plenty of sky about.' With many bows and smiles he placed their drinks in front of them. 'I thought the princesses had gone to a better pub,' he said.

'What's a better pub without you, handsome?' said the blonde girl.

'This is the "Ritz" and the "Savoy", isn't it, garçon darling?' the girl from the Gardens said, and kissed her hand to him.

The young man in the window seat, still bewildered by the first sudden sight of her entering the darkening room, caught the kiss to himself and blushed. He thought to run out of the room and through the miracle-making Gardens, to rush into his house and hide his head in the bedclothes and lie all night there, dressed and trembling, her voice in his ears, her green eyes wide awake under his closed eyelids. But only a sick boy with tossed blood would run from his proper love into a dream, lie down in a bedroom that was full of his shames, and sob against the feathery, fat breast and face on the damp pillow. He remembered his age and poems, and would not move.

'Tanks a million, Lou,' said the barman.

Her name was Lou, Louise, Louisa. She must be Spanish or French or a gypsy, but he could tell the street that her voice came from; he knew where her friends lived by the rise and fall of their sharp voices, and the name of the middle-aged woman was Mrs Emerald Franklin. She was to be seen every night in the 'Jew's Harp', sipping and spying and watching the clock.

'We've been listening to Matthews Hellfire on the sands. Down with this and down with that, and he used to drink a pint of biddy before his breakfast,' Mrs Franklin said. 'Oh, there's a nerve!'

'And his eye on the fluff all the time,' said the blonde girl. 'I wouldn't trust him any further than Ramon Navarro behind the counter.'

'Whoops! I've gone up in the world. Last week I was Charley Chase,' said the barman.

Mrs Franklin raised her empty glass in a gloved hand and shook it like a bell. 'Men are deceivers ever,' she said. 'And a drop of mother's ruin right around.'

'Especially Mr Franklin,' said the barman.

'But there's a lot in what the preacher says, mind,' Mrs Franklin said, 'about the carrying on. If you go for a constitutional after stop-tap along the sands you might as well be in Sodom and Gomorrah.'

The blonde girl laughed. 'Hark to Mrs Grundy! I see her with a black man last Wednesday, round by the museum.'

'He was an Indian,' said Mrs Franklin, 'from the university college, and I'd thank you to remember it. Everyone's brothers under the skin, but there's no tarbrush in my family.'

'Oh, dear! oh, dear!' said Lou. 'Lay off it, there's loves. This is my birthday. It's a holiday. Put a bit of fun in it. Miaow! miaow! Marjorie, kiss Emerald and be friends.' She smiled and laughed at them both. She winked at the barman, who was filling their glasses to the top. 'Here's to your blue eyes, garçon!' She had not noticed the young man in the corner. 'And one for grandad there,' she said, smiling at the swaying, drunk man. 'He's twenty-one today. There! I've made him smile.'

The drunk man made a deep, dangerous bow, lifted his hat, stumbled against the mantelpiece, and his full pint in his free hand was steady as a rock. 'The prettiest girl in Carmarthenshire,' he said.

'This is Glamorganshire, dad,' she said, 'where's your geography? Look at him waltzing! mind your glasses! He's got that Kruschen feeling. Come on, faster! give us the Charleston.'

The drunk man, with his pint held high, danced until he fell, and all the time he never spilled a drop. He lay at Lou's feet on the dusty floor and grinned up at her in confidence and affection. 'I fell,' he said. 'I could dance like a trooper when I had a beatyem.'

'He lost his bottom at the last trump,' the barman explained.

'When did he lose his bottom?' said Mrs Franklin.

'When Gabriel blew his whistle down in Dowlais.'

'You're pulling my leg.'

'It's a pleasure, Mrs Em. Hoi, you! get up from the vomitorium.'

The man wagged his end like a tail, and growled at Lou's feet.

'Put your head on my foot. Be comfy. Let him lie there,' she said.

He went to sleep at once.

'I can't have drunks on the premises.'

'You know where to go then.'

'Cru-el Mrs Franklin!'

'Go on, attend to your business. Serve the young man in the corner, his tongue's hanging out.'

'Cru-el lady!'

As Mrs Franklin called attention to the young man, Lou peered short-sightedly across the saloon and saw him sitting with his back to the window.

'I'll have to get glasses,' she said.

'You'll have plenty of glasses before the night's out.'

'No, honest, Marjorie, I didn't know anyone was there. I do beg your pardon, you in the corner,' she said.

The barman switched on the light. 'A bit of *lux in tenebris*.'

'Oh!' said Lou.

The young man dared not move for fear that he might break the long light of her scrutiny, the enchantment shining like a single line of light between them, or startle her into speaking; and he did not conceal the love in his eyes, for she could pierce through to it as easily as she could turn his heart in his chest and make it beat above the noises of the two friends' hurried conversation, the rattle of glasses behind the counter where the barman spat and polished and missed nothing, and the snores of the comfortable sleeper. Nothing can hurt me. Let the barman jeer. Giggle in your glass, our Em. I'm telling the world, I'm walking in clover. I'm staring at Lou like a fool, she's my girl, she's my lily. Oh love! O love! She's no lady, with her sing-song Tontine voice, she drinks like a deep-sea diver; but Lou, I'm yours, and Lou, you're mine. He refused to meditate on her calmness now and twist her beauty into words. She was nothing under the sun or moon but his. Unashamed and certain, he smiled at her; and, though he was prepared for all, her answering smile made his fingers tremble again, as they had trembled in the Gardens, and reddened his cheeks and drove his heart to a gallop.

'Harold, fill the young man's glass up,' Mrs Franklin said.

The barman stood still, a duster in one hand and a dripping glass in the other.

'Have you got water in your ears? Fill the young man's glass!'

The barman put the duster to his eyes. He sobbed. He wiped away the mock tears.

'I thought I was attending a première and this was the royal box,' he said.

'He's got water on the brain, not in his earhole,' said Marjorie.

'I dreamt it was a beautiful tragicomedy entitled *Love at First Sight*, or, *Another Good Man Gone Wrong*. Act one in a boozer by the sea.'

The two women tapped their foreheads.

Lou said, still smiling: 'Where was the second act?'

Her voice was as gentle as he had imagined it to be before her gay and nervous playing with the over-familiar barman and the inferior women. He saw her as a wise, soft girl whom no hard company could spoil, for her soft self, bare to the heart, broke through every defence of her sensual falsifiers. As he thought this, phrasing her gentleness, faithlessly running to words away from the real room and his love in the middle, he woke with a start and saw her lively body six steps from him, no calm heart dressed in a sentence, but a pretty girl, to be got and kept. He must catch hold of her fast. He got up to cross to her.

'I woke before the second act came on,' said the barman. 'I'd sell my dear old mother to see that. Dim light. Purple couches. Ecstatic bliss: Là, là chérie!'

The young man sat down at the table, next to her.

Harold, the barman, leaned over the counter and cupped his hand to his ear.

The man on the floor rolled in his sleep, and his head lay in the spittoon.

'You should have come and sat here a long time ago,' Lou whispered. 'You should have stopped to talk to me in the Gardens. Were you shy?'

'I was too shy,' the young man whispered.

'Whispering isn't manners. I can't hear a word,' said the barman.

At a sign from the young man, a flick of the fingers that sent the waiters in evening dress bustling with oysters about the immense room, the barman filled the glasses with port, gin, and Nutbrown.

'We never drink with strangers,' Mrs Franklin said, laughing.

'He isn't a stranger,' said Lou, 'are you, Jack?'

He threw a pound note on the table: 'Take the damage.'

The evening that had been over before it began raced along among the laughter of the charming women sharp as knives, and the stories of the barman, who should be on the stage, and Lou's delighted smiles and silences at his side. Now she is safe and sure, he thought, after her walking like my doubtful walking, around the lonely distances of the holiday. In the warm, spinning middle they were close and alike. The town and the sea and the last pleasure makers drifted into the dark that had nothing to do with them, and left this one room burning.

One by one, some lost men from the dark shuffled into the bar, drank sadly, and went out. Mrs Franklin, flushed and dribbling, waved her glass at their departures. Harold winked behind their backs. Marjorie showed them her long, white legs.

'Nobody loves us except ourselves,' said Harold. 'Shall I shut the bar and keep the riffraff out?'

'Lou is expecting Mr O'Brien, but don't let that stop you,' Marjorie said. 'He's her sugar daddy from old Ireland.'

'Do you love Mr O'Brien?' the young man whispered.

'How could I, Jack?'

He could see Mr O'Brien as a witty, tall fellow of middle age, with waved greying hair and a clipped bit of dirt on his upper lip, a flash ring on his marriage finger, a pouched, knowing eye, dummy dressed with a whaleboned waist, a broth of a man about Cardiff. Lou's horrible lover tearing towards her now down the airless streets in the firm's car. The young man clenched his hand on the table covered with dead, and sheltered her in the warm strength of his fist. 'My round, my round,' he said, 'up again, plenty! Doubles, trebles, Mrs Franklin is a jibber.'

'My mother never had a jibber.'

'Oh, Lou,' he said, 'I am more than happy with you.'

'Coo! coo! hear the turtledoves.'

'Let them coo,' said Marjorie. 'I could coo, too.'

The barman looked around him in surprise. He raised his hands, palms up, and cocked his head.

'The bar is full of birds,' he said.

'Emerald's laying an egg,' he said, as Mrs Franklin rocked in her chair.

Soon the bar was full of customers. The drunk man woke up and ran out, leaving his cap in a brown pool. Sawdust dropped from his hair. A small, old, round, red-faced, cheery man sat facing the young man and Lou, who held hands under the table and rubbed their legs against each other.

'What a night for love!' said the old man. 'On such a night as this did Jessica steal from the wealthy Jew. Do you know where that comes from?'

'*The Merchant of Venice*,' Lou said. 'But you're an Irishman, Mr O'Brien.'

'I could have sworn you were a tall man with a little tish,' said the young man gravely.

'What's the weapons, Mr O'Brien?'

'Brandies at dawn, I should think, Mrs Franklin.'

'I never described Mr O'Brien to you at all. You're dreaming!' Lou whispered. 'I wish this night could go on forever.'

'But not here. Not in the bar. In a room with a big bed.'

'A bed in a bar,' said the old man, 'if you'll pardon me hearing you, that's what I've always wanted. Think of it, Mrs Franklin.'

The barman bobbed up from behind the counter.

'Time, gentlemen and others!'

The sober strangers departed to Mrs Franklin's laughter.

The lights went out.

'Lou, don't you lose me.'

'I've got your hand.'

'Press it hard, hurt it.'

'Break his bloody neck,' Mrs Franklin said in the dark. 'No offence meant.'

'Marjorie smack hand,' said Marjorie. 'Let's get out of the dark. Harold's a rover in the dark.'

'And the girl guides.'

'Let's take a bottle each and go down to Lou's,' she said.

'I'll buy the bottles,' said Mr O'Brien.

'It's you don't lose me now,' Lou whispered. 'Hold on to me, Jack. The others won't stay long. Oh, Mr Christ, I wish it was just you and me!'

'Will it be just you and me?'

'You and me and Mr Moon.'

Mr O'Brien opened the saloon door. 'Pile into the Rolls, you ladies. The gentlemen are going to see to the medicine.'

The young man felt Lou's quick kiss on his mouth before she followed Marjorie and Mrs Franklin out.

'What do you say we split the drinks?' said Mr O'Brien.

'Look what I found in the lavatory,' said the barman, 'he was singing on the seat.' He appeared behind the counter with the drunk man leaning on his arm.

They all climbed into the car.

'First stop, Lou's.'

The young man, on Lou's knee, saw the town in a daze spin by them, the funnelled and masted smoke-blue outline of the still, droning docks, the lightning lines of the poor streets growing longer, and the winking shops that were snapped out one by one. The car smelled of scent and powder and flesh. He struck with his elbow, by accident, Mrs Franklin's upholstered breast. Her thighs, like cushions, bore the drunk man's rolling weight. He was bumped and tossed on a lump of women. Breasts, legs, bellies, hands, touched, warmed, and smothered him. On through the night, towards Lou's bed, towards the unbelievable end of the dying holiday, they tore past black houses and bridges, a station in a smoke cloud, and drove up a steep side-street with one weak lamp in a circle of railings at the top, and swerved into a space where a tall tenement house stood surrounded by cranes, standing ladders, poles and girders, barrows, brick heaps.

They climbed to Lou's room up many flights of dark, perilous stairs. Washing hung on the rails outside closed doors. Mrs Franklin, fumbling alone with the drunk man, behind the others, trod in a bucket, and a lucky black cat ran over her foot. Lou led the young man by the hand through a passage marked with names and doors, lit a match, and whispered: 'It won't be very long. Be good and patient with Mr O'Brien. Here it is. Come in first. Welcome to you, Jack!' She kissed him again at the door of her room.

She turned on the light, and he walked with her proudly into her own room, into the room that he could come to know, and saw a wide bed, a gramophone on a chair, a wash-basin half hidden in a corner, a gas fire and a cooking ring, a closed cupboard, and her photograph in a cardboard frame on the chest of drawers with no handles. Here she slept and ate. In the double bed she lay all night, pale and curled, sleeping on her left side. When he lived with her always, he would not allow her to dream. No other men must lie and love in her head. He spread his fingers on her pillow.

'Why do you live at the top of the Eiffel Tower?' said the barman, coming in.

'What a climb!' said Mr O'Brien. 'But it's very nice and private when you get here.'

'If you get here!' said Mrs Franklin. 'I'm dead beat. This old nuisance weighs a ton. Lie down, lie down on the floor and go to sleep. The old nuisance!' she said fondly. 'What's your name?'

'Ernie,' the drunk man said, raising his arm to shield his face.

'Nobody's going to bite you, Ernie. Here, give him a nip of whisky. Careful! Don't pour it on your waistcoat; you'll be squeezing your waistcoat in the morning. Pull the curtains, Lou, I can see the wicked old moon,' she said.

'Does it put ideas in your head?'

'I love the moon,' said Lou.

'There never was a young lover who didn't love the moon.' Mr O'Brien gave the young man a cheery smile, and patted his hand. His own hand was red and hairy. 'I could see at the flash of a glance that Lou and this nice young fellow were made for each other. I could see it in their eyes. Dear me, no! I'm not so old and blind I can't see love in front of my nose. Couldn't you see it, Mrs Franklin? Couldn't you see it, Marjorie?'

In the long silence, Lou collected glasses from the cupboard as though she had not heard Mr O'Brien speak. She drew the curtains, shut out the moon, sat on the edge of her bed with her feet tucked under her, looked at her photograph as at a stranger, folded her hands as she had folded them, on the first meeting, before the young man's worship in the Gardens.

'A host of angels must be passing by,' said Mr O'Brien. 'What a silence there is! Have I said anything out of place? Drink and be merry, tomorrow we die. What do you think I bought these lovely shining bottles for?'

The bottles were opened. The dead were lined on the mantelpiece. The whisky went down. Harold the barman and Marjorie, her dress lifted, sat in the one armchair together. Mrs Franklin; with Ernie's head on her lap, sang in a sweet, trained contralto voice *The Shepherd's Lass*. Mr O'Brien kept rhythm with his foot.

I want Lou in my arms, the young man said to himself, watching Mr O'Brien tap and smile and the barman draw Marjorie down deep. Mrs Franklin's voice sang sweetly in the small bedroom where he and Lou should be lying in the white bed without any smiling company to see them drown. He and Lou could go down together, one cool body weighted with a boiling stone, on to the falling, blank white, entirely empty sea, and never rise. Sitting on their bridal bed, near enough to hear his breath, she was farther from him than before they met. Then he had everything but her body; now she had given him two kisses, and everything had vanished by that beginning. He must be good and patient with Mr O'Brien. He could wipe away the embracing, old smile with the iron back of his hand. Sink lower, lower, Harold and Marjorie, tumble like whales at Mr O'Brien's feet.

He wished that the light would fail. In the darkness he and Lou could creep beneath the clothes and imitate the dead. Who would look for them there, if they were dead still and soundless? The others would shout to them down the dizzy stairs or rummage in the silence about the narrow, obstacled corridors or stumble out into the night to search for them among the cranes and ladders in the desolation of the destroyed houses. He could hear, in the made-up dark, Mr O'Brien's voice cry, 'Lou, where are you? Answer! answer!' the hollow answer of the echo, 'answer!' and hear her lips in the cool pit of the bed secretly move around another name, and feel them move.

'A fine piece of singing, Emerald, and very naughty words. That was a shepherd, that was,' Mr O'Brien said.

Ernie, on the floor, began to sing in a thick, sulking voice but Mrs Franklin placed her hand over his mouth and he sucked and nuzzled it.

'What about this young shepherd?' said Mr O'Brien, pointing his glass at the young man. 'Can he sing as well as make love? You ask him kindly, girlie,' he said to Lou, 'and he'll give us a song like a nightingale.'

'Can you sing, Jack?'

'Like a crow, Lou.'

'Can't he even talk poetry? What a young man to have who can't spout the poets to his lady!' Mr O'Brien said.

From the cupboard Lou brought out a red-bound book and gave it to the young man, saying: 'Can you read us a piece out of here? The second volume's in the hatbox. Read us a dreamy piece, Jack. It's nearly midnight.'

'Only a love poem, no other kind,' said Mr O'Brien. 'I won't hear anything but a love poem.'

'Soft and sweet,' Mrs Franklin said. She took her hand away from Ernie's mouth and looked at the ceiling.

The young man read, but not aloud, lingering on her name, the inscription on the fly-leaf of the first volume of the collected poems of Tennyson: 'To Louisa, from her Sunday School teacher, Miss Gwyneth Forbes. God's in His Heaven, all's right with the world.'

'Make it a love poem, don't forget.'

The young man read aloud, closing one eye to steady the dancing print, 'Come into the Garden, Maud'. And when he reached the beginning of the fourth verse his voice grew louder:

> 'I said to the lily, "There is but one
> With whom she has heart to be gay.
> When will the dancers leave her alone?
> She is weary of dance and play."
> Now half to the setting moon are gone,
> And half to the rising day;
> Low on the sand and loud on the stone
> The last wheel echoes away.
> I said to the rose, "The brief night goes
> In babble and revel and wine.
> O young lord-lover, what sighs are those,
> For one that will never be thine?
> But mine, but mine," so I sware to the rose,
> "For ever and ever, mine." '

At the end of the poem, Harold said, suddenly, his head hanging over the arm of the chair, his hair made wild, and his mouth red with lipstick: 'My grandfather remembers seeing Lord Tennyson, he was a little man with a hump.'

'No,' said the young man, 'he was tall and he had long hair and a beard.'

'Did you ever see him?'

'I wasn't born then.'

'My grandfather saw him. He had a hump.'

'Not Alfred Tennyson.'

'Lord Alfred Tennyson was a little man with a hump.'

'It couldn't have been the same Tennyson.'

'You've got the wrong Tennyson, this was the famous poet with a hump.'

Lou, on the wonderful bed, waiting for him alone of all the men, ugly or handsome, old or young, in the wide town and the small world that would be bound to fall, lowered her head and kissed her hand to him and held her hand in the river of light on the counterpane. The hand, to him, became transparent, and the light on the counterpane glowed up steadily through it in the thin shape of her palm and fingers.

'Ask Mr O'Brien what Lord Tennyson was like,' said Mrs Franklin. 'We appeal to you, Mr O'Brien, did he have a hump or not?'

Nobody but the young man, for whom she lived and waited now, noticed Lou's little loving movements. She put her glowing hand to her left breast. She made a sign of secrecy on her lips.

'It depends,' Mr O'Brien said.

The young man closed one eye again, for the bed was pitching like a ship: a sickening, hot storm out of a cigarette cloud unsettled cupboard and chest. The motions of the sea-going bedroom were calmed with the cunning closing of his eye, but he longed for night air. On sailor's legs he walked to the door.

'You'll find the House of Commons on the second floor at the end of the passage,' said Mr O'Brien.

At the door, he turned to Lou and smiled with all his love, declaring it to the faces of the company and making her, before Mr O'Brien's envious regard, smile back and say: 'Don't be long, Jack. Please! You mustn't be long.'

Now everyone knew. Love had grown up in an evening.

'One minute, my darling,' he said. 'I'll be here.'

The door closed behind him. He walked into the wall of the passage. He lit a match. He had three left. Down the stairs, clinging to the sticky, shaking rails, rocking on seesaw floorboards, bruising his shin on a bucket, past the noises of secret lives behind doors he slid and stumbled and swore and heard Lou's voice in a fresh fever drive him on, call him to return, speak to him with such passion and abandonment that even in the darkness and the pain of his haste he was dazzled and struck still. She spoke, there on the rotting stairs in the middle of the poor house, a frightening rush of love words; from her mouth, at his ear, endearments were burned out. Hurry! hurry! Every moment is being killed. Love, adored, dear, run back and whistle to me, open the door, shout my name, lay me down. Mr O'Brien has his hands on my side.

He ran into a cavern. A draught blew out his matches. He lurched into a room where two figures on a black heap on the floor lay whispering, and ran from there in a panic. He made water at the dead end of the passage and hurried back towards Lou's room, finding himself at last on a silent patch of stairway at the top of the house: he put out his hand, but the rail was broken and nothing there prevented a long drop to the ground down a twisted shaft that would echo and double his cry, bring out from their holes in the wall the sleeping or stirring families, the whispering figures, the blind startled turners of night into day. Lost in a tunnel near the roof, he fingered the damp walls for a door; he found a handle and gripped it hard, but it came off in his hand. Lou had led him down a longer passage than this. He remembered the number of doors: there were three on each side. He ran down the broken-railed flight into another passage and dragged his hand along the wall. Three doors, he counted. He opened the third door, walked into darkness, and groped for the switch on the left. He saw, in the sudden light, a bed and a cupboard and a chest of drawers with no handles, a gas fire, a washbasin in the corner. No bottles. No glasses. No photograph of Lou. The red counterpane on the bed was smooth. He could not remember the colour of Lou's counterpane.

He left the light burning and opened the second door, but a strange woman's voice cried, half-asleep: 'Who is there? Is it you, Tom? Tom, put the light on.' He looked for a line of light at the foot of the next door, and stopped to listen for voices. The woman was still calling in the second room.

'Lou, where are you?' he cried. 'Answer! answer!'

'Lou, what Lou? There's no Lou here,' said a man's voice through the open door of the first dark room at the entrance to the passage.

He scampered down another flight and counted four doors with his scratched hand. One door opened and a woman in a nightdress put out her head. A child's head appeared below her.

'Where does Lou live? Do you know where Lou lives?'

The woman and child stared without speaking.

'Lou! Lou! her name is Lou!' he heard himself shout. 'She lives here, in this house! Do you know where she lives?'

The woman caught the child by the hair and pulled her into the room. He clung to the edge of her door. The woman thrust her arm round the edge and brought down a bunch of keys sharply on his hands. The door slammed.

A young woman with a baby in a shawl stood at an open door on the opposite side of the passage, and caught his sleeve as he ran by. 'Lou who? You woke my baby.'

'I don't know her other name. She's with Mrs Franklin and Mr O'Brien.'

'You woke my baby.'

'Come in and find her in the bed,' a voice said from the darkness behind the young woman.

'He's woken up the baby.'

He ran down the passage, holding his wet hand to his mouth. He fell against the rails of the last flight of stairs. He heard Lou's voice in his head once more whisper to him to return as the ground floor rose, like a lift full of dead, towards the rails. Hurry! hurry! I can't, I won't wait, the bridal night is being killed.

Up the rotten, bruising, mountainous stairs he climbed, in his sickness, to the passage where he had left the one light burning in an end room. The light was out. He tapped all the doors and whispered her name. He beat on the doors and shouted, and a woman, dressed in a vest and a hat, drove him out of the passage with a walking stick.

For a long time he waited on the stairs, though there was no love now to wait for and no bed but his own too many miles away to lie in, and only the approaching day to remember his discovery. All around him the disturbed inhabitants of the house were falling back into sleep. Then he walked out of the house onto the waste space and under the leaning cranes and ladders. The light of the one weak lamp in a rusty circle fell across the brick heaps and the broken wood and the dust that had been houses once, where the small and hardly known and never-to-be-forgotten people of the dirty town had lived and loved and died and, always, lost.

RICHARD WRIGHT was born in 1908 in Mississippi and died in 1960, in France, where he had lived as an expatriate for the latter part of his career. His first published novel, *Native Son* (1940), established him as the spokesman for his generation of American blacks. His other works include *Uncle Tom's Children*, a collection of four novellas; *Eight Men*, a collection of short stories; *Black Boy*, an autobiography of his youth; and *White Man, Listen!* a tract on the evils of racial inequality.

the man who
went to chicago

RICHARD WRIGHT

When I rose in the morning the temperature had dropped below zero. The house was as cold to me as the Southern streets had been in winter. I dressed, doubling my clothing. I ate in a restaurant, caught a streetcar, and rode south, rode until I could see no more black faces on the sidewalks. I had now crossed the boundary line of the Black Belt and had entered the territory where jobs were perhaps to be had from white folks. I walked the streets and looked into shop windows until I saw a sign in a delicatessen: PORTER WANTED.

I went in and a stout white woman came to me.

'Vat do you vant?' she asked.

The voice jarred me. She's Jewish, I thought, remembering with shame the obscenities I used to shout at Jewish storekeepers in Arkansas.

'I thought maybe you needed a porter?' I said.

'Meester 'Offman, he eesn't here yet,' she said. 'Vill you vait?'

'Yes, ma'am.'

'Seet down.'

'No, ma'am, I'll wait outside.'

'But eet's cold out zhere,' she said.

'That's all right,' I said.

She shrugged. I went to the sidewalk. I waited for half an hour in the bitter cold, regretting that I had not remained in the warm store, but unable to go back inside. A bald, stoutish white man went into the store and pulled off his coat. Yes, he was the boss man . . .

'Zo you vant a job?' he asked.

'Yes, sir,' I answered, guessing at the meaning of his words.

'Vhere you vork before?'

'In Memphis, Tennessee.'

'My brudder-in-law vorked in Tennessee vonce,' he said.

I was hired. The work was easy, but I found to my dismay that I could not understand a third of what was said to me. My slow Southern ears were baffled by their clouded, thick accents. One morning Mrs Hoffman asked me to go to a neighbouring store – it was owned by a cousin of hers – and get a can of chicken *à la* king. I had never heard the phrase before and I asked her to repeat it.

'Don't you know nosing?' she demanded of me.

'If you would write it down for me, I'd know what to get,' I ventured timidly.

'I can vite!' she shouted in a sudden fury. 'Vat kinda boy iss you?'

I memorized the separate sounds that she had uttered and went to the neighbouring store.

'Mrs Hoffman wants a can Cheek Keeng Awr Lar Keeng,' I said slowly, hoping he would not think I was being offensive.

'All vite,' he said, after staring at me a moment.

He put a can into a paper bag and gave it to me; outside in the street I opened the bag and read the label: Chicken *à la* King. I cursed, disgusted with myself. I knew those words. It had been her thick accent that had thrown me off. Yet I was not angry with her for speaking broken English; my English, too, was broken. But why could she not have taken more patience? Only one answer came to my mind. I was black and she did not care. Or so I thought . . . I was persisting in reading my present environment in the light of my old one. I reasoned thus: though English was my native tongue and America my native land, she, an alien, could operate a store and earn a living in a neighbourhood where I could not even live. I reasoned further that she was aware of this and was trying to protect her position against me.

It was not until I had left the delicatessen job that I saw how grossly I had misread the motives and attitudes of Mr Hoffman and his wife. I had not yet learned anything that would have helped me to thread my way through these perplexing racial relations. Accepting my environment at its face value, trapped by my own emotions, I kept asking myself what had black people done to bring this crazy world upon them?

The fact of the separation of white and black was clear to me; it was its effect upon the personalities of people that stumped and dismayed me. I did not feel that I was a threat to anybody; yet, as soon as I had grown old enough to think, I had learned that my entire personality, my aspirations, had long ago been discounted; that, in a measure, the very meaning of the words I spoke could not be fully understood.

And when I contemplated the area of No Man's Land into which the Negro mind in America had been shunted I wondered if there had ever been in all human history a more corroding and devastating attack upon the personalities of men than the idea of racial discrimination. In order to escape the racial attack that went to the roots of my life, I would have gladly accepted any way of life but the one in which I found myself. I would have agreed to live under a system of feudal oppression, not because I preferred feudalism but because I felt that feudalism made use of a limited part of a man, defined man, his rank, his function in society. I would have consented to live under the most rigid type of dictatorship, for I felt that dictatorships, too, defined the use of men, however degrading that use might be.

While working as a porter in Memphis I had often stood aghast as a friend of mine had offered himself to be kicked by the white men; but now, while working in Chicago, I was learning that perhaps even a kick was better than uncertainty ... I had elected, in my fevered search for honourable adjustment to the American scene, not to submit and in doing so I had embraced the daily horror of anxiety, of tension, of eternal disquiet. I could now sympathize with – though I could never bring myself to approve – those tortured blacks who had given up and had gone to their white tormentors and had said: 'Kick me, if that's all there is for me; kick me and let me feel at home, let me have peace!'

Colour hate defined the place of black life as below that of white life; and the black man, responding to the same dreams as the white man, strove to bury within his heart his awareness of this difference because it made him lonely and afraid. Hated by whites and being an organic part of the culture that hated him, the black man grew in turn to hate in himself that which others hated in him. But pride would make him hate his self-hate, for he would not want whites to know that he was so thoroughly conquered by them that his total life was conditioned by their attitude; but in the act of hiding his self-hate, he could not help but hate those who evoked his self-hate in him. So each part of his day would be consumed in a war with himself, a good part of his energy would be spent in keeping control of his unruly emotions, emotions which he had not wished to have, but could not help having. Held at bay by the hate of others, preoccupied with his own feelings, he was continuously at war with reality. He became inefficient, less able to see and judge the objective world. And when he reached that state, the white people looked at him and laughed and said:

'Look, didn't I tell you niggers were that way?'

To solve this tangle of balked emotion, I loaded the empty part of the ship of my personality with fantasies of ambition to keep it from toppling over into the sea of senselessness. Like any other American, I dreamed of going into business and making money; I dreamed of working for a firm that would allow me to advance until I reached an important position; I even dreamed of organizing secret groups of blacks to fight all whites . . . and if the blacks would not agree to organize, then they would have to be fought. I would end up again with self-hate, but it was now a self-hate that was projected outward upon other blacks. Yet I knew – with that part of my mind that the whites had given me – that none of my dreams were possible. Then I would hate myself for allowing my mind to dwell upon the unattainable. Thus the circle would complete itself.

Slowly I began to forge in the depths of my mind a mechanism that repressed all the dreams and desires that the Chicago streets, the newspapers, the movies were evoking in me. I was going through a second childhood; a new sense of the limit of the possible was being born in me. What could I dream of that had the barest possibility of coming true? I could think of nothing. And slowly, it was upon exactly that nothingness that my mind began to dwell, that constant sense of wanting without having, of being hated without reason. A dim notion of what life meant to a Negro in America was coming to consciousness in me, not in terms of external events, lynchings, Jim Crowism, and the endless brutalities, but in terms of crossed-up feeling, of emotional tension. I sensed that Negro life was a sprawling land of unconscious suffering, and there were but few Negroes who knew the meaning of their lives, who could tell their story.

Word reached me that an examination for postal clerk was impending, and at once I filed an application and waited. As the date for the examination drew near, I was faced with another problem. How could I get a free day without losing my job? In the South it would have been an unwise policy for a Negro to have gone to his white boss and asked for time to take an examination for another job. It would have implied that the Negro did not like to work for the white boss, that he felt he was not receiving just consideration and, inasmuch as most jobs that Negroes held in the South involved a personal, paternalistic relationship, he would have been risking an argument that might have led to violence.

I now began to speculate about what kind of man Mr Hoffman was, and I found that I did not know him: that is, I did not know his basic attitude towards Negroes. If I asked him, would he be sympathetic enough to allow me time off with pay? I needed the money. Perhaps he would say: 'Go home and stay home if you don't like this job!' I was not sure of him. I decided, therefore, that I had better not risk it. I would forfeit the money and stay away without telling him.

The examination was scheduled to take place on a Monday; I had been working steadily and I would be too tired to do my best if I took the examination without benefit of rest. I decided to stay away from the shop Saturday, Sunday, and Monday. But what could I tell Mr Hoffman? Yes, I would tell him that I had been ill. No, that was too thin. I would tell him that my mother had died in Memphis and that I had gone down to bury her. That lie might work.

I took the examination, and when I came to the store on Tuesday, Mr Hoffman was astonished, of course.

'I didn't sink you vould ever come back,' he said.

'I'm awfully sorry, Mr Hoffman.'

'Vat happened?'

'My mother died in Memphis and I had to go down and bury her,' I lied.

He looked at me, then shook his head.

'Rich, you lie,' he said.

'I'm not lying,' I lied stoutly.

'You vanted to do somesink, zo you zayed ervay,' he said, shrugging.

'No, sir. I'm telling you the truth,' I piled another lie upon the first one.

'No. You lie. You disappoint me,' he said.

'Well, all I can do is tell you the truth,' I lied indignantly.

'Vy didn't you use the phone?'

'I didn't think of it,' I told a fresh lie.

'Rich, if your mudder die, you vould tell me,' he said.

'I didn't have time. Had to catch the train,' I lied yet again.

'Vhere did you get the money?'

'My aunt gave it to me,' I said, disgusted that I had to lie and lie again.

'I don't vant a boy vat tells lies,' he said.

'I don't lie,' I lied passionately to protect my lies.

Mrs Hoffman joined in and both of them hammered at me.
'Ve know. You come from ze Zouth. You feel you can't tell us ze truth. But ve don't bother you. Ve don't feel like people in ze Zouth. Ve treat you nice, don't ve?' they asked.
'Yes, ma'am,' I mumbled.
'Zen vy lie?'
'I'm not lying,' I lied with all my strength.

I became angry because I knew that they knew that I was lying. I had lied to protect myself, and then I had to lie to protect my lie. I had met so many white faces that would have violently disapproved of my taking the examination that I could not have risked telling Mr Hoffman the truth. But how could I tell him that I had lied because I was so unsure of myself? Lying was bad, but revealing my own sense of insecurity would have been worse. It would have been shameful, and I did not like to feel ashamed.

Their attitudes had proved utterly amazing. They were taking time out from their duties in the store to talk to me, and I had never encountered anything like that from whites before. A Southern white man would have said: 'Get to hell out of here!' or 'All right, nigger. Get to work.' But no white people had ever stood their ground and probed at me, questioned me at such length. It dawned upon me that they were trying to treat me as an equal, which made it even more impossible for me ever to tell them that I had lied, why I had lied. I felt that if I confessed I would be giving them a moral advantage over me that would have been unbearable.

'All vight, zay and vork,' Mr Hoffman said. 'I know you're lying, but I don't care, Rich.'

I wanted to quit. He had insulted me. But I liked him in spite of myself. Yes, I had done wrong; but how on earth could I have known the kind of people I was working for? Perhaps Mr Hoffman would have gladly consented for me to take the examination; but my hopes had been far weaker than my powerful fears.

Working with them from day to day and knowing that they knew I had lied from fear crushed me. I knew that they pitied me and pitied the fear in me. I resolved to quit and risk hunger rather than stay with them. I left the job that following Saturday, not telling them that I would not be back, not possessing the heart to say goodbye. I just wanted to go quickly and have them forget that I had ever worked for them.

After an idle week, I got a job as a dishwasher in a North Side café that had just opened. My boss, a white woman, directed me in unpacking barrels of dishes, setting up new tables, painting, and so on. I had charge of serving breakfast; in the late afternoon I carted trays of food to patrons in the hotel who did not want to come down to eat. My wages were fifteen dollars a week; the hours were long, but I ate my meals on the job.

The cook was an elderly Finnish woman with a sharp, bony face. There were several white waitresses. I was the only Negro in the café. The waitresses were a hard, brisk lot, and I was keenly aware of how their attitudes contrasted with those of Southern white girls. They had not been taught to keep a gulf between me and themselves; they were relatively free of the heritage of racial hate.

One morning as I was making coffee, Cora came forward with a tray loaded with food and squeezed against me to draw a cup of coffee.

'Pardon me, Richard,' she said.

'Oh, that's all right,' I said in an even tone.

But I was aware that she was a white girl and that her body was pressed closely against mine, an incident that had never happened to me before in my life, an incident charged with the memory of dread. But she was not conscious of my blackness or of what her actions would have meant in the South. And had I not been born in the South, her trivial act would have been as unnoticed by me as it was by her. As she stood close to me, I could not help thinking that if a Southern white girl had wanted to draw a cup of coffee, she would have commanded me to step aside so that she might not come in contact with me. The work of the hot and busy kitchen would have had to cease for a moment so that I could have taken my tainted body far enough away to allow the Southern white girl a chance to get a cup of coffee. There lay a deep emotional safety in knowing that the white girl who was now leaning carelessly against me was not thinking of me, had no deep, vague, irrational fright that made her feel that I was a creature to be avoided at all costs.

One summer morning a white girl came late to work and rushed into the pantry where I was busy. She went into the women's room and changed her clothes; I heard the door open and a second later I was surprised to hear her voice:

'Richard, quick! Tie my apron!'

She was standing with her back to me and the strings of her apron dangled loose. There was a moment of indecision on my part, then I took the two loose strings and carried them around her body and brought them again to her back and tied them in a clumsy knot.

'Thanks a million,' she said, grasping my hand for a split second, and was gone.

I continued my work, filled with all the possible meanings that the tiny, simple, human event could have meant to any Negro in the South where I had spent most of my hungry days.

I did not feel any admiration or any hate for the girls. My attitude was one of abiding and friendly wonder. For the most part I was silent with them, though I knew that I had a firmer grasp of life than most of them. As I worked I listened to their talk and perceived its puzzled, wandering, superficial fumbling with the problems and facts of life. There were many things they wondered about that I could have explained to them, but I never dared.

During my lunch hour, which I spent on a bench in a nearby park, the waitresses would come and sit beside me, talking at random, laughing, joking, smoking cigarettes. I learned about their tawdry dreams, their simple hopes, their home lives, their fear of feeling anything deeply, their sex problems, their husbands. They were an eager, restless, talkative, ignorant bunch, but casually kind and impersonal for all that. They knew nothing of hate and fear, and strove instinctively to avoid all passion.

I often wondered what they were trying to get out of life, but I never stumbled upon a clue, and I doubt if they themselves had any notion. They lived on the surface of their days; their smiles were surface smiles, and their tears were surface tears. Negroes lived a truer and deeper life than they, but I wished that Negroes, too, could live as thoughtlessly, serenely, as they. The girls never talked of their feelings; none of them possessed the insight or the emotional equipment to understand themselves or others. How far apart in culture we stood! All my life I had done nothing but feel and cultivate my feelings; all their lives they had done nothing but strive for petty goals, the trivial material prizes of American life. We shared a common tongue, but my language was a different language from theirs.

It was in the psychological distance that separated the races that the deepest meaning of the problem of the Negro lay for me. For these poor, ignorant white girls to have understood my life would have meant nothing short of a vast revolution in theirs. And I was convinced that what they needed to make them complete and grown-up in their living was the inclusion in their personalities of a knowledge of lives such as I lived and suffered containedly.

As I, in memory, think back now upon those girls and their lives I feel that for white America to understand the significance of the problem of the Negro will take a bigger and tougher America than any we have yet known. I feel that America's past is too shallow, her national character too superficially optimistic, her very morality too suffused with colour hate for her to accomplish so vast and complex a task. Culturally the Negro represents a paradox: though he is an organic part of the nation, he is excluded by the entire tide and direction of American culture. Frankly, it is felt to be right to exclude him, and it is felt to be wrong to admit him freely. Therefore, if within the confines of its present culture the nation ever seeks to purge itself of its colour hate, it will find itself at war with itself, convulsed by a spasm of emotional and moral confusion. If the nation ever finds itself examining its real relation to the Negro, it will find itself doing infinitely more than that; for the anti-Negro attitude of whites represents but a tiny part — though a symbolically significant one — of the moral attitude of the nation. Our too-young and too-new America, lusty because it is lonely, aggressive because it is afraid, insists upon seeing the world in terms of good and bad, the holy and the evil, the high and the low, the white and the black; our America is frightened by fact, by history, by processes, by necessity. It hugs the easy way of damning those whom it cannot understand, of excluding those who look different; and it salves its conscience with a self-draped cloak of righteousness. Am I damning my native land? No; for I, too, share these faults of character! And I really do not think that America, adolescent and cocksure, a stranger to suffering and travail, an enemy of passion and sacrifice, is ready to probe into its most fundamental beliefs.

I knew that not race alone, not colour alone, but the daily values that gave meaning to life stood between me and those white girls with whom I worked. Their constant outward-looking, their mania for radios, cars, and a thousand other trinkets, made them dream and fix their eyes upon the trash of life, made it impossible for them to learn a language that could have taught them to speak of what was in their or others' hearts. The words of their souls were the syllables of popular songs.

The essence of the irony of the plight of the Negro in America, to me, is that he is doomed to live in isolation, while those who condemn him seek the basest goals of any people on the face of the earth. Perhaps it would be possible for the Negro to become reconciled to his plight if he could be made to believe that his sufferings were for some remote, high, sacrificial end; but sharing the culture that condemns him, and seeing that a lust for trash is what blinds the nation to his claims, is what sets storms to rolling in his soul.

Though I had fled the pressure of the South, my outward conduct had not changed. I had been schooled to present an unalteringly smiling face, and I continued to do so despite the fact my environment allowed more open expression. I hid my feelings and avoided all relationships with whites that might cause me to reveal them.

Tillie, the Finnish cook, was a tall, ageless, red-faced, raw-boned woman with long snow-white hair, which she balled in a knot at the nape of her neck. She cooked expertly and was superbly efficient. One morning, as I passed the sizzling stove I thought I heard Tilly cough and spit, but I saw nothing; her face, obscured by steam, was bent over a big pot. My senses told me that Tillie had coughed and spat into that pot, but my heart told me that no human being could possibly be so filthy. I decided to watch her. An hour or so later I heard Tillie clear her throat with a grunt, saw her cough and spit into the boiling soup. I held my breath; I did not want to believe what I had seen.

Should I tell the boss lady? Would she believe me? I watched Tillie for another day to make sure that she was spitting into the food. She was; there was no doubt about it. But who would believe me if I told them what was happening? I was the only black person in the café. Perhaps they would think that I hated the cook. I stopped eating my meals there and bided my time.

The business of the café was growing rapidly and a Negro girl was hired to make salads. I went to her at once.

'Look, can I trust you?' I asked.

'What are you talking about?' she asked.

'I want you to say nothing, but watch that cook.'

'For what?'

'Now, don't get scared. Just watch the cook.'

She looked at me as though she thought I was crazy; and, frankly, I felt that perhaps I ought not say anything to anybody.

'What do you mean?' she demanded.

'All right,' I said. 'I'll tell you. That cook spits in the food.'

'What are you saying?' she asked aloud.

'Keep quiet,' I said.

'Spitting?' she asked me in a whisper. 'Why would she do that?'

'I don't know. But watch her.'

She walked away from me with a funny look in her eye. But half an hour later she came rushing to me, looking ill, sinking into a chair.

'Oh, God, I feel awful!'

'Did you see it?'

'She *is* spitting in the food!'

'What ought we do?' I asked.

'Tell the lady,' she said.

'She wouldn't believe me,' I said.

She widened her eyes as she understood. We were black and the cook was white.

'But I can't work here if she's going to do that,' she said.

'Then you tell her,' I said.

'She wouldn't believe me either,' she said.

She rose and ran to the women's room. When she returned she stared at me. We were two Negroes and we were silently asking ourselves if the white boss lady would believe us if we told her that her expert white cook was spitting in the food all day long as it cooked on the stove.

'I don't know,' she wailed, in a whisper, and walked away.

I thought of telling the waitresses about the cook, but I could not get up enough nerve. Many of the girls were friendly with Tillie. Yet I could not let the cook spit in the food all day. That was wrong by any human standard of conduct. I washed dishes, thinking, wondering; I served breakfast, thinking, wondering; I served meals in the apartments of patrons upstairs, thinking, wondering. Each time I picked up a tray of food I felt like retching. Finally the Negro salad girl came to me and handed me her purse and hat.

'I'm going to tell her and quit, goddamn,' she said.

'I'll quit too, if she doesn't fire her,' I said.

'Oh, she won't believe me,' she wailed, in agony.

'You tell her. You're a woman. She might believe you.'

Her eyes welled with tears and she sat for a long time; then she rose and went abruptly into the dining-room. I went to the door and peered. Yes, she was at the desk, talking to the boss lady. She returned to the kitchen and went into the pantry; I followed her.

'Did you tell her?' I asked.

'Yes.'

'What did she say?'

'She said I was crazy.'

'Oh, God!' I said.

'She just looked at me with those grey eyes of hers,' the girl said. 'Why would Tillie do that?'

'I don't know,' I said.

The boss lady came to the door and called the girl; both of them went into the dining-room. Tillie came over to me; a hard, cold look was in her eyes.

'What's happening here?' she asked.

'I don't know,' I said, wanting to slap her across the mouth.

She muttered something and went back to the stove, coughed, and spat into a bubbling pot. I left the kitchen and went into the back areaway to breathe. The boss lady came out.

'Richard,' she said.

Her face was pale. I was smoking a cigarette and I did not look at her.

'Is this true?'

'Yes, ma'am.'

'It couldn't be. Do you know what you're saying?'

'Just watch her,' I said.

'I don't know,' she moaned.

She looked crushed. She went back into the dining-room, but I saw her watching the cook through the doors. I watched both of them, the boss lady and the cook, praying that the cook would spit again. She did. The boss lady came into the kitchen and stared at Tillie, but she did not utter a word. She burst into tears and ran back into the dining-room.

'What's happening here?' Tillie demanded.

No one answered. The boss lady came out and tossed Tillie her hat, coat, and money.

'Now, get out of here, you dirty dog!' she said.

Tillie stared, then slowly picked up her hat, coat, and the money; she stood a moment, wiped sweat from her forehead with her hand, then spat — this time on the floor. She left.

Nobody was ever able to fathom why Tillie liked to spit into the food.

Brooding over Tillie, I recalled the time when the boss man in Mississippi had come to me and had tossed my wages to me and said:

'Get out, nigger! I don't like your looks.'

And I wondered if a Negro who did not smile and grin was as morally loathsome to whites as a cook who spat into the food.

The following summer I was called for temporary duty in the post office, and the work lasted into the winter. Aunt Cleo succumbed to a severe cardiac condition and, hard on the heels of her illness, my brother developed stomach ulcers. To rush my worries to a climax, my mother also became ill. I felt that I was maintaining a private hospital. Finally, the post-office work ceased altogether and I haunted the city for jobs. But when I went into the streets in the morning I saw sights that killed my hope for the rest of the day. Unemployed men loitered in doorways with blank looks in their eyes, sat dejectedly on front steps in shabby clothing, congregated in sullen groups on street corners, and filled all the empty benches in the parks of Chicago's South Side.

Luck of a sort came when a distant cousin of mine, who was a superintendent for a Negro burial society, offered me a position on his staff as an agent. The thought of selling insurance policies to ignorant Negroes disgusted me.

'Well, if you don't sell them, somebody else will,' my cousin told me. 'You've got to eat, haven't you?'

During that year I worked for several burial and insurance societies that operated among Negroes, and I received a new kind of education. I found that the burial societies, with some exceptions, were mostly 'rackets'. Some of them conducted their business legitimately, but there were many that exploited the ignorance of their black customers.

I was paid under a system that netted me fifteen dollars for every dollar's worth of new premiums that I placed upon the company's books, and for every dollar's worth of old premiums that lapsed I was penalized fifteen dollars. In addition, I was paid a commission of ten per cent on total premiums collected, but during the Depression it was extremely difficult to persuade a black family to buy a policy carrying even a dime premium. I considered myself lucky if, after subtracting lapses from new business, there remained fifteen dollars that I could call my own.

This 'gambling' method of remuneration was practised by some of the burial companies because of the tremendous 'turnover' in policy-holders, and the companies had to have a constant stream of new business to keep afloat. Whenever a black family moved or suffered a slight reverse in fortune, it usually let its policy lapse and later bought another policy from some other company.

Each day now I saw how the Negro in Chicago lived, for I visited hundreds of dingy flats filled with rickety furniture and ill-clad children. Most of the policy-holders were illiterate and did not know that their policies carried clauses severely restricting their benefit payments, and as an insurance agent, it was not my duty to tell them.

After tramping the streets and pounding on doors to collect pre-miums, I was dry, strained, too tired to read or write. I hungered for relief, and as a salesman of insurance to many young black girls, I found it. There were many comely black housewives who, trying desperately to keep up their insurance payments, were willing to make bargains to escape paying a ten-cent premium. I had a long, tortured affair with one girl by paying her ten-cent premium each week. She was an illiterate black child with a baby whose father she did not know. During the entire period of my relationship with her, she had but one demand to make of me: she wanted me to take her to a circus. Just what significance circuses had for her, I was never able to learn.

After I had been with her one morning – in exchange for the dime premium – I sat on the sofa in the front-room and began to read a book I had with me. She came over shyly.

'Lemme see that,' she said.

'What?' I asked.

'That book,' she said.

I gave her the book; she looked at it intently. I saw that she was holding it upside down.

'What's in here you keep reading?' she asked.

'Can't you really read?' I asked.

'Naw,' she giggled. 'You know I can't read.'

'You can read *some*,' I said.

'Naw,' she said.

I stared at her and wondered just what a life like hers meant in the scheme of things, and I came to the conclusion that it meant absolutely nothing. And neither did my life mean anything.

'How come you looking at me that way for?'

'Nothing.'

'You don't talk much.'

'There isn't much to say.'

'I wish Jim was here,' she sighed.

'Who's Jim?' I asked, jealous. I knew that she had other men, but I resented her mentioning them in my presence.

'Just a friend,' she said.

I hated her then, then hated myself for coming to her.

'Do you like Jim better than you like me?' I asked.

'Naw. Jim just likes to talk.'

'Then why do you be with me, if you like Jim better?' I asked, trying to make an issue and feeling a wave of disgust because I wanted to.

'You all right,' she said, giggling. 'I like you.'

'I could kill you,' I said.

'What?' she exclaimed.

'Nothing,' I said, ashamed.

'Kill me, you said? You crazy, man,' she said.

'Maybe I am,' I muttered, angry that I was sitting beside a human being to whom I could not talk, angry with myself for coming to her, hating my wild and restless loneliness.

'You oughta go home and sleep,' she said. 'You tired.'

'What do you ever think about?' I demanded harshly.

'Lotta things.'

'What, for example?'

'You,' she said, smiling.

'You know I mean just one dime to you each week,' I said.

'Naw, I think a lotta you.'

'Then what do you think?'

' 'Bout how you talk when you talk. I wished I could talk like you,' she said seriously.

'Why?' I taunted her.

'When you gonna take me to a circus?' she demanded suddenly.

'You ought to be in a circus,' I said.

'I'd like it,' she said, her eyes shining.

I wanted to laugh, but her words sounded so sincere that I could not.

'There's no circus in town,' I said.

'I bet there is and you won't tell me 'cause you don't wanna take me,' she said, pouting.

'But there's no circus in town, I tell you!'

'When will one come?'

'I don't know.'

'Can't you read it in the papers?' she asked.

'There's nothing in the papers about a circus.'

'There is,' she said. 'If I could read, I'd find it.'

I laughed, and she was hurt.

'There *is* a circus in town,' she said stoutly.

'There's no circus in town,' I said. 'But if you want to learn to read, then I'll teach you.'

She nestled at my side, giggling.

'See that word?' I said, pointing.

'Yeah.'

'That's an "and",' I said.

She doubled, giggling.

'What's the matter?' I asked.

She rolled on the floor, giggling.

'What's so funny?' I demanded.

'You,' she giggled. 'You so funny.'

I rose.

'The hell with you,' I said.

'Don't you go and cuss me now,' she said. 'I don't cuss you.'

'I'm sorry,' I said.

I got my hat and went to the door.

'I'll see you next week?' she asked.

'Maybe,' I said.

When I was on the sidewalk, she called to me from a window.

'You promised to take me to a circus, remember?'

'Yes.' I walked close to the window. 'What is it you like about a circus?'

'The animals,' she said simply.

I felt that there was a hidden meaning, perhaps, in what she had said, but I could not find it. She laughed and slammed the window shut.

Each time I left her I resolved not to visit her again. I could not talk to her; I merely listened to her passionate desire to see a circus. She was not calculating; if she liked a man, she just liked him. Sex relations were the only relations she had ever had; no others were possible with her, so limited was her intelligence.

Most of the other agents also had their bought girls, and they were extremely anxious to keep other agents from tampering with them. One day a new section of the South Side was given to me as a part of my collection area, and the agent from whom the territory had been taken suddenly became very friendly with me.

'Say, Wright,' he asked, 'did you collect from Ewing on Champlain Avenue yet?'

'Yes,' I answered, after consulting my book.

'How did you like her?' he asked, staring at me.

'She's a good-looking number,' I said.

'You had anything to do with her yet?' he asked.

'No, but I'd like to,' I said laughing.

'Look,' he said. 'I'm a friend of yours.'

'Since when?' I countered.

'No, I'm really a friend,' he said.

'What's on your mind?'

'Listen, that gal's sick,' he said seriously.

'What do you mean?'

'She's got the clap,' he said. 'Keep away from her. She'll lay with anybody.'

'Gee, I'm glad you told me,' I said.

'You had your eye on her, didn't you?' he asked.

'Yes, I did,' I said.

'Leave her alone,' he said. 'She'll get you down.'

That night I told my cousin what the agent had said about Miss Ewing. My cousin laughed.

'That gal's all right,' he said. 'That agent's been fooling around with her. He told you she had a disease so that you'd be scared to bother her. He was protecting her from you.'

That was the way the black women were regarded by the black agents. Some of the agents were vicious; if they had claims to pay to a sick black woman and if the woman was able to have sex relations with them, they would insist upon it, using the claims money as a bribe. If the woman refused, they would report to the office that the woman was a malingerer. The average black woman would submit because she needed the money badly.

As an insurance agent it was necessary for me to take part in one swindle. It appears that the burial society had originally issued a policy that was – from their point of view – too liberal in its provisions, and the officials decided to exchange the policies then in the hands of their clients for other policies carrying stricter clauses. Of course, this had to be done in a manner that would not allow the policy-holder to know that his policy was being switched – that he was being swindled. I did not like it, but there was only one thing I could do to keep from being a party to it: I could quit and starve. But I did not feel that being honest was worth the price of starvation.

The swindle worked in this way. In my visits to the homes of the policy-holders to collect premiums, I was accompanied by the superintendent, who claimed to the policy-holder that he was making a routine inspection. The policy-holder, usually an illiterate black woman, would dig up her policy from the bottom of a trunk or chest and hand it to the superintendent. Meanwhile I would be marking the woman's premium book, an act which would distract her from what the superintendent was doing. The superintendent would exchange the old policy for a new one which was identical in colour, serial number, and beneficiary, but which carried smaller payments. It was dirty work and I wondered how I could stop it. And when I could think of no safe way I would curse myself and the victims and forget about it. (The black owners of the burial societies were leaders in the Negro communities and were respected by whites.)

When I reached the relief station, I felt that I was making a public confession of my hunger. I sat waiting for hours, resentful of the mass of hungry people about me. My turn finally came and I was questioned by a middle-class Negro woman who asked me for a short history of my life. As I waited, I became aware of something happening in the room. The black men and women were mumbling quietly among themselves; they had not known one another before they had come here, but now their timidity and shame were wearing off and they were exchanging experiences. Before this they had lived as individuals, each somewhat afraid of the other, each seeking his own pleasure, each staunch in that degree of Americanism that had been allowed him. But now life had tossed them together, and they were learning to know the sentiments of their neighbours for the first time; their talking was enabling them to sense the collectivity of their lives, and some of their fear was passing.

Did the relief officials realize what was happening? No. If they had, they would have stopped it. But they saw their 'clients' through the eyes of the profession, saw only what their 'science' allowed them to see. As I listened to the talk, I could see black minds shedding many illusions. These people now knew that the past had betrayed them, had cast them out; but they did not know what the future would be like, did not know what they wanted. Yes, some of the things that the Communists said were true; they maintained that there came times in history when a ruling class could no longer rule. And now I sat looking at the beginnings of anarchy. To permit the birth of this new consciousness in these people was proof that those who ruled did not quite know what they were doing, assuming that they were trying to save themselves and their class. Had they understood what was happening, they would never have allowed millions of perplexed and defeated people to sit together for long hours and talk, for out of their talk was rising a new realization of life. And once this new conception of themselves had formed, no power on earth could alter it.

I left the relief station with the promise that food would be sent to me, but I also left with a knowledge that the relief officials had not wanted to give to me. I had felt the possibility of creating a new under-standing of life in the minds of people rejected by the society in which they lived, people to whom the Chicago *Tribune* referred con-temptuously as the 'idle' ones, as though these people had deliberately sought their present state of helplessness.

Who would give these people a meaningful way of life? Communist theory defined these people as the moulders of the future of mankind, but the Communist speeches I had heard in the park had mocked that definition. These people, of course, were not ready for a revolution; they had not abandoned their past lives by choice, but because they simply could not live the old way any longer. Now, what new faith would they embrace? The day I begged bread from the city officials was the day that showed me I was not alone in my loneliness; society had cast millions of others with me. But how could I be with them? How many understood what was happening? My mind swam with questions that I could not answer.

I was slowly beginning to comprehend the meaning of my environ-ment; a sense of direction was beginning to emerge from the conditions of my life. I began to feel something more powerful than I could express. My speech and manner changed. My cynicism slid from me. I grew open and questioning. I wanted to know.

If I were a member of the class that rules, I would post men in all the neighbourhoods of the nation, not to spy upon or club rebellious workers, not to break strikes or disrupt unions, but to ferret out those who no longer respond to the system under which they live. I would make it known that the real danger does not stem from those who seek to grab their share of wealth through force, or from those who try to defend their property through violence, for both of these groups, by their affirmative acts, support the values of the system under which they live. The millions that I would fear are those who do not dream of the prizes that the nation holds forth, for it is in them, though they may not know it, that a revolution has taken place and is biding its time to translate itself into a new and strange way of life.

I feel that the Negroes' relation to America is symbolically peculiar, and from the Negroes' ultimate reactions to their trapped state a lesson can be learned about America's future. Negroes are told in a language they cannot possibly misunderstand that their native land is not their own; and when, acting upon impulses which they share with whites, they try to assert a claim to their birthright, whites retaliate with terror, never pausing to consider the consequences should the Negroes give up completely. The whites never dream that they would face a situation far more terrifying if they were confronted by Negroes who made no claims at all than by those who are buoyed up by social aggressiveness. My knowledge of how Negroes react to their plight makes me declare that no man can possibly be individually guilty of treason, that an insurgent act is but a man's desperate answer to those who twist his environment so that he cannot fully share the spirit of his native land. Treason is a crime of the State.

Christmas came and I was once more called to the post office for temporary work. This time I met many young white men and we discussed world happenings, the vast armies of unemployed, the rising tide of radical action. I now detected a change in the attitudes of the whites I met; their privations were making them regard Negroes with new eyes, and for the first time, I was invited to their homes.

When the work in the post office ended, I was assigned by the relief system as an orderly to a medical research institute in one of the largest and wealthiest hospitals in Chicago. I cleaned operating rooms, dog, rat, mice, cat, and rabbit pans, and fed guinea pigs. Four of us Negroes worked there and we occupied an underworld position, remembering that we must restrict ourselves – when not engaged upon some task – to the basement corridors, so that we would not mingle with white nurses, doctors, or visitors.

The sharp line of racial division drawn by the hospital authorities came to me the first morning, when I walked along an underground corridor and saw two long lines of women coming towards me. A line of white girls marched past, clad in starched uniforms that gleamed white; their faces were alert, their step quick, their bodies lean and shapely, their shoulders erect, their faces lit with the light of purpose. And after them came a line of black girls, old, fat, dressed in ragged gingham, walking loosely, carrying tin cans of soap powder, rags, mops, brooms . . . I wondered what law of the universe kept them from being mixed? The sun would not have stopped shining had there been a few black girls in the first line, and the earth would not have stopped whirling on its axis had there been a few white girls in the second line. But the two lines I saw graded social status in purely racial terms.

Of the three Negroes who worked with me, one was a boy about my own age, Bill, who was either sleepy or drunk most of the time. Bill straightened his hair and I suspected that he kept a bottle hidden somewhere in the piles of hay which we fed to the guinea pigs. He did not like me and I did not like him, though I tried harder than he to conceal my dislike. We had nothing in common except that we were both black and lost. While I contained my frustration, he drank to drown his. Often I tried to talk to him, tried in simple words to convey to him some of my ideas, and he would listen in sullen silence. Then one day he came to me with an angry look on his face.

'I got it,' he said.

'You've got what?' I asked.

'This old race problem you keep talking about,' he said.

'What about it?'

'Well, it's this way,' he explained seriously. 'Let the government give every man a gun and five bullets, then let us all start over again. Make it just like it was in the beginning. The ones who come out on top, white or black, let them rule.'

His simplicity terrified me. I had never met a Negro who was so irredeemably brutalized. I stopped pumping my ideas into Bill's brain for fear that the fumes of alcohol might send him reeling towards some fantastic fate.

The two other Negroes were elderly and had been employed in the institute for fifteen years or more. One was Brand, a short, black, morose bachelor; the other was Cooke, a tall, yellow, spectacled fellow who spent his spare time keeping track of world events through the Chicago *Tribune*. Brand and Cooke hated each other for a reason that I was never able to determine, and they spent a good part of each day quarrelling.

When I began working at the institute, I recalled my adolescent dream of wanting to be a medical research worker. Daily I saw young Jewish boys and girls receiving instruction in chemistry and medicine that the average black boy or girl could never receive. When I was alone, I wandered and poked my fingers into strange chemicals, watched intricate machines trace red and black lines on ruled paper. At times I paused and stared at the walls of the rooms, at the floors, at the wide desks at which the white doctors sat; and I realized – with a feeling that I could never quite get used to – that I was looking at the world of another race.

My interest in what was happening in the institute amused the three other Negroes with whom I worked. They had no curiosity about 'white folks' things', while I wanted to know if the dogs being treated for diabetes were getting well; if the rats and mice in which cancer had been induced showed any signs of responding to treatment. I wanted to know the principle that lay behind the Aschheim-Zondek tests that were made with rabbits, the Wassermann tests that were made with guinea pigs. But when I asked a timid question I found that even Jewish doctors had learned to imitate the sadistic method of humbling a Negro that the others had cultivated.

'If you know too much, boy, your brains might explode,' a doctor said one day.

Each Saturday morning I assisted a young Jewish doctor in slitting the vocal cords of a fresh batch of dogs from the city pound. The object was to devocalize the dogs so that their howls would not disturb the patients in the other parts of the hospital. I held each dog as the doctor injected Nembutal into its veins to make it unconscious; then I held the dog's jaws open as the doctor inserted the scalpel and severed the vocal cords. Later, when the dogs came to, they would lift their heads to the ceiling and gape in a soundless wail. The sight became lodged in my imagination as a symbol of silent suffering.

To me Nembutal was a powerful and mysterious liquid, but when I asked questions about its properties I could not obtain a single intelligent answer. The doctor simply ignored me with:

'Come on. Bring me the next dog. I haven't got all day.'

One Saturday morning, after I had held the dogs for their vocal cords to be slit, the doctor left the Nembutal on a bench. I picked it up, uncorked it, and smelled it. It was odourless. Suddenly Brand ran to me with a stricken face.

'What're you doing?' he asked.

'I was smelling this stuff to see if it had any odour,' I said.

'Did you really smell it?' he asked me.

'Yes.'

'Oh, God!' he exclaimed.

'What's the matter?' I asked.

'You shouldn't've done that!' he shouted.

'Why?'

He grabbed my arm and jerked me across the room.

'Come on!' he yelled, snatching open the door.

'What's the matter?' I asked.

'I gotta get you to a doctor 'fore it's too late,' he gasped.

Had my foolish curiosity made me inhale something dangerous?

'But — is it poisonous?'

'Run, boy!' he said, pulling me. 'You'll fall dead.'

Filled with fear, with Brand pulling my arm, I rushed out of the room, raced across a rear area-way, into another room, then down a long corridor. I wanted to ask Brand what symptoms I must expect, but we were running too fast. Brand finally stopped, gasping for breath. My heart beat wildly and my blood pounded in my head. Brand then dropped to the concrete floor, stretched out on his back, and yelled with laughter, shaking all over. He beat his fists against the concrete; he moaned, giggled, he kicked.

I tried to master my outrage, wondering if some of the white doctors had told him to play the joke. He rose and wiped tears from his eyes, still laughing. I walked away from him. He knew that I was angry, and he followed me.

'Don't get mad,' he gasped through his laughter.

'Go to hell,' I said.

'I couldn't help it,' he giggled. 'You looked at me like you'd believe anything I said. Man, you was scared.'

He leaned against the wall, laughing again, stomping his feet. I was angry, for I felt that he would spread the story. I knew that Bill and Cooke never ventured beyond the safe bounds of Negro living, and they would never blunder into anything like this. And if they heard about this, they would laugh for months.

'Brand, if you mention this, I'll kill you,' I swore.

'You ain't mad?' he asked, laughing, staring at me through tears.

Sniffing, Brand walked ahead of me. I followed him back into the room that housed the dogs. All day, while at some task, he would pause and giggle, then smother the giggling with his hand, looking at me out of the corner of his eyes, shaking his head. He laughed at me for a week. I kept my temper and let him amuse himself. I finally found out the properties of Nembutal by consulting medical books; but I never told Brand.

One summer morning, just as I began work, a young Jewish boy came to me with a stopwatch in his hand.

'Dr — wants me to time you when you clean a room,' he said. 'We're trying to make the institute more efficient.'

'I'm doing my work, and getting through on time,' I said.

'This is the boss's order,' he said.

'Why don't you work for a change?' I blurted, angry.

'Now, look,' he said. '*This* is my work. Now *you* work.'

I got a mop and pail, sprayed a room with disinfectant, and scrubbed at coagulated blood and hardened dog, rat, and rabbit faeces. The normal temperature of a room was ninety, but as the sun beat down upon the skylights, the temperature rose above a hundred. Stripped to my waist, I slung the mop, moving steadily like a machine, hearing the boy press the button on the stopwatch as I finished cleaning a room.

'Well, how is it?' I asked.

'It took you seventeen minutes to clean that last room,' he said. 'That ought to be the time for each room.'

'But that room was not very dirty,' I said.

'You have seventeen rooms to clean,' he went on as though I had not spoken. 'Seventeen times seventeen make four hours and forty-nine minutes.' He wrote upon a little pad. 'After lunch, clean the five flights of stone stairs. I timed a boy who scrubbed one step and multiplied that time by the number of steps. You ought to be through by six.'

'Suppose I want relief?' I asked.

'You'll manage,' he said and left.

Never had I felt so much the slave as when I scoured those stone steps each afternoon. Working against time, I would wet five steps, sprinkle soap powder, and then a white doctor or a nurse would come along and, instead of avoiding the soapy steps, would walk on them and track the dirty water onto the steps that I had already cleaned. To obviate this, I cleaned but two steps at a time, a distance over which a ten-year-old child could step. But it did no good. The white people still plopped their feet down into the dirty water and muddied the other clean steps. If I ever really hotly hated unthinking whites, it was then. Not once during my entire stay at the institute did a single white person show enough courtesy to avoid a wet step. I would be on my knees, scrubbing, sweating, pouring out what limited energy my body could wring from my meagre diet, and I would hear feet approaching. I would pause and curse with tense lips:

'These sonofabitches are going to dirty these steps again, goddamn their souls to hell!'

Sometimes a sadistically observant white man would notice that he had tracked dirty water up the steps, and he would look back down at me and smile and say:

'Boy, we sure keep you busy, don't we?'

And I would not be able to answer.

The feud that went on between Brand and Cooke continued. Although they were working daily in a building where scientific history was being made, the light of curiosity was never in their eyes. They were conditioned to their racial 'place', had learned to see only a part of the whites and the white world; and the whites, too, had learned to see only a part of the lives of the blacks and their world.

Perhaps Brand and Cooke, lacking interests that could absorb them, fuming like children over trifles, simply invented their hate of each other in order to have something to feel deeply about. Or perhaps there was in them a vague tension stemming from their chronically frustrating way of life, a pain whose cause they did not know; and like those devocalized dogs, they would whirl and snap at the air when their old pain struck them. Anyway, they argued about the weather, sports, sex, war, race, politics, and religion; neither of them knew much about the subjects they debated, but it seemed that the less they knew the better they could argue.

The tug of war between the two elderly men reached a climax one winter day at noon. It was incredibly cold, and an icy gale swept up and down the Chicago streets with blizzard force. The door of the animal-filled room was locked, for we always insisted that we be allowed one hour in which to eat and rest. Bill and I were sitting on wooden boxes, eating our lunches out of paper bags. Brand was washing his hands at the sink. Cooke was sitting on a rickety stool, munching an apple and reading the Chicago *Tribune*.

Now and then a devocalized dog lifted his nose to the ceiling and howled soundlessly. The room was filled with many rows of high steel tiers. Perched upon each of these tiers were layers of steel cages containing the dogs, rats, mice, rabbits, and guinea pigs. Each cage was labelled in some indecipherable scientific jargon. Along the walls of the room were long charts with zigzagging red and black lines that traced the success or failure of some experiment. The lonely piping of guinea pigs floated unheeded about us. Hay rustled as a rabbit leaped restlessly about in its pen. A rat scampered around in its steel prison. Cooke tapped the newspaper for attention.

'It says here,' Cooke mumbled through a mouthful of apple, 'that this is the coldest day since 1888.'

Bill and I sat unconcerned. Brand chuckled softly.

'What in hell you laughing about?' Cooke demanded of Brand.

'You can't believe what that damn *Tribune* says,' Brand said.

'How come I can't?' Cooke demanded. 'It's the world's greatest newspaper.'

Brand did not reply; he shook his head pityingly and chuckled again.

'Stop that damn laughing at me!' Cooke said angrily.

'I laugh as much as I wanna,' Brand said. 'You don't know what you talking about. The *Herald-Examiner* says it's the coldest day since 1873.'

'But the *Trib* oughta know,' Cooke countered. 'It's older'n that *Examiner*.'

'That damn *Trib* don't know nothing!' Brand drowned out Cooke's voice.

'How in hell you know?' Cooke asked with rising anger.

The argument waxed until Cooke shouted that if Brand did not shut up he was going to 'cut his black throat'.

Brand whirled from the sink, his hands dripping soapy water, his eyes blazing.

'Take that back,' Brand said.

'I take nothing back! What you wanna do about it?' Cooke taunted.

The two elderly Negroes glared at each other. I wondered if the quarrel was really serious, or if it would turn out harmlessly as so many others had done.

Suddenly Cooke dropped the Chicago *Tribune* and pulled a long knife from his pocket; his thumb pressed a button and a gleaming steel blade leaped out. Brand stepped back quickly and seized an ice pick that was stuck in a wooden board above the sink.

'Put that knife down,' Brand said.

'Stay 'way from me, or I'll cut your throat,' Cooke warned.

Brand lunged with the ice pick. Cooke dodged out of range. They circled each other like fighters in a prize ring. The cancerous and tubercular rats and mice leaped about in their cages. The guinea pigs whistled in fright. The diabetic dogs bared their teeth and barked soundlessly in our direction. The Aschheim-Zondek rabbits flopped their ears and tried to hide in the corners of their pens. Cooke now crouched and sprang forward with the knife. Bill and I jumped to our feet, speechless with surprise. Brand retreated. The eyes of both men were hard and unblinking; they were breathing deeply.

'Say, cut it out!' I called in alarm.

'Them damn fools is really fighting,' Bill said in amazement.

Slashing at each other, Brand and Cooke surged up and down the aisles of steel tiers. Suddenly Brand uttered a bellow and charged into Cooke and swept him violently backwards. Cooke grasped Brand's hand to keep the ice pick from sinking into his chest. Brand broke free and charged Cooke again, sweeping him into an animal-filled steel tier. The tier balanced itself on its edge for an indecisive moment, then toppled.

Like kingpins, one steel tier lammed into another, then they all crashed to the floor with a sound as of the roof falling. The whole aspect of the room altered quicker than the eye could follow. Brand and Cooke stood stock-still, their eyes fastened upon each other, their pointed-weapons raised; but they were dimly aware of the havoc that churned about them.

The steel tiers lay jumbled; the doors of the cages swung open. Rats and mice and dogs and rabbits moved over the floor in wild panic. The Wassermann guinea pigs were squealing as though judgement day had come. Here and there an animal had been crushed beneath a cage.

All four of us looked at one another. We knew what this meant. We might lose our jobs. We were already regarded as black dunces; and if the doctors saw this mess they would take it as final proof. Bill rushed to the door to make sure that it was locked. I glanced at the clock and saw that it was 12.30. We had one half-hour of grace.

'Come on,' Bill said uneasily. 'We got to get this place cleaned.'

Brand and Cooke stared at each other, both doubting.

'Give me your knife, Cooke,' I said.

'Naw! Take Brand's ice pick *first*,' Cooke said.

'The hell you say!' Brand said. 'Take his knife *first*!'

A knock sounded at the door.

'Sssssh,' Bill said.

We waited. We heard footsteps going away. We'll all lose our jobs, I thought.

Persuading the fighters to surrender their weapons was a difficult task, but at last it was done and we could begin to set things right. Brand stooped and tugged at one end of a steel tier. Cooke stooped to help him. Both men seemed to be acting in a dream. Soon, however, all four of us were working frantically, watching the clock.

As we laboured we conspired to keep the fight a secret; we agreed to tell the doctors – if any should ask – that we had not been in the room during our lunch hour; we felt that that lie would explain why no one had unlocked the door when the knock had come.

We righted the tiers and replaced the cages; then we were faced with the impossible task of sorting the cancerous rats and mice, the diabetic dogs, the Aschheim-Zondek rabbits, and the Wassermann guinea pigs. Whether we kept our jobs or not depended upon how shrewdly we could cover up all evidence of the fight. It was pure guesswork, but we had to try to put the animals back into the correct cages. We knew that certain rats or mice went into certain cages, but we did not know *what* rat or mouse went into *what* cage. We did not know a tubercular mouse from a cancerous mouse – the white doctors had made sure that we would not know. They had never taken time to answer a single question; though we worked in the institute, we were as remote from the meaning of the experiments as if we lived on the moon. The doctors had laughed at what they felt was our childlike interest in the fate of the animals.

First we sorted the dogs; that was fairly easy, for we could remember the size and colour of most of them. But the rats and mice and guinea pigs baffled us completely.

We put our heads together and pondered, down in the underworld of the great scientific institute. It was a strange scientific conference; the fate of the entire medical research institute rested in our ignorant, black hands.

We remembered the number of rats, mice, or guinea pigs – we had to handle them several times a day – that went into a given cage, and we supplied the number helter-skelter from those animals that we could catch running loose on the floor. We discovered that many rats, mice, and guinea pigs were missing – they had been killed in the scuffle. We solved that problem by taking healthy stock from other cages and putting them into cages with sick animals. We repeated this process until we were certain that, numerically at least, all the animals with which the doctors were experimenting were accounted for.

The rabbits came last. We broke the rabbits down into two general groups; those that had fur on their bellies and those that did not. We knew that all those rabbits that had shaven bellies – our scientific knowledge adequately covered this point because it was our job to shave the rabbits – were undergoing the Aschheim-Zondek tests. But in what pen did a given rabbit belong? We did not know. I solved the problem very simply. I counted the shaven rabbits; they numbered seventeen. I counted the pens labelled 'Aschheim-Zondek', then proceeded to drop a shaven rabbit into each pen at random. And again we were numerically successful. At least white America had taught us how to count . . .

Lastly we carefully wrapped all the dead animals in newspapers and hid their bodies in a garbage can.

At a few minutes to one the room was in order; that is, the kind of order that we four Negroes could figure out. I unlocked the door and we sat waiting, whispering, vowing secrecy, wondering what the reaction of the doctors would be.

Finally a doctor came, grey-haired, white-coated, spectacled, efficient, serious, taciturn, bearing a tray upon which sat a bottle of mysterious fluid and a hypodermic needle.

'My rats, please.'

Cooke shuffled forward to serve him. We held our breath. Cooke got the cage which he knew the doctor always called for at that hour and brought it forward. One by one, Cooke took out the rats and held them as the doctor solemnly injected the mysterious fluid under their skins.

'Thank you, Cooke,' the doctor murmured.

'Not at all, sir,' Cooke mumbled with a suppressed gasp.

When the doctor had gone we looked at one another, hardly daring to believe that our secret would be kept. We were so anxious that we did not know whether to curse or laugh. Another doctor came.

'Give me A–Z rabbit number 14.'

'Yes, sir,' I said.

I brought him the rabbit and he took it upstairs to the operating room. We waited for repercussions. None came.

All that afternoon the doctors came and went. I would run into the room – stealing a few seconds from my step-scrubbing – and ask what progress was being made and would learn that the doctors had detected nothing. At quitting time we felt triumphant.

'They won't ever know,' Cooke boasted in a whisper.

I saw Brand stiffen. I knew that he was aching to dispute Cooke's optimism, but the memory of the fight he had just had was so fresh in his mind that he could not speak.

Another day went by and nothing happened. Then another day. The doctors examined the animals and wrote in their little black books, in their big black books, and continued to trace red and black lines upon the charts.

A week passed and we felt out of danger. Not one question had been asked.

Of course, we four black men were much too modest to make our contribution known, but we often wondered what went on in the laboratories after that secret disaster. Was some scientific hypothesis, well on its way to validation and ultimate public use, discarded because of unexpected findings on that cold winter day? Was some tested principle given a new and strange refinement because of fresh, remarkable evidence? Did some brooding research worker – those who held stopwatches and slopped their feet carelessly in the water of the steps I tried so hard to keep clean – get a wild, if brief, glimpse of a new scientific truth? Well, we never heard . . .

I brooded upon whether I should have gone to the director's office and told him what had happened, but each time I thought of it I remembered that the director had been the man who had ordered the boy to stand over me while I was working and time my movements with a stopwatch. He did not regard me as a human being. I did not share his world. I earned thirteen dollars a week and I had to support four people with it, and should I risk that thirteen dollars by acting idealistically? Brand and Cooke would have hated me and would have eventually driven me from the job had I 'told' on them. The hospital kept us four Negroes as though we were close kin to the animals we tended, huddled together down in the underworld corridors of the hospital, separated by a vast psychological distance from the significant processes of the rest of the hospital – just as America had kept us locked in the dark underworld of American life for three hundred years – and we had made our own code of ethics, values, loyalty.

our contemporaries

ambrose his mark

JOHN BARTH

Owing to the hectic circumstances of my birth, for some months I had no proper name. Mother had seen Garbo in *Anna Christie* at the Dorset Opera House during her pregnancy and come to hope for a daughter, to be named by some logic Christine in honour of that lady. When I was brought home, after Father's commitment to the Eastern Shore Asylum, she made no mention of a name nor showed any interest in selecting one, and the family were too concerned for her well-being to press the matter. She grew froward – by turns high-spirited and listless, voluble and dumb, doting and cynical. Some days she would permit no hands but hers to touch me, would haul me about from room to room, crooning and nuzzling: a photograph made by Uncle Karl on such a day shows her posed before our Concord vines, her pretty head thrown back, scarfed and earringed like a gypsy; her eyes are closed, her mouth laughs gaily behind her cigarette; one hand holds a cup of coffee, the other steadies a scowling infant on her hip. Other times she would have none of me, or even suffer me in her sight. About my feeding there was ever some unease: if I cried, say, when the family was at the table, forks would pause and eyes turn furtively to Andrea. For in one humour she would fetch out her breast in any company and feed me while she smoked or strolled the garden – nor nurse me quietly at that, but demand of Aunt Rosa whether I hadn't Hector's eyes . . .

'Ja, well.'

'And Poppa Tom's appetite. Look, Konrad, how he wolfs it. There's a man for you.'

Grandfather openly relished these performances; he chuckled at the mentions of himself, teased Uncle Konrad for averting his eyes, and never turned his own from my refections.

'Now there is Beauty's picture, *nicht wahr*, Konrad? Mother and child.'

But his entertainment was not assured: just as often Andrea would say, 'Lord, there goes Christine again. Stick something in his mouth, Rosie, would you?' or merely sigh – a rueful expiration that still blows fitful as her ghost through my memory – and say nothing, but let Aunt Rosa (always nervously at hand) prepare and administer my bottle, not even troubling to make her kindless joke about the grand unsuckled bosoms of that lady.

To Rosa I was *Honig*; Mother too, when 'Christine' seemed unfunny, called me thus, and in the absence of anything official, *Honey* soon lost the quality of endearment and took the neutral function of a proper name. Uncle Konrad privately held out for *Hector*, but no one ventured to bring up her husband's name in Mother's presence. Uncle Karl was not in town to offer an opinion. Aunt Rosa believed that calling me *Thomas* might improve relations between Grandfather and his youngest son; but though he'd made no secret of his desire to have my older brother be his namesake, and his grievance at the choice of *Peter*, Grandfather displayed no more interest than did Andrea in naming me. Rosa attributed his indifference to bruised pride; in any case, given Mother's attitude, the question of my nomination was academic. Baptism was delayed, postponed, anon forgot.

Only once did Mother allude to my namelessness, some two or three months after my birth. I was lying in Aunt Rosa's lap, drinking from a bottle; dinner was just done; the family lingered over coffee. Suddenly Andrea, on one of her impulses, cried 'Give him here, Rosa!' and snatched me up. I made a great commotion.

'Now, you frightened it,' Rosa chided.

Andrea ignored her. ' 'E doesn't want Rosie's old bottle, does Christine.'

Her croon failed to console me. 'Hold him tight till I unbutton,' she said – not to Rosa but to Uncle Konrad. Her motives, doubtless, were the usual: to make Aunt Rosa envious, amuse Grandfather, and mortify Uncle Konrad, who could not now readily look away. She undid her peignoir, casually bemoaning her abundance of milk: it was making her clothes a sight, it was hurting her besides, she must nurse me more regularly. She did not at once retrieve me but with such chatter as this bent forward, cupped her breast, invited me to drink the sweet pap already beading and spreading under her fingers. Uncle Konrad, it was agreed, at no time before or after turned so crimson.

'Here's what the Honey wants,' Andrea said, relieving him finally of his charge. To the company in general she declared, 'It does feel good, you know: there's a nerve or something runs from here right to you-know-where.'

'*Schämt euch!*' Aunt Rosa cried.

'*Ja* sure,' Grandfather said merrily. 'You named it!'

'No, really, she knows as well as I do what it's like. Doesn't she, Christine. Sure Mother likes to feed her little mannie, look how he grabs, poor darling ...' Here she was taken unexpectedly with grief; pressed me fiercely to her, drew the peignoir about us; her tears warmed my forehead and her breast. 'Who will he ever be, Konrad? Little orphan of the storm, who is he now?'

'Ah! Ah!' Rosa rushed to hug her. Grandfather drew and sucked upon his meerschaum, which however had gone dead out.

'Keep up like you have been,' Konrad said stiffly; 'soon he'll be old enough to pick his own name.' My uncle taught fifth grade at East Dorset School, of which Hector had been principal until his commitment, and in summers was a vendor of encyclopaedias and tuner of pianos. To see things in their larger context was his gentle aim; to harmonize part with part, time with time; and he never withheld from us what he deemed germane or helpful. The American Indians, he declared now, had the right idea. 'They never named a boy right off. What they did, they watched to find out who he was. They'd look for the right sign to tell them what to call him.'

Grandfather scratched a kitchen match on his thumbnail and relit his pipe.

'There's sense in that,' Uncle Konrad persevered. 'How can you tell what name'll suit a person when you don't know him yet?'

Ordinarily Rosa was his audience; preoccupied now with Andrea, she did not respond.

'There's some name their kids for what they want them to be. A brave hunter, et cetera.'

'Or a movie star,' Mother offered, permitting Rosa to wipe her eyes.

'Same principle exactly,' Konrad affirmed, and was grateful enough to add in her behalf, despite his late embarrassment: 'It's an important thing, naming a child. If I had a boy, I'd be a good long time about it.'

'*Ach,*' Grandfather said. 'You said that right.'

Andrea sniffed sympathy but did not reply, and so Uncle Konrad enlarged no further. Too bad for Grandfather his restlessness moved him from the table, for by this time my mother was herself sufficiently to turn back the veil she'd drawn about us.

'Well,' she sighed to me. 'You've caused the devil's mischief so far. Your daddy in the crazy-house; people saying Lord knows what about your mother.'

'Thank Almighty God you got him,' Aunt Rosa said. 'And born perfect only for his little mark. Look how wide and clear his eyes!'

Uncle Konrad unbent so far as to pat my head while I nursed, a boldness without known precedent in his biography. 'That's a sign of brains,' he declared. 'This boy could be our pride and saving.'

Mother's laugh took on a rougher note. But she caressed my cheek with her knuckle, and I nursed on. Her temper was gay and fond now; yet her breast still glistened with the tears of a minute past. Not just that once was what I drank from her thus salted.

Grandfather would have no whisky or other distillation in the house, but drank grandly of wines and beers which he made himself in the whitewashed sheds behind the summer-kitchen. His yeast and earliest grapestock were German, imported for him by the several families he'd brought to the county. The vines never flourished: anon they fell victim to anthracnose and phylloxera and were replaced by our native Delawares, Nortons, Lenoirs; but the yeast – an ancient culture from Sachsen-Altenburg – throve with undiminished vigour in our cellar. With it he would brew dark Bavarian lager, pellucid Weiss, and his cherished Dortmund, pale gold and strongly hopped. Yet vinting was his forte, even Hector agreed. What he drew from the red and white grapes was splendid enough, but in this pursuit as in some others he inclined to variety and experiment: without saccharimeter or any other aid than a Rhenish intuition, he filled his crocks as the whim took him with anything fermentable – rice, cherries, dandelions, elderberries, rose petals, raisins, coconut – and casked unfailingly a decent wine.

Now it was Uncle Konrad's pleasure to recite things on occasion to the family, and in 1929, hearing by this means verses of Macpherson's *Ossian,* Grandfather had been inspired with a particular hankering for mead. From a farmer whose payments on a foot-stone were in arrears, he accepted in lieu of cash a quantity of honey, and his fermentation was an entire success. The craving got hold of him, he yearned to crush walnuts in the golden wort – but honey was dear, and dollars, never plentiful in the family, there were none for such expenditure. The stock market had fallen, the tomato canners were on strike, hard times were upon the nation; if funerals were a necessity, gravestones were not;

Uncle Karl, Grandfather's right-hand man, had left town two years past to lay bricks in Baltimore; our business had seldom been poorer.

'There is a trick for finding bee trees,' Grandfather asserted. One exposed a pan of sugar water in the woods, waited until a number of honeybees assembled at it, and trapped them by covering the pan with cheesecloth. One then released a single bee and followed it, pan in hand, till it was lost from sight, whereupon one released another bee, and another, and another, and was fetched at length to their common home. It remained then only to smoke out the colony and help oneself to their reserves of honey. All that winter, as I grew in Mother's womb, Grandfather fretted with his scheme; when the spring's first bees appeared on our pussywillows, on our alder catkins, he was off with Hector and Konrad, saucepan and cheesecloth. Their researches led them through fresh-marsh, through pinewoods, over stile and under trestle — but never a bee tree they discovered, only swampy impasses or the hives of some part-time apiarist.

My birth — more exactly, Hector's notion that someone other than himself had fathered me; his mad invasion of the delivery room; his wild assertion, as they carried him off, that the port-wine stain near my eye was a devil's mark — all this commotion, naturally, ended the quest. Not, however, the general project. Out of scrap pine Grandfather fashioned a box-hive of his own, whitewashed and established it among the lilacs next to the goat-pen, and bade Uncle Konrad keep his eyes open for a migrant swarm, the season being opportune.

His expectation was not unreasonable, even though East Dorset was by 1930 a proper residential ward with sidewalks, sewers, and street-lights. To maintain a goat might be judged eccentric, even vulgar, by neighbours with flush toilets and daily milk service; chickens, likewise, were *non grata* on Seawall Street (if not on Hayward or Franklin, where roosters crowed to the end of the Second World War); but there was nothing unseemly about a stand of sweetcorn, for example, if one had ground enough, or a patch of cucumbers, or a hive of bees. These last, in fact, were already a feature of our street's most handsome yard: I mean Erdmann's, adjacent but for an alley to our own. Upon Willy Erdmann's three fine skeps, braided of straw and caned English-fashion, Grandfather had brooded all winter. Two were inhabited and prosperous; the third, brand new, stood vacant against the day when a swarm would take wing from the others in search of new quarters.

Lilac honey, Grandfather declared, was more pleasing than any other to his taste; moreover it was essential that the hive be placed as far as possible from the house, not to disturb the occupants of either. Though no one pressed him to explain, he insisted it was for these reasons only (one or both of which must have been Erdmann's also) that he located his hive in the extreme rear corner of our property, next to the alley.

Our neighbour plainly was unhappy with this arrangement. Not long from the Asylum himself, whither he'd repaired to cure a sudden dipsomania, Erdmann was convalescing some months at home before he reassumed direction of his business. Pottering about his yard he'd seen our box-hives built and situated: as April passed he came to spend more time on the alley side of his lot – cultivating his tulips, unmulching his roses, chewing his cigar, glaring from his beehives to ours.

'Yes, well,' Grandfather observed. 'Willy's bees have been for years using our lilacs. Have I begrutched?'

He made it his tactic at first to stroll hiveward himself whenever Erdmann was standing watch: he would examine his grape-canes, only just opening their mauve-and-yellow buds; he would make pleasantries in two tongues to Gretchen the goat; Erdmann soon would huff indoors.

But with both Hector and Karl away, Grandfather was obliged to spend more time than usual at the stoneyard, however slack the business; throughout whole weekday mornings and afternoons his apiary interests lay under Erdmann's scrutiny.

'A swarm in May is worth a load of hay,' Uncle Konrad recalled:

'A swarm in June is worth a silver spoon.
But a swarm in July is not worth a fly.'

May was cool, the lilacs and japonica had never blossomed so; then June broke out on the peninsula like a fire, everything flowered together, in Erdmann's skeps the honey flow was on.

'What you need,' Grandfather said to Andrea, 'you need peace and quiet and fresh air this summer. Leave Rosa the housework; you rest and feed your baby.'

'What the hell have I *been* doing?' Mother asked. But she did not protest her father-in-law's directive or his subsequent purchase of a hammock for her comfort, an extraordinary munificence. Even when his motive was revealed to be less than purely chivalrous – he strung the hammock between a Judas tree and a vine post, in view of the alley – she did not demur. On the contrary, though she teased Grandfather without mercy, she was diverted by the stratagem and cooperated beyond his expectation. Not only did she make it her custom on fine days to loll in the hammock, reading, dozing, and watching casually for a bee swarm; she took to nursing me there as well. Aunt Rosa and certain of the neighbours murmured; Uncle Konrad shook his head; but at feeding times I was fetched to the hammock and suckled in the sight

of any. At that time my mother had lost neither her pretty face and figure nor her wanton spirit: she twitted the schoolboys who gawked along
the fence and the trashmen lingering at our cans; merrily she remarked
upon rerouting and delays on the part of delivery wagons, which seldom
before had used our alley. And she was as pleased as Grandfather, if not
for the same reason, by the discomfiture of Mr Erdmann, who now was
constrained to keep what watch he would from an upstairs window.

'Willy's bashful as Konrad,' she said to Rosa. 'Some men, I swear,
you'd think they'd never seen anything.'

Grandfather chuckled. 'Willy's just jealous. Hector he's got used to,
but he don't like sharing you with the trashman.'

But Mother could not be daunted by any raillery. 'Listen to the pot
call the kettle!'

'Ja sure,' said Grandfather, and treated her to one of the pinches for
which he was famed among East Dorset housewives.

Mr Erdmann's response to the hammock was a bee-bob: he threaded
dead bees into a cluster and mounted it on a pole, which he then erected
near his skeps to attract the swarm.

'He knows they won't swarm for a naughty man,' Grandfather explained. 'It wonders me he can even handle them.' In the old country, he
declared, couples tested each other's virtue by walking hand in hand
among the hives, the chaste having nothing to fear.

Mother was sceptical. 'If bees were like that, not a man in Dorset
could keep a hive. Except Konrad.'

My uncle, as if she were not fondling the parting in the middle of his
hair, began to discourse upon the prophetic aspect of swarming among
various peoples – eg, that a swarm on the house was thought by the
Austrians to augur good fortune, by the Romans to warn of ill, and by
the Greeks to herald strangers; that in Switzerland a swarm on a dry
twig presaged the death of someone in the family, et cetera – but before
ever he had got to the Bretons and Transylvanians his wife was his only
auditor: Andrea was back in her magazine, and Grandfather had gone
off to counter Erdmann's bee-bob by rubbing the inside of his own hive
with elder flowers.

The last Sunday of the month but one dawned bright, hot, still. Out
on the river not even the bell buoy stirred, whose clang we heard in
every normal weather; in its stead the bell of Grace, M-P Southern, mark
of a straiter channel, called forth East Dorseters in their cords and
worsteds. But ours was a family mired in apostasy. There was no athe-
ism in the house; in truth there was no talk of religion at all, except in
Hector's most cynical moods. It was generally felt that children should
be raised in the church, and so when the time came Peter and I would be
enrolled in the Sunday school and the Junior Christian Endeavour.

More, Grandfather had lettered, gratis, *In Remembrance of Me* on the oak communion table and engraved the church cornerstone as well. We disapproved of none of the gentlemen who ministered the charge, although Grace, not the plum of the conference, was served as a rule by preachers very young or very old. Neither had we doctrinal differences with Methodism – Southern or Northern, Protestant or Episcopal: Aunt Rosa sometimes said, as if in explanation of our backsliding, 'Why it is, we were all Lutherans in the old country'; but it would have been unkind to ask her the distinction between the faiths of Martin Luther and John Wesley. Yet though Konrad, with a yellow rosebud in his lapel, went faithfully to Bible class, none of us went to church. God served us on our terms and in our house (we were with a few exceptions baptized, wed, and funeralled in the good parlour); for better or worse it was not in our make-up to serve Him in His.

By eleven, then, this Sunday morning, Aunt Rosa had brought Peter home from Cradle Roll, Konrad was back from Bible class, and the family were about their separate pleasures. Grandfather, having inspected the bee situation earlier and found it not apparently changed, had settled himself on the side porch to carve a new drive-wheel for Peter's locomotive; my brother watched raptly, already drawn at three to what would be his trade. Rosa set to hammering dough for Maryland biscuits; Konrad was established somewhere with the weighty *Times*; Mother was in her hammock. There she had lazed since breakfast, dressed only in a sachless kimono to facilitate nursing; oblivious to the frowns of passing Christians, she had chain-smoked her way through the Sunday crossword, highlight of her week. At eleven, when the final bell of the morning sounded, I was brought forth. Cradled against her by the sag of the hammock, I drank me to a drowse; and she too, just as she lay – mottled by light and leaf shadow, lulled by my work upon her and by wafting organ chords from the avenue – soon slept soundly.

What roused her was a different tone, an urgent, resonating thrum. She opened her eyes: all the air round about her was aglint with bees. Thousand on thousand, a roaring gold sphere, they hovered in the space between the hammock and the overhanging branches.

Her screams brought Grandfather from the porch; he saw the clouds of bees and ducked at once into the summer-kitchen, whence he rushed a moment later banging pie-tin cymbals.

'*Mein Schwarm! Mein Schwarm!*'

Now Rosa and Konrad ran at his heels, he in his trousers and BVDs, she with flour half to her elbows; but before they had cleared the backhouse arbour there was an explosion in the alley, and Willy Erdmann burst like a savage through our hollyhocks. His hair was tousled, expression wild; in one hand he brandished a smoking shot-gun, in the

other his bee-bob, pole and all; mother-of-pearl opera glasses swung
from a black cord around his neck. He leaped about the hammock as if
bedemoned.

'Not a bee, Thomas!'

Aunt Rosa joined her shrieks to Andrea's, who still lay under the
snarling cloud. 'The *Honig*! Ai!' And my brother Peter, having made his
way to the scene in the wake of the others, blinked twice or thrice and
improved the pandemonium by the measure of his wailings.

Uncle Konrad dashed hammockward with rescue in his heart, but
was arrested by shouts from the other men.

'*Nein*, don't dare!' Grandfather cautioned. 'They'll sting!'

Mr Erdmann agreed. 'Stay back!' And dropping the bee-bob shouldered his gun as if Konrad's design was on the bees.

'Lie still, Andy,' Grandfather ordered. 'I *spritz* them once.'

He ran to fetch the garden hose, a spray of water being, like a charge
of bird shot, highly regarded among beekeepers as a means to settle
swarms. But Mr Erdmann chose now to let go at blue heaven with his
other barrel and brought down a shower of Judas leaves upon the
company; at the report Grandfather abandoned his plan, whether fear-
ing that Konrad had been gunned down or merely realizing, what was
the case, that our hose would not reach half the distance. In any event
his instructions to Mother were carried out: even as he turned
she gave a final cry and swooned away. Mercifully, providentially! For
now the bees, moved by their secret reasons, closed ranks and settled
upon her chest. Ten thousand, twenty thousand strong they clustered.
Her bare bosoms, my squalling face – all were buried in the golden
swarm.

Fright undid Rosa's knees; she sat down hard on the grass and wailed,
'*Grosser Gott! Grosser Gott!*' Uncle Konrad went rigid. Erdmann too
stood transfixed, his empty weapon at port arms. Only Grandfather
seemed undismayed; without a wondering pause he rushed to the hammock and scooped his bare hands under the cluster.

'Take the *Honig*,' he said to Konrad.

In fact, though grave enough, the situation was more spectacular
than dangerous, since bees at swarming time are not disposed to sting.
The chiefest peril was that I might suffocate under the swarm, or in
crying take a mouthful of bees. And even these misfortunes proved
unlikely, for when Grandfather lifted two handfuls of the insects from
my head and replaced them gently on another part of the cluster, he
found my face pressed into Mother's side and shielded by her breast.
Konrad plucked me from the hammock and passed me to Aunt Rosa,
still moaning where she sat.

'Open the hive,' Grandfather bade him further, and picked up half the swarm in one trailing mass. The gesture seemed also to lift Mr Erdmann's spell.

'Now, by God, Tom, you shan't have my bees!'

'Your bees bah.' Grandfather walked quickly to the open hive to deposit his burden.

'I been watching with the glasses! It's my skeps they came from!'

'It's my girl they lit on. I know what you been watching.' He returned for the rest of the bees. Erdmann, across the hammock from him, laid his shotgun on the grass and made as if to snatch the cluster himself – but the prospect of removing it bare-handed, and from that perch, stayed him.

Seeing the greatest danger past and his rival unnerved, Grandfather affected nonchalance. 'We make a little gamble,' he offered benignly. 'I take all on her right one, you take all on her left. Whoever draws the queen wins the pot.'

Our neighbour was not amused. He maintained his guard over the hammock.

'Ordinary thievery!'

Grandfather shrugged. 'You take them then, Willy. But quick, don't they'll sting her.'

'By damn ' Mr Erdmann glowered with thwart and crestfall. 'I got to have gloves on.'

'Gloves!' My father's father feigned astonishment. 'Ach, Andy don't care! Well then, look out.'

Coolly as if packing a loose snowball he scraped up the second pile. Mother stirred and whimpered. Only isolated bees in ones and twos now wandered over her skin or darted about in quest of fellows. Konrad moved to brush them away, murmured something reassuring, discreetly drew the kimono together. I believe he even kissed my mother, lightly, on the brow. Grandfather lingered to watch, savouring his neighbour's agitation and his own indifference to the bees. Then he turned away in high humour.

'Alle Donner! Got to have an opera glass to see her and gloves on to touch her! We don't call you bashful no more, Konrad, after Willy! Wait till Karl hears!'

Uncle Konrad one daresays was used to these unsubtleties; in any case he was busy with Mother's reviving. But Erdmann, stung as never before by his pilfered bees, went now amok; seized up his bee-bob with a wrathful groan and lunging – for Grandfather had strode almost out of range – brought it down on his old tormentor's shoulder. Futile was Konrad's shout, worse than futile his interception: Erdmann's thrust careered him square into the hammock, and when Konrad put his all into a body block from the other side, both men fell more or less athwart

T–E

my mother. The hammock parted at its headstring; all piled as one into the clover. But Grandfather had spun raging, bees in hand: the smite *en route* to his shoulder had most painfully glanced his ear. Not his own man, he roared in perfect ectasy and hurled upon that tangle of the sinned against and sinning his golden bolt.

Now the fact of my salvation and my plain need for a pacifier had by this time brought Aunt Rosa to her feet; she alone beheld the whole quick sequence of attack, parry, collapse, and indiscriminating vengeance. But with me and Peter in her care her knees did not fail her: she snatched my brother's hand and fled with us from the yard.

In Grace meanwhile the service had proceeded despite shotgun blast and clang of pans, which however were acknowledged with small stirs and meetings of eyes. Through hymn, creed, and prayer, through anthem, lesson, and gloria the order of worship had got, as far as to the notices and offertory. There being among the congregation a baby come for christening, the young minister had called its parents and god-parents to the font.

'Dearly beloved,' he had exhorted, 'forasmuch as all men, though fallen in Adam, are born into this world in Christ the Redeemer, heirs of life eternal and subjects of the saving grace of the Holy Spirit; and that our Saviour Christ saith: "Suffer the little children to come unto me, and forbid them not, for of such is the kingdom of God"; I beseech you to call upon God the Father through our Lord Jesus Christ, that of His bounteous goodness He will so grant unto this child, now to be baptized, the continual replenishing of His grace . . .'

Here the ritual gave way before a grand ado in the rear of the church: Aunt Rosa's conviction that the family's reckoning was at hand had fetched her across the avenue and up the stone steps, only to abandon her on the threshold of the sanctuary. She stood with Peter and me there in the vestibule, and we raised a caterwaul the more effective for every door's being stopped open to cool the faithful.

'First-degree murder!' Rosa shrieked, the urgentest alarum she could muster. Organ ceased, minister also; all eyes turned; ushers and back-pew parishioners hurried to investigate, but could not achieve a more lucid account of what ailed us. The names Poppa Tom and Willy Erdmann, however, came through clearly enough to suggest the location of the emergency. Mrs Mayne, the preacher's wife, led us from the vestibule towards shelter in the parsonage; a delegation of lay-leaders hastened to our house, and the Reverend Dr Mayne, having given instructions that he be summoned if needed, bade his distracted flock pray.

Grandfather's victims had not been long discovering their fresh affliction, for the bees' docility was spent. Where the cluster fell, none knew for certain, but on impact it had resolved into separate angry bees.

There was a howling and a flurrying of limbs. Konrad and Willy Erdmann scrambled apart to flail like epileptics in the grass. Grandfather rushed in batting his hands and shouting '*Nein lieber Gott,* sting Willy just!' Only Mother made no defence; having swooned from one fright and wakened to another, she now lay weeping where she'd been dumped: up-ended, dazed, and sore exposed.

But whom neither pain nor the fear of it can move, shame still may. The bees were already dispersing when the Methodists reached our fence; at sight of them the principals fell to accusation.

'Stole my swarm and sicked 'em on me!' Erdmann hollered from the grass.

'Bah, it was my bees anyhow,' Grandfather insisted. He pointed to Andrea. 'You see what he done. And busted the hammock yet!'

My mother's plight had not escaped their notice, nor did their notice now escape hers: she sprang up at once, snatched together the kimono, sprinted a-bawl for the summer-kitchen. Her departure was regarded by all except Erdmann, who moved to answer Grandfather's last insinuation with a fresh assault, and Uncle Konrad, who this time checked him effectively until others came over the fence to help.

'Thieves and whores!' Erdmann cried trembling. 'Now he steals my bees!'

'It's all a great shame,' Konrad said to the company, who as yet had no clear notion what had occurred. His explanation was cut off by Erdmann, not yet done accusing Grandfather.

'Thinks he's God Almighty!'

Joe Voegler the blacksmith said, 'Nah, Willy, whoa down now.'

Mr Erdmann wept. 'Nobody's safe! Takes what he pleases!'

Grandfather was examining his hands with interest. 'Too quick they turned him loose, he ain't cured yet.'

'Would you see him home, Joe?' Uncle Konrad asked. 'We'll get it straightened out. I'm awful sorry, Willy.'

'You talk!' Erdmann shrieked at him. 'You been in on it too!'

Grandfather clucked his tongue.

'Come on, Willy!' Voegler said. A squat-muscled, gentle man with great arms and lower lip, he led Erdmann respectfully towards the alley.

'What you think drove Hector nuts?' Erdmann appealed. 'He knows what's what!'

'So does Willy,' Grandfather remarked aside. 'That's why the opera glasses.'

The onlookers smiled uncertainly. Uncle Konrad shook his head. 'I'm sorry, everybody.'

Our neighbour's final denunciation was delivered from his back steps as Voegler ushered him to the door. 'Brat's got no more father'n a drone bee! Don't let them tell you I done it!'

Grandfather snorted. 'What a man won't say. Excuse me, I go wash the bee stings.'

He had, it seems, been stung on the hands and fingers a number of times — all, he maintained, in those last seconds when he flung the cluster. Konrad, himself unstung, remained behind to explain what had happened and apologized once more. The group then dispersed to spread the story, long to be recounted in East Dorset. Aunt Rosa, Peter, and I were retrieved from the parsonage; Uncle Konrad expressed the family's regret to Dr Mayne, a friend of his and not devoid of wit.

' "The Lord shall hiss for the fly that is in Egypt," ' the minister quoted, ' "and for the bee that is in Assyria, and they shall come and rest all of them in the desolate valleys." There's an omen here someplace.'

At Konrad's suggestion the two went that afternoon on embassies of peace to both houses. There was no question of litigation, but Dr Mayne was concerned for the tranquillity of future worship services, and disturbed by the tenor of Erdmann's charge.

'So. Tell Willy I forgive him his craziness,' Grandfather instructed them. 'I send him a gallon of mead when it's ready.'

'You don't send him a drop,' Dr Mayne said firmly. 'Not when we just got him cured. And Willy's not the first to say things about you-all. I'm not sure you don't want some forgiving yourself.'

Grandfather shrugged. 'I could tell things on people, but I don't hold grutches. Tell Willy I forgive him his trespasses, he should forgive mine too.'

Dr Mayne sighed.

Of the interview with Erdmann I can give no details; my uncle, who rehearsed these happenings until the year of his death, never dwelt on it. This much is common knowledge in East Dorset: that Willy never got his bees back, and in fact disposed of his own hives not long after; that if he never withdrew his sundry vague accusations, he never repeated them either, so that the little scandal presently subsided; finally, that he was cured for good and all of any interest he might have had in my mother, whom he never spoke to again, but not, alas, of his dipsomania, which revisited him at intervals during my youth, impaired his business, made him reclusive, and one day killed him.

The extraordinary swarming was variously interpreted. Among our neighbours it was regarded as a punishment of Andrea in particular for her wantonness, of our family in general for its backsliding and eccentricity. Even Aunt Rosa maintained there was more to it than mere chance, and could not be induced to taste the product of our hive.

Grandfather on the contrary was convinced that a change in our fortunes was imminent – so striking an occurrence could not but be significant – and on the grounds that things were as bad as they could get, confidently expected there to be an improvement.

Portentous or not, the events of that morning had two notable consequences for me, the point and end of their chronicling here: first, it was discovered that my mother's bawling as she fled from the scene had not been solely the effect of shame: in her haste to cover herself, she had trapped beneath the kimono one bee, which single-handedly, so to speak, had done what the thousands of his kindred had refrained from: his only charge he had fired roundly into their swarming place, fount of my sustenance. It was enflamed with venom and grotesquely swollen; Mother was prostrate with pain. Aunt Rosa fetched cold compresses, aspirins, and the family doctor, who after examining the wound prescribed aspirins and cold compresses.

'And do your nursing on the porch,' he recommended. 'Goodness gracious.'

But Andrea had no further use for that aspect of motherhood. Though the doctor assured her that the swelling would not last more than a few days, during which she could empty the injured breast by hand and nurse with the other, she refused to suckle me again; a diet free of butterfat was prescribed to end her lactation. As of that Sunday I was weaned not only from her milk but from her care; thenceforth it was Rosa who bathed and changed, soothed and burped me, after feeding me from a bottle on her aproned lap.

As she went about this the very next morning, while Mother slept late, she exclaimed to her husband, 'It's a bee!'

Uncle Konrad sprang from his eggs and rushed around the table to our aid, assuming that another fugitive had been turned up. But it was my birthmark Rosa pointed out: the notion had taken her that its three lobes resembled the wings and abdomen of a bee in flight.

'Oh boy,' Konrad sighed.

'Nah, it is a bee! A regular bee! I declare.'

My uncle returned to his breakfast, opining that no purple bee ought to be considered regular who moreover flew upside down without benefit of head.

'You laugh; there's more to this than meets the eye,' his wife said. 'All the time he was our *Honig*, that's what drew the bees. Now his mark.'

Grandfather entered at this juncture, and while unable to share Aunt Rosa's interpretation of my birthmark, he was willing to elaborate on her conceit.

'*Ja*, sure, he was the *Honig*, and Andy's the queen, hah? And Hector's a drone that's been kicked out of the hive.'

Aunt Rosa lightly fingered my port-wine mark. 'What did Willy Erd-mann mean about the *Honig* was a drone bee?'

'Never mind Willy,' Konrad said. 'Anyhow we poor worker-ones have to get to it.'

But all that forenoon as he plied his wrench and dinged his forks he smiled at his wife's explanation of the swarm; after lunch it turned in his fancy as he pedalled through West End on behalf of *The Book of Knowledge*. By suppertime, whether drawing on his own great fund of lore or the greater of his stock-in-trade, he had found a number of historical parallels to my experience in the hammock.

'It's as clear a naming sign as you could ask for,' he declared to Andrea.

'I don't even want to think about it,' Mother said. She was still in some pain, not from the venom but from superfluous lactation, which her diet had not yet checked.

'No, really,' he said. 'For instance, a swarm of bees lit on Plato's mouth when he was a kid. They say that's where he got his way with words.'

'Is that a fact now,' Aunt Rosa marvelled, who had enlarged all day to Mother on the coincidence of my nickname, my birthmark, and my immersion in the bees. 'I never did read him yet.'

'No kid of mine is going to be called Plato,' Andrea grumbled. 'That's worse than Christine.'

Uncle Konrad was not discouraged. 'Plato isn't the end of it. They said the exact same thing about Sophocles, that wrote all the tra-gedies.'

Mother allowed this to be more to the point. 'Tragedies is all it's been, one after the other.' But Sophocles pleased her no more than Plato as a given name. Xenophon, too, was rejected, whose *Anabasis*, though my uncle had not read it himself, was held to have been sweet-ened by the same phenomenon.

'If his name had been Bill or Percy,' said my mother. 'But *Xenophon* for Christ' sake.'

Grandfather had picked his teeth throughout this discussion. 'A Greek named Percy,' he now growled.

Aunt Rosa, whose grip on the thread of conversation was ever less strong than her desire to be helpful, volunteered that the Greek street-pedlar from whom Konrad had purchased her a beautiful Easter egg at the Oberammergau Passion play in 1910 had been named Leonard Something-or-other.

'It was on his pushcart, that stood all the time by our hotel,' she explained, and not to appear over-authoritative, added: 'But Konrad said he was a Jew.'

'Look here,' said Uncle Konrad. 'Call him Ambrose.'

'Ambrose?'

'Sure Ambrose.' Quite serious now, he brushed back with his hand his straight blond hair and regarded Mother gravely. 'Saint Ambrose had the same thing happen when he was a baby. All these bees swarmed on his mouth while he was asleep in his father's yard, and everybody said he'd grow up to be a great speaker.'

'Ambrose,' Rosa considered. 'That ain't bad, Andy.'

My mother admitted that the name had a not unpleasant sound, at least by contrast with Xenophon.

'But the bees was more on this baby's eyes and ears than on his mouth,' Grandfather observed for the sake of accuracy. 'They was all over the side of his face there where the mark is.'

'One of them sure wasn't,' Mother said.

'So he'll grow up to see things clear,' said Uncle Konrad.

Andrea sniffed and lit a cigarette. 'Long as he grows up to be a saint like his Uncle Konrad, huh Rosa? Saints we can use in this family.'

The conversation turned to other matters, but thenceforward I was called Saint Ambrose, in jest, as often as *Honig*, and Ambrose by degrees became my name. Yet years were to pass before anyone troubled to have me christened or to correct my birth certificate, whereon my surname was preceded by a blank. And seldom was I ever to be called anything but *Honig*, Honey-bee (after my ambiguous birthmark), or other nicknames.

As towards one's face, one's body, one's self, one feels complexly towards the name he's called by, which too one had no hand in choosing. It was to be my fate to wonder at that moniker, relish and revile it, ignore it, stare it out of countenance into hieroglyph and gibber, and come finally if not to embrace at least to accept it with the cold neutrality of self-recognition, whose expression is a thin-lipped smile. Vanity frets about his name. Pride vaunts it, Knowledge retches at its sound, Understanding sighs; all live outside it, knowing well that I and my sign are neither one nor quite two.

Yet only give it voice: whisper 'Ambrose', as at rare times certain people have – see what-all leaves off to answer! Ambrose, Ambrose, Ambrose, Ambrose! Regard that beast, ungraspable, most queer, pricked up in my soul's crannies!

DONALD BARTHELME was born in Pennsylvania in 1931 and now lives in Greenwich Village, New York. He is the author of an experimental novella, *Snow White*, and three collections of short stories, *Come Back, Dr Caligari; Unspeakable Practices, Unnatural Acts;* and *City Life.*

me and miss mandible

DONALD BARTHELME

13 September

Miss Mandible wants to make love to me but she hesitates because I am officially a child; I am, according to the records, according to the grade-book on her desk, according to the card index in the principal's office, eleven years old. There is a misconception here, one that I haven't quite managed to get cleared up yet. I am in fact thirty-five, I've been in the Army, I am six feet one, I have hair in the appropriate places, my voice is a baritone, I know very well what to do with Miss Mandible if she ever makes up her mind.

In the meantime we are studying common fractions. I could, of course, answer all the questions, or at least most of them (there are things I don't remember). But I prefer to sit in this too-small seat with the desk-top cramping my thighs and examine the life around me. There are thirty-two in the class, which is launched every morning with the pledge of allegiance to the flag. My own allegiance, at the moment, is divided between Miss Mandible and Sue Ann Brownly, who sits across the aisle from me all day long and is, like Miss Mandible, a fool for love. Of the two I prefer, today, Sue Ann; although between eleven and eleven and a half (she refuses to reveal her exact age), she is clearly a woman, with a woman's disguised aggression and a woman's peculiar contradictions. Strangely neither she nor any of the other children seems to see any incongruity in my presence here.

15 September

Happily our geography text, which contains maps of all the principal land-masses of the world, is large enough to conceal my clandestine journal-keeping, accomplished in an ordinary black composition book. Every day I must wait until Geography to put down such thoughts as I may have had during the morning about my situation and my fellows. I have tried writing at other times and it does not work. Either the teacher is walking up and down the aisles (during this period, luckily, she sticks close to the map rack in the front of the room) or Bobby Vanderbilt, who sits behind me, is punching me in the kidneys and wanting to know what I am doing. Vanderbilt, I have found out from certain desultory conversation on the playground, is hung up on sports cars, a veteran consumer of *Road and Track*. This explains the continual roaring sounds which seem to emanate from his desk; he is reproducing a record album called *Sounds of Sebring*.

19 September

Only I, at times (only at times), understand that somehow a mistake has been made, that I am in a place where I don't belong. It may be that Miss Mandible also knows this, at some level, but for reasons not fully understood by me she is going along with the game. When I was first assigned to this room I wanted to protest, the error seemed obvious, the stupidest principal could have seen it; but I have come to believe it was deliberate, that I have been betrayed again.

Now it seems to make little difference. This life role is as interesting as my former life role, which was that of a claims adjuster for the Great Northern Insurance Company, a position which compelled me to spend my time amid the debris of our civilization: rumpled fenders, roofless sheds, gutted warehouses, smashed arms and legs. After ten years of this one had a tendency to see the world as a vast junkyard, looking at a man and seeing only his (potentially) mangled parts, entering a house only to trace the path of the inevitable fire. Therefore when I was installed here, although I knew an error had been made, I countenanced it, I was shrewd; I was aware that there might well be some kind of advantage to be gained from what seemed a disaster. The role of The Adjuster teaches one much.

22 September

I am being solicited for the volleyball team. I decline, refusing to take unfair profit from my height.

23 September

Every morning the roll is called: Bestvina, Bokenfohr, Broan, Brownly, Cone, Coyle, Crecelius, Darin, Durbin, Geiger, Guiswite, Heckler, Jacobs, Kleinschmidt, Lay, Logan, Masei, Mitgang, Pfeilsticker. It is like the litany chanted in the dim miserable dawns of Texas by the cadre sergeant of our basic training company.

In the Army, too, I was ever so slightly awry. It took me a fantastically long time to realize what the others grasped almost at once: that much of what we were doing was absolutely pointless, to no purpose. I kept wondering why. Then something happened that proposed a new question. One day we were commanded to whitewash, from the ground to the topmost leaves, all of the trees in our training area. The corporal who relayed the order was nervous and apologetic. Later an off-duty captain sauntered by and watched us, white-splashed and totally weary, strung out among the freakish shapes we had created. He walked away swearing. I understood the principle (orders are orders), but I wondered: who decides?

29 September

Sue Ann is a wonder. Yesterday she viciously kicked my ankle for not paying attention when she was attempting to pass me a note during History. It is swollen still. But Miss Mandible was watching me, there was nothing I could do. Oddly enough Sue Ann reminds me of the wife I had in my former role, while Miss Mandible seems to be a child. She watches me constantly, trying to keep sexual significance out of her look; I am afraid the other children have noticed. I have already heard, on that ghastly frequency that is the medium of classroom communication, the words *'Teacher's Pet!'*

2 October

Sometimes I speculate on the exact nature of the conspiracy which brought me here. At times I believe it was instigated by my wife of former days, whose name was . . . I am only pretending to forget. I know her name very well, as well as I know the name of my former motor oil (Quaker State) or my old Army serial number (US 54109268). Her name was Brenda, and the conversation I recall best, the one which makes me suspicious now, took place on the day we parted. 'You have the soul of a whore,' I said on that occasion, stating nothing less than literal, unvarnished fact. 'You,' she replied, 'are a pimp, a poop, and a child. I am leaving you forever and I trust that without me you will perish of your own inadequacies. Which are considerable.'

I squirm in my seat at the memory of this conversation, and Sue Ann watches me with malign compassion. She has noticed the discrepancy between the size of my desk and my own size, but apparently sees it only as a token of my glamour, my dark man-of-the-world-ness.

7 October

Once I tiptoed up to Miss Mandible's desk (when there was no one else in the room) and examined its surface. Miss Mandible is a clean-desk teacher, I discovered. There was nothing except her gradebook (the one in which I exist as a sixth-grader) and a text, which was open at a page headed *Making the Processes Meaningful*. I read: 'Many pupils enjoy working fractions when they understand what they are doing. They have confidence in their ability to take the right steps and to obtain correct answers. However, to give the subject full social significance, it is necessary that many realistic situations requiring the processes be found. Many interesting and lifelike problems involving the use of fractions should be solved . . .'

8 October

I am not irritated by the feeling of having been through all this before. Things are done differently now. The children, moreover, are in some ways different from those who accompanied me on my first voyage through the elementary schools. *'They have confidence in their ability to take the right steps and to obtain correct answers.'* This is surely true. When Bobby Vanderbilt, who sits behind me, and has the great tactical advantage of being able to manoeuvre in my disproportionate shadow, wishes to bust a classmate in the mouth he first asks Miss Mandible to lower the blind, saying that the sun hurts his eyes. When she does so, *bip!* My generation would never have been able to con authority so easily.

13 October

It may be that on my first trip through the schools I was too much under the impression that what the authorities (who decides?) had ordained for me was right and proper, that I confused authority with life itself. My path was not particularly of my own choosing. My career stretched out in front of me like a paper chase, and my role was to pick up the clues. When I got out of school, the first time, I felt that this estimate was substantially correct, and eagerly entered the hunt. I found clues abundant: diplomas, membership cards, campaign buttons, a marriage licence, insurance forms, discharge papers, tax returns, Certificates of Merit. They seemed to prove, at the very least, that I was *in the running*. But that was before my tragic mistake on the Mrs Anton Bichek claim.

I misread a clue. Do not misunderstand me: it was a tragedy only from the point of view of the authorities. I conceived that it was my duty to obtain satisfaction for the injured, for this elderly lady (not even one of our policy-holders, but a claimant against Big Ben Transfer and Storage, Inc), from the company. The settlement was $165,000; the claim, I still believe, was just. But without my encouragement Mrs Bichek would never have had the self-love to prize her injury so highly. The company paid, but its faith in me, in my efficacy in the role, was broken. Henry Goodykind, the district manager, expressed this thought in a few not altogether unsympathetic words, and told me at the same time that I was to have a new role. The next thing I knew I was here, at Horace Greeley Elementary, under the lubricious eye of Miss Mandible.

17 October

Today we are to have a fire drill. I know this because I am a Fire Marshal, not only for our room but for the entire right wing of the second floor. This distinction, which was awarded shortly after my arrival, is interpreted by some as another mark of my somewhat dubious relations with our teacher. My armband, which is red and decorated with white felt letters reading FIRE, sits on the little shelf under my desk, next to the brown paper bag containing the lunch I carefully make for myself each morning. One of the advantages of packing my own lunch (I have no one to pack it for me) is that I am able to fill it with things I enjoy. The peanut butter sandwiches that my mother made in my former existence, many years ago, have been banished in favour of ham and cheese. I have found that my diet has mysteriously adjusted to my new situation; I no longer drink, for instance, and when I smoke, it is in the boys' john, like everybody else. When school is out I hardly smoke at all. It is only in the matter of sex that I feel my own true age; this is apparently something that, once learned, can never be forgotten. I live in fear that Miss Mandible will one day keep me after school, and when we are alone, create a compromising situation. To avoid this I have become a model pupil: another reason for the pronounced dislike I have encountered in certain quarters. But I cannot deny that I am singed by those long glances from the vicinity of the chalk-board; Miss Mandible is in many ways, notably about the bust, a very tasty piece.

24 October

There are isolated challenges to my largeness, to my dimly realized position in the class as Gulliver. Most of my classmates are polite about this matter, as they would be if I had only one eye, or wasted, metal-wrapped legs. I am viewed as a mutation of some sort but essentially a peer. However Harry Broan, whose father has made himself rich manufacturing the Broan Bathroom Vent (with which Harry is frequently reproached; he is always being asked how things are in Ventsville), today inquired if I wanted to fight. An interested group of his followers had gathered to observe this suicidal undertaking. I replied that I didn't feel quite up to it, for which he was obviously grateful. We are now friends forever. He has given me to understand privately that he can get me all the bathroom vents I will ever need, at a ridiculously modest figure.

25 October

'*Many interesting and lifelike problems involving the use of fractions should be solved* . . .' The theorists fail to realize that everything that is either interesting or lifelike in the classroom proceeds from what they would probably call interpersonal relations: Sue Ann Brownly kicking me in the ankle. How lifelike, how womanlike, is her tender solicitude after the deed! Her pride in my newly acquired limp is transparent; everyone knows that she has set her mark upon me, that it is a victory in her unequal struggle with Miss Mandible for my great, overgrown heart. Even Miss Mandible knows, and counters in perhaps the only way she can, with sarcasm, 'Are you wounded, Joseph?' Conflagrations smoulder behind her eyelids, yearning for the Fire Marshal clouds her eyes. I mumble that I have bumped my leg.

30 October

I return again and again to the problem of my future.

4 November

The underground circulating library has brought me a copy of *Movie–TV Secrets*, the multicolour cover blazoned with the headline 'Debbie's Date Insults Liz!' It is a gift from Frankie Randolph, a rather plain girl who until today has had not one word for me, passed on via Bobby Vanderbilt. I nod and smile over my shoulder in acknowledgement; Frankie hides her head under her desk. I have seen these magazines being passed around among the girls (sometimes one of the boys will condescend to inspect a particularly lurid cover). Miss Mandible confiscates them whenever she finds one. I leaf through *Movie–TV Secrets* and get an eyeful. 'The exclusive picture on these pages isn't what it seems. We know how it looks and we know what the gossipers will do. So in the interest of a nice guy, we're publishing the facts first. Here's what really happened!' The picture shows a rising young movie idol in bed, pyjama-ed and bleary-eyed, while an equally blowzy young woman looks startled beside him. I am happy to know that the picture is not really what it seems; it seems to be nothing less than divorce evidence.

What do these hipless eleven-year-olds think when they come across, in the same magazine, the full-page ad for Maurice de Paree, which features 'Hip Helpers' or what appear to be padded rumps? ('A real undercover agent that adds appeal to those hips and derrière, both!') If they cannot decipher the language the illustrations leave nothing to the imagination. 'Drive him frantic . . .' the copy continues. Perhaps this explains Bobby Vanderbilt's preoccupation with Lancias and Maseratis; it is a defence against being driven frantic.

Sue Ann has observed Frankie Randolph's overture, and catching my eye, she pulls from her satchel no less than seventeen of these magazines, thrusting them at me as if to prove that anything any of her rivals has to offer, she can top. I shuffle through them quickly, noting the broad editorial perspective:

'Debbie's Kids Are Crying'
'Eddie asks Debbie: Will You . . .?'
'The Nightmares Liz Has About Eddie!'
'The Things Debbie Can Tell about Eddie'
'The Private Life of Eddie and Liz'
'Debbie Gets her Man Back?'
'A New Life for Liz'
'Love Is a Tricky Affair'
'Eddie's Taylor-Made Love Nest'
'How Liz Made a Man of Eddie'
'Are They Planning to Live Together?'
'Isn't It Time to Stop Kicking Debbie Around?'
'Debbie's Dilemma'
'Eddie Becomes a Father Again'
'Is Debbie Planning to Re-wed?'
'Can Liz Fulfil Herself?'
'Why Debbie Is Sick of Hollywood'

Who are these people, Debbie, Eddie, Liz, and how did they get themselves in such a terrible predicament? Sue Ann knows, I am sure; it is obvious that she has been studying their history as a guide to what she may expect when she is suddenly freed from this drab, flat classroom.

I am angry and I shove the magazines back at her with not even a whisper of thanks.

5 November

The sixth grade at Horace Greeley Elementary is a furnace of love, love, love. Today it is raining, but inside the air is heavy and tense with passion. Sue Ann is absent; I suspect that yesterday's exchange has driven her to her bed. Guilt hangs about me. She is not responsible, I know, for what she reads, for the models proposed to her by a venal publishing industry; I should not have been so harsh. Perhaps it is only the flu.

Nowhere have I encountered an atmosphere as charged with aborted sexuality as this. Miss Mandible is helpless; nothing goes right today. Amos Darin has been found drawing a dirty picture in the cloakroom. Sad and inaccurate, it was offered not as a sign of something else but as an act of love in itself. It has excited even those who have not seen it, even those who saw but understood only that it was dirty. The room buzzes with imperfectly comprehended titillation. Amos stands by the door, waiting to be taken to the principal's office. He wavers between fear and enjoyment of his temporary celebrity. From time to time Miss Mandible looks at me reproachfully, as if blaming me for the uproar. But I did not create this atmosphere, I am caught in it like all the others.

8 November

Everything is promised my classmates and I, most of all the future. We accept the outrageous assurances without blinking.

9 November

I have finally found the nerve to petition for a larger desk. At recess I can hardly walk; my legs do not wish to uncoil themselves. Miss Mandible says she will take it up with the custodian. She is worried about the excellence of my themes. Have I, she asks, been receiving help? For an instant I am on the brink of telling her my story. Something, however, warns me not to attempt it. Here I am safe, I have a place; I do not wish to entrust myself once more to the whimsy of authority. I resolve to make my themes less excellent in the future.

11 November

A ruined marriage, a ruined adjusting career, a grim interlude in the Army when I was almost not a person. This is the sum of my existence to date, a dismal total. Small wonder that re-education seemed my only hope. It is clear even to me that I need reworking in some fundamental way. How efficient is the society that provides thus for the salvage of its clinkers!

Plucked from my unexamined life among other pleasant, desperate, money-making young Americans, thrown backward in space and time, I am beginning to understand how I went wrong, how we all go wrong. (Although this was far from the intention of those who sent me here; they require only that I *get right*.)

14 November

The distinction between children and adults, while probably useful for some purposes, is at bottom a specious one, I feel. There are only individual egos, crazy for love.

15 November

The custodian has informed Miss Mandible that our desks are all the correct size for sixth-graders, as specified by the Board of Estimate and furnished the schools by the Nu-Art Educational Supply Corporation of Englewood, California. He has pointed out that if the desk size is correct, then the pupil size must be incorrect. Miss Mandible, who has already arrived at this conclusion, refuses to press the matter further. I think I know why. An appeal to the administration might result in my removal from the class, in a transfer to some sort of set-up for 'exceptional children'. This would be a disaster of the first magnitude. To sit in a room with child geniuses (or, more likely, children who are 'retarded') would shrivel me in a week. Let my experience here be that of the common run, I say; let me be, please God, typical.

20 November

We read signs as promises. Miss Mandible understands by my great height, by my resonant vowels, that I will one day carry her off to bed. Sue Ann interprets these same signs to mean that I am unique among her male acquaintances, therefore most desirable, therefore her special property as is everything that is Most Desirable. If neither of these propositions work out then life has broken faith with them.

I myself, in my former existence, read the company motto ('Here to Help in Time of Need') as a description of the duty of the adjuster, drastically mislocating the company's deepest concerns. I believed that because I had obtained a wife who was made up of wife-signs (beauty, charm, softness, perfume, cookery) I had found love. Brenda, reading the same signs that have now misled Miss Mandible and Sue Ann Brownly, felt she had been promised that she would never be bored again. All of us, Miss Mandible, Sue Ann, myself, Brenda, Mr Goodykind, still believe that the American flag betokens a kind of general righteousness.

But I say, looking about me in this incubator of future citizens, that signs are signs, and that some of them are lies. This is the great discovery of my time here.

23 November

It may be that my experience as a child will save me after all. If only I can remain quietly in this classroom, making my notes while Napoleon plods through Russia in the droning voice of Harry Broan, reading aloud from our history text. All of the mysteries that perplexed me as an adult have their origins here, and one by one I am numbering them, exposing their roots.

2 December

Miss Mandible will refuse to permit me to remain ungrown. Her hands rest on my shoulders too warmly, and for too long.

7 December

It is the pledges that this place makes to me, pledges that cannot be redeemed, that confuse me later and make me feel I am not *getting anywhere*. Everything is presented as the result of some knowable process; if I wish to arrive at four I get there by way of two and two. If I wish to burn Moscow the route I must travel has already been marked out by another visitor. If, like Bobby Vanderbilt, I yearn for the wheel of the Lancia 2·4-litre coupé, I have only to go through the appropriate process, that is, get the money. And if it is money itself that I desire, I have only to make it. All of these goals are equally beautiful in the sight of the Board of Estimate; the proof is all around us, in the no-nonsense ugliness of this steel and glass building, in the straightline matter-of-factness with which Miss Mandible handles some of our less reputable wars. Who points out that arrangements sometimes slip, that errors are made, that signs are misread? '*They have confidence in their ability to take the right steps and to obtain correct answers.*' I take the right steps, obtain correct answers, and my wife leaves me for another man.

8 December

My enlightenment is proceeding wonderfully.

9 December

Disaster once again. Tomorrow I am to be sent to a doctor, for observation. Sue Ann Brownly caught Miss Mandible and me in the cloakroom, during recess, and immediately threw a fit. For a moment I thought she was actually going to choke. She ran out of the room weeping, straight for the principal's office, certain now which of us was Debbie, which Eddie, which Liz. I am sorry to be the cause of her disillusionment, but I know that she will recover. Miss Mandible is ruined but fulfilled. Although she will be charged with contributing to the delinquency of a minor, she seems at peace; *her* promise has been kept. She knows now that everything she has been told about life, about America, is true.

I have tried to convince the school authorities that I am a minor only in a very special sense, that I am in fact mostly to blame – but it does no good. They are as dense as ever. My contemporaries are astounded that I present myself as anything other than an innocent victim. Like the Old Guard marching through the Russian drifts, the class marches to the conclusion that truth is punishment.

Bobby Vanderbilt has given me his copy of *Sounds of Sebring*, in farewell.

LEONARD COHEN was born in 1934 in Montreal, Canada. He is the author of three volumes of poetry, including *The Spice-Box of Earth*, and two novels, *The Favourite Game* and *Beautiful Losers*, the latter the source of the following excerpt.

from a long letter from f

LEONARD COHEN

Later

Among the bars in my soap collection. I paid big cash for it. Argentine vacation hotel weekend shack-up with Edith. Never mind that. I paid equivalent US $635. Waiter giving me the eye for days. He not cute little recent immigrant. Former Lord of few miserable European acres. Transaction beside swimming pool. I wanted it. I wanted it. My lust for secular grey magic. Human soap. A full bar, minus the wear of one bath in which I plunged myself, for better or for worse.

Mary, Mary, where are you, my little Abishag?

My dear friend, take my spirit hand.

I am going to show you everything *happening*. That is as far as I can take you. I cannot bring you into the middle of action. My hope is that I have prepared *you* for this pilgrimage. I didn't suspect the pettiness of my dream. I believed that I had conceived the vastest dream of my generation: I wanted to be a magician. That was my idea of glory. Here is a plea based on my whole experience: do not be a magician, be magic.

That weekend when I arranged for you to work in the Archives, Edith and I flew down to Argentine for a little sun and experiments. Edith was having trouble with her body: it kept changing sizes, she even feared that it might be dying.

We took a large air-conditioned room overlooking the sea, double-locking the door as soon as the porter had left with his hand full of tip.

Edith spread a large rubber sheet over the double bed, carefully moving from corner to corner to smooth it out. I loved to watch her bend over. Her buttocks were my masterpiece. Call her nipples an eccentric extravagance, but the bum was perfect. It's true that from year to year it required electronic massage and applications of hormone mould, but the conception was perfect.

Edith took off her clothes and lay down on the rubber sheet. I stood over her. Her eyes blazed.

—I hate you, F. I hate you for what you've done to me and my husband. I was a fool to get mixed up with you. I wish he'd known me before you—

—Hush, Edith. We don't want to go over all that again. You wanted to be beautiful.

—I can't remember anything now. I'm all confused. Perhaps I was beautiful before.

—Perhaps, I echoed in a voice as sad as hers.

Edith shifted her brown hips to make herself comfortable, and a shaft of sunlight infiltrated her pubic hair, giving it a rust-coloured tint. Yes, that was beauty beyond my craft.

Sun on Her Cunt
Wispy Rusty Hair
Her Tunnels Sunk in Animal
Her Kneecaps Round and Bare

I knelt beside the bed and laid one of my thin arms on the little sunlit orchard, listening to the tiny swamp machinery.

—You've meddled, F. You've gone against God.

—Hush, my little chicken. There is some cruelty even I cannot bear.

—You should have left me like you found me. I'm no good to anyone now.

—I could suck you forever, Edith.

She made the shaved hairs on the back of my neck tingle with the grazing of her lovely brown fingers.

—Sometimes I feel sorry for you, F. You might have been a great man.

—Stop talking, I bubbled.

—Stand up, F. Get your mouth off me. I'm pretending that you are someone else.

—Who?

—The waiter.
—Which one? I demanded.
—With the moustache and the raincoat.
—I thought so, I thought so.
—You noticed him, too, didn't you, F?
—Yes.

I stood up too suddenly. Dizziness twirled my brain like a dial and formerly happy chewed food in my stomach turned into vomit. I hated my life, I hated my meddling, I hated my ambition. For a second I wanted to be an ordinary bloke cloistered in a tropical hotel room with an Indian orphan.

> Take from me my Camera
> Take from me my Glass
> The Sun the Wet Forever
> Let the Doctors Pass

—Don't cry, F. You knew it had to happen. You wanted me to go all the way. Now I'm no good to anyone and I'll try anything.

I stumbled to the window but it was hermetically sealed. The ocean was deep green. The beach was polka-dotted with beach umbrellas. How I longed for my old teacher, Charles Axis. I strained my eyes for an immaculate white bathing suit, unshadowed by topography of genitalia.

—Oh, come here, F. I can't stand watching a man vomit and cry.

She cradled my head between her bare breasts, stuffing a nipple into each ear.

—There now.

Thankyou, thankyou, thankyou, thankyou.

—Listen, F. Listen the way you wanted us all to listen.

—I'm listening, Edith.

> Let me let me follow
> Down the Sticky Caves
> Where embryonic Cities
> Form Scum upon the Waves

—You're not listening, F.
—I'm trying.
—I feel sorry for you, F.
—Help me, Edith.
—Then get back to work. That's the only thing that can help you. Try to finish the work you began on all of us.

She was right. I was the Moses of our little exodus. I would never cross. My mountain might be very high but it rises from the desert. Let it suffice me.

I recovered my professional attitude. Her lower perfume was still in my nostrils but that was my business. I surveyed the nude girl from my Pisgah. Her soft lips smiled.

—That's better, F. Your tongue was nice but you do better as a doctor.

—All right, Edith. What seems to be the trouble now?

—I can't make myself come any more.

—Of course you can't. If we're going to perfect the panorgasmic body, extend the erogenous zone over the whole fleshy envelope, popularize the Telephone Dance, then we've got to begin by diminishing the tyranny of the nipples, lips, clitoris, and asshole.

—You're going against God, F. You say dirty words.

—I'll take my chances.

—I feel so lost since I can't make myself come any more. I'm not ready for the other stuff yet. It makes me too lonely. I feel blurred. Sometimes I forget where my cunt is.

—You make me weary, Edith. To think I've pinned all my hopes on you and your wretched husband.

—Give it back to me, F.

—All right, Edith. It's a very simple matter. We do it with books. I thought this might happen, so I brought the appropriate ones along. I also have in this trunk a number of artificial phalli (used by women), Vaginal Vibrators, the Rin-No-Tam and Godemiche or Dildo.

—Now you're talking.

—Just lie back and listen. Sink into the rubber sheet. Spread your legs and let the air-conditioning do its filthy work.

—OK, shoot.

I cleared my famous throat. I chose a swollen book, frankly written, which describes various Auto-Erotic practices as indulged in by humans and animals, flowers, children and adults, and women of all ages and cultures. The areas covered included: Why Wives Masturbate, What We Can Learn From the Anteater, Unsatisfied Women, Abnormalities and Eroticism, Techniques of Masturbation, Latitude of Females, Genital Shaving, Clitoral Discovery, Club Masturbation, Female Metal, Nine Rubber, Frame Caress, Urethral Masturbation, Individual Experiments, Masturbation in and of Children, Thigh-Friction Technique, Mammary Stimulation, Auto-Eroticism in Windows.

—Don't stop, F. I feel it coming back.

Her lovely brown fingers inched down her silky rounded belly. I continued reading in my slow, tantalizing, weather-reporting tones. I read to my deep-breathing protégée of the unusual sex practices, when Sex

Becomes 'Different'. An 'Unusual' sex practice is one where there is some greater pleasure than orgasm through intercourse. Most of these bizarre practices involve a measure of mutilation, shock, voyeurism, pain, or torture. The sex habits of the average person are relatively free of such sadistic or masochistic traits. NEVERTHELESS, the reader will be shocked to see how abnormal are the tastes of the so-called normal person. CASE HISTORIES and intensive field work. Filled with chapters detailing ALL ASPECTS of the sex act. SAMPLE HEADINGS: Rubbing, Seeing, Silk Rings, Satyriasis, Bestiality in Others. The average reader will be surprised to learn how 'Unusual' practices are passed along by seemingly innocent, normal sex partners.

—It's so good, F. It's been so long.

Now it was late afternoon. The sky had darkened somewhat. Edith was touching herself everywhere, smelling herself shamelessly. I could hardly keep still myself. The texts had got to me. Goose pimples rose on her young form. I stared dumbly at Original drawings: male and female organs, both external and internal, drawings indicating correct and incorrect methods of penetration. Wives will benefit from seeing how the penis is received.

—Please, F. Don't leave me like this.

My throat was burning with the hunger of it. Love fondled. Edith writhed under her squeezes. She flipped over on her stomach, wielding her small beautiful fists in anal stimulation. I threw myself into a Hand book of Semi-Impotence. There were important pieces woven into the theme: how to enlarge the erect penis, penis darkness, use of lubricants, satisfaction during menstruation, abusing the menopause, a wife's manual assistance in overcoming semi-impotence.

—Don't touch me, F. I'll die.

I blurted out a piece of Fellatio and Cunnilingus between Brother and Sister, and others. My hands were almost out of control. I stumbled through a new concept for an exciting sex life. I didn't miss the section on longevity. Thrilling culminations possible for all. Lesbians by the hundreds interviewed and bluntly questioned. Some tortured for coy answers. Speak up, you cheap dyke. An outstanding work showing the sex offender at work. Chemicals to get hair off palms. Not models! Actual Photos of Male and Female Sex Organs and Excrement. Explored Kissing. The pages flew. Edith mumbling bad words through froth. Her fingers were bright and glistening, her tongue bruised from the taste of her waters. I spoke the books in everyday terms, the most sensitivity, cause of erection. Husband-Above 1–17, Wife-Above 18–29, Seated 30–34, On-The-Side 35–38, Standing & Kneeling Positions 39–53, Miscellaneous Squats 54–109, Coital Movement In All Directions, both for Husband and Wife.

—Edith! I cried. Let me have Foreplay.

—Never.

I sped through a glossary of Sexual Terms. In 1852, Richard Burton (d aet 69) submitted calmly to circumcision at the age of 31. 'Milkers.' Detailed Library of Consummated Incest. Ten Steps on Miscegenation. Techniques of Notorious Photographers. The Evidence of Extreme Acts. Sadism, Mutilation, Cannibalism, Cannibalism of Oralists, How To Match Disproportionate Organs. See the vivid birth of the new American woman. I shouted the recorded facts. She will not be denied the pleasures of sex. CASE HISTORIES show the changing trends. Filled with accounts of college girls eager to be propositioned. Women no longer inhibited by oral intimacy. Men masturbated to death. Cannibalism during Foreplay. Skull Coition. Secrets of 'Timing' and Climax. Foreskin, Pro, Con, and Indifferent. The Intimate Kiss. What are the benefits of sexual experimentation? Own and other's sexual make-up. Sin has to be taught. Kissing Negroes on their Mouths. Thigh Documents. Styles of Manual Pressure in Voluntary Indulgence. Death Rides a Camel. I gave her everything. My voice cried the Latex. I hid no laces, nor a pair of exciting open-front pants, nor soft elasticized bra instead of sagging, heavy wide bust, therefore youthful separation. O'er Edith's separate nipples I blabbed the full record. Santa Pants, Fire Alarm Snow, Glamour Tip, plain wrapper Thick Bust Jelly, washable leather Kinsey Doll, Smegma Discipline, the LITTLE SQUIRT ashtray, 'SEND ME ANOTHER Rupture-Easer so I will have one to change off with. It is enabling me to work top speed at my press machine 8 hrs a day,' this I threw in for sadness, for melancholy soft flat groin pad which might lurk in Edith's memory swamp as soiled lever, as stretched switch to bumpy apotheosis wet rocket come out of the fine print slum where the only trumpet solo is grandfather's stringy cough and underwear money problems.

Edith was wiggling her saliva-covered kneecaps, bouncing on the rivulets of lubrication. Her thighs were aglow with froth, and her pale anus was excavated by cruel false fingernails. She screamed for deliverance, the flight her imagination commanded denied by a half-enlightened cunt.

—Do something, F. I beg you. But don't touch me.

—Edith, darling! What have I done to you?

—Stand back, F!

—What can I do?

—Try.

—Torture story?

—Anything, F. Hurry.

—The Jews?

—No. Too foreign.

—1649? Brébeuf and Lalemant?

—Anything.

So I began to recite my schoolboy lesson of how the Iroquois killed the Jesuits Brébeuf and Lalemant, whose scorched and mangled relics were discovered the morning of the twentieth by a member of the Society and seven armed Frenchmen. 'Ils y trouvèrent un spectacle d'horreur . . .'

On the afternoon of the sixteenth the Iroquois had bound Brébeuf to a stake. They commenced to scorch him from head to foot.

—Everlasting flames for those who persecute the worshippers of God, Brébeuf threatened them in the tone of a master.

As the priest spoke the Indians cut away his lower lip and forced a red-hot iron down his throat. He made no sign or sound of discomfort.

Then they led out Lalemant. Around his naked body they had fastened strips of bark, smeared with pitch. When Lalemant saw his Superior, the bleeding unnatural aperture exposing his teeth, the handle of the heated implement still protruding from the seared and ruined mouth, he cried out in the words of St Paul:

—We are made a spectacle to the world, to angels, and to men

Lalemant flung himself at Brébeuf's feet. The Iroquois took him, bound him to a stake, and ignited the vegetation in which he was trussed. He screamed for heaven's help, but he was not to die so quickly.

They brought a collar made of hatchets heated red-hot and conferred it on Brébeuf. He did not flinch.

An exconvert, who had backslid, now shouldered forward and demanded that hot water be poured on their heads, since the missionaries had poured so much cold water on them. A kettle was slung, water boiled, and then poured slowly on the heads of the captive priests.

—We baptize you, they laughed, that you may be happy in heaven. You told us that the more one suffers on earth, the happier he is in heaven.

Brébeuf stood like a rock. After a number of revolting tortures they scalped him. He was still alive when they laid open his breast. A crowd came forward to drink the blood of so courageous an enemy and to devour his heart. His death astonished his murderers. His ordeal lasted four hours.

Lalemant, physically weak from childhood, was taken back to the house. There he was tortured all night, until sometime after dawn, one Indian wearied of the extended entertainment and administered a fatal blow with his hatchet. There was no part of his body which was not burned, 'even to his eyes, in the sockets of which these wretches had placed live coals'. His ordeal lasted seventeen hours.

—How do you feel, Edith?

There was no need for me to ask. My recitals had served only to bring her closer to a summit she could not achieve. She moaned in terrible hunger, her gooseflesh shining in supplication that she might be freed from the unbearable coils of secular pleasure, and soar into that blind realm, so like sleep, so like death, that journey of pleasure beyond pleasure, where each man travels as an orphan towards an atomic ancestry, more anonymous, more nourishing than the arms of blood or foster family.

I knew she would never make it.

—F, get me out of this, she moaned pitifully.

I plugged in the Danish Vibrator. A degrading spectacle followed. As soon as those delicious electric oscillations occupied my hand like an army of trained seaweed, weaving, swathing, caressing – I was reluctant to surrender the instrument to Edith. Somehow, in the midst of her juicy ordeal, she noticed me trying to slip the Perfected Suction Bracers down into the shadows of my underwear.

She lifted herself out of her pools and lunged at me.

—Give me that. You rat!

Bearlike (some ancestral memory?) she swung at me. I had not had the opportunity to fasten the Improved Wonder Straps, and the Vibrator flew out of my embrace. Thus the bear, with a swipe of his clawed paw, scoops the fish from the bosom of the stream. Crablike, the DV scuttled across the polished floor, humming like an overturned locomotive.

—You're selfish, F, Edith snarled.

—That's the observation of a liar and an ingrate, I said as gently as possible.

—Get out of my way.

—I love you, I said as I inched my way towards the DV. I love you, Edith. My methods may have been wrong, but I never stopped loving you. Was it selfish of me to try to end your pain, yours and his (you, dear old comrade)? I saw pain everywhere. I could not bear to look into your eyes, so maggoty were they with pain and desire. I could not bear to kiss either of you, for each of your embraces disclosed a hopeless, mordant plea. In your laughter, though it were for money or for sunsets, I heard your throats ripped with greed. In the midst of the high jump, I saw the body wither. Between the spurts of come, you launched your tidings of regret. Thousands built, thousands lay squashed beneath tubes of highway. You were not happy to brush your teeth. I gave you breasts with nipples: could you nourish anyone? I gave you prick with separate memory: could you train a race? I took you to a complete movie of the Second World War: did you feel any lighter when we walked out? No, you threw yourselves upon the thorns of research. I sucked you, and you howled to dispense me something more than poison. With every hand-shake you wept for a lost garden. You found a cutting edge for every object. I couldn't stand the racket of your pain. You were smeared with blood and tortured scabs. You needed bandages – there was no time to boil the germs out of them – I grabbed what was at hand. Caution was a luxury. There was no time for me to examine my motives. Self-purification would have been an alibi. Beholding such a spectacle of misery, I was free to try anything. I can't answer for my own erection. I have no explanation for my own vile ambitions. Confronted with your pus, I could not stop to examine my direction, whether or not I was aimed at a star. As I limped down the street every window broadcast a command: Change! Purify! Experiment! Cauterize! Reverse! Burn! Pre-serve! Teach! Believe me, Edith, I had to act, and act fast. That was my nature. Call me Dr Frankenstein with a deadline. I seemed to wake up in the middle of a car accident, limbs strewn everywhere, detached voices screaming for comfort, severed fingers pointing homeward, all the debris withering like sliced cheese out of cellophane – and all I had in the wrecked world was a needle and thread, so I got down on my knees, I pulled pieces out of the mess and I started to stitch them together. I had an idea of what a man should look like, but it kept changing. I couldn't devote a lifetime to discovering the ideal physique. All I heard was pain, all I saw was mutilation. My needle going so madly, sometimes I found I'd run the thread right through my own flesh and I was joined to one of my own grotesque creations – I'd rip us apart – and then I heard my own voice howling with the others, and I knew that I was also truly part of the disaster. But I also realized that I was not the only one on my knees sewing frantically. There were others like me, making the same mon-strous mistakes, driven by the same impure urgency, stitching them-selves into the ruined heap, painfully extracting themselves—

—F, you're weeping.

—Forgive me.

—Stop blubbering. See, you've lost your hard-on.

—It's all breaking down now. My discipline is collapsing. Have you any idea how much discipline I had to use in training the two of you?

We both leaped for the Vibrator at the same instant. Her fluids made her slippery. For a second in our struggle, I wished we were making love, for all her nozzles were stiff and fragrant. I grabbed her around the waist; before I knew it her bum popped out of my bearhug like a wet watermelon seed, her thighs went by like a missed train, and there I was with empty lubricated arms, nose squashed against the expensive ma-hogany floor.

Old friend, are you still with me? Do not despair. I promised you that this would end in ecstasy. Yes, your wife was naked during this story.

Somewhere in the dark room, draped over the back of a chair like a huge exhausted butterfly, her Gal panties, stiffened by the slightest masonry of sweat, dreamed of ragged fingernails, and I dreamed with them – large, fluttering, descending dreams crisscrossed with vertical scratches. For me it was the end of Action. I would keep on trying, but I knew I had failed the both of you, and that both of you had failed me. I had one trick left, but it was a dangerous one, and I'd never used it. Events, as I will show, would force me into it, and it would end with Edith's suicide, my hospitalization, your cruel ordeal in the treehouse. How many times did I warn you that you would be whipped by loneliness?

So I lay there in Argentine. The Danish Vibrator hummed like a whittler as it rose and fell over Edith's young contours. It was cold and black in the room. Occasionally one of her glistening kneecaps would catch a glint of moonlight as she jerked her box up and down in desperate supplication. She had stopped moaning; I assumed she had approached the area of intense breathless silence which the orgasm loves to flood with ventriloquist gasps and cosmic puppet plots.

—Thank God, she whispered at last.

—I'm glad you could come, Edith. I'm very happy for you.

—Thank God it's off me. I had to blow it. It made me do oral intimacy.

—Wha—?

Before I could question her further it was upon my buttocks, its idiot hum revved up to a psychotic whine. The detachable crotch piece inserted itself between my hairy thighs, ingeniously providing soft support for my frightened testicles. I had heard of these things happening before, and I knew it would leave me bitter and full of self-loathing. Like a cyanide egg dropped into the gas chamber the DV released a glob of Formula Cream at the top of the muscular cleavage I had laboured so hard to define. As my body heat melted it to the trickle which would grease its shameful entry, several comfortable Latex cups assumed exciting holds here and there. The elastic Developer seemed to have a life of its own, and the Fortune Straps spread everything apart, and I felt the air-conditioning coolly evaporating sweat and cream *from tiny surfaces I hardly knew existed*. I was ready to lie there for ten days. I was not even surprised. I knew it would be insatiable but I was ready to submit. I heard Edith faintly calling to me just as the Foam Pad rose the full length. After that I heard nothing. It was like a thousand Sex Philosophers working over me with perfect cooperation. I may have screamed at the first thud of the White Club, but the Formula Cream kept coming, and I think a cup was converted to handle excreta. It hummed in my ears like alabaster lips.

I don't know how long it swarmed among my private pieces.
Edith made it to a light switch. She couldn't bear to look at me.
—Are you happy, F?
I did not answer.
—Should I do something, F?
Perhaps the DV answered with a sated whir. It pulled in the American
Laces fast as an Italian eater, the suck went out of the cups, my scrotum
dropped unceremoniously, and the machine slipped off my quivering
body meat. I think I was happy . . .
—Should I pull out the plug, F?
—Do what you want, Edith. I'm washed up.
Edith yanked at the electric cord. The DV shuddered, fell silent, and
stopped. Edith sighed with relief, but too soon. The DV began to pro-
duce a shattering sonic whistle.
—Does it have batteries?
—No, Edith. It doesn't have batteries.
She covered her breasts with crossed arms.
—You mean—?
Yes. It's learned to feed itself.
Edith backed into a corner as the Danish Vibrator advanced towards
her. She stooped queerly, as if she were trying to hide her cunt between
her thighs. I could not stir from the puddle of jelly in which I had been
buggered by countless improvements. It made its way across the hotel
room in a leisurely fashion, straps and cups flowing behind it, like a
Hawaiian skirt made of grass and brassières.
It had learned to feed itself.
(O Father, Nameless and Free of Description, lead me from the Desert
of the Possible. Too long I have dealt with Events. Too long I laboured to
become an Angel. I chased Miracles with a bag of Power to salt their
wild Tails. I tried to dominate Insanity so I could steal its Information. I
tried to programme the Computers with Insanity. I tried to create Grace
to prove that Grace existed. Do not punish Charles Axis. We could not
see the Evidence so we stretched our Memories. Dear Father, accept this
confession: we did not train ourselves to Receive because we believed
there wasn't Anything to Receive and we could not endure with this
Belief.)
—Help, help me, F.
But I was fastened to the floor with a tingling nail, the head of which
was my anus.
It took its time getting to her. Edith, meanwhile, her back squeezed
into the right angle, had sunk to a defenceless sitting position, her
lovely legs spread apart. Numbed by horror and the prospect of disgusting thrills, she was ready to submit. I have stared at many orifices,

but never have I seen one wear such an expression. The soft hairs were thrown back from the dripping lips like a Louis Quartorze sunburst. The layers of lip spread and gathered like someone playing with a lens opening. The Danish Vibrator mounted her slowly, and soon the child (Edith was twenty) was doing things with her mouth and fingers that no one, believe me, old friend, no one has ever done to you. Perhaps this was what you wanted from her. But you did not know how to encourage her, and this was not your fault. No one could. That is why I tried to lead the fuck away from mutual dialling.

The whole assault lasted maybe twenty-five minutes. Before the tenth minute passed she was begging the thing to perform in her armpits, specifying which nipple was hungriest, twisting her torso to offer it hidden pink terrain — until the Danish Vibrator began to command. Then Edith, quite happily, became nothing but a buffet of juice, flesh, excrement, muscle to serve its appetite.

Of course, the implications of her pleasure are enormous.

The Danish Vibrator slipped off her face, uncovering a bruised soft smile.

—Stay, she whispered.

It climbed onto the window sill, purring deeply, revved up to a sharp moan, and launched itself through the glass, which broke and fell over its exit like a fancy stage curtain.

—Make it stay.

—It's gone.

We dragged our strange bodies to the window. The perfumed sticky tropical night wafted into the room as we leaned out to watch the Danish Vibrator move down the marble storeys of the hotel. When it reached the ground it crossed the parking lot and soon achieved the beach.

—Oh, God, F, it was beautiful. Feel this.

—I know, Edith. Feel this.

A curious drama began to unfold beneath us on the deserted moonlit sand. As the DV made slowly towards the waves breaking in dark flowers on the bright shore, a figure emerged from a grove of ghostly palms. It was a man wearing an immaculate white bathing suit. I do not know whether he was running to intercept the Danish Vibrator with the intention of violently disabling it, or merely wished to observe at closer range its curiously graceful progress towards the Atlantic.

How soft the night seemed, like the last verse of a lullaby. With one hand on his hip and the other scratching his head, the tiny figure beneath us watched, as did we, the descent of the apparatus into the huge rolling sea, which closed over its luminous cups like the end of a civilization.

—Will it come back, F? To us?

—It doesn't matter. It's in the world.

We stood close to each other in the window, two figures on a rung of a high marble ladder built into the vast cloudless night, leaning on nothing.

A small breeze detached a wisp of her hair and I felt its tiny fall across my cheek.

—I love you, Edith.

—I love you, F.

—And I love your husband.

—So do I.

—Nothing is as I planned it, but now I know what will happen.

—So do I, F.

—Oh, Edith, something is beginning in my heart, a whisper of rare love, but I will never be able to fulfil it. It is my prayer that your husband will.

—He will, F.

—But he will do it alone. He can only do it alone.

—I know, she said. We must not be with him.

A great sadness overtook us as we looked out over the miles of sea, an egoless sadness that we did not own or claim. Here and there the restless water kept an image of the shattered moon. We said goodbye to you, old lover. We did not know when or how the parting would be completed, but it began that moment

There was a professional knock on the blond door.

—It must be him, I said.

—Should we put our clothes on?

—Why bother?

We did not even have to open the door. The waiter had a pass-key. He was wearing the old raincoat and moustache, but underneath he was perfectly nude. We turned towards him.

—Do you like Argentine? I asked for the sake of civil conversation.

—I miss the news-reels, he said.

—And the parades? I offered.

—And the parades. But I can get everything else here. Ah!

He noticed our reddened organs and began to fondle them with great interest.

—Wonderful! Wonderful! I see you have been well prepared.

What followed was old hat. I have no intention of adding to any pain which might be remaindered to you, by a minute description of the excesses we performed with him. Lest you should worry for us, let me say that we had, indeed, been well prepared, and we hardly cared to resist his sordid exciting commands, even when he made us kiss the whip.

—I have a treat for you, he said at last.

—He has a treat for us, Edith.

—Shoot, she replied wearily.

From the pocket of his overcoat he withdrew a bar of soap.

—Three in a tub, he said merrily in his heavy accent.

So we splashed around with him. He lathered us from head to foot, proclaiming all the while the special qualities of the soap, which, as you must now understand, was derived from melted human flesh.

That bar is now in your hands. We were baptized by it, your wife and I. I wonder what you will do with it.

You see. I have shown you *how it happens*, from style to style, from kiss to kiss.

There is more, there is the history of Catherine Tekakwitha – you shall have all of it.

Wearily we dried each other with the opulent towels of the hotel. The waiter was very careful with our parts.

—I had millions of these at my disposal, he said without a trace of nostalgia.

He slipped into his raincoat and spent some time before the full-length mirror playing with his moustache and slanting his hair across his forehead in just the way he liked.

—And don't forget to inform the *Police Gazette*. We'll bargain over the soap later.

—Wait!

As he opened the door to go, Edith threw her arms about his neck, pulled him to the dry bed, and cradled his famous head against her breasts.

—What did you do that for? I demanded of her after the waiter had made his stiff exit, and nothing remained of him but the vague stink of his sulphurous flatulence.

—For a second I thought he was an A—.

—Oh, Edith!

I sank to my knees before your wife, and I laid my mouth on her toes. The room was a mess, the floor spotted with pools of fluid and suds, but she rose from it all like a lovely statue with epaulets and nipple tips of moonlight.

—Oh, Edith! It doesn't matter what I've done to you, the tits, the cunt, the hydraulic buttock failure, all my Pygmalion tampering, it means nothing, I know now. Acne and all, you were out of my reach, you were beyond my gadgetry. Who are you?

—Ισιξ ἐγὼ εἰμί πάντα γεγονόξ καί ὄν καί ἐσόμενον καὶ τό ἐμόν πέπλου ουδείξ τῶν θνητῶν ἀπεκαλυψεν!

—You're not joking? Then I'm only fit to suck your toes.

—Wiggle.

ROBERT COOVER is the author of two novels: *The Origin of the Brunists*, which won the William Faulkner Award for the best first novel of 1966, and *The Universal Baseball Association, Inc, J. Henry Waugh, Prop*; and one volume of short stories, *Pricksongs and Descants*.

the babysitter

ROBERT COOVER

She arrives at 7.40, ten minutes late, but the children, Jimmy and Bitsy, are still eating supper, and their parents are not ready to go yet. From other rooms come the sounds of a baby screaming, water running, a television musical (no words: probably a dance number – patterns of gliding figures come to mind). Mrs Tucker sweeps into the kitchen, fussing with her hair, and snatches a baby bottle full of milk out of a pan of warm water, rushes out again. 'Harry!' she calls. 'The babysitter's here already!'

o   o   o

That's My Desire? I'll Be Around? He smiles toothily, beckons faintly with his head, rubs his fast-balding pate. *Bewitched*, maybe? Or, *What's the Reason?* He pulls on his shorts, gives his hips a slap. The baby goes silent in mid-scream. Isn't this the one who used their tub last time? *Who's Sorry Now*, that's it.

o   o   o

Jack is wandering around town, not knowing what to do. His girlfriend is babysitting at the Tuckers', and later, when she's got the kids in bed, maybe he'll drop over there. Sometimes he watches TV with her when

T–F

she's babysitting, it's about the only chance he gets to make out a little since he doesn't own wheels, but they have to be careful because most people don't like their sitters to have boyfriends over. Just kissing her makes her nervous. She won't close her eyes because she has to be watching the door all the time. Married people really have it good, he thinks.

o   o   o

'Hi,' the babysitter says to the children, and puts her books on top of the refrigerator. 'What's for supper?' The little girl, Bitsy, only stares at her obliquely. She joins them at the end of the kitchen table. 'I don't have to go to bed until nine,' the boy announces flatly, and stuffs his mouth full of potato chips. The babysitter catches a glimpse of Mr Tucker hurrying out of the bathroom in his underwear.

o   o   o

Her tummy. Under her arms. And her feet. Those are the best places. She'll spank him, she says sometimes. Let her.

o   o   o

That sweet odour that girls have. The softness of her blouse. He catches a glimpse of the gentle shadows amid her thighs, as she curls her legs up under her. He stares hard at her. He has a lot of meaning packed into that stare, but she's not even looking. She's popping her gum and watching television. She's sitting right there, inches away, soft, fragrant, and ready: but what's his next move? He notices his buddy Mark in the drugstore, playing the pinball machine, and joins him. 'Hey, this mama's cold, Jack baby! She needs your touch!'

o   o   o

Mrs Tucker appears at the kitchen doorway, holding a rolled-up diaper. 'Now, don't just eat potato crisps, Jimmy! See that he eats his hamburger, dear.' She hurries away to the bathroom. The boy glares sullenly at the babysitter, silently daring her to carry out the order. 'How about a little of that good hamburger now, Jimmy?' she says perfunctorily. He lets half of it drop to the floor. The baby is silent and a man is singing a love song on the TV. The children crunch chips.

o   o   o

He loves her. She loves him. They whirl airily, stirring a light breeze, through a magical landscape of rose and emerald and deep blue. Her light-brown hair coils and wisps softly in the breeze, and the soft folds of her white gown tug at her body and then float away. He smiles in a pulsing crescendo of sincerity and song.

o   o   o

'You mean she's alone?' Mark asks. 'Well, there's two or three kids,' Jack says. He slides the coin in. There's a rumble of steel balls tumbling, lining up. He pushes a plunger with his thumb, and one ball pops up in place, hard and glittering with promise. His stare? to say he loves her. That he cares for her and would protect her, would shield her, if need be, with his own body. Grinning, he bends over the ball to take careful aim: he and Mark have studied this machine and have it figured out, but still it's not that easy to beat.

o   o   o

On the drive to the party, his mind is partly on the girl, partly on his own high school days, long past. Sitting at the end of the kitchen table there with his children, she had seemed to be self-consciously arching her back, jutting her pert breasts, twitching her thighs: and for whom if not for him? So she'd seen him coming out of there, after all. He smiles. Yet what could he ever do about it? Those good times are gone, old man. He glances over at his wife, who, readjusting a garter, asks: 'What do you think of our babysitter?'

o   o   o

He loves her. She loves him. And then the babies come. And dirty diapers and one goddamn meal after another. Dishes. Noise. Clutter. And fat. Not just tight, her girdle actually hurts. Somewhere recently she's read about women getting heart attacks or cancer or something from too-tight girdles. Dolly pulls the car door shut with a grunt, strangely irritated, not knowing why. Party mood. Why is her husband humming, *Who's Sorry Now?* Pulling out of the drive, she glances back at the lighted kitchen window. 'What do you think of our babysitter?' she asks. While her husband stumbles all over himself trying to answer, she pulls a stocking tight, biting deeper with the garters.

o   o   o

'Stop it!' she laughs. Bitsy is pulling on her skirt and he is tickling her in the ribs. 'Jimmy! Don't!' But she is laughing too much to stop him. He leaps on her, wrapping his legs around her waist, and they all fall to the carpet in front of the TV, where just now a man in a tuxedo and a little girl in a flouncy white dress are doing a tap-dance together. The baby-sitter's blouse is pulled out of her skirt, showing a patch of bare tummy: the target. 'I'll spank!'

o   o   o

Jack pushes the plunger, thrusting up a steel ball, and bends studiously over the machine. 'You getting any off her?' Mark asks, and clears his throat, flicks ash from his cigarette. 'Well, not exactly, not yet,' Jack says, grinning awkwardly, but trying to suggest more than he admits to, and fires. He heaves his weight gently against the machine as the ball bounds off a rubber bumper. He can feel her warming up under his hands, the flippers suddenly coming alive, delicate rapid-fire patterns emerging in the flashing of the lights. 1000 WHEN LIT: *now!* 'Got my hand on it, that's about all.' Mark glances up from the machine, cigarette dangling from his lip. 'Maybe you need some help,' he suggests with a wry one-sided grin. 'Like maybe together, man, we could do it.'

o   o   o

She likes the big tub. She uses the Tuckers' bath salts, and loves to sink into the hot fragrant suds. She can stretch out, submerged, up to her chin. It gives her a good sleepy tingly feeling.

o   o   o

'What do you think of our babysitter?' Dolly asks, adjusting a garter. 'Oh, I hardly noticed,' he says. 'Cute girl. She seems to get along fine with the kids. Why?' 'I don't know.' His wife tugs her skirt down, glances at a lighted window they are passing, adding: 'I'm not sure I trust her completely, that's all. With the baby, I mean. She seems a little careless. And the other time, I'm almost sure she had a boyfriend over.' He grins, claps one hand on his wife's broad gartered thigh. 'What's wrong with that?' he asks. Still in anklets, too. Bare thighs, no girdles, nothing up there but a flimsy pair of panties and soft adolescent flesh. He's flooded with vague remembrances of football rallies and movie balconies.

o   o   o

How tiny and rubbery it is! she thinks, soaping between the boy's legs, giving him his bath. Just a funny jiggly little thing that looks like it shouldn't even be there at all. Is that what all the songs are about?

O   O   O

Jack watches Mark lunge and twist against the machine. Got her running now, racking them up. He's not too excited about the idea of Mark fooling around with his girlfriend, but Mark's a cooler operator than he is, and maybe, doing it together this once, he'd get over his own timidity. And if she didn't like it, there were other girls around. If Mark went too far, he could cut him off, too. He feels his shoulders tense: enough's enough, man . . . but sees the flesh, too. 'Maybe I'll call her later,' he says.

O   O   O

'Hey, Harry! Dolly! Glad you could make it!' 'I hope we're not late.' 'No, no, you're one of the first, come on in! By golly, Dolly, you're looking younger every day! How do you do it? Give my wife your secret, will you?' He pats her on her girdled bottom behind Mr Tucker's back, leads them in for drinks.

O   O   O

8.00. The babysitter runs water in the tub, combs her hair in front of the bathroom mirror. There's a western on television, so she lets Jimmy watch it while she gives Bitsy her bath. But Bitsy doesn't want a bath. She's angry and crying because she had to be first. The babysitter tells her if she'll take her bath quickly, she'll let her watch television while Jimmy takes his bath, but it does no good. The little girl fights to get out of the bathroom, and the babysitter has to squat with her back against the door and forcibly undress the child. There are better places to babysit. Both children mind badly, and then, sooner or later, the baby is sure to wake up for a diaper change and more bottle. The Tuckers do have a good colour TV, though, and she hopes things will be settled down enough to catch the 8.30 programme. She thrusts the child into the tub, but she's still screaming and thrashing around. 'Stop it now, Bitsy, or you'll wake the baby!' 'I have to go potty!' the child wails, switching tactics. The babysitter sighs, lifts the girl out of the tub and onto the toilet, getting her skirt and blouse all wet in the process. She glances at herself in the mirror. Before she knows it, the girl is off the seat and out of the bathroom. 'Bitsy! Come back here!'

O   O   O

'Okay, that's enough!' Her skirt is ripped and she's flushed and crying. 'Who says?' 'I do, man!' The bastard goes for her, but he tackles him. They roll and tumble. Tables tip, lights topple, the TV crashes to the floor. He slams a hard right to the guy's gut, clips his chin with a rolling left.

o   o   o

'We hope it's a girl.' That's hardly surprising, since they already have four boys. Dolly congratulates the woman like everybody else, but she doesn't envy her, not a bit. That's all she needs about now. She stares across the room at Harry, who is slapping backs and getting loud, as usual. He's spreading out through the middle, so why the hell does he have to complain about her all the time? 'Dolly, you're looking younger every day!' was the nice greeting she got tonight. 'What's your secret?' And Harry: 'It's all those calories. She's getting back her baby fat.' 'Haw haw! Harry, have a heart!'

o   o   o

'Get her feet!' he hollers at Bitsy, his fingers in her ribs, running over her naked tummy, tangling in the underbrush of straps and strange clothing. 'Get her shoes off!' He holds her pinned by pressing his head against her soft chest. 'No! No, Jimmy! Bitsy, stop!' But though she kicks and twists and rolls around, she doesn't get up, she can't get up, she's laughing too hard, and the shoes come off, and he grabs a stockinged foot and scratches the sole ruthlessly, and she raises up her legs, trying to pitch him off, she's wild, boy, but he hangs on, and she's laughing, and on the screen there's a rattle of hooves, and he and Bitsy are rolling around and around on the floor in a crazy rodeo of long bucking legs.

o   o   o

He slips the coin in. There's a metallic fall and a sharp click as the dial tone begins. 'I hope the Tuckers have gone,' he says. 'Don't worry, they're at our place,' Mark says. 'They're always the first ones to come and the last ones to go home. My old man's always bitching about them.' Jack laughs nervously and dials the number. 'Tell her we're coming over to protect her from getting raped,' Mark suggests, and lights a cigarette. Jack grins, leaning casually against the door jamb of the phone-booth, chewing gum, one hand in his pocket. He's really pretty uneasy, though. He has the feeling he's somehow messing up a good thing.

o   o   o

Bitsy runs naked into the living-room, keeping a hassock between herself and the babysitter. 'Bitsy ...!' the babysitter threatens. Artificial reds and greens and purples flicker over the child's wet body, as hooves clatter, guns crackle, and stagecoach wheels thunder over rutted terrain. 'Get outa the way, Bitsy!' the boy complains. 'I can't see!' Bitsy streaks past and the babysitter chases, cornering the girl in the back bedroom. Bitsy throws something that hits her softly in the face: a pair of men's undershorts. She grabs the girl scampering by, carries her struggling to the bathroom, and with a smart crack on her glistening bottom, pops her back into the tub. In spite, Bitsy peepees in the bathwater.

o   o   o

Mr Tucker stirs a little water into his bourbon and kids with his host and another man, just arrived, about their golf games. They set up a match for the weekend, a threesome looking for a fourth. Holding his drink in his right hand, Mr Tucker swings his left through the motion of a tee-shot. 'You'll have to give me a stroke a hole,' he says. 'I'll give you a stroke!' says the host: 'Bend over!' Laughing, the other man asks: 'Where's your boy Mark tonight?' 'I don't know,' replies the host, gathering up a trayful of drinks. Then he adds in a low growl: 'Out chasing tail probably.' They chuckle loosely at that, then shrug in commiseration and return to the living-room to join their women.

o   o   o

Shades pulled. Door locked. Watching the TV. Under a blanket maybe. Yes, that's right, under a blanket. Her eyes close when he kisses her. Her breasts, under both their hands, are soft and yielding.

o   o   o

A hard blow to the belly. The face. The dark beardy one staggers. The lean-jawed sheriff moves in, but gets a spurred boot in his face. The dark one hurls himself forward, drives his shoulder into the sheriff's hard midriff, her own tummy tightens, withstands, as the sheriff smashes the dark man's nose, slams him up against a wall, slugs him again! and again! The dark man grunts rhythmically, backs off, then plunges suicidally forward – her own knees draw up protectively – the sheriff staggers! caught low! but instead of following through, the other man steps back – a pistol! the dark one has a pistol! the sheriff draws! shoots from the hip! explosions! she clutches her hands between her thighs – no! the sheriff spins! wounded! the dark man hesitates, aims, her legs stiffen towards the set, the sheriff rolls desperately in the straw, fires: dead! the dark man is dead! groans, crumples, his pistol drooping in his collapsing hand, dropping, he drops. The sheriff, spent, nicked, watches weakly from the floor where he lies. Oh, to be whole! to be good and strong and right! to embrace and be embraced by harmony and wholeness! The sheriff, drawing himself painfully up on one elbow, rubs his bruised mouth with the back of his other hand.

o   o   o

'Well, we just sorta thought we'd drop over,' he says, and winks broadly at Mark. 'Who's we?' 'Oh, me and Mark here.' 'Tell her, good thing like her, gotta pass it around,' whispers Mark, dragging on his smoke, then flicking the butt over under the pinball machine. 'What's that?' she asks. 'Oh, Mark and I were just saying, like two's company, three's an orgy,' Jack says, and winks again. She giggles. 'Oh, Jack!' Behind her, he can hear shouts and gunfire. 'Well, okay, for just a little while, if you'll both be good.' Way to go, man.

o   o   o

Probably some damn kid over there right now. Wrestling around on the couch in front of his TV. Maybe he should drop back to the house. Just to check. None of that stuff, she was there to do a job! Park the car a couple of doors down, slip in the front door before she knows it. He sees the disarray of clothing, the young thighs exposed to the flickering television light, hears his baby crying. 'Hey, what's going on here! Get outa here, son, before I call the police!' Of course, they haven't really been doing anything. They probably don't even know how. He stares benignly down upon the girl, her skirt rumpled loosely around her thighs. Flushed, frightened, yet excited, she stares back at him. He smiles. His finger touches a knee, approaches the hem. Another couple arrives. Filling up here with people. He wouldn't be missed. Just slip out, stop back casually to pick up something or other he'd forgot, never mind what. He remembers that the other time they had this babysitter, she took a bath in their house. She had a date afterwards, and she'd just come from cheerleading practice or something. Aspirin maybe. Just drop quietly and casually into the bathroom to pick up some aspirin. 'Oh, excuse me, dear! I only . . .!' She gazes back at him, astonished, yet strangely moved. Her soft wet breasts rise and fall in the water, and her tummy looks pale and ripply. He recalls that her pubic hairs, left in the tub, were brown. Light brown.

o   o   o

She's no more than stepped into the tub for a quick bath, when Jimmy announces from outside the door that he has to go to the bathroom. She sighs: just an excuse, she knows. 'You'll have to wait.' The little nuisance. 'I can't wait.' 'Okay, then come ahead, but I'm taking a bath.' She supposes that will stop him, but it doesn't. In he comes. She slides down into the suds until she's eye-level with the edge of the tub. He hesitates. 'Go ahead, if you have to,' she says, a little awkwardly, 'but I'm not getting out.' 'Don't look,' he says. She: 'I will if I want to.'

o   o   o

She's crying. Mark is rubbing his jaw where he's just slugged him. A lamp lies shattered. 'Enough's enough, Mark! Now get outa here!' Her skirt is ripped to the waist, her bare hip bruised. Her panties lie on the floor like a broken balloon. Later, he'll wash her wounds, help her dress, he'll take care of her. Pity washes through him, giving him a sudden hard-on. Mark laughs at it, pointing. Jack crouches, waiting, ready for anything.

o   o   o

Laughing, they roll and tumble. Their little hands are all over her, digging and pinching. She struggles to her hands and knees, but Bitsy leaps astride her neck, bowing her head to the carpet. 'Spank her, Jimmy!' His swats sting: is her skirt up? The phone rings. 'The cavalry to the rescue!' she laughs, and throws them off to go answer.

o   o   o

Kissing Mark, her eyes closed, her hips nudge towards Jack. He stares at the TV screen, unsure of himself, one hand slipping cautiously under her skirt. Her hand touches his arm as though to resist, then brushes on by to rub his leg. This blanket they're under was a good idea. 'Hi! This is Jack!'

o   o   o

Bitsy's out and the water's running. 'Come on, Jimmy, your turn!' Last time, he told her he took his own baths, but she came in anyway. 'I'm not gonna take a bath,' he announces, eyes glued on the set. He readies for the struggle. 'But I've already run your water. Come on, Jimmy, please!' He shakes his head. She can't make him, he's sure as strong as she is. She sighs. 'Well, it's up to you. I'll use the water myself then,' she says. He waits until he's pretty sure she's not going to change her mind, then sneaks in and peeks through the keyhole in the bathroom door: just in time to see her big bottom as she bends over to stir in the bubblebath. Then she disappears. Trying to see as far down as the keyhole will allow, he bumps his head on the knob. 'Jimmy, is that you?' 'I – I have to go to the bathroom!' he stammers.

o   o   o

Not actually in the tub, just getting in. One foot on the mat, the other in the water. Bent over slightly, buttocks flexed, teats swaying, holding on to the edge of the tub. 'Oh, excuse me! I only wanted . . .!' He passes over her astonishment, the awkward excuses, moves quickly to the part where he reaches out to— 'What on earth are you doing, Harry?' his wife asks, staring at his hand. His host, passing, laughs. 'He's practising his swing for Sunday, Dolly, but it's not going to do him a damn bit of good!' Mr Tucker laughs, sweeps his right hand on through the air as though lifting a seven-iron shot onto the green. He makes a *dok!* sound with his tongue. 'In there!'

o   o   o

'No, Jack, I don't think you'd better.' 'Well, we just called, we just, uh, thought we'd, you know, stop by for a minute, watch television for thirty minutes, or, or something.' 'Who's we?' 'Well, Mark's here, I'm with him, and he said he'd like to, you know, like if it's all right, just—' 'Well, it's *not* all right. The Tuckers said no.' 'Yeah, but if we only—' 'And they seemed awfully suspicious about last time.' 'Why? We didn't—I mean, I just thought—' 'No, Jack, and that's period.' She hangs up. She returns to the TV, but the commercial is on. Anyway, she's missed most of the show. She decides maybe she'll take a quick bath. Jack might come by anyway, it'd make her mad, that'd be the end as far as he was concerned, but if he should, she doesn't want to be all sweaty. And besides, she likes the big tub the Tuckers have.

o   o   o

He is self-conscious and stands with his back to her, his little neck flushed. It takes him forever to get started, and when it finally does come, it's just a tiny trickle. 'See, it was just an excuse,' she scolds, but she's giggling inwardly at the boy's embarrassment. 'You're just a nuisance, Jimmy.' At the door, his hand on the knob, he hesitates, staring timidly down on his shoes. 'Jimmy?' She peeks at him over the edge of the tub, trying to keep a straight face, as he sneaks a nervous glance back over his shoulder. 'As long as you bothered me,' she says, 'you might as well soap my back.'

o   o   o

'The aspirin . . .' They embrace. She huddles in his arms like a child. Lovingly, paternally, knowledgeable, he wraps her nakedness. How compact, how tight and small her body is! Kissing her ear, he stares down past her rump at the still clear water. 'I'll join you,' he whispers hoarsely.

o   o   o

She picks up the shorts Bitsy threw at her. Men's underwear. She holds them in front of her, looks at herself in the bedroom mirror. About twenty sizes too big for her, of course. She runs her hand inside the opening in front, pulls out her thumb. How funny it must feel!

o   o   o

'Well, man, I say we just go rape her,' Mark said flatly, and swings his weight against the pinball machine. 'Uff! Ahh! Get in there, you mother! Look at that! Hah! Man, I'm gonna turn this baby over!' Jack is embarrassed about the phone conversation. Mark just snorted in disgust when he hung up. He cracks down hard on his gum, angry that he's such a chicken. 'Well, I'm game if you are,' he says coldly.

o   o   o

8.30. 'Okay, come on, Jimmy, it's time.' He ignores her. The western gives way to a spy show. Bitsy, in pyjamas, pads into the living-room. 'No, Bitsy, it's time to go to bed.' 'You said I could watch!' the girl whines, and starts to throw another tantrum. 'But you were too slow and it's late. Jimmy, you get in that bathroom, and right now!' Jimmy stares sullenly at the set, unmoving. The babysitter tries to catch the opening scene of the television programme so she can follow it later, since Jimmy gives himself his own baths. When the commercial interrupts, she turns off the sound, stands in front of the screen. 'Okay, into the tub, Jimmy Tucker, or I'll take you in there and give you your bath myself!' 'Just try it,' he says, 'and see what happens.'

o   o   o

They stand outside, in the dark, crouched in the bushes, peeking in. She's on the floor, playing with the kids. Too early. They seem to be tickling her. She gets to her hands and knees, but the little girl leaps on her head, pressing her face to the floor. There's an obvious target, and the little boy proceeds to beat on it. 'Hey, look at that kid go!' whispers Mark, laughing and snapping his fingers softly. Jack feels uneasy out here. Too many neighbours, too many cars going by, too many people in the world. That little boy in there is one up on him, though: he's never thought about tickling her as a starter.

o   o   o

His little hand, clutching the bar of soap, lathers shyly a narrow space between her shoulderblades. She is doubled forward against her knees, buried in rich suds, peeking at him over the edge of her shoulder. The soap slithers out of his grip and plunks into the water. 'I . . . I dropped the soap,' he whispers. She: 'Find it.'

o   o   o

'I dream of Jeannie with the light-brown pubic hair!' 'Harry! Stop that! You're drunk!' But they're laughing, they're all laughing, damn! he's feeling pretty goddamn good at that, and now he just knows he needs that aspirin. Watching her there, her thighs spread for him, on the couch, in the tub, hell, on the kitchen table for that matter, he tees off on Number Nine, and – *whap!* – swats his host's wife on the bottom. 'Hole in one!' he shouts. 'Harry!' Why can't his goddamn wife Dolly ever get happy-drunk instead of sour-drunk all the time? 'Gonna be tough Sunday, old buddy!' 'You're pretty tough right now, Harry,' says his host.

o   o   o

The babysitter lunges forward, grabs the boy by the arms and hauls him off the couch, pulling two cushions with him, and drags him towards the bathroom. He lashes out, knocking over an endtable full of magazines and ashtrays. 'You leave my brother alone!' Bitsy cries and grabs the sitter around the waist. Jimmy jumps on her and down they all go. On the silent screen, there's a fade-in to a dark passageway in an old apartment building in some foreign country. She kicks out and somebody falls between her legs. Somebody else is sitting on her face. 'Jimmy! Stop that!' the babysitter laughs, her voice muffled.

o   o   o

She's watching television. All alone. It seems like a good time to go in. Just remember: really, no matter what she says, she wants it. They're standing in the bushes, trying to get up the nerve. 'We'll tell her to be good,' Mark whispers, 'and if she's not good, we'll spank her.' Jack giggles softly, but his knees are weak. She stands. They freeze. She looks right at them. 'She can't see us,' Mark whispers tensely. 'Is she coming out?' 'No,' says Mark, 'she's going into — that must be the bathroom!' Jack takes a deep breath, his heart pounding. 'Hey, is there a window back there?' Mark asks.

o o o

The phone rings. She leaves the tub, wrapped in a towel. Bitsy gives a tug on the towel. 'Hey, Jimmy, get the towel!' she squeals. 'Now stop that, Bitsy!' the babysitter hisses, but too late: with one hand on the phone, the other isn't enough to hang on to the towel. Her sudden nakedness awes them and it takes them a moment to remember about tickling her. By then, she's in the towel again. 'I hope you got a good look,' she says angrily. She feels chilled and oddly a little frightened. 'Hello?' No answer. She glances at the window — is somebody out there? Something, she saw something, and a rustling — footsteps?

o o o

'Okay, I don't care, Jimmy, don't take a bath,' she says irritably. Her blouse is pulled out and wrinkled, her hair is all mussed, and she feels sweaty. There's about a million things she'd rather be doing than baby-sitting with these two. Three: at least the baby's sleeping. She knocks on the overturned endtable for luck, rights it, replaces the magazines and ashtrays. The one thing that really makes her sick is a dirty diaper. 'Just go on to bed.' 'I don't have to go to bed until nine,' he reminds her. Really, she couldn't care less. She turns up the volume on the TV, settles down on the couch, poking her blouse back into her skirt, pushing her hair out of her eyes. Jimmy and Bitsy watch from the floor. She wishes Jack would come by. The man, no doubt the spy, is following a woman, but she doesn't know why. The woman passes another man. Something seems to happen, but it's not clear what. She's probably already missed too much. The phone rings.

o o o

Mark is kissing her. Jack is under the blanket, easing her panties down over her squirming hips. Her hand is in his pants, pulling it out, pulling it towards her, pulling it hard. She knew just where it was! Mark is stripping, too. God, it's really happening! he thinks with a kind of pious joy, and notices the open door. 'Hey! What's going on here?'

o   o   o

He soaps her back, smooth and slippery under his hand. She is doubled over, against her knees, between his legs. Her light-brown hair, reaching to her gleaming shoulders, is wet at the edges. The soap slips, falls between his legs. He fishes for it, finds it, slips it behind him. 'Help me find it,' he whispers in her ear. 'Sure Harry,' says his host, going around behind him. 'What'd you lose?'

o   o   o

Soon be nine, time to pack the kids off to bed. She clears the table, dumps paper plates and left-over hamburgers into the garbage, puts glasses and silverware into the sink, and the mayonnaise, mustard, and ketchup in the refrigerator. Neither child has eaten much supper finally, mostly potato chips and ice-cream, but it's really not her problem. She glances at the books on the refrigerator. Not much chance she'll get to them, she's already pretty worn out. Maybe she'd feel better if she had a quick bath. She runs water into the tub, tosses in bubblebath salts, undresses. Before pushing down her panties she stares for a moment at the smooth silken panel across her tummy, fingers the place where the opening would be if there were one. Then she steps quickly out of them, feeling somehow ashamed, unhooks her brassière. She weighs her breasts in the palm of her hands, watching herself in the bathroom mirror, where in the open window behind her, she sees a face. She screams.

o   o   o

She screams: 'Jimmy! Give me that!' 'What's the matter?' asks Jack on the other end. 'Jimmy! Give me my towel! Right now!' 'Hello? Hey, are you still there?' 'I'm sorry, Jack,' she says, panting. 'You caught me in the tub. I'm just wrapped in a towel and these silly kids grabbed it away!' 'Gee, I wish I'd been there!' 'Jack—!' 'To protect you, I mean.' 'Oh, sure,' she says, giggling. 'Well, what do you think, can I come over and watch TV with you?' 'Well, not right this minute,' she says. He laughs lightly. He feels very cool. 'Jack?' 'Yeah?' 'Jack, I . . . I think there's somebody outside the window!'

o   o   o

She carries him, fighting all the way, to the tub, Bitsy pummelling her in the back and kicking her ankles. She can't hang on to him and undress him at the same time. 'I'll throw you in, clothes and all, Jimmy Tucker!' she gasps. 'You better not!' he cries. She sits on the toilet seat, locks her legs around him, whips his shirt up over his head before he knows what's happening. The pants are easier. Like all little boys his age, he has almost no hips at all. He hangs on desperately to his underpants, but when she succeeds in snapping these down out of his grip, too, he gives up, starts to bawl, and beats her wildly in the face with his fists. She ducks her head, laughing hysterically, oddly entranced by the spectacle of that pale little thing down there, bobbing and bouncing rubberily about with the boy's helpless fury and anguish.

o   o   o

'Aspirin? Whaddaya want aspirin for, Harry? I'm sure they got aspirin here, if you—' 'Did I say aspirin? I meant, uh, my glasses. And, you know, I thought, well, I'd sorta check to see if everything was okay at home.' Why the hell is it his mouth feels like it's got about six sets of teeth packed in there, and a tongue the size of that liverwurst his host's wife is passing around? 'Whaddaya want your glasses for, Harry? I don't understand you at all!' 'Aw, well, honey, I was feeling kind of dizzy or something, and I thought—' 'Dizzy is right. If you want to check on the kids, why don't you just call on the phone?'

o   o   o

They can tell she's naked and about to get into the tub, but the bathroom window is frosted glass, and they can't see anything clearly. 'I got an idea,' Mark whispers. 'One of us goes and calls her on the phone, and the other watches when she comes out.' 'Okay, but who calls?' 'Both of us, we'll do it twice. Or more.'

o   o   o

Down forbidden alleys. Into secret passageways. Unlocking the world's terrible secrets. Sudden shocks: a trapdoor! a fall! or the stunning report of a rifle shot, the *whaaii-ii-iing!* of the bullet biting concrete by your ear! Careful! Then edge forward once more, avoiding the light, inch at a time, now a quick dash for an open doorway – *look out!* there's a knife! a struggle! no! the long blade glistens! jerks! thrusts! *stabbed!* No, no, it missed! The assailant's down, yes! the spy's on top, pinning him, a terrific thrashing about, the spy rips off the assailant's mask; *a woman!*

o   o   o

Fumbling behind her, she finds it, wraps her hand around it, tugs. 'Oh!' she gasps, pulling her hand back quickly, her ears turning crimson. 'I ... thought it was the soap!' He squeezes her close between his thighs, pulls her back towards him, one hand sliding down her tummy between her legs. *I Dream of Jeannie*— 'I have to go to the bathroom!' says someone outside the door.

o   o   o

She's combing her hair in the bathroom when the phone rings. She hurries to answer it before it wakes the baby. 'Hello, Tuckers.' There's no answer. 'Hello?' A soft click. Strange. She feels suddenly alone in the big house, and goes in to watch TV with the children.

o   o   o

'Stop it!' she screams. 'Please, stop!' She's on her hands and knees, trying to get up, but they're too strong for her. Mark holds her head down. 'Now, baby, we're gonna teach you how to be a nice girl,' he says coldly, and nods at Jack. When she's doubled over like that, her skirt rides up her thighs to the leg bands of her panties. 'C'mon, man, go! This baby's cold! She needs your touch!'

o   o   o

Parks the car a couple of blocks away. Slips up to the house, glances in his window. Just like he's expected. Her blouse is off and the kid's shirt is unbuttoned. He watches, while slowly, clumsily, childishly, they fumble with each other's clothes. My God, it takes them forever. 'Some party!' 'You said it!' When they're more or less naked, he walks in. 'Hey! what's going on here?' They go white as bleu cheese, Haw haw! 'What's the little thing you got sticking out there, boy?' 'Harry, behave yourself!' No, he doesn't let the kid get dressed, he sends him home bare-assed. 'Bare-assed!' He drinks to that. 'Promises, promises,' says his host's wife. 'I'll mail you your clothes, son!' He gazes down on the naked little girl on his couch. 'Looks like you and me, we got a little secret to keep, honey,' he says coolly. 'Less you wanna go home the same way your boyfriend did!' He chuckles at his easy wit, leans down over her, and unbuckles his belt. 'Might as well make it two secrets, right?' 'What in God's name are you talking about, Harry?' He staggers out of there, drink in hand, and goes to look for his car.

o   o   o

'Hey! What's going on here?' They huddle half-naked under the blanket, caught utterly unawares. On television: the clickety-click of frightened running feet on foreign pavements. Jack is fumbling for his shorts, tangled somehow around his ankles. The blanket is snatched away. 'On your feet there!' Mr Tucker, Mrs Tucker, Mark's mom and dad, the police, the neighbours, everybody comes crowding in. Hopelessly, he has a terrific erection. So hard it hurts. Everybody stares down at it.

o o o

Bitsy's sleeping on the floor. The babysitter is taking a bath. For more than an hour now, he's had to use the bathroom. He doesn't know how much longer he can wait. Finally, he goes to knock on the bathroom door. 'I have to use the bathroom.' 'Well, come ahead, if you have to.' 'Not while you're in there.' She sighs loudly. 'Okay, okay, just a minute,' she says, 'but you're a real nuisance, Jimmy!' He's holding on, pinching it as tight as he can. 'Hurry!' He holds his breath, squeezing shut his eyes. No. Too late. At last, she opens the door. 'Jimmy!' 'I told you to hurry!' he sobs. She drags him into the bathroom and pulls his pants down.

o o o

He arrives just in time to see her emerge from the bathroom, wrapped in a towel, to answer the phone. His two kids sneak up behind her and pull the towel away. She's trying to hang on to the phone and get the towel back at the same time. It's quite a picture. She's got a sweet ass. Standing there in the bushes, pawing himself with one hand, he lifts his glass with the other and toasts her sweet ass, which his son now swats. Haw haw, maybe that boy's gonna shape up, after all.

o o o

They're in the bushes, arguing about their next move, when she comes out of the bathroom, wrapped in a towel. They can hear the baby crying. Then it stops. They see her running, naked, back to the bathroom like she's scared or something. 'I'm going in after her, man, whether you're with me or not!' Mark whispers, and he starts out of the bushes. But just then, a light comes sweeping up through the yard, as a car swings in the drive. They hit the dirt, hearts pounding. 'Is it the cops?' 'I don't know!' 'Do you think they saw us?' 'Sshh!' A man comes staggering up the walk from the drive, a drink in his hand, stumbles on in the kitchen door and then straight into the bathroom. 'It's Mr Tucker!' Mark whispers. A scream. 'Let's get outa here, man!'

o o o

9.00 Having missed most of the spy show anyway and having little else to do, the babysitter has washed the dishes and cleaned the kitchen up a little. The books on the refrigerator remind her of her better intentions, but she decides that first she'll see what's next on TV. In the living-room, she finds little Bitsy sound asleep on the floor. She lifts her gently, carries her into her bed, and tucks her in. 'Okay, Jimmy, it's nine o'clock, I've let you stay up, now be a good boy.' Sullenly, his sleepy eyes glued still to the set, the boy backs out of the room towards his bedroom. A drama comes on. She switches channels. A ball-game and a murder mystery. She switches back to the drama. It's a love story of some kind. A man married to an ageing invalid wife, but in love with a younger girl. 'Use the bathroom and brush your teeth before going to bed, Jimmy!' she calls, but as quickly regrets it, for she hears the baby stir in its crib.

o   o   o

Two of them are talking about mothers they've salted away in rest homes. Oh boy, that's just wonderful, this is one helluva party. She leaves them to use the john, takes advantage of the retreat to ease her girdle down awhile, get a few good deep breaths. She has this picture of her three kids carting her off to a rest home. In a wheelbarrow. That sure is something to look forward to, all right. When she pulls her girdle back up, she can't seem to squeeze into it. The host looks in. 'Hey, Dolly, are you all right?' 'Yeah, I just can't get into my damn girdle, that's all.' 'Here, let me help.'

o   o   o

She pulls them on, over her own, standing in front of the bedroom mirror, holding her skirt bundled up around the waist. About twenty sizes too big for her, of course. She pulls them tight from behind, runs her hand inside the opening in front, pulls out her thumb. 'And what a good boy am I!' She giggles: how funny it must feel! Then, in the mirror, she sees him: in the doorway behind her, sullenly watching. 'Jimmy! You're supposed to be in bed!' 'Those are my daddy's!' the boy says. 'I'm gonna tell!'

o   o   o

'Jimmy!' She drags him into the bathroom and pulls his pants down. 'Even your shoes are wet! Get them off!' She soaps up a warm wash-cloth she's had with her in the bathtub, scrubs him from the waist down with it. Bitsy stands in the doorway, staring. 'Get out! Get out!' the boy screams at his sister. 'Go back to bed, Bitsy. It's just an accident.' 'Get out!' The baby wakes and starts to howl.

o   o   o

The young lover feels sorry for her rival, the invalid wife; she believes the man has a duty towards the poor woman and insists she is willing to wait. But the man argues that he also has a duty towards himself: his life, too, is short, and he could not love his wife now even were she well. He embraces the young girl feverishly; she twists away in anguish. The door opens. They stand there grinning, looking devilish, but pretty silly at the same time. 'Jack! I thought I told you not to come!' She's angry, but she's also glad in a way: she was beginning to feel a little too alone in the big house, with the children all sleeping. She should have taken that bath, after all. 'We just came by to see if you were being a good girl,' Jack says and blushes. The boys glance at each other nervously.

o   o   o

She's just sunk down into the tubful of warm fragrant suds, ready for a nice long soaking, when the phone rings. Wrapping a towel around her, she goes to answer: no one there. But now the baby's awake and bawling. She wonders if that's Jack bothering her all the time. If it is, brother, that's the end. Maybe it's the end anyway. She tries to calm the baby with the half-empty bottle, not wanting to change it until she's finished her bath. The bathroom's where the diapers go dirty, and they make it stink to high heaven. 'Shush, shush!' she whispers, rocking the crib. The towel slips away, leaving an airy empty tingle up and down her backside. Even before she stoops for the towel, even before she turns around, she knows there's somebody behind her.

o   o   o

'We just came by to see if you were being a good girl,' Jack says, grinning down at her. She's flushed and silent, her mouth half open. 'Lean over,' says Mark amiably. 'We'll soap your back, as long as we're here.' But she just huddles there, down in the suds, staring up at them with big eyes.

o   o   o

'Hey! What's going on here?' It's Mr Tucker, stumbling through the door with a drink in his hand. She looks up from the TV. 'What's the matter, Mr Tucker?' 'Oh, uh, I'm sorry, I got lost – no, I mean, I had to get some aspirin. Excuse me!' And he rushes past her into the bathroom, caroming off the living-room door jamb on the way. The baby wakes.

o   o   o

'Okay, get off her, Mr Tucker!' 'Jack!' she cries, 'what are *you* doing here?' He stares hard at them a moment: so that's where it goes. Then, as Mr Tucker swings heavily off, he leans into the bastard with a right to the belly. Next thing he knows, though, he's got a face full of an old man's fist. He's not sure, as the lights go out, if that's his girlfriend screaming or the baby . . .

o   o   o

Her host pushes down on her fat fanny and tugs with all his might on her girdle, while she bawls on his shoulder: 'I don't *wanna* go to a rest home!' 'Now, now, take it easy, Dolly, nobody's gonna make you—' 'Ouch! Hey, you're hurting!' 'You should buy a bigger girdle, Dolly.' 'You're telling me?' Some other guy pokes his head in. 'Whatsamatter? Dolly fall in?' 'No, she fell out. Give me a hand.'

o   o   o

By the time she's chased Jack and Mark out of there, she's lost track of the programme she's been watching on television. There's another woman in the story now for some reason. That guy lives a very complicated life. Impatiently, she switches channels. She hates ballgames, so she settles for the murder mystery. She switches just in time, too: there's a dead man sprawled out on the floor of what looks like an office or a study or something. A heavy-set detective gazes up from his crouch over the body: 'He's been strangled.' Maybe she'll take that bath, after all.

o   o   o

She drags him into the bathroom and pulls his pants down. She soaps up a warm washcloth she's had in the tub with her, but just as she reaches between his legs, it starts to spurt, spraying her arms and hands. 'Oh, Jimmy! I thought you were done!' she cries, pulling him towards the toilet and aiming it into the bowl. How moist and rubbery it is! And you can turn it every which way. How funny it must feel!

o   o   o

'Stop it!' she screams. 'Please stop!' She's on her hands and knees and Jack is holding her head down. 'Now we're gonna teach you how to be a nice girl,' Mark says and lifts her skirt. 'Well, I'll be damned!' 'What's the matter?' asks Jack, his heart pounding. 'Look at this big pair of men's underpants she's got on!' 'Those are my daddy's!' says Jimmy, watching them from the doorway. 'I'm gonna tell!'

o   o   o

People are shooting at each other in the murder mystery, but she's so mixed up, she doesn't know which ones are the good guys. She switches back to the love story. Something seems to have happened, because now the man is kissing his invalid wife tenderly. Maybe she's finally dying. The baby wakes, begins to scream. Let it. She turns up the volume on the TV.

o   o   o

Leaning down over her, unbuckling his belt. It's all happening just like he's known it would. Beautiful! The kid is gone, though his pants, poor lad, remain. 'Looks like you and me, we got a secret to keep, child!' But he's cramped on the couch and everything is too slippery and small. 'Lift your legs up, honey. Put them around my back.' But instead, she screams. He rolls off, crashing to the floor. There they all come, through the front door. On television, somebody is saying: 'Am I a burden to you, darling?' 'Dolly! My God! Dolly, I can explain . . .'

o   o   o

The game of the night is Get Dolly Tucker Back in Her Girdle Again. They've got her down on her belly in the living room and the whole damn crowd is working on her. Several of them are stretching the girdle, while others try to jam the fat inside. 'I think we made a couple inches on this side! Roll her over!' Harry?

o   o   o

She's just stepped into the tub, when the phone rings, waking the baby. She sinks down in the suds, trying not to hear. But that baby doesn't cry, it screams. Angrily, she wraps a towel around herself, stamps peevishly into the baby's room, just letting the phone jangle. She tosses the baby down on its back, unpins its diapers hastily, and gets yellowish baby stool all over her hands. Her towel drops away. She turns to find

Jimmy staring at her like a little idiot. She slaps him in the face with her dirty hand, while the baby screams, the phone rings, and nagging voices argue on the TV. There are better things she might be doing.

o   o   o

What's happening? Now there's a young guy in it. Is he after the young girl or the old invalid? To tell the truth, it looks like he's after the same man the women are. In disgust, she switches channels. 'The strangler again,' growls the fat detective, hands on hips, staring down at the body of a half-naked girl. She's considering either switching back to the love story or taking a quick bath, when a hand suddenly clutches her mouth.

o   o   o

'You're both chicken,' she says, staring up at them. 'But what if Mr Tucker comes home?' Mark asks nervously.

o   o   o

How did he get here? He's standing pissing in his own goddamn bathroom, his wife is still back at the party, the three of them are, like good kids, sitting in there in the living-room watching TV. One of them is his host's boy Mark. 'It's a good murder mystery, Mr Tucker,' Mark said, when he came staggering in on them a minute ago. 'Sit still!' he shouted. 'I'm just home for a moment!' Then whump whump on into the bathroom. Long hike for a weewee, Mister. But something keeps bothering him. Then it hits him: the girl's panties, hanging like a broken balloon from the rabbit-ear antennae on the TV! He barges back in there, giving his shoulder a helluva crack on the living-room door jamb on the way – but they're not hanging there any more. Maybe he's only imagined it. 'Hey, Mr Tucker,' Mark says flatly. 'Your fly's open.'

o   o   o

The baby's dirty. Stinks to high heaven. She hurries back to the living-room, hearing sirens and gunshots. The detective is crouched outside a house, peering in. Already, she's completely lost. The baby screams at the top of its lungs. She turns up the volume. But it's all confused. She hurries back in there, claps an angry hand to the baby's mouth. 'Shut up!' she cries. She throws the baby down on its back, starts to unpin the diaper, as the baby tunes up again. The phone rings. She answers it, one eye on the TV. *'What?'* The baby cries so hard it starts to choke. Let it. 'I said, hi, this is Jack!' Then it hits her: oh no! the diaper pin!

O   O   O

'The aspirin . . .' But she's already in the tub. Way down in the tub. Staring at him through the water. Her tummy looks pale and ripply. He hears sirens, people on the porch.

O   O   O

Jimmy gets up to go to the bathroom and gets his face slapped and smeared with baby poop. Then she hauls him off to the bathroom, yanks off his pyjamas, and throws him into the tub. That's okay, but next she gets naked and acts like she's gonna get in the tub, too. The baby's screaming and the phone's ringing like crazy and in walks his dad. Saved! he thinks, but no, his dad grabs him right back out of the tub and whales the dickens out of him, no questions asked, while she watches, then sends him – *whack!* – back to bed. So he's lying there, wet and dirty and naked and sore, and he still has to go to the bathroom, and outside his window he hears two older guys talking. 'Listen, you know where to do it if we get her pinned?' 'No! Don't you?'

O   O   O

'Yo ho heave ho! *Ugh!*' Dolly's on her back and they're working on the belly side. Somebody got the great idea of buttering her down first. Not to lose the ground they've gained, they've shot it inside with a basting syringe. But now suddenly there's this big tug-of-war under way between those who want to stuff her in and those who want to let her out. Something rips, but she feels better. The odour of hot butter makes her think of movie theatres and popcorn. 'Hey, has anybody seen Harry?' she asks. 'Where's Harry?'

O   O   O

Somebody's getting chased. She switches back to the love story, and now the man's back kissing the young lover again. What's going on? She gives it up, decides to take a quick bath. She's just stepping into the tub, one foot in, one foot out, when Mr Tucker walks in. 'Oh, excuse me! I only wanted some aspirin . . .' She grabs for a towel, but he yanks it away. 'Now, that's not how it's supposed to happen, child,' he scolds. 'Please! Mr Tucker . . .!' He embraces her savagely, his calloused old

hands clutching roughly at her backside. 'Mr Tucker!' she cries, squirming. 'Your wife called—' He's pushing something between her legs, hurting her. She slips, they both slip – something cold and hard slams her in
the back, cracks her skull, she seems to be sinking down into a sea . . .

o   o   o

They've got her over the hassock, skirt up and pants down. 'Give her a
little lesson there, Jack baby!' The television lights flicker and flash over
her glossy flesh. 1,000 WHEN LIT Whack! Slap! Bumper to bumper! He
leans into her, feeling her come alive.

o   o   o

The phone rings, waking the baby. 'Jack, is that you? Now, you listen to
me—!' 'No dear, this is Mrs Tucker. Isn't the TV awfully loud?' 'Oh, I'm
sorry, Mrs Tucker! I've been getting—' 'I tried to call you before, but I
couldn't hang on. To the phone I mean. I'm sorry, dear.' 'Just a minute,
Mrs Tucker, the baby's—' 'Honey, listen! Is Harry there? Is Mr Tucker
there, dear?'

o   o   o

'Stop it!' she screams and claps a hand over the baby's mouth. 'Stop it!
Stop it! *Stop it!*' Her other hand is full of baby stool and she's afraid
she's going to be sick. The phone rings. 'No!' she cries. She's hanging on
to the baby, leaning woozily away, listening to the phone ring. 'Okay,
okay,' she sighs, getting a hold of herself. But when she lets go of the
baby, it isn't screaming any more. She shakes it. Oh no . . .

o   o   o

'Hello?' No answer. Strange. She hangs up and, wrapped only in a towel,
stares out the window at the cold face staring in – she screams!

o   o   o

She screams, scaring the hell out of him. He leaps out of the tub, glances
up at the window she's gaping at just in time to see two faces duck
away, then slips on the bathroom tiles, and crashes to his ass, whacking
his head on the sink on the way down. She stares down at him,
trembling, a towel over her narrow shoulders. 'Mr Tucker! Mr Tucker,
are you all right . . .?' *Who's Sorry Now?* Yessir, whose back is breaking
with each . . . He stares up at the little tufted locus of all his woes, and
passes out, dreaming of Jeannie . . .

o   o   o

The phone rings. 'Dolly! It's for you!' 'Hello?' 'Hello, Mrs Tucker?' 'Yes, speaking.' 'Mrs Tucker, this is the police calling . . .'

o   o   o

It's cramped and awkward and slippery, but he's pretty sure he got it in her, once anyway. When he gets the suds out of his eyes, he sees her staring up at them. Through the water. 'Hey, Mark! Let her up!'

o   o   o

Down in the suds. Feeling sleepy. The phone rings, startling her. Wrapped in a towel, she goes to answer. 'No, he's not here, Mrs Tucker.' Strange. Married people act pretty funny sometimes. The baby is awake and screaming. Dirty, a real mess. Oh boy, there's a lot of things she'd rather be doing than babysitting in this madhouse. She decides to wash the baby off in her own bathwater. She removes her towel, unplugs the tub, lowers the water level so the baby can sit. Glancing back over her shoulder, she sees Jimmy staring at her. 'Go back to bed, Jimmy!' 'I have to go to the bathroom.' 'Good grief, Jimmy! It looks like you already have!' The phone rings. She doesn't bother with the towel what can Jimmy see he hasn't already seen? – and goes to answer. 'No, Jack, and that's final.' Sirens, on the TV, as the police move in. But wasn't that the channel with the love story? Ambulance maybe. Get this over with so she can at least catch the news. 'Get those wet pyjamas off, Jimmy, and I'll find clean ones. Maybe you better get in the tub, too.' 'I think something's wrong with the baby,' he says. 'It's down in the water and it's not swimming or anything.'

o   o   o

She's staring up at them from the rug. They slap her. Nothing happens. 'You just tilted her, man!' Mark says softly. 'We gotta get outa here!' Two little kids are standing wide-eyed in the doorway. Mark looks hard at Jack. 'No, Mark, they're just little kids . . .!' 'We gotta, man, or we're dead.'

o   o   o

'Dolly! My God! Dolly, I can explain!' She glowers down at them, her ripped girdle around her ankles. 'What the four of you are doing in the bathtub with *my* babysitter?' she says sourly. 'I can hardly wait!'

o   o   o

Police sirens wail, lights flash. 'I heard the scream!' somebody shouts. 'There were two boys!' 'I saw a man!' 'She was running with the baby!' 'My God!' somebody screams, 'they're *all* dead!' Crowds come running. Spotlights probe the bushes.

o   o   o

'Harry, where the hell you been?' his wife whines, glaring blearily up at him from the carpet. 'I can explain,' he says. 'Hey, whatsamatter, Harry?' his host asks, smeared with butter for some goddamn reason. 'You look like you just seen a ghost!' Where did he leave his drink! Everybody's laughing, everybody except Dolly, whose cheeks are streaked with tears. 'Hey, Harry, you won't let them take me to a rest home, will you, Harry?'

o   o   o

10.00. The dishes done, children to bed, her books read, she watches the news on television. Sleepy. The man's voice is gentle, soothing. She dozes – awakes with a start: a babysitter? Did the announcer say something about a babysitter?

o   o   o

'Just want to catch the weather,' the host says, switching on the TV. Most of the guests are leaving, but the Tuckers stay to watch the news. As it comes on, the announcer is saying something about a babysitter. The host switches channels. 'They got a better weatherman on four,' he explains. 'Wait!' says Mrs Tucker. 'There was something about a babysitter . . .!' The host switches back. 'Details have not yet been released by the police,' the announcer says. 'Harry, maybe we'd better go . . .'

o   o   o

They stroll casually out of the drugstore, run into a buddy of theirs. 'Hey! Did you hear about the babysitter?' the guy asks. Mark grunts, glances at Jack. 'Got a smoke?' he asks the guy.

o   o   o

'I think I hear the baby screaming!' Mrs Tucker cries, running across the lawn from the drive.

o   o   o

She wakes, startled, to find Mr Tucker hovering over her. 'I must have dozed off!' she exclaims. 'Did you hear the news about the babysitter?' Mrs Tucker asks. 'Part of it,' she says, rising. 'Too bad, wasn't it?' Mr Tucker is watching the report of the ball scores and golf tournaments. 'I'll drive you home in just a minute, dear,' he says. 'Why, how nice!' Mrs Tucker exclaims from the kitchen. 'The dishes are all done!'

o   o   o

'What can I say, Dolly?' the host says with a sigh, twisting the buttered strands of her ripped girdle between his fingers. 'Your children are murdered, your husband gone, a corpse in your bathtub, and your house is wrecked. I'm sorry. But what can I say?' On the TV, the news is over, and they're selling aspirin. 'Hell, I don't know,' she says. 'Let's see what's on the late late movie.'

CARLOS FUENTES, born in 1929, is perhaps the best known of the Mexican novelists. Most of his work has been strongly socially and politically oriented, including *Where the Air Is Clear* and *The Death of Artemio Cruz*. Fuentes has also published short stories, many in the style of Henry James. His latest collection, as yet untranslated, is *Cantar de Ciegos* (1964).

aura

CARLOS FUENTES

Man hunts and struggles. Woman intrigues and dreams; she is the mother of fantasy, the mother of the gods. She has second sight, the wings that enable her to fly to the infinite of desire and the imagination ... The gods are like men: they are born and they die on a woman's breast ...

JULES MICHELET

I

You're reading the advertisement: an offer like this isn't made every day. You read it and reread it. It seems to be addressed to you and nobody else. You don't even notice when the ash from your cigarette falls into the cup of tea you ordered in this cheap, dirty café. You read it again. 'Wanted, young historian, conscientious, neat. Perfect knowledge of colloquial French. Youth ... knowledge of French, preferably after living in France for a while ... Four thousand pesos a month, all meals, comfortable bedroom-study.' All that's missing is your name. The advertisement should have two more words, in bigger, blacker type: Felipe

Montero. Wanted, Felipe Montero, formerly on scholarship at the Sorbonne, historian full of useless facts, accustomed to digging among yellowed documents, part-time teacher in private schools, nine hundred pesos a month. But if you read that, you'd be suspicious, and take it as a joke. 'Address, Donceles 815.' No telephone; come in person.

You leave a tip, reach for your briefcase, get up. You wonder if another young historian, in the same situation you are, has seen this same advertisement, has got ahead of you and taken the job already. You walk down to the corner, trying to forget this idea. As you wait for the bus, you run over the dates you must have on the tip of your tongue so that your sleepy pupils will respect you. The bus is coming now, and you're staring at the tips of your black shoes. You've got to be prepared. You put your hand in your pocket, search among the coins, and finally take out thirty centavos. You've got to be prepared. You grab the handrail – the bus slows down but doesn't stop – and jump aboard. Then you shove your way forward, pay the driver the thirty centavos, squeeze yourself in among the passengers already standing in the aisle, hang on to the overhead rail, press your briefcase tighter under your left arm, and automatically put your left hand over the back pocket where you keep your wallet.

This day is just like any other day, and you don't remember the advertisement until the next morning, when you sit down in the same café and order breakfast and open your newspaper. You come to the advertising section and there it is again: *young historian*. The job is still open. You reread the advertisement, lingering over the final words: four thousand pesos.

It's surprising to know that anyone lives on Donceles Street. You always thought that nobody lived in the old centre of the city. You walk slowly, trying to pick out the number 815 in that conglomeration of old colonial mansions, all of them converted into repair shops, jewellery shops, shoe stores, drugstores. The numbers have been changed, painted over, confused. A 13 next to a 200. An old plaque reading 47 over a scrawl in blurred charcoal: *now* 924. You look up at the second stories. Up there, everything is the same as it was. The jukeboxes don't disturb them. The mercury streetlights don't shine in. The cheap merchandise on sale along the street doesn't have any effect on that upper level . . . on the Baroque harmony of the carved stones; on the battered stone saints with pigeons clustering on their shoulders; on the latticed balconies, the copper gutters, the sandstone gargoyles; on the greenish curtains that darken the long windows; on that window from which someone draws back when you look at it. You gaze at the fanciful vines carved over the doorway, then lower your eyes to the peeling wall and discover 815, *formerly* 69.

You rap vainly with the knocker, that copper head of a dog, so worn and smooth that it resembles the head of a canine foetus in a museum of natural science. It seems as if the dog is grinning at you and you let go of the cold metal. The door opens at the first light push of your fingers, but before going in you give a last look over your shoulder, frowning at the long line of stalled cars that growl, honk, and belch out the unhealthy fumes of their impatience. You try to retain some single image of that indifferent outside world.

You close the door behind you and peer into the darkness of a roofed alleyway. It must be a patio of some sort, because you can smell the mould, the dampness of the plants, the rotting roots, the thick drowsy aroma. There isn't any light to guide you, and you're searching in your coat pocket for the box of matches when a sharp, thin voice tells you, from a distance: 'No, it isn't necessary. Please. Walk thirteen steps forward and you'll come to a stairway at your right. Come up, please. There are twenty-two steps. Count them.'

Thirteen. To the right. Twenty-two.

The dank smell of the plants is all around you as you count out your steps, first on the paving stones, then on the creaking wood, spongy from the dampness. You count to twenty-two in a low voice and then stop, with the matchbox in your hand, the briefcase under your arm. You knock on a door that smells of old pine. There isn't any knocker. Finally you push it open. Now you can feel a carpet under your feet, a thin carpet, badly laid. It makes you trip and almost fall. Then you notice the greyish, filtered light that reveals some of the humps.

'Señora,' you say, because you seem to remember a woman's voice. 'Señora . . .'

'Now turn to the left. The first door. Please be so kind.'

You push the door open: you don't expect any of them to be latched, you know they all open at a push. The scattered lights are braided in your eyelashes, as if you were seeing them through a silken net. All you can make out are the dozens of flickering lights. At last you can see that they're votive lights, all set on brackets or hung between unevenly spaced panels. They cast a faint glow on the silver objects, the crystal flasks, the gilt-framed mirrors. Then you see the bed in the shadows beyond, and the feeble movement of a hand that seems to be beckoning to you.

But you can't see her face until you turn your back on that galaxy of religious lights. You stumble to the foot of the bed, and have to go around it in order to get to the head of it. A tiny figure is almost lost in its immensity. When you reach out your hand, you don't touch another hand, you touch the ears and thick fur of a creature that's chewing silently and steadily, looking up at you with its glowing red eyes. You smile and stroke the rabbit that's crouched beside her hand. Finally you shake hands, and her cold fingers remain for a long while in your sweating palm.

'I'm Felipe Montero. I read your advertisement.'

'Yes, I know. I'm sorry, there aren't any chairs.'

'That's all right. Don't worry about it.'

'Good. Please let me see your profile. No, I can't see it well enough. Turn towards the light. That's right. Excellent.'

'I read your advertisement . . .'

'Yes, of course. Do you think you're qualified? *Avez-vous fait des études?*'

'*A Paris, Madame.*'

'*Ah, oui, ça me fait plaisir, toujours, toujours, d'entendre . . . oui . . . vous savez . . . on était tellement habitué . . . et après . . .*'

You move aside so that the light from the candles and the reflections from the silver and crystal show you the silk coif that must cover a head of very white hair and that frames a face so old it's almost childlike. Her whole body is covered by the sheets and the feather pillows and the high, tightly buttoned white collar, all except for her arms, which are wrapped in a shawl, and her pallid hands resting on her stomach. You can only stare at her face until a movement of the rabbit lets you glance furtively at the crusts and bits of bread scattered on the worn-out red silk of the pillows.

'I'll come directly to the point. I don't have many years ahead of me, Señor Montero, and therefore I decided to break a lifelong rule and place an advertisement in the newspaper . . .'

'Yes, that's why I'm here.'

'Of course. So you accept.'

'Well, I'd like to know a little more . . .'

'Yes. You're wondering.'

She sees you glance at the night table, the different-coloured bottles, the glasses, the aluminium spoons, the row of pill-boxes, the other glasses – all stained with whitish liquids – on the floor within reach of her hand. Then you notice that the bed is hardly raised above the level of the floor. Suddenly the rabbit jumps down and disappears in the shadows.

'I can offer you four thousand pesos.'

'Yes, that's what the advertisement said today.'

'Ah, then it came out.'

'Yes, it came out.'

'It has to do with the memoirs of my husband, General Llorente. They must be put in order before I die. I want them to be published. I decided that a short time ago.'

'But the General himself? Wouldn't he be able to . . .'

'He died sixty years ago, Señor. They're his unfinished memoirs. They have to be completed before I die.'

'But . . .'

'I can tell you everything. You'll learn to write in my husband's own style. You'll only have to arrange and read his manuscripts to become fascinated by his style . . . his clarity . . . his . . .'

'Yes, I understand.'

'Saga, Saga. Where are you? *Ici*, Saga . . .'

'Who?'

'My companion.'

'The rabbit?'

'Yes. She'll come back.'

When you raise your eyes, which you've been keeping lowered, her lips are closed but you can hear her words again — 'She'll come back' — as if the old lady were pronouncing them at that instant. Her lips remain still. You look behind you and you're almost blinded by the gleam from the religious objects. When you look at her again you see that her eyes have opened very wide, and that they're clear, liquid, enormous, almost the same colour as the yellowish whites around them, so that only the black dots of the pupils mar that clarity. It's lost a moment later in the heavy folds of her lowered eyelids, as if she wanted to protect that glance which is now hiding at the back of its dry cave.

'Then you'll stay here. Your room is upstairs. It's sunny there.'

'It might be better if I didn't trouble you, Señora. I can go on living where I am and work on the manuscripts there.'

'My conditions are that you have to live here. There isn't much time left.'

'I don't know if . . .'

'Aura . . .'

The old woman moves for the first time since you entered her room. As she reaches out her hand again you sense that agitated breathing beside you, and another hand reaches out to touch the Señora's fingers. You look around and a girl is standing there, a girl whose whole body you can't see because she's standing so close to you and her arrival was so unexpected, without the slightest sound — not even those sounds that can't be heard but are real anyway because they're remembered immediately afterwards, because in spite of everything they're louder than the silence that accompanies them.

'I told you she'd come back.'

'Who?'

'Aura. My companion. My niece.'

'Good afternoon.'

The girl nods and at the same instant the old lady imitates her gesture.

'This is Señor Montero. He's going to live with us.'

You move a few steps so that the light from the candles won't blind you. The girl keeps her eyes closed, her hands folded at her side. She doesn't look at you at first, then little by little she opens her eyes as if she were afraid of the light. Finally you can see that those eyes are sea-green and that they surge, break to foam, grow calm again, then surge again like a wave. You look into them and tell yourself it isn't true, because they're beautiful green eyes just like all the beautiful green eyes you've ever known. But you can't deceive yourself: those eyes do surge, do change, as if offering you a landscape that only you can see and desire.

'Yes. I'm going to live with you.'

II

The old woman laughs sharply and tells you that she is grateful for your kindness and the girl will show you to your room. You're thinking about the salary of four thousand pesos, and how the work should be pleasant because you like these jobs of careful research that don't include physical effort or going from one place to another or meeting people you don't want to meet. You're thinking about this as you follow her out of the room, and you discover that you've got to follow her with your ears instead of your eyes: you follow the rustle of her skirt, the rustle of taffeta, and you're anxious now to look into her eyes again. You climb the stairs behind that sound in the darkness, and you're still unused to the obscurity. You remember it must be about six in the afternoon, and the flood of light surprises you when Aura opens the door to your bedroom – another door without a latch – and steps aside to tell you: 'This is your room. We'll expect you for supper in an hour.'

She moves away with that same faint rustle of taffeta, and you weren't able to see her face again.

You close the door and look up at the skylight that serves as a roof. You smile when you find that the evening light is blinding compared with the darkness in the rest of the house, and smile again when you try out the mattress on the gilded metal bed. Then you glance around the room: a red wool rug, olive-and-gold wallpaper, an easy chair covered in red velvet, an old walnut desk with a green leather top, an old Argand lamp with its soft glow for your nights of research, and a bookshelf over the desk in reach of your hand. You walk over to the other door, and on pushing it open you discover an outmoded bathroom: a four-legged bathtub with little flowers painted on the porcelain, a blue hand-basin, an old-fashioned toilet. You look at yourself in the large oval mirror on the door of the wardrobe – it's also walnut – in the bathroom hallway. You move your heavy eyebrows and wide thick lips, and your breath fogs the mirror. You close your black eyes, and when you open them again the mirror has cleared. You stop holding your breath and run your hand through your dark, limp hair; you touch your fine profile, your lean cheeks; and when your breath hides your face again you're repeating her name: 'Aura'.

After smoking two cigarettes while lying on the bed, you get up, put on your jacket, and comb your hair. You push the door open and try to remember the route you followed coming up. You'd like to leave the door open so that the lamplight could guide you, but that's impossible because the springs close it behind you. You could enjoy playing with that door, swinging it back and forth. You don't do it. You could take the lamp down with you. You don't do it. This house will always be in darkness, and you've got to learn it and relearn it by touch. You grope your way like a blind man, with your arms stretched out wide, feeling your way along the wall, and by accident you turn on the light switch. You stop and blink in the bright middle of that long, empty hall. At the end of it you can see the banister and the spiral staircase.

You count the stairs as you go down: another custom you've got to learn in Señora Llorente's house. You take a step backward when you see the reddish eyes of the rabbit, which turns its back on you and goes hopping away.

You don't have time to stop in the lower hallway because Aura is waiting for you at a half-open stained-glass door, with a candelabra in her hand. You walk towards her, smiling, but you stop when you hear the painful yowling of a number of cats – yes, you stop to listen, next to Aura, to be sure that they're cats – and then follow her to the parlour.

'It's the cats,' Aura tells you. 'There's lots of rats in this part of the city.'

You go through the parlour: furniture upholstered in faded silk; glass-fronted cabinets containing porcelain figurines, musical clocks, medals, glass balls; carpets with Persian designs; pictures of rustic scenes; green velvet curtains. Aura is dressed in green.

'Is your room comfortable?'

'Yes. But I have to get my things from the place where . . .'

'It won't be necessary. The servant has already gone for them.'

'You shouldn't have bothered.'

You follow her into the dining-room. She places the candelabra in the middle of the table. The room feels damp and cold. The four walls are panelled in dark wood, carved in Gothic style, with fretwork arches and large rosettes. The cats have stopped yowling. When you sit down, you notice that four places have been set. There are two large, covered plates and an old, grimy bottle.

Aura lifts the cover from one of the plates. You breathe in the pungent odour of the liver and onions she serves you, then you pick up the old bottle and fill the cut-glass goblets with that thick red liquid. Out of curiosity you try to read the label on the wine bottle, but the grime has obscured it. Aura serves you some whole boiled tomatoes from the other plate.

'Excuse me,' you say, looking at the two extra places, the two empty chairs, 'but are you expecting someone else?'

Aura goes on serving the tomatoes. 'No. Señora Consuelo feels a little ill tonight. She won't be joining us.'

'Señora Consuelo? Your aunt?'

'Yes. She'd like you to go in and see her after supper.'

You eat in silence. You drink that thick wine, occasionally shifting your glance so that Aura won't catch you in the hypnotized stare that you can't control. You'd like to fix the girl's features in your mind. Every time you glance away you forget them again, and an irresistible urge forces you to look at her once more. As usual, she has her eyes lowered. While you're searching for the pack of cigarettes in your coat pocket, you run across that big key, and remember, and say to Aura: 'Ah I forgot that one of the drawers in my desk is locked. I've got my papers in it.'

And she murmurs: 'Then you want to go out?' She says it as a reproach.

You feel confused, and reach out your hand to her with the key dangling from one finger.

'It isn't important. The servants can go for them tomorrow.'

But she avoids touching your hand, keeping her own hands on her lap. Finally she looks up, and once again you question your senses, blaming the wine for your bewilderment, for the dizziness brought on by those shining, clear green eyes, and you stand up after Aura does, running your hand over the wooden back of the Gothic chair, without daring to touch her bare shoulder or her motionless head.

You make an effort to control yourself, diverting your attention away from her by listening to the imperceptible movement of a door behind you – it must lead to the kitchen – or by separating the two different elements that make up the room: the compact circle of light around the candelabra, illuminating the table and one carved wall, and the larger circle of darkness surrounding it. Finally you have the courage to go up to her, take her hand, open it, and place your key-ring in her smooth palm as a token.

She closes her hand, looks up at you, and murmurs, 'Thank you.' Then she rises and walks quickly out of the room.

You sit down in Aura's chair, stretch your legs, and light a cigarette, feeling a pleasure you've never felt before, one that you knew was part of you but that only now you're experiencing fully, setting it free, bringing it out because this time you know it'll be answered and won't be lost . . . And Señora Consuelo is waiting for you, as Aura said. She's waiting for you after supper . . .

You leave the dining-room, and with the candelabra in your hand you walk through the parlour and the hallway. The first door you come to is the old lady's. You rap on it with your knuckles, but there isn't any answer. You knock again. Then you push the door open because she's waiting for you. You enter cautiously, murmuring: 'Señora . . . Señora . . .'

She doesn't hear you, for she's kneeling in front of that wall of religious objects, with her head resting on her clenched fists. You see her from a distance: she's kneeling there in her coarse woollen nightgown, with her head sunk into her narrow shoulders; she's thin, even emaciated, like a medieval sculpture; her legs are like two sticks, and they're inflamed with erysipelas. While you're thinking of the continual rubbing of that rough wool against her skin, she suddenly raises her fists and strikes feebly at the air, as if she were doing battle against the images you can make out as you tiptoe closer: Christ, the Virgin, St Sebastian, St Lucia, the Archangel Michael, and the grinning demons in an old print, the only happy figures in that iconography of sorrow and wrath, happy because they're jabbing their pitchforks into the flesh of the damned, pouring cauldrons of boiling water on them, violating the women, getting drunk, enjoying all the liberties forbidden to the saints. You approach that central image, which is surrounded by the tears of Our Lady of Sorrows, the blood of Our Crucified Lord, the delight of Lucifer, the anger of the Archangel, the viscera preserved in bottles of alcohol, the silver heart: Señora Consuelo, kneeling, threatens them with her fists, stammering the words you can hear as you move even closer: 'Come, City of God! Gabriel, sound your trumpet! Ah, how long the world takes to die!'

She beats her breast until she collapses in front of the images and candles in a spasm of coughing. You raise her by the elbow, and as you gently help her to the bed you're surprised at her smallness: she's almost a little girl, bent over almost double. You realize that without your assistance she'd have had to get back to bed on her hands and knees. You help her into that wide bed with its bread crumbs and old feather pillows, and cover her up, and wait till her breathing is back to normal, while the involuntary tears run down her parchment cheeks.

'Excuse me . . . excuse me, Señor Montero . . . Old ladies have nothing left but . . . the pleasures of devotion . . . Give me my handkerchief, please.'

'Señorita Aura told me . . .'

'Yes, of course. I don't want to lose any time. We should . . . we should begin working as soon as possible . . . Thank you . . .'

'You should try to rest.'

'Thank you . . . Here . . .'

The old lady raises her hand to her collar, unbuttons it, and lowers her head to remove the frayed purple ribbon that she hands to you. It's heavy because there's a copper key hanging from it.

'Over in that corner . . . Open that trunk and bring me the papers at the right, on top of the others . . . They're tied with a yellow ribbon . . .'

'I can't see very well . . .'

'Ah, yes . . . it's just that I'm so accustomed to the darkness. To my right . . . keep going till you come to the trunk . . . They've walled us in, Señor Montero. They've built up all around us and blocked off the light. They've tried to force me to sell, but I'll die first. This house is full of memories for us. They won't take us out of here till I'm dead . . . Yes, that's it. Thank you. You can begin reading this part. I'll give you the others later. Goodnight, Señor Montero. Thank you. Look, the candelabra has gone out. Light it outside the door, please. No, no, you can keep the key. I trust you.'

'Señora, there's a rat's nest in that corner . . .'

'Rats? I never go over there . . .'

'You should bring the cats in here.'

'The cats? What cats? Goodnight. I'm going to sleep. I'm very tired.'

'Goodnight.'

III

That same evening you read those yellow papers written in mustard-coloured ink, some of them with holes where a careless ash had fallen, others heavily flyspecked. General Llorente's French doesn't have the merits his wife attributed to it. You tell yourself you can make considerable improvements in the style, can tighten up his rambling account of past events: his childhood on an *hacienda* in Oaxaca, his military studies in France, his friendship with the Duke of Morny and the intimates of Napoleon III, his return to Mexico on the staff of Maximilian, the imperial ceremonies and gatherings, the battles, the defeat in 1867, his exile in France. Nothing that hasn't been described before. As you undress you think of the old lady's distorted notions, the value she attributes to these memoirs. You smile as you get into bed, thinking of the four thousand pesos.

You sleep soundly until a flood of light wakes you up at six in the morning; that glass roof doesn't have any curtains. You bury your head under the pillow and try to go back to sleep. Ten minutes later you give it up and walk into the bathroom, where you find all your things neatly arranged on a table and your few clothes hanging in the wardrobe. Just as you finish shaving the early morning silence is broken by that painful, desperate yowling.

You try to find out where it's coming from: you open the door to the hallway, but you can't hear anything from there: those cries are coming from up above, from the skylight. You jump up on the chair, from the chair on to the desk, and by supporting yourself on the bookshelf you can reach the skylight. You open one of the windows and pull yourself up to look out at that side garden, that square of yew trees and brambles where five, six, seven cats – you can't count them, can't hold yourself up there for more than a second – are all twined together, all writhing in flames and giving off a dense smoke that reeks of burnt fur. As you get down again you wonder if you really saw it: perhaps you only imagined it from those dreadful cries that continue, grow less, and finally stop.

You put on your shirt, brush off your shoes with a piece of paper, and listen to the sound of a bell that seems to run through the passageways of the house until it arrives at your door. You look out into the hallway: Aura is walking along it with a bell in her hand. She turns her head to look at you and tells you that breakfast is ready. You try to detain her but she goes down the spiral staircase, still ringing that black-painted bell as if she were trying to wake up a whole asylum, a whole boarding school.

You follow her in your shirt sleeves, but when you reach the down-stairs hallway you can't find her. The door of the old lady's bedroom opens behind you and you see a hand that reaches out from behind the partly opened door, sets a chamberpot in the hallway, and disappears again, closing the door.

In the dining-room your breakfast is already on the table, but this time only one place has been set. You eat quickly, return to the hallway, and knock at Señora Consuelo's door. Her sharp, weak voice tells you to come in. Nothing has changed: the perpetual shadows, the glow of the votive lights and the silver objects.

'Good morning, Señor Montero. Did you sleep well?'

'Yes. I read till quite late.'

The old lady waves her hand as if in a gesture of dismissal. 'No, no, no. Don't give me your opinion. Work on those pages and when you've finished I'll give you the others.'

'Very well. Señora, would I be able to go into the garden?'

'What garden, Señor Montero?'

'The one that's outside my room.'

'This house doesn't have any garden. We lost our garden when they built up all around us.'

'I think I could work better outdoors.'

'This house has only got that dark patio where you came in. My niece is growing some shade plants there. But that's all.'

'It's all right, Señora.'

'I'd like to rest during the day. But come to see me tonight.'

'Very well, Señora.'

You spend all morning working on the papers, copying out the passages you intend to keep, rewriting the ones you think are especially bad, smoking one cigarette after another, and reflecting that you ought to space your work so that the job lasts as long as possible. If you can manage to save at least twelve thousand pesos, you can spend a year on nothing but your own work, which you've postponed and almost forgotten. Your great, inclusive work on the Spanish discoveries and conquests in the New World. A work that sums up all the scattered chronicles, makes them intelligible, and discovers the resemblances among all the undertakings and adventures of Spain's Golden Age and all the human prototypes and major accomplishments of the Renaissance. You end up by putting aside the General's tedious pages and starting to compile the dates and summaries of your own work. Time passes and you don't look at your watch until you hear the bell again. Then you put on your coat and go down to the dining-room.

Aura is already seated. This time Señora Llorente is at the head of the table, wrapped in her shawl and nightgown and coif, hunching over her plate. But the fourth place has also been set. You note it in passing: it doesn't bother you any more. If the price of your future creative liberty is to put up with all the manias of this old woman, you can pay it easily. As you watch her eating her soup you try to figure out her age. There's a time after which it's impossible to detect the passing of the years, and Señora Consuelo crossed that frontier a long time ago. The General hasn't mentioned her in what you've already read of the memoirs. But if the General was 42 at the time of the French invasion, and died in 1901, forty years later, he must have died at the age of 82. He must have married the Señora after the defeat at Querétaro and his exile. But she would only have been a girl at that time . . .

The dates escape you because now the Señora is talking in that thin, sharp voice of hers, that birdlike chirping. She's talking to Aura and you listen to her as you eat, hearing her long list of complaints, pains, suspected illnesses, more complaints about the cost of medicines, the dampness of the house, and so forth. You'd like to break in on this domestic conversation to ask about the servant who went for your things yesterday, the servant you've never even glimpsed and who never waits on table. You're about to ask about him but you're suddenly surprised to realize that up to this moment Aura hasn't said a word and is eating with a sort of mechanical fatality, as if she were waiting for some outside impulse before picking up her knife and fork, cutting a piece of liver – yes, it's liver again, apparently the favourite dish in this house – and carrying it to her mouth. You glance quickly from the aunt to the niece, but at that moment the Señora becomes motionless and at the same moment Aura puts her knife on her plate and also becomes motionless, and you remember that the Señora had put down her knife only a fraction of a second earlier.

There are several minutes of silence: you finish eating while they sit there rigid as statues, watching you. At last the Señora says, 'I'm very tired. I ought not to eat at the table. Come, Aura, help me to my room.'

The Señora tries to hold your attention: she looks directly at you so that you'll keep looking at her, although what she's saying is aimed at Aura. You have to make an effort in order to evade that look, which once again is wide, clear, and yellowish, free of the veils and wrinkles that usually obscure it. Then you glance at Aura, who is staring fixedly at nothing and silently moving her lips. She gets up with a motion like those you associate with dreaming, takes the arm of the bent old lady, and slowly helps her from the dining-room.

Alone now, you help yourself to the coffee that has been there since the beginning of the meal, the cold coffee you sip as you wrinkle your brow and ask yourself if the Señora doesn't have some secret power over her niece: if the girl, your beautiful Aura in her green dress, isn't kept in this dark old house against her will. But it would be so easy for her to escape while the Señora was asleep in her shadowy room. You tell yourself that her hold over the girl must be terrible. And you consider the way out that occurs to your imagination: perhaps Aura is waiting for you to release her from the chains in which the perverse, insane old lady, for some unknown reason, has bound her. You remember Aura as she was a few moments ago, spiritless, hypnotized by her terror, incapable of speaking in front of the tyrant, moving her lips in silence as if she were silently begging you to set her free; so enslaved that she imitated every gesture of the Señora, as if she were permitted to do only what the Señora did.

You rebel against this tyranny: you walk towards the other door, the one at the foot of the staircase, the one next to the old lady's room: that's where Aura must live, because there's no other room in the house. You push the door open and go in. This room is dark also, with whitewashed walls, and the only decoration is an enormous black

Christ. At the left there's a door that must lead into the widow's bedroom. You go up to it on tiptoe, put your hands against it, then decide not to open it: you should talk with Aura alone.

And if Aura wants your help she'll come to your room. You go up there for a while, forgetting the yellowed manuscripts and your own notebooks, thinking only about the beauty of your Aura. And the more you think about her, the more you make her yours, not only because of her beauty and your desire, but also because you want to set her free: you've found a moral basis for your desire, and you feel innocent and self-satisfied. When you hear the bell again you don't go down to supper because you can't bear another scene like the one at the middle of the day. Perhaps Aura will realize it and come up to look for you after supper.

You force yourself to go on working on the papers. When you're bored with them you undress slowly, get into bed, and fall asleep at once, and for the first time in years you dream, dream of only one thing, of a fleshless hand that comes towards you with a bell, screaming that you should go away, everyone should go away; and when that face with its empty eye sockets comes close to yours, you wake up with a muffled cry, sweating, and feel those gentle hands caressing your face, those lips murmuring in a low voice, consoling you and asking you for affection. You reach out your hands to find that other body, that naked body with a key dangling from its neck, and when you recognize the key you recognize the woman who is lying over you, kissing you, kissing your whole body. You can't see her in the black of the starless night, but you can smell the fragrance of the patio plants in her hair, can feel her smooth, eager body in your arms: you kiss her again and don't ask her to speak.

When you free yourself, exhausted, from her embrace, you hear her first whisper: 'You're my husband.' You agree. She tells you it's daybreak, then leaves you, saying that she'll wait for you that night in her room. You agree again and then fall asleep, relieved, unburdened, emptied of desire, still feeling the touch of Aura's body, her trembling, her surrender.

It's hard for you to wake up. There are several knocks on the door, and at last you get out of bed, groaning and still half-asleep. Aura, on the other side of the door, tells you not to open it: she says that Señora Consuelo wants to talk with you, is waiting for you in her room.

Ten minutes later you enter the widow's sanctuary. She's propped up against the pillows, motionless, her eyes hidden by those drooping, wrinkled, dead-white lids; you notice the puffy wrinkles under her eyes, the utter weariness of her skin.

Without opening her eyes she asks you, 'Did you bring the key to the trunk?'

'Yes, I think so . . . Yes, here it is.'

'You can read the second part. It's in the same place. It's tied with a blue ribbon.'

You go over to the trunk, this time with a certain disgust: the rats are swarming around it, peering at you with their glittering eyes from the cracks in the rotted floorboards, galloping towards the holes in the rotted walls. You open the trunk and take out the second batch of papers, then return to the foot of the bed. Señora Consuelo is petting her white rabbit. A sort of croaking laugh emerges from her buttoned-up throat, and she asks you, 'Do you like animals?'

'No, not especially. Perhaps because I've never had any.'

'They're good friends. Good companions. Above all when you're old and lonely.'

'Yes, they must be.'

'They're always themselves, Señor Montero. They don't have any pretensions.'

'What did you say his name is?'

'The rabbit? She's Saga. She's very intelligent. She follows her instincts. She's natural and free.'

'I thought it was a male rabbit.'

'Oh? Then you still can't tell the difference.'

'Well, the important thing is that you don't feel all alone.'

'They want us to be alone, Señor Montero, because they tell us that solitude is the only way to achieve saintliness. They forget that in solitude the temptation is even greater.'

'I don't understand, Señora.'

'Ah, it's better that you don't. Get back to work now, please.'

You turn your back on her, walk to the door, leave her room. In the hallway you clench your teeth. Why don't you have courage enough to tell her that you love the girl? Why don't you go back and tell her, once and for all, that you're planning to take Aura away with you when you finish the job? You approach the door again and start pushing it open, still uncertain, and through the crack you see Señora Consuelo standing up, erect, transformed, with a military tunic in her arms: a blue tunic with gold buttons, red epaulets, bright medals with crowned eagles – a tunic the old lady bites ferociously, kisses tenderly, drapes over her shoulders as she performs a few teetering dance steps. You close the door.

Yes: 'She was fifteen years old when I met her,' you read in the second part of the memoirs. '*Elle avait quinze ans lorsque je l'ai connue et, si j'ose le dire, ce sont ses yeux verts qui ont fait ma perdition.*' Consuelo's green eyes, Consuelo who was only fifteen in 1867, when General Llorente married her and took her with him into exile in Paris. '*Ma jeune poupée,*' he wrote in a moment of inspiration, '*ma jeune poupée aux yeux verts; je t'ai comblée d'amour.*' He described the house they lived in, the outings, the dances, the carriages, the world of the Second Empire, but all in a dull enough way. '*J'ai même supporté ta haine des chats, moi qui aimais tellement les jolies bêtes . . .*' One day he found her torturing a cat; she had it between her legs, with her crinoline skirt pulled up, and he didn't know how to attract her attention because it seemed to him that '*tu faisais ça d'une façon si innocente, par pur enfantillage*', and in fact it excited him so much that if you can believe what he wrote, he made love to her that night with extraordinary passion, '*parce que tu m'avais dit que torturer les chats était ta manière à toi de rendre notre amour favorable, par un sacrifice symbolique . . .*' You've figured it up: Señora Consuelo must be 109. Her husband died fifty-nine years ago. '*Tu sais si bien t'habiller, ma douce Consuelo, toujours drappée dans de velours verts, verts comme tes yeux. Je pense que tu seras toujours belle, même dans cent ans . . .*' Always dressed in green. Always beautiful, even after a hundred years. '*Tu es si fière de ta beauté; que ne ferais tu pas pour rester toujours jeune?*'

IV

Now you know why Aura is living in this house: to perpetuate the illusion of youth and beauty in that poor, crazed old lady. Aura, kept here like a mirror, like one more icon on that votive wall with its clustered offerings, preserved hearts, imagined saints and demons.

You put the manuscript aside and go downstairs, suspecting there's only one place Aura could be in the morning: the place that greedy old woman has assigned to her.

Yes, you find her in the kitchen, at the moment she's beheading a kid: the vapour that rises from the open throat, the smell of spilt blood, the animal's glazed eyes, all give you nausea. Aura is wearing a ragged blood-stained dress and her hair is dishevelled; she looks at you without recognition and goes on with her butchering.

You leave the kitchen: this time you'll really speak to the old lady, really throw her greed and tyranny in her face. When you push open the door she's standing behind the veil of lights, performing a ritual with the empty air: one hand stretched out and clenched, as if holding something up, and the other clasped around an invisible object, striking again and again at the same place. Then she wipes her hands against her breast, sighs, and starts cutting the air again, as if – yes, you can see it clearly – as if she were skinning an animal . . .

You run through the hallway, the parlour, the dining-room, to where

Aura is slowly skinning the kid, absorbed in her work, heedless of your entrance or your words, looking at you as if you were made of air.

You climb up to your room, go in, and brace yourself against the door as if you were afraid someone would follow you: panting, sweating, victim of your horror, of your certainty. If something or someone should try to enter, you wouldn't be able to resist, you'd move away from the door, you'd let it happen. Frantically you drag the armchair over to that latchless door, push the bed up against it, then fall onto the bed, exhausted, drained of your willpower, with your eyes closed and your arms wrapped around your pillow ... the pillow that isn't yours ... nothing is yours.

You fall into a stupor, into the depths of a dream that's your only escape, your only means of saying no to insanity. 'She's crazy, she's crazy,' you repeat again and again to make yourself sleepy, and you can hear her again as she skins the imaginary kid with an imaginary knife. 'She's crazy, she's crazy ...'

in the depths of the dark abyss, in your silent dream with its mouths opening in silence, you see her coming towards you from the blackness of the abyss, you see her crawling towards you,

in silence,

moving her fleshless hand, coming towards you until her face touches yours and you see the old lady's bloody gums, her toothless gums, and you scream and she goes away again, moving her hand, sowing the abyss with the yellow teeth she carries in her bloodstained apron:

your scream is an echo of Aura's, she is standing in front of you in your dream, and she's screaming because someone's hands have ripped her green taffeta skirt in two, and then

she turns her head towards you

with the torn folds of the skirt in her hands, turns towards you and laughs silently, with the old lady's teeth superimposed on her own, while her legs, her naked legs, shatter into bits and fly towards the abyss ...

There's a knock at the door, then the sound of the bell, the supper bell. Your head aches so much that you can't make out the hands on the clock, but you know it must be late: above your head you can see the night clouds beyond the skylight. You get up painfully, dazed and hungry. You hold the glass pitcher under the faucet, wait for the water to run, fill the pitcher, then pour it into the basin. You wash your face, brush your teeth with your worn toothbrush that's clogged with greenish paste, dampen your hair – you don't notice you're doing all this in the wrong order – and comb it meticulously in front of the oval mirror on the walnut wardrobe. Then you tie your tie, put on your jacket, and go down to the empty dining-room, where only one place has been set: yours.

Beside your plate, under your napkin, there's an object you start caressing with your fingers: a clumsy little rag doll, filled with a powder that trickles from its badly sewn shoulder; its face is drawn with indian ink, and its body is naked, sketched with a few brushstrokes. You eat the cold supper – liver, tomatoes, wine – with your right hand while holding the doll in your left.

You eat mechanically, without noticing at first your own hypnotized attitude, but later you glimpse a reason for your oppressive sleep, your nightmare, and finally identify your sleepwalking movements with those of Aura and the old lady. You're suddenly disgusted by that horrible little doll, in which you begin to suspect a secret illness, a contagion. You let it fall to the floor. You wipe your lips with the napkin, look at your watch, and remember that Aura is waiting for you in her room.

You go cautiously up to Señora Consuelo's door, but there isn't a sound from within. You look at your watch again: it's barely nine o'clock. You decide to feel your way down to that dark, roofed patio you haven't been in since you came through it, without seeing anything, on the day you arrived here.

You touch the damp, mossy walls, breathe the perfumed air, and try to isolate the different elements you're breathing, to recognize the heavy, sumptuous aromas that surround you. The flicker of your match lights up the narrow, empty patio, where various plants are growing on each side in the loose, reddish earth. You can make out the tall, leafy forms that cast their shadows on the walls in the light of the match; but it burns down, singeing your fingers, and you have to light another one to finish seeing the flowers, fruits and plants you remember reading about in old chronicles, the forgotten herbs that are growing here so fragrantly and drowsily: the long, broad, downy leaves of the hen-bane; the twining stems with flowers that are yellow outside, red inside; the pointed, heart-shaped leaves of the nightshade; the ash-coloured down of the grape-mullein with its clustered flowers; the bushy gatheridge with its white blossoms; the belladonna. They come to life in the flare of your match, swaying gently with their shadows, while you recall the uses of these herbs that dilate the pupils, alleviate pain, reduce the pangs of childbirth, bring consolation, weaken the will, induce a voluptuous calm.

You're all alone with the perfumes when the third match burns out. You go up to the hallway slowly, listen again at Señora Consuelo's door, then tiptoe on to Aura's. You push it open without knocking and go into that bare room, where a circle of light reveals the bed, the huge Mexican crucifix, and the woman who comes towards you when the door is closed. Aura is dressed in green, in a green taffeta robe from which, as she approaches, her moon-pale thighs reveal themselves. The woman, you repeat as she comes close, the woman, not the girl of yesterday: the girl of yesterday – you touch Aura's fingers, her waist – couldn't have been more than 20; the woman of today – you caress her loose black hair, her pallid cheeks – seems to be 40. Between yesterday and today, something about her green eyes has turned hard; the red of her lips has strayed beyond their former outlines, as if she wanted to fix them in a happy grimace, a troubled smile: as if, like that plant in the patio, her smile combined the taste of honey and the taste of gall. You don't have time to think of anything more.

'Sit down on the bed, Felipe.'

'Yes.'

'We're going to play. You don't have to do anything. Let me do everything myself.'

Sitting on the bed, you try to make out the source of that diffuse, opaline light that hardly lets you distinguish the objects in the room, and the presence of Aura, from the golden atmosphere that surrounds them. She sees you looking up, trying to find where it comes from. You can tell from her voice that she's kneeling down in front of you.

'The sky is neither high nor low. It's over us and under us at the same time.'

She takes off your shoes and socks and caresses your bare feet.

You feel the warm water that bathes the soles of your feet, while she washes them with a heavy cloth, now and then casting furtive glances at that Christ carved from black wood. Then she dries your feet, takes you by the hand, fastens a few violets in her loose hair, and begins to hum a melody, a waltz, to which you dance with her, held by the murmur of her voice, gliding around to the slow, solemn rhythm she's setting, very different from the light movements of her hands, which unbutton your shirt, caress your chest, reach around to your back and grasp it. You also murmur that wordless song, that melody rising naturally from your throat: you glide around together, each time closer to the bed, until you muffle the song with your hungry kisses on Aura's mouth, until you stop the dance with your crushing kisses on her shoulders and breasts.

You're holding the empty robe in your hands. Aura, squatting on the bed, places an object against her closed thighs, caressing it, summoning you with her hand. She caresses that thin wafer, breaks it against her thighs, oblivious of the crumbs that roll down her hips: she offers you half of the wafer and you take it, place it in your mouth at the same time she does, and swallow it with difficulty. Then you fall on Aura's naked body, you fall on her naked arms, which are stretched out from one side of the bed to the other like the arms of the crucifix hanging on the wall, the black Christ with that scarlet silk wrapped around his thighs, his spread knees, his wounded side, his crown of thorns set on a tangled black wig with silver spangles. Aura opens up like an altar.

You murmur her name in her ear. You feel the woman's full arms against your back. You hear her warm voice in your ear: 'Will you love me forever?'

'Forever, Aura. I'll love you forever.'

'Forever? Do you swear it?'

'I swear it.'

'Even though I grow old? Even though I lose my beauty? Even though my hair turns white?'

'Forever, my love, forever.'

'Even if I die, Felipe? Will you love me forever, even if I die?'

'Forever, forever. I swear it. Nothing can separate us.'

'Come, Felipe, come . . .'

When you wake up, you reach out to touch Aura's shoulder, but you only touch the still-warm pillow and the white sheet that covers you.

You murmur her name.

You open your eyes and see her standing at the foot of the bed, smiling but not looking at you. She walks slowly towards the corner of the room, sits down on the floor, places her arms on the knees that emerge from the darkness you can't peer into, and strokes the wrinkled hand that comes forward from the lessening darkness: she's sitting at the feet of the old lady, of Señora Consuelo, who is seated in an armchair you hadn't noticed earlier: Señora Consuelo smiles at you, nodding her head, smiling at you along with Aura, who moves her head in rhythm with the old lady's; they both smile at you, thanking you. You lie back, without any will, thinking that the old lady has been in the room all the time;

you remember her movements, her voice, her dance,
though you keep telling yourself she wasn't there.

The two of them get up at the same moment, Consuelo from the chair, Aura from the floor. Turning their backs on you, they walk slowly towards the door that leads to the widow's bedroom, enter that room where the lights are forever trembling in front of the images, close the door behind them, and leave you to sleep in Aura's bed.

V

Your sleep is heavy and unsatisfying. In your dreams you had already felt the same vague melancholy, the weight on your diaphragm, the sadness that won't stop oppressing your imagination. Although you're sleeping in Aura's room, you're sleeping all alone, far from the body you believe you've possessed.

When you wake up, you look for another presence in the room, and realize it's not Aura who disturbs you but rather the double presence of something that was engendered during the night. You put your hands on your forehead, trying to calm your disordered senses: that dull melancholy is hinting to you in a low voice, the voice of memory and premonition, that you're seeking your other half, that the sterile conception last night engendered your own double.

And you stop thinking, because there are things even stronger than the imagination: the habits that force you to get up, look for a bathroom off this room without finding one, go out into the hallway rubbing your eyelids, climb the stairs tasting the thick bitterness of your tongue, enter your own room feeling the rough bristles on your chin, turn on the bathroom faucets and then slide into the warm water, letting yourself relax into forgetfulness.

But while you're drying yourself, you remember the old lady and the girl as they smiled at you before leaving the room arm in arm; you recall that whenever they're together they always do the same things: they embrace, smile, eat, speak, enter, leave, at the same time, as if one were imitating the other, as if the will of one depended on the existence of the other . . . You cut yourself lightly on one cheek as you think of these things while you shave; you make an effort to get control of yourself. When you finish shaving you count the objects in your travelling case, the bottles and tubes which the servant you've never seen brought over from your boarding house: you murmur the names of these objects, touch them, read the contents and instructions, pronounce the names of the manufacturers, keeping to those objects in order to forget that other one, the one without a name, without a label, without any rational consistency. What is Aura expecting of you? you ask yourself, closing the travelling case. What does she want, what does she want?

In answer you hear the dull rhythm of her bell in the corridor telling you breakfast is ready. You walk to the door without your shirt on. When you open it you find Aura there: it must be Aura because you see the green taffeta she always wears, though her face is covered with a green veil. You take her by the wrist, that slender wrist which trembles at your touch . . .

'Breakfast is ready,' she says, in the faintest voice you've ever heard.

'Aura. Let's stop pretending.'

'Pretending?'

'Tell me if Señora Consuelo keeps you from leaving, from living your own life. Why did she have to be there when you and I . . . Please tell me you'll go with me when . . .'

'Go away? Where?'

'Out of this house. Out into the world, to live together. You shouldn't feel bound to your aunt forever . . . Why all this devotion? Do you love her that much?'

'Love her?'

'Yes. Why do you have to sacrifice yourself this way?'

'Love her? She loves me. She sacrifices herself for me.'

'But she's an old woman, almost a corpse. You can't . . .'

'She has more life than I do. Yes, she's old and repulsive . . . Felipe, I don't want to become . . . to be like her . . . another . . .'

'She's trying to bury you alive. You've got to be reborn, Aura.'

'You have to die before you can be reborn . . . No, you don't understand. Forget about it, Felipe. Just have faith in me.'

'If you'd only explain.'

'Just have faith in me. She's going to be out today for the whole day . . .'

'She?'

'Yes, the other.'

'She's going out? But she never . . .'

'Yes, sometimes she does. She makes a great effort and goes out. She's going out today. For all day . . . You and I could . . .'

'Go away?'

'If you want to.'

'Well . . . perhaps not yet. I'm under contract. But as soon as I can finish the work, then . . .'

'Ah, yes. But she's going to be out all day. We could do something . . .'

'What?'

'I'll wait for you this evening in my aunt's bedroom. I'll wait for you as always.'

She turns away, ringing her bell like the lepers who use a bell to announce their approach, telling the unwary: 'Out of the way, out of the way.' You put on your shirt and coat and follow the sound of the bell calling you to the dining-room. In the parlour the widow Llorente comes towards you, bent over, leaning on a knobby cane; she's dressed in an old white gown with a stained and tattered gauze veil. She goes by without looking at you, blowing her nose into a handkerchief, blowing her nose and spitting. She murmurs, 'I won't be at home today, Señor Montero. I have complete confidence in your work. Please keep at it. My husband's memoirs must be published.'

She goes away, stepping across the carpets with her tiny feet, which are like those of an antique doll, and supporting herself with her cane, and spitting and sneezing as if she wanted to clear something from her congested lungs. It's only by an effort of will that you keep yourself from following her with your eyes, despite the curiosity you feel at seeing the yellowed bridal gown she's taken from the bottom of that old trunk in her bedroom . . .

You scarcely touch the cold coffee that's waiting for you in the dining-room. You sit for an hour in the tall arch-back chair, smoking, waiting for the sounds you never hear, until finally you're sure the old lady has left the house and can't catch you at what you're going to do. For the last hour you've had the key to the trunk clutched in your hand, and now you get up and silently walk through the parlour into the hallway, where you wait for another fifteen minutes — your watch tells you how long — with your ear against Señora Consuelo's door. Then you slowly push it open until you can make out, beyond the spider's web of candles, the empty bed on which her rabbit is gnawing at a carrot: the bed that's always littered with scraps of bread, and that you touch gingerly as if you thought the old lady might be hidden among the rumples of the sheets. You walk over to the corner where the trunk is, stepping on the tail of one of those rats; it squeals, escapes from your feet, and scampers off to warn the others. You fit the copper key into the rusted padlock, remove the padlock, and then raise the lid, hearing the creak of the old, stiff hinges. You take out the third portion of the memoirs — it's tied with a red ribbon — and under it you discover those photographs, those old, brittle, dog-eared photographs. You pick them up without looking at them, clutch the whole treasure to your breast, and hurry out of the room without closing the trunk, forgetting the hunger of the rats. You close the door, lean against the wall in the hallway until you catch your breath, then climb the stairs to your room.

Up there you read the new pages, the continuation, the events of an agonized century. In his florid language General Llorente describes the personality of Eugenia de Montijo, pays his respects to Napoleon the Small, summons up his most martial rhetoric to declare the Franco-Prussian War, fills whole pages with his sorrow at the defeat, harangues all men of honour about the Republican monster, sees a ray of hope in General Boulanger, sighs for Mexico, believes that in the Dreyfus affair the honour — always that word 'honour'! — of the Army has asserted itself again . . .

The brittle pages crumble at your touch: you don't respect them now, you're only looking for a reappearance of the woman with green eyes. 'I know why you weep at times, Consuelo. I have not been able to give you children, although you are so radiant with life . . .' And later: 'Consuelo, you should not tempt God. We must reconcile ourselves. Is not my affection enough? I know that you love me; I feel it. I am not asking you for resignation, because that would offend you. I am only asking you to see, in the great love which you say you have for me, something sufficient, something that can fill both of us, without the need of turning to sick imaginings . . .'

On another page: 'I told Consuelo that those medicines were utterly useless. She insists on growing her own herbs in the garden. She says she is not deceiving herself. The herbs are not to strengthen the body, but rather the soul . . .' Later: 'I found her in a delirium, embracing the pillow. She cried, "Yes, yes, yes, I've done it, I've recreated her! I can invoke her, I can give her life with my own life!" It was necessary to call the doctor. He told me he could not quiet her, because the truth was that she was under the effects of narcotics, not of stimulants . . .' And finally: 'Early this morning I found her walking barefooted through the hallways. I wanted to stop her. She went by without looking at me, but her words were directed to me. "Don't stop me," she said. "I'm going towards my youth, and my youth is coming towards me. It's coming in, it's in the garden, it's come back . . ." Consuelo, my poor Consuelo, even the devil was an angel at one time . . .'

There isn't any more. The memoirs of General Llorente end with that sentence: 'Consuelo, le démon aussi était un ange, avant . . .'

And after the last page, the portraits. The portrait of an elderly gentleman in a military uniform, an old photograph with these words in one corner: 'Moulin, Photographe, 35 Boulevard Haussmann' and the date '1894'. Then the photograph of Aura, of Aura with her green eyes, her black hair gathered in ringlets, leaning against a Doric column with a painted landscape in the background: the landscape of a Lorelei in the Rhine. Her dress is buttoned up to the collar, there's a handkerchief in her hand, she's wearing a bustle: Aura, and the date '1876' in white ink, and on the back of the daguerrotype, in spidery handwriting: 'Fait pour notre dixième anniversaire de mariage', and a signature in the same hand, 'Consuelo Llorente'. In the third photograph you see both Aura and the old gentleman, but this time they're dressed in outing clothes, sitting on a bench in a garden. The photograph has become a little blurred: Aura doesn't look as young as she did in the other picture, but it's she, it's he, it's . . . it's you. You stare and stare at the photographs, then hold them up to the skylight. You cover General Llorente's beard with your finger, and imagine him with black hair, and you only discover yourself: blurred, lost, forgotten, but you, you, you.

Your head is spinning, overcome by the rhythm of that distant waltz, by the odour of damp, fragrant plants; you fall exhausted on the bed, touching your cheeks, your eyes, your nose, as if you were afraid that some invisible hand had ripped off the mask you've been wearing for twenty-seven years, the cardboard features that hid your true face, your real appearance, the appearance you once had but then forgot. You bury your face in the pillow, trying to keep the wind of the past from tearing away your own features, because you don't want to lose them. You lie there with your face in the pillow, waiting for what has to come, for what you can't prevent. You don't look at your watch again, that useless object tediously measuring time in accordance with human vanity, those little hands marking out the long hours that were invented to disguise the real passage of time, which races with a mortal and insolent swiftness no clock could ever measure. A life, a century, fifty years: you can't imagine these lying measurements any longer, you can't hold that bodiless dust within your hands.

When you look up from the pillow, you find you're in darkness. Night has fallen.

Night has fallen. Beyond the skylight the swift black clouds are hiding the moon, which tries to free itself, to reveal its pale, round, smiling face. It escapes for only a moment, then the clouds hide it again. You haven't got any hope left. You don't even look at your watch. You hurry down the stairs, out of that prison cell with its old papers and faded daguerrotypes, and stop at the door of Señora Consuelo's room, and listen to your own voice, muted and transformed after all those hours of silence. 'Aura . . .'

Again: 'Aura . . .'

You enter the room. The votive lights have gone out. You remember that the old lady has been away all day; without her faithful attention the candles have all burned up. You grope forward in the darkness to the bed.

And again: 'Aura.'

You hear a faint rustle of taffeta, and the breathing that keeps time with your own. You reach out your hand to touch Aura's green robe.

'No . . . Don't touch me . . . Lie down at my side.'

You find the edge of the bed, swing up your legs, and remain there stretched out and motionless. You can't help feeling a shiver of fear: 'She might come back any minute.'

'She won't come back.'

'Never?'

'I'm exhausted. She's already exhausted. I've never been able to keep her with me for more than three days.'

'Aura . . .'

You want to put your hand on Aura's breasts. She turns her back: you can tell by the difference in her voice.

'No . . . Don't touch me . . .'

'Aura . . . I love you.'

'Yes. You love me. You told me yesterday that you'd always love me.'

'I'll always love you, always. I need your kisses, your body . . .'

'Kiss my face. Only my face.'

You bring your lips close to the head that's lying next to yours. You stroke Aura's long black hair. You grasp that fragile woman by the shoulders, ignoring her sharp complaint. You tear off her taffeta robe, embrace her, feel her small and lost and naked in your arms, despite her moaning resistance, her feeble protests, kissing her face without thinking, without distinguishing, and you're touching her withered breasts when a ray of moonlight shines in and surprises you, shines in through a chink in the wall that the rats have chewed open, an eye that lets in a beam of silvery moonlight. It falls on Aura's eroded face, as brittle and yellowed as the memoirs, as creased with wrinkles as the photographs. You stop kissing those fleshless lips, those toothless gums: the ray of moonlight shows you the naked body of the old lady, of Señora Consuelo, limp, spent, tiny, ancient, trembling because you touch her, you love her, you too have come back . . .

You plunge your face, your open eyes, into Consuelo's silver-white hair, and you'll embrace her again when the clouds cover the moon, when you're both hidden again, when the memory of youth, of youth reembodied, rules the darkness.

'She'll come back, Felipe. We'll bring her back together. Let me recover my strength and I'll bring her back . . .'

JOHN BART GERALD was born in New York City in 1940 and is both novelist and short-story writer. His novel, *A Thousand, Thousand Mornings*, appeared in 1966.

blood letting

JOHN BART GERALD

The incident itself didn't last long. The wall behind his desk was covered with framed awards, commendations, pictures of colonels and generals shaking hands, chiefs of staff, and up top against the flag was our President. The Major said, 'Why aren't you in uniform, Sergeant?' And I said, 'I have something to show you, sir.' 'Well what is it, Blake?' he said, for in a military way we were friends. With an edge cutting in my hand I pulled the blade down the middle of my chest through the T-shirt and hair down to the bone. And as the blood sprang into the split flesh I drew another cut across the top of my chest to make a cross. And stood there with the warm seeping down into my pants, looking at him, realizing he would never see me, or any of us.

My mother was an artist from Milwaukee and my father left Charleston. They met at a picnic and went to New York to build their lives together. They had ideals. But my mother painted less when she had children. And my father became very successful in business and protected us. I went to all the good schools, and finally Harvard. My sister made her debut at the Junior League Ball. And at times when I had nothing else I thought back to that world and to those names like symbols of the days when I was better than everyone else.

At the Guards' Ball the beautiful, intelligent daughter of a paper manufacturer broke down crying with me. I patted her bare back and took her out for a cup of coffee. We walked down to Lexington Avenue, she barefoot, carrying her shoes though it was mid-winter, me with a white turban around my head set with a glass jewel, walked into a drugstore, and sat at the counter. She couldn't stop crying. She kept saying it was a sham, it had no meaning. Everyone on the counter stools was staring at us, and I wanted her to speak more softly.

At first I didn't do very well at Harvard. I tried hard. I always tried hard, but I felt I had blinders on and didn't know how to take them off. I was asked to join a club. People in clubs ignored you if you were not. I joined. Mine was regarded as one of the best, if not blue blood or polo-playing particularly, then vaguely intellectual. It was the only one that accepted one or two Jews each year, and I thought that was right. I studied classics and English. I fell in love with an undergraduate actress, and when she was no longer amused, tired of Harvard and myself, I left.

I reached the doorstep of Doctor Schweitzer's hospital in Lambaréné and worked there for close to a year with lepers. But faced with a humanity in the natives as deep or maybe deeper than my own, and afraid of dying or never leaving, I grew hungry for learning just who in hell I was, so I went back to school.

Elections were held around the club's large banquet table. Three room-mates were asked to join and a fourth was not because he had the wrong colour. The alumni would have objected. I didn't want to belong any longer. When I sent in my resignation I was told I couldn't resign, any more than I could resign from being a gentleman. I was not sure. When the resignation was refused again I walked into the club's leather-upholstered leather-bound library to the book where members had signed in on election night over the past two hundred years. And I looked through page after page of neat signatures, finding a President and other names of government, finance, and industry, without a smudge, until I came to my own name and drew a thin line through the name in ink, initialled and dated it.

Not many club men talked to me again. On the other hand I began studying and learning and didn't think about the club again for a long time. I finished strong at Harvard, still running a race, and went right into six months with the Air Force Reserve. Since I already knew so much officer material, I wanted to learn what it was like to be an enlisted man. Later I went to monthly meetings, married my girl from college, wrote earnest short stories, and began to teach school.

It was awkward to feel that the war starting was immoral and would ultimately be disastrous to the people of my country, and to belong at the same time to the military. It was awkward teaching that stories and ideals were as real as life's blood when some of my students would graduate into war. It was awkward paying taxes. It was awkward distrusting my government. I found a number of things awkward. What amazed me was how much awkwardness I could live with.

I was always intrigued by the father of a college friend who became a cabinet minister in one of the countries Hitler conquered until he could no longer face the crimes his own government found expedient and went off to die on the Russian front. I always thought if I had been in Germany in the thirties, white Anglo-Saxon Protestant as I am, I would have had the sense to leave rather than be trapped by circumstance. But I wouldn't. I would have stayed long enough to discover whether I was the blind middle class, the Jew, or the storm-trooper.

The annual two-week tour of duty was spent learning how to load bombs. After three days I pulled my back lifting and was taken to the base hospital. In the other beds were casualties back from the war zone, men who had played dead, men with parts of their bodies gone. One told what it was like to shoot a woman. Another talked only of prisoners. They told their stories late at night, stories not asked for, told in blood.

At the peace demonstration in Washington, I marched and laughed with my friends, with my students, but the wounded were still more real to me. I couldn't forget them, they knew what the war was. They were sent out to be killed. They knew how strong their rights were even to live. I remembered a black man without legs who looked in my eyes and said, 'Don't go'.

In basic training a friend was ordered to clean out the ovens when the KP sergeant found he was Jewish. The ovens were still hot, and he cleaned them out on his hands and knees while I watched. All through training I didn't say a word. The military taught me how to survive, just survive until it was all over. Because I still hoped to be square with myself, I stared at my cowardice and the moments of compromise so that finally I would not betray myself. I learned the uses of anonymity. I learned stupidity. I learned to keep my mouth shut. I learned men do not obey out of love. I learned to be jovial with a stupid officer. I learned that the military could do what it wanted, and if my rights were protected in regulations, business was carried out behind their façade. I learned respect for sergeants. I learned to be more clever. I knew my fear kept me free as long as and if I was free.

I survived. At times I was impressed by my lack of stature as the war continued to escalate and civilian casualties rose and the other country and her people were destroyed. And our own men were killed for a mistake. In five years of monthly meetings I became a sergeant. And went out to the firing range with the rest of the guys and shot expert with such a splitting headache I could barely see the target.

I wanted to avoid prison. In civilian life I did not break any law or sign a pledge to. When my students asked if they should go to jail, I turned them back to their own consciences. Because I would not go to jail. I did not want to go. All I had to do was oversleep my monthly meetings to face disciplinary call-up. Refusal meant military prison. I had lived through it many times in my head, but I didn't think I could live through the years in prison. They kept me running. The only price I had to pay for my freedom was the continual admission of my own cowardice.

I preferred not to look at it that way. I explored areas of my life where I secretly considered myself a hero. I thought at times I was a hero to my marriage, though that was not fair to my wife. I remembered my moments with the civil rights movement, especially as I believed more and more in man's right to live free. I remembered walking through the Alabama countryside singing 'Before I'll be a slave, I'll be buried in my grave, and go home to the Lord and be free'. And being thrown in jail for breaking no law at all, and beaten for it.

It was hard to admit I preferred heroism without having to pay too much too often. Christ, whom I admired, only went up on his cross once. I wondered if I didn't admire more the TV or movie hero who could make a career out of heroic acts. I liked myself less. I dreamed of prison and the Air Force confused in the same dream.

At times I thought I was too hard on myself. At my monthly meetings I only sat and watched Driver Safety lectures, or played with wooden dummies. In military prison I would have emptied garbage cans for the war effort. I saw others like me. And if it was hard to do absolutely nothing for a bad war, I was doing no harm. Wooden bombs weren't real bombs. But then one supported the system finally or one did not, as a fighting man, a reservist, or civilian. Those closer to the flame just took more risk in getting burned.

I decided the argument with a note to myself. 'Men don't choose to spend five years in jail. They go because they have to follow their conscience. Whatever it says about me I still have the choice.' I always had the choice. Life offered me so many choices, my difficulty was in choosing. I hoped I would never have to confront this choice. I knew if I did I would learn something that frightened me.

My wife began the pork chops and spinach. I sat at the kitchen table with the late paper before me, and looked through the list of activated reserve units until I found my unit's name. Then I read an account of the latest incident when there was some doubt who was telling the truth.

I asked Linda not to answer the phone because I wanted time to think before I was caught up in the network binding me to the military. Maybe I was caught already. I went to the bedroom and lay down. My mind began a useless meandering of logic through the alternatives before me. I was aware of a slow steady pulse of survival beating under the surface of my life. Linda's aunt in Montreal would hide me, then find me a job up north or passage out. We had some good friends in Canada. I would be AWOL, then a deserter. I laughed suddenly. I was always realizing I was American, no great patriot, but the country was part of myself. I couldn't ignore it. I couldn't resign from my whole life. I couldn't resign from myself.

Then I thought serving might not be so bad. I was paid fairly well and the officers left me alone. I liked the people in my unit. I might not be sent to the war zone. And maybe I could switch into administrative work and not load the bombs myself. That's what I thought.

I knew if I served two years straight in the Air Force, it wouldn't matter from then on what I thought was right or wrong because I would have to accept in my heart I would do anything, or be part of anything. And then my sense of right and wrong wasn't worth much. My whole life wasn't worth much. And the words I used were worth nothing. I grasped at that and tried to accept. I wanted to accept it. I couldn't go to jail. Not just because I would lose Linda and life, but prison was my private terror, as if I had lived with it since the day I was born. Until my thoughts broke down and I was thrown back on several incidents which I suddenly saw very clearly because they were all I had left.

I was marching over the bridge out of Selma into the Alabama countryside with my legs trembling, afraid someone would shoot at us from the woods. I was huddled on the cement floor while the cons kicked me. I sat on that floor scared of the jailers, scared of the cons, their razors, taking my wedding ring, what went on behind the blankets they stretched around their steel bunks and threatened me with, scared I wouldn't get out, scared I would start screaming and never stop. I never left that jail in Alabama completely. The prison was still in my head. I used to pray, 'God let me be free.'

When I left the hospital in Africa, Schweitzer gave me a letter for the authorities. I never gave it to the government. I kept it in the back of my journal. Because it said I was a good and honest person, with the Doctor's cramped signature at the bottom of the page. Because the words said I was worth something, when I wasn't always sure. I remembered 'reverence for life', and all the clichés fashionable people associated with the old man. But I saw him trying to work them out in life, awkward and clumsily at times, as out of place as organ music in the jungle night, a man trying to make his conscience real.

I remember saying the Lord's Prayer hundreds of times in my boarding-school chapel. And my tutor at college whose blood was literature. And Linda looking at me in the days when we were in love.

She was standing by the door looking at me. The phone rang and rang and rang.

Once in a bad time my father gave me a piece of paper with his father's name on it and his father's father, back six or seven generations of ministers and doctors in small Southern towns. And my father said, 'You'll be all right. We always have been. And you're one of us.'

She stood by the bed crying. I wanted to comfort her but there wasn't anything to say. She kept touching me. She didn't ask what I was going to do. When I was ready I hugged her as strong as I could but I didn't feel her. There was a knot tied in my chest pulling tighter and tighter and tighter. I said 'See you.' And when I walked out the door I fell into America.

JAMES LEO HERLIHY was born in 1927, in Detroit, Michigan. Although his name has been mainly associated with the novel *Midnight Cowboy*, he has worked successfully in other forms, having written the plays *Blue Denim* and *Crazy October*; an earlier novel, *All Fall Down*; and two collections of short fiction, *The Sleep of Baby Filbertson and Other Stories* and *A Story That Ends With a Scream*.

love and the buffalo

JAMES LEO HERLIHY

Mr Highet was disposed of yesterday. The other two men in here have already been . . . No, let's just say the rest of the ward is empty.

Anyway, now that I'm alone I can take some notes. I don't know how I'll get them outside. But the first real task is to get them on paper and keep them well hidden. Time enough later to worry about getting them into the hands of someone who can put them to good use.

The minute I opened my eyes this morning I knew this was it, my last day. I knew even before Miss Z came in and did her smile. How, I don't know. The only oddness I remember was the sky. It looked peculiar, a little too leaden; they've probably done something to it. But that wasn't it either. I don't know. A man simply senses these things. And once he does, the actual evidence begins to pile up so fast he hardly has time to collect and interpret it. That's what these notes are for. I've got to jot down certain things before they're forgotten and lost to us.

First of all – if it isn't already clear – I'm in a hoZpital. H-o-z-pital. That's right, Z.

I'm in the obZervation ward. O-b-z. Z again.

I can't possibly list all the zees connected with this case. Here and there I'll indicate the more subtle ones that might otherwise be missed, but I'll have to rely upon the reader to catch the more obvious ones. As I said, there's this time problem.

Back to this morning: I knew when Miss Z came towards my bed with her thermometer she was bringing the clue with her. And I knew that at the instant my eyes connected with her face, she'd present me with the first real signal. If you can understand that. It's fairly subtle, rather mysterious. Which is one of the problems, so many subtleties in this thing.

I couldn't look at her, not at first. I didn't dare. I had to arrange this awareness carefully in my mind and prepare a reaction to it. For instance, if I'd shown surprise, or fear, I'd have been finished. Instinctively I knew it was important to keep her from realizing I'd caught the signal. It's better if you see it, and get it, but don't let them know you've got it. Just play dumb. I could give a thousand reasons why this is the best way to play it, but I don't have time. Just take my word for it.

So. Finally I did look at her, my own face a carefully set blank. And of course Miss Z was looking at me. (Later, you'll appreciate the irony of this particular Z. It's not her real name. It's what I call her in my mind. Z for Zoe. Zoe means *life* in Greek. You'll see how bitter this irony gets.)

The minute she caught my eye, she opened her mouth and smiled, and there it was: her upper lip, plus a kind of, how can I describe it, a diagonal, almost invisible shadow formed perhaps by her tongue, and then her lower lip. Taken altogether they formed a perfect, a deliberate, a malicious Z.

Oh, she was so pleased with herself. It was written all over her face, the delight she took in her own exquisite cleverness, placing the Z in a smile. So easy to deny later if anyone accused her openly. No evidence to be caught with, you see. She wouldn't have dared put it in a note or say it out loud for witnesses to hear.

She was disappointed when I didn't lose control of myself. I felt like shuddering or screaming. But I didn't. I smiled right back. And without a Z, as if I hadn't caught the signal at all. This would give me about three minutes, while the thermometer was in my mouth, to think. I had to think. And fast.

She lingered by the bed, fussing with her charts, nearly falling over with nonchalance. I wanted to hit her.

'I've got an idea!' she said. 'Why don't you shave today?' She spoke like some nitwit kindergarten teacher proposing a lovely game of mud-pies in a bed of quicksand. 'You have such a handsome face, but it's all hidden by those whiskers.'

I said nothing. The thermometer was in my mouth. Miss Z only asks questions when your mouth is full.

'Suppose I just bring the razor,' she said, 'and put it on that table. Then if the mood strikes you, you can simply plug it in! How's that sound?'

(Is it necessary to point out that an electric raZor, *simply plugged in,* makes an absolutely distinct zzzzzz?)

'Would you like that?' she said, the cruelty too deliberate to ignore.

I pointed to my mouth, as if the thermometer were my reason for not speaking. Thank heaven I'm used to living by my wits.

'All right then, meanie,' she said playfully, '*don't* answer. But that's exactly what I'm going to do.'

This is what evil is, I thought as she walked away from me, her rear end stiff and secretive. From a certain point of view, Miss Z is beautiful. Blonde hair, high bosoms, dark eyelashes, red lips, the works. Everything where it's supposed to be and of the right proportions. The sort of beauty they throw together in those big super drugstores. And I'm certain that making love to her would be disastrous. Only an insane person would dare, or perhaps a drunk or someone brutally insensitive. When I first saw her, of course, I allowed such a prospect to move once, quickly, through my own imagination. It was horrible. I realized at once that her juices were pure acid. At the very instant of penetration, the male member disintegrates entirely, the testicles, too, and the scrotum simply hangs there for ever more, as empty and useless as a pauper's purse.

My mind, as I've already indicated, works brilliantly under fire. The more danger there is, the greater its agility. Now, for instance, even before the winds of Miss Z's exit had subsided in the room, the plan had formed itself with no real effort at all.

I knew I'd kill her. And what's more, I knew exactly how I'd go about it.

If these notes are going to do any good at all, I suppose they should include a few autobiographical touches.

I'm 46. I was a boy during the twenties, a young man during the depression, a soldier during World War II. One day, while killing time behind a clump of banana trees in a very pretty tropical place, I heard a ZZZZZ sound. There was an explosion. I was hurt. Not badly though. They made a big do over it but if you ask me the damage was extremely slight. However this is not my point. I'm not telling a war story here. I merely wish to note that during the zzzzzz that preceded that explosion I came to know something, something important. I gained (all in a flash and through no effort of my own) a certain view of life as it is lived in the American century. And since then my own life has been more or less dedicated, I say this modestly, to the gathering of data, evidence, etc, in support of that view. Only recently have I begun to understand what might be done with these materials, how *urgent* it is, in fact, that I do what I can to initiate some sort of movement to counter this direction that everything has taken in recent decades. It was only this morning – I'm ashamed to admit this – only this morning have I actually taken pen and paper to make these notes. And the horror of it is, there may not be time to finish!

But here goes:

Concentrate. This may require concentration. Think back to the twenties and thirties. Remember the sound of a car door closing. It went Ka-Kloonk. And the horn went Ow-*oo*-ga. Today's car door goes *gloozhe*, and the horn, difficult to spell, is actually a shrill, baritone zzzzzzz. And recall please how in those days one *klomp-klomped* up a stairway. Now one ascends in an elevator, zzzzzz. The sound of men working used to be KLONGang. My father was a blacksmith. KLONG-*ang*, went his hammer as it touched the anvil. Now, however, a rivet gun, a drill, an electric saw, all go *dzzzzt dzzzt*.

This may sound trivial. It is. I am purposely starting with things that aren't what you'd call crucial. But note, please, the general *softening* of everything, the tendency towards Z sounds.

(A word to the fainthearted: I'm trying to do this gradually, tastefully. I'm trying not to offend. But I must warn you, the thing itself gets pretty hairy. Remember, please, I don't like it any better than you do.)

People, and not just the rich, used to live in fairly big rooms with high ceilings, and when they laughed and talked they'd go *ha-ha-ha* and *talk-talk-talk*, good and loud and real. Now, living in these little cardboard shelves with paper walls, and under ceilings they can reach up and touch (a man should never be able to touch his own ceiling without a ladder) the talk is nothing more than *bzzzzz, bzzzzz, bzzzzz*. And it is well known that nothing of importance or size can be said in a situation where voices cannot be raised. Whispering, which is all that can take place in these rooms, lends itself best to the telling of petty secrets and the bearing of false witness against one's neighbour.

Interruptions: Miss Z just came in for the thermometer. And of course she brought the razor. The hideous thing is lying not two feet from my head at this very moment. But that's all right, that's just fine. You will see in due course how the razor has become a part of my plan.

I can tell, by the way, that Miss Z suspects nothing. It delights me to realize the wicked bitch will be dead by teatime, sawdust spilling from her heart, betsy-wetsy-doll eyes rolling back in her drugstore head. Alas, I have no time to indulge myself with these pretty images. Back to the low ceilings.

It is important here to touch upon a related matter: while the rooms men live in are shrinking in size, men themselves are actually becoming larger. (Not bigger, please; larger.) There is a village in West Germany where the average height of a 14-year-old boy is six-foot-four. Similar figures exist throughout Europe and America. I have no time – and surely there's no need! – to suggest what will result when this size-of-man size-of-room ratio, already absurd, reaches its ultimate limits; the intelligent reader will have seized the picture without assistance. I must now proceed to the question of why people are growing to such ungainly proportions.

To put it bluntly, this food thing has gotten entirely out of hand.

They've found ways of creating fruits and vegetables without the sun, and the results of these techniques, to put it as simply as possible, create monsters. In appearance they are as perfect and handsome and enticing as Snow White's apple – a fairly lucky simile, for wasn't that article produced with poisons and gases in a dungeon under the palace, with no exposure whatever to true sunlight? As for fowl, there is no longer any night in the life of a chicken. It grows at a regulated speed in the light of a perpetual electronic sun, laying eggs of a grotesquely predictable size and quality. In death, this bird which has never seen sky or earth is interred in a block of ice and gift-wrapped by machines in see-through paper. Even on the table, the stuff looks splendid. And since the American century is the century of surfaces, people eat first with their eyes, seldom even noticing the absence of flavour and sweetness and mystery. The trouble is – at the risk of overworking the legend of Miss White and her fatal apple – the stuff induces in us a witch's sleep of death. Zzzzzz, Zzzzzz.

One note before we leave the kitchen: When was the last time anyone heard a cleaver going KLUNK, the *snap-snap* of a pea, the *whack* of a carrot being cut, or milk bottles going *klonk* against one another in an icebox that went *drip-drip*? In place of these, there is one endless deadly *zzzzzzz* of refrigeration and an occasional *dzzt* as some pretty-coloured frozen falsehood hits boiling water – in the kitchen*ette*.

Enough has been said that the reader may have guessed what sort of place this is, this hospital. It's a place for the recalcitrant, for the few who refuse to succumb to Z. We reZist. And we are gathered up, one by one, and placed in these institutions for processing and ultimate dispoZal. We are slowly Z-ed away to nothing, or practically nothing.

For instance, the night before last, Mr Highet reached the end of his processing. Yesterday morning, Miss Z carried him out in the palm of her hand.

I said, 'What have you got there, nurse?' I knew, but I wondered what she'd say.

'What have I got *where?*' was her brilliant rejoinder.

'Oh, in the palm of your hand,' I said casually.

'This?' She opened her plaster-of-paris fingers. 'It's just a capsule.'

Obviously they had Mr Highet in this capsule. When they finally Z you out for good, it makes you very small in every way. You look like a bit of dust. Sometimes the orderly carries out the remains, hidden in a bucket of scrub water or a dustpan. I've seen them hauled out of here every which way, in pillow cases, in bits of Kleenex, in water glasses, ashtrays, slop jars, bedpans. They don't care how: *get them out*, that's all that matters. But I will say this is the first time in memory of someone being hauled out in a capsule. Apparently, sensing I'd caught on to their other methods, they felt called upon really to tax their meagre ingenuity.

'May I see it?' I said.

'*Why* on earth?'

'Oh, just curious.'

She thought for a while. 'Well, all right. Why not?' She lowered her palm. 'See?'

The capsule was fairly large, and black as death. I wondered how she'd got him in there so quickly – although I had observed that these people are fairly good with their fingers.

'What kind of capsule is it?' I said.

'Vitamin,' she answered quick as a wink.

'Oh, I see. Well, if it's a vitamin, why don't you swallow it?'

That got her. I felt her shuddering. I laughed. I don't blame her for loathing me. I *am* difficult. They're not used to my kind in here.

'I don't need it,' she said. 'I've had my vitamin today.'

'Yes,' I said, 'I thought you had.'

She smiled and began to leave.

I said, 'Nurse?'

She stopped.

'Nurse, where is that gentleman today?' I pointed to the bed by the window.

'Mr Highet? Why, he went home this morning.'

'Oh? Well, isn't that curious, because I didn't see him leave.'

'You mean you don't believe me, is that it?' she said. The same old smile: *come, kiddies, mud-pie time!*

'I didn't say that, I didn't say anything at all, I just said I didn't see him leave.'

'Tell me,' she said, 'where do you think Mr Highet is?'

I just looked at her. I'd already pressed the point too far and I knew it. She stopped smiling and something happened in her face that told me they were going to close in and finish me off next.

However, I didn't think *immediately*. I thought I'd have a few weeks or at least a few days. But then this morning, as I've already described, it became inescapably clear that they intend to get me tonight.

Intend.

I have a few intentions of my own, thanks.

The plan is simple, and foolproof. At first blush it may seem to constitute a complete reversal of my initial stand, but that's actually the genius of it: I will create the impression that I have ceased all resistance. (I take no credit for this strategy, it's an ancient one: give the enemy false confidence, it's as simple as that.)

When Miss Z returns to the ward, I intend to make a zzzzz sound at her. I'll repeat this every time she passes my bed. This will give her the impression that I have accepted her signal from this morning, and therefore my fate.

Secondly, I'll shave. With a concerted effort of the will, this can be done without the zzzzz actually entering the brain. Shaving is important. To their kind of mind, it will seem to be the ultimate capitulation. The psychiatrist here has been prattling on vomitously for weeks now about the beard being a father imitation that will 'fall away' – if you can stand the expression – 'when the father within comes to birth'. Understand please, he's deadly serious about all this tripe.

Thirdly, at just the right moment, probably late this afternoon, I'll place a bit of dust on the sheet and hide myself under the bed. Miss Z, finding the dust on her next tour of the wards, will assume my processing has concluded a few hours in advance of their calculations. And while she's gathering up my proxy for disposal, I'll seize her legs from under the bed. There'll be a brief struggle and in a matter of seconds she'll be dead from strangulation.

Reading over these notes, I realize I may seem somewhat overwrought, a bit too vexed by the more trivial aspects of this Z-situation: television, the constant electronic bzzzzzz of today's world, all the subtle new zees the Bell System has been introducing into long-distance telephoning, etc. I've said too much, perhaps, and risked running out of time before I get to what is important: the zeeing of love.

My attitude in this connexion was the *specific* reason for my being brought here in the first place. Therefore, even at the peril of allowing these notes to descend to the level of a woe that is merely personal, I'll deftly sketch in at least the rough outlines of my own situation.

To begin with, love has been done away with, damn near. I've been watching it happen since World War II. At first it seemed fairly gradual, but one should realize that the gradual, seen by some standards other than the purely optical, might indeed be quite appallingly rapid. The death of a rose for example cannot be observed by the naked eye but it takes place nonetheless overnight. And so it has been with love. People still prate and blab and sing about it a good deal, perhaps even more than ever, like homage to the dead; but the article itself is well-nigh gone from the world. And where did it go?

Like everything else of value, it's being Z-processed in a thousand insidious ways, but mostly it's being tranquillized out of existence.

The process is simple: love is caring. Tranquillizers subdue, mute, deaden, the caring centres in the brain. That's all there is to it. A tranquillizer is a lobotomy in pill form. Or to say it more accurately, it is a soporific for the soul. Zzzzz-zzzzz-zzzzz, sleep the soul. While love dies.

Why is this being done? First of all, it isn't love *per se* that's under attack. It's the trouble it brings. This American time of the world is a deadly efficient time. For instance, instead of using architecture to solve the housing problem, it seeks to solve the housing problem by destroying architecture. Why? Well, no one has ever succeeded in measuring or even naming the precise function of beauty. All that's known is the price of maintaining it and how much space it occupies. In our times these figures have been declared to be too great.

Love is in a similar fix. Its function, like that of an old Park Avenue mansion, eludes these tragic new mathematics. Love's measurable products, eg, songs and babies, can be produced in quantity by quite other means. Therefore the trouble it brings, anxiety, the blues, jealousy, inconvenience, etc, is thought to be insupportable. A person simply turns off the telephone and munches little white pills until the danger is past and the troublemaker is dead in him. From a certain point of view, this works. One might even say it has worked so well that love on the contemporary landscape constitutes no more of a threat to the public safety than the buffalo. Nowadays neither is likely to be allowed to gather in sufficient force for a stampede. Both, for all practical purposes, both love and the buffalo, have had it.

Miss Z just came in.

I said, 'Bzzzzzz,' as per plan.

'Oh!' she said, 'that's the sound a razor makes!' The bitch. I nodded.

'Does that mean you're going to shave for me?'

I nodded again, docile as a poodle. Miss Z smiled. She looked genuinely, profoundly relieved, like a junkie who's been promised a fix.

Evil evil evil.

I gritted my teeth and returned her smile. 'Zzzzzz,' I said.

'Uh-huh, and zzzz zzzz zzzz,' she said. It's-the-loveliest-game was her attitude. 'Would you like me to plug it in for you?'

I started to shake my head, but caught the gesture just in time to turn it into a nod.

She plugged in the razor and handed it to me. I waited for her to leave, but she just stood there watching.

She said, 'Wouldn't you like me to do it for you?' When things are going their way, they become unbelievably bold. But I had to say no this time, I just couldn't risk it.

Finally, she left the room, and I shaved. I'm absolutely certain the zzzz of the razor did not really penetrate. I kept saying K-K-K-K-K-Kill, K-K-K-Kill over and over again the whole time, and I'm sure those good hard sounds counteracted the zzzz almost entirely.

It will now be seen how certain events in my own life perfectly illustrate my thesis on the subject of love in the 1960s. I am here because I refused to allow my love to be demolished. Specifically, when my ex-wife refused to see me or even to answer the telephone, I broke into the apartment. I went to the roof and down the fire escape and kicked in the bedroom window. The place was *thick* with electronic rays. She was in the living-room using the television, the air conditioner, and the hair dryer *simultaneously*! But still she heard me enter and ran screaming down the halls. Busybody neighbours, roused momentarily from their zzz-slumbers, called the police. *Who* of course were lurking somewhere nearby in a squad car full of radio waves. I was apprehended.

My entrance into the apartment that night was in violation of something called a peace bond my wife had acquired in court some weeks earlier. She got it by claiming I tried to kill her.

Which wasn't the case at all. I was simply trying to awaken her, as she had fallen slowly, almost imperceptibly at first, into the clutches of this Z-thing.

The poor woman – Bennington, class of '48, formerly the world's most tiresome exponent of natural childbirth, and the only debutante in history to insist upon a barefooted outdoor wedding – this woman was actually strangling in appliances by the time I discovered the Z-pills. There were quarrels. That is, *I* quarrelled. She gulped pills. Couldn't have been more agreeable, went around with a perfectly asinine, beatific grin all the time, and I couldn't bear it. The simple fact was she was dying. I knew it and tried to save her and somehow in the process happened to leave a few little blue marks on her throat. Anyway, here I am.

(Just for one wild moment, in the interest of looking under every little pebble for truth, let's consider that I *was* trying to kill her that night. Isn't there something to be said for real death as opposed to living death? And isn't that precisely what Z amounts to? Has anyone, anywhere, ever postulated an even faintly valid reason for enduring a life from which love is gone forever? Is there anyone – I do not here address myself to the dying, which includes of course the virtually millions of Z-puppets who clutter the world – is there anyone among the living few who knows a way to continue the labour of breathing without at least some small hope that love might one day be revived in him? Of course not.)

Teatime approaches.

I found my proxy, my effigy, on the bathroom floor. It's not the kind of dust I'd hoped for, a fine, fuzzy, grey little tumbleweed of the sort that gathers under beds. They don't seem to have that kind here; undoubtedly it reminds them of their sins. What I did find looks like a bit of mud from someone's shoe. But it'll do nicely. I've placed it in the middle of the bed and it looks rather peculiar there, this tiny fragment of clay against the white of the sheet.

I think perhaps it's the saddest thing I've ever seen.

But it's time now to get under the bed.

How nice this is. I had no idea I'd be able to write under here. Hospital beds are fairly high, so there's plenty of room. I'm lying on my stomach. It's not really comfortable, but it's cool and pleasant in other ways. I'm exhausted now. When I look up, I can see that peculiar sky out the window.

I wonder if it's really winter. They could easily have put that snow effect out there, any good stage-hand could show them how. But then, why would they do that, how can it be to their advantage to make me think it's winter? I've been thinking so much today I can't quite piece everything together now. But I do hope the snow is real. It's in my head now and I don't want anything false in there. And then, too, real snow can have such peace in it. My mother, the foolish old dear, used to say it was torn up notes from God. She didn't say what was written on them. Or why He tore them up. Maybe if I knew I wouldn't be under this bed.

Funny, but I can't remember any more what I'm doing here. I only remember something about it being urgent.

I hear footsteps. A lot of them.

Oh, God!

snow

TED HUGHES

And let me repeat this over and over again: beneath my feet is the earth, some part of the surface of the earth. Beneath the snow beneath my feet, that is. What else could it be? It is firm, I presume, and level. If it is not actually soil and rock, it must be ice. It is very probably ice. Whichever it may be, it is proof – the most substantial proof possible – that I am somewhere on the earth, the known earth. It would be absurd to dig down through the snow, just to determine exactly what is underneath, earth or ice. This bedded snow may well be dozens of feet deep. Besides, the snow filling all the air and rivering along the ground would pour into the hole as fast as I could dig, and cover me too – very quickly.

This could be no other planet: the air is perfectly natural, perfectly good.

Our aircraft was forced down by this unusual storm. The pilot tried to make a landing, but misjudged the extraordinary power of the wind and the whereabouts of the ground. The crash was violent. The fuselage buckled and gaped, and I was flung clear. Unconscious of everything save the need to get away from the disaster, I walked farther off into the blizzard and collapsed, which explains why when I came to full consciousness and stood up out of the snow that was burying me I could see nothing of either the aircraft or my fellow passengers. All around me was what I have been looking at ever since. The bottomless dense motion of snow. I started to walk.

Of course, everything previous to that first waking may have been entirely different since I don't remember a thing about it. Whatever chance dropped me here in the snow evidently destroyed my memory. That's one thing of which there is no doubt whatsoever. It is, so to speak, one of my facts. The aircraft crash is a working hypothesis, that merely.

There's no reason why I should not last quite a long time yet. I seem to have an uncommon reserve of energy. To keep my mind firm, that is the essential thing, to fix it firmly in my reasonable hopes, and lull it there, encourage it. Mesmerize it slightly with a sort of continuous prayer. Because when my mind is firm, my energy is firm. And that's the main thing here – energy. No matter how circumspect I may be, or how lucid, without energy I am lost on the spot. Useless to think about it. Where my energy ends I end, and all circumspection and all lucidity end with me. As long as I have energy I can correct my mistakes, outlast them, outwalk them – for instance the unimaginable error that as far as I know I am making at this very moment. This step, this, the next five hundred, or five thousand – all mistaken, all absolute waste, back to where I was ten hours ago. But we recognize that thought. My mind is not my friend. My support, my defence, but my enemy too – not perfectly intent on getting me out of this. If I were mindless perhaps there would be no difficulty whatsoever. I would simply go on aware of nothing but my step-by-step success in getting over the ground. The thing to do is to keep alert, keep my mind fixed in alertness, recognize these treacherous paralysing, yes, lethal thoughts the second they enter, catch them before they can make that burrowing plunge down the spinal cord.

Then gently and without any other acknowledgement push them back – out into the snow where they belong. And that *is* where they belong. They are the infiltrations of the snow, encroachments of this immensity of lifelessness. But they enter so slyly! We are true, they say, or at least very probably true, and on that account you must entertain us and even give us the run of your life, since above all things you are dedicated to the truth. That is the air they have, that's how they come in. What do I know about the truth? As if simple-minded dedication to truth were the final law of existence! I only know more and more clearly what is good for me. It's my mind that has this contemptible awe for the probably true, and my mind, I know, I prove it every minute, is not me and is by no means sworn to help me. Am I a lie? I must survive – that's a truth sacred as any, and as the hungry truths devour the sleepy truths I shall digest every other possible truth to the substance and health and energy of my own, and the ones I can't digest I shall spit out, since in this situation my intention to survive is the one mouth, the one digestive tract, so to speak, by which I live. But those others! I relax for a moment, I leave my mind to itself for a moment — and they are in complete possession. They plunge into me, exultantly, mercilessly. There is no question of their intention or their power. Five seconds of carelessness, and they have struck. The strength melts from me, my bowels turn to water, my consciousness darkens and shrinks, I have to stop.

What are my facts? I do have some definite facts.

Taking six steps every five seconds, I calculate — allowing for my brief regular sleeps — that I have been walking through this blizzard for five months and during that time have covered something equal to the breadth of the Atlantic between Southampton and New York. Two facts, and a third: throughout those five months this twilight of snow has not grown either darker or brighter.

So.

There seems no reason to doubt that I am somewhere within either the Arctic or the Antarctic Circle. That's a comfort. It means my chances of survival are not uniquely bad. Men have walked the length of Asia simply to amuse themselves.

Obviously I am not travelling in a straight line. But that needn't give me any anxiety. Perhaps I made a mistake when I first started walking, setting my face against the wind instead of down-wind. Coming against the wind I waste precious energy and there is always this wearisome snow blocking my eyes and mouth. But I had to trust the wind. This resignation to the wind's guidance is the very foundation of my firmness of mind. The wind is not simply my compass. In fact, I must not think of it as a compass at all. The wind is my law. As a compass nothing could be more useless. No need to dwell on that. It's extremely probable indeed and something I need not hide from myself that this wind is leading me to and fro in quite a tight little maze — always shifting too stealthily for me to notice the change. Or if the sun is circling the horizon, it seems likely that the wind is swinging with it through the three hundred and sixty degrees once in every twenty-four hours, turning me as I keep my face against it in a perfect circle not more than seven miles across. This would explain the otherwise strange fact that in spite of the vast distance I have covered the terrain is still dead level, exactly as when I started. A frozen lake, no doubt. This is a strong possibility and I must get used to it without letting it overwhelm me, and without losing sight of its real advantages.

The temptation to trust to luck and instinct and cut out across wind is to be restricted. The effect on my system of confidence would be disastrous. My own judgement would naturally lead me in a circle. I would have to make deliberate changes of direction to break out of that circle – only to go in a larger circle or a circle in the opposite direction. So more changes. Wilder and more sudden changes, changes of my changes – all to evade an enemy that showed so little sign of itself it might as well not have existed. It's clear where all that would end. Shouting and running and so on. Staggering round like a man beset by a mob. Falling, grovelling. So on. The snow.

No. All I have to do is endure: that is, keep my face to the wind. My face to the wind, a firm grip on my mind, and everything else follows naturally. There is not the slightest need to be anxious. Any time now the Polar night will arrive, bringing a drastic change of climate – inevitable. Clearing the sky and revealing the faultless compass of the stars.

The facts are overwhelmingly on my side. I could almost believe in Providence. After all, if one single circumstance were slightly – only slightly – other than it is! If, for instance, instead of waking in a blizzard on a firm level place I had come to consciousness falling endlessly through snow cloud. Then I might have wondered very seriously whether I were in the gulf or not. Or if the atmosphere happened to consist of, say, ammonia. I could not have existed. And in the moment before death by asphyxiation I would certainly have been convinced I was out on some lifeless planet. Or if I had no body but simply arms and legs growing out of a head, my whole system of confidence would have been disoriented from the start. My dreams, for instance, would have been meaningless to me, or rather an argument of my own meaninglessness. I would have died almost immediately, out of sheer bewilderment. I wouldn't need nearly such extreme differences either. If I had been without these excellent pigskin boots, trousers, jacket, gloves and hood, the cold would have extinguished me at once.

And even if I had double the clothing that I have, where would I be without my chair? My chair is quite as important as one of my lungs. As both my lungs, indeed, for without it I should be dead. Where would I have slept? Lying in the snow. But lying flat, as I have discovered, I am buried by the snow in just under a minute, and the cold begins to take over my hands and my feet and my face. Sleep would be impossible. In other words, I would very soon collapse of exhaustion and be buried. As it is, I unsnap my chair harness, plant the chair in the snow, sit on it, set my feet on the rung between the front legs, my arms folded over my knees and my head resting on my arms, and am able in this way to take a sleep of fully ten minutes before the snow piles over me.

The chain of providential coincidences is endless. Or rather, like a chain mail, it is complete without one missing link to betray and annul the rest. Even my dreams are part of it. They are as tough and essential a link as any, since there can no longer be any doubt that they are an accurate reproduction of my whole previous life, of the world as it is and as I knew it – all without one contradictory detail. Yet if my amnesia had been only a little bit stronger! – it needed only that. Because without this evidence of the world and my identity I could have known no purpose in continuing the ordeal. I could only have looked, breathed, and died, like a nestling fallen from the nest.

Everything fits together. And the result – my survival, and my determination to survive. I should rejoice.

The chair is of conventional type: nothing in the least mystifying about it. A farmhouse sort of chair: perfectly of a piece with my dreams, as indeed are my clothes, my body, and all the inclinations of my mind. It is of wood, painted black, though in places showing a coat of brown beneath the black. One of the nine struts in the back is missing and some child – I suppose it was a child – has stuck a dab of chewing gum into the empty socket. Obviously the chair has been well used, and not too carefully. The right foreleg has been badly chewed, evidently by a puppy, and on the seat both black and brown paints are wearing through, showing the dark grain of the pale wood. If all this is not final evidence of a reality beyond my own, of the reality of the world it comes from, the world I redream in my sleeps – I might as well lie down in the snow and be done with.

The curious harness needn't worry me. The world, so far as I've dreamed it at this point, contains no such harness, true. But since I've not yet dreamed anything from after my twenty-sixth birthday, the harness might well have been invented between that time and the time of my disaster. Probably it's now in general use. Or it may be the paraphernalia of some fashionable game that came in during my twenty-seventh or later year, and to which I got addicted. Sitting on snow peaks in nineteenth-century chairs. Or perhaps I developed a passion for painting polar scenery and along with that a passion for this particular chair as my painting seat, and had the harness designed specially. A lucky eccentricity! It is perfectly adapted to my present need. But all that's in the dark still. There's a lot I haven't dreamed yet. From my twenty-third and twenty-fourth years I have almost nothing – a few insignificant episodes. Nothing at all after my twenty-sixth birthday. The rest, though, is about complete, which suggests that any time now I ought to be getting my twenty-third and twenty-fourth years in full and, more important, my twenty-seventh year, or as much of it as there is, along with the accurate account of my disaster and the origin of my chair.

There seems little doubt of my age. Had I been dreaming my life chronologically there would have been real cause for worry. I could have had no idea how much was still to come. Of course, if I were suddenly to dream something from the middle of my sixtieth year I would have to reorganize all my ideas. What really convinces me of my youth is my energy. The appearance of my body tells me nothing. Indeed, from my hands and feet — which are all I have dared to uncover — one could believe I was several hundred years old, or even dead, they are so black and shrunken on the bone. But the emaciation is understandable, considering that for five months I have been living exclusively on willpower, without the slightest desire for food.

I have my job to get back to, and my mother and father will be in despair. And God knows what will have happened to Helen. Did I marry her? I have no wedding ring. But we were engaged. And it is another confirmation of my youth that my feelings for her are as they were then — stronger, in fact, yes, a good deal stronger, though speaking impartially these feelings that seem to be for her might easily be nothing but my desperate longing to get back to the world in general — a longing that is using my one-time affection for Helen as a sort of form or model. It's possible, very possible, that I have in reality forgotten her, even that I am sixty years old, that she has been dead for thirty-four years. Certain things may be very different from what I imagine. If I were to take this drift of thoughts to the logical extreme there is no absolute proof that my job, my parents, Helen, and the whole world are not simply my own invention, fantasies my imagination has improvised on the simple themes of my own form, my clothes, my chair, and the properties of my present environment. I am in no position to be sure about anything.

But there is more to existence, fortunately, than consideration of possibilities. There is conviction, faith. If there were not, where would I be? The moment I allow one of these 'possibilities' the slightest intimacy — a huge futility grips me, as it were physically, by the heart, as if the organ itself were despairing of this life and ready to give up.

Courageous and calm. That should be my prayer. I should repeat that, repeat it like the Buddhists with their 'O jewel of the lotus'. Repeat it till it repeats itself in my very heart, till every heartbeat drives it through my whole body. Courageous and calm. This is the world, think no more about it.

My chair will keep me sane. My chair, my chair, my chair — I might almost repeat that. I know every mark on it, every grain. So near and true! It alone predicates a universe, the entire universe, with its tough carpentering, its sprightly, shapely design — so delicate, so strong. And while I have the game I need be afraid of nothing. Though it is dangerous. Tempting, dangerous, but — it is enough to know that the joy is mine. I set the chair down in the snow, letting myself think I am going to sleep, but instead of sitting I step back a few paces into the snow. How did I think of that? The first time, I did not dare look away from it. I had never before let it out of my hand, never let it go for a fraction between unbuckling it and sitting down on it. But then I let it go and stepped back into the snow. I had never heard my voice before. I was astonished at the sound that struggled up out of me. Well, I need the compensations. And this game does rouse my energies, so it is, in a sense, quite practical. After the game, I could run. That's the moment of danger, though, the moment of overpowering impatience when I could easily lose control and break out, follow my instinct, throw myself on luck, run out across the wind.

But there is a worse danger. If I ran out across the wind I would pretty soon come to my senses, turn my face back into the wind. It is the game itself, the stage of development it has reached, that is dangerous now. I no longer simply step back. I set the chair down, turn my face away, and walk off into the blizzard, counting my steps carefully. At fourteen paces I stop. Fifteen is the limit of vision in this dense flow of snow, so at fourteen I stop and turn. Let those be the rules. Let me fix the game at that. Because at first I see nothing. That should be enough for me. Everywhere, pouring silent grey, a silence like a pressure, like the slow coming to bear of some incalculable pressure, too gradual to detect. If I were simply to stand there my mind would crack in a few moments. But I concentrate, I withdraw my awe from the emptiness and look pointedly into it. At first, everything is as usual – as I have seen it for five months. Then my heart begins to thump unnaturally, because I seem to make out a dimness, a shadow that wavers deep in the grey turmoil, vanishes and darkens, rises and falls. I step one pace forward and using all my willpower stop again. The shadow is as it was. Another step. The shadow seems to be a little darker. Then it vanishes and I lunge two steps forward but immediately stop because there it is, quite definite, no longer moving. Slowly I walk towards it. The rules are that I keep myself under control, that I restrain all sobs or shouts though of course it is impossible to keep the breathing regular – at this stage at least, and right up to the point where the shadow resolves into a chair. In that vast grey dissolution – my chair! The snowflakes are drifting against the legs and gliding between the struts, bumping against them, clinging and crawling over the seat. To control myself then is not within human power. Indeed I seem to more or less lose consciousness at that point. I'm certainly not responsible for the weeping, shouting thing that falls on my chair, embracing it, kissing it, bruising his cheeks against it. As the snowflakes tap and run over my gloves and over the chair I begin to call them names. I peer into each one as if it were a living face, full of speechless recognition, and I call to them – Willy, Joanna, Peter, Jesus, Ferdinand, anything that comes into my head, and shout to them and nod and laugh. Well, it's harmless enough madness.

The temptation to go beyond the fourteen paces is now becoming painful. To go deep into the blizzard. Forty paces. Then come back, peering. Fifteen paces, twenty paces. Stop. A shadow.

That would not be harmless madness. If I were to leave my chair like that the chances are I would never find it again. My footprints do not exist in this undertow of snow. Weeks later, I would still be searching, casting in great circles, straining at every moment to pry a shadow out of the grey sameness. My chair meanwhile a hundred miles away in the blizzard, motionless – neat legs and elegant back, sometimes buried, sometimes uncovering again. And for centuries, long after I'm finished, still sitting there, intact with its tooth-marks and missing strut, waiting for a darkening shape to come up out of the nothingness and shout to it and fall on it and possess it.

But my chair is here, on my back, here. There's no danger of my ever losing it. Never so long as I keep control, keep my mind firm. All the facts are on my side. I have nothing to do but endure.

LEROI JONES (Imamu Aneer Baraka) was born in 1934 in Newark, New Jersey, where he now lives. As a novelist, poet, essayist, and short-story writer, he has been preoccupied chiefly with themes about his fellow blacks and the nature of racial degradation. His work includes *The Dead Lecturer* and other poems; the plays, *Dutchman, The Slave*, and *The Toilet*; a novel, *The System of Dante's Hell*; and a book on jazz, *Blues People*.

answers in progress

LEROI JONES

Can you die in air-raid jiggle
torn arms flung through candystores
Touch the edge of answer. The waves of nausea
as change sweeps the frame of breath and meat.

'Stick a knife through his throat,'
          he slid
           in the blood
         got up running towards
      the blind newsdealer. He screamed
    about 'Cassius Clay', and slain there in the
  street, the whipped figure of jesus, head opened
eyes flailing against his nose. They beat him to
pulpy answers. We wrote Muhammad Ali across his
face and chest, like a newspaper of bleeding meat.

The next day the spaceships landed. Art Blakey records was what they were looking for. We gave them Buttercorn Lady and they threw it back at us. They wanted to know what happened to the Jazz Messengers. And right in the middle, playing the Sun-Ra tape, the blanks staggered out of the department store. Omar had missed finishing the job, and they staggered out, falling in the snow, red all over the face chest, the stab wounds in one in the top of an Adam hat.

The spacemen thought that's what was really happening. One beeped (Ali mentioned this in the newspapers) that this was evolution. Could we dig it? Shit, yeh. We were laughing. Some blanks rounded one corner, Yaa and Dodua were behind them, to take them to the Centre. Nationalized on the spot.

The spacemen could dig everything. They wanted to take one of us to a spot and lay for a minute, to dig what they were into. Their culture and shit. Whistles Newark was broke up in one section. The dead mayor and other wops carried by in black trucks. Wingo, Rodney, and them waving at us. They stopped the first truck and Cyril wanted to know about them thin cats hopping around us. He's always very fast finger.

Spacemen wanted to know what happened after Blakey. They'd watched but couldn't get close enough to dig exactly what was happening. Albert Ayler they dug immediately from Russell's mouth imitation. That's later. Red spam came in their throats with the voices, and one of them started to scat. It wigged me. Bamberger's burning down, dead blancos all over and a cat from Sigma Veda, and his brothers, hopping up and down asking us what was happening.

We left Rachel and Lefty there to keep explaining. Me and Pinball had to go back to headquarters, and report Market Street Broad Street rundown. But we told them we'd talk to them. I swear one of those cats had a hip walk. Even though they was hoppin and bopadoppin up and down, like they had to pee. Still this one cat had a stiff tentacle, when he walked. Yeh; long blue winggly cats, with soft liquid sounds out of their throats for voices. Like, 'You know where Art Blakey, Buhainia, is working?' We fell out.

Walk through life
beautiful more than anything
stand in the sunlight
walk through life
love all the things
that make you strong, be lovers, be anything
for all the people of
earth.

You have brothers

you love each other, change up
and look at the world
now, it's
ours, take it slow
we've long time, a long way
to go,

we have
each other, and the
world
don't be sorry
walk on out through sunlight life, and know
we're on the go
for love
to open
our lives
to walk
tasting the sunshine
of life.

Boulevards played songs like that and we rounded up blanks where we had to. Spacemen were on the south side laying in some of the open houses. Some brothers came in from the west, Chicago, they had a bad thing going out there. Fires were still high as the buildings, but Ram sent a couple of them out to us, to dig what was happening. One of them we sent to the blue cats, to take that message back. Could W dig what was happening with them? We sent our own evaluation back, and when I finished the report me and Pinball started weaving through the dead cars and furniture. Waving at the brothers, listening to the sounds, we had piped through the streets.

Smokey Robinson was on now. But straight up fast and winging. No more unrequited love. Damn Smokey got his thing together too. No more tracks or mirages. Just the beauty of the whole. I hope they play Sun-Ra for them blue cats, so they can dig where we at.

Magic City played later. By time we got to the courthouse, the whole top of that was out. Like you could look inside from fourth or fifth floor of the Hall of Records. Cats were all over that joint. Ogun wanted the records intact.

Past the playgrounds and all them blanks in the cold standing out there or laying on the ground crying. The rich ones really were funny. This ol cat me an Pinball recognized still had a fag thing going for him. In a fur coat, he was some kind of magistrate. Bobby and Moosie were questioning him about some silver he was supposed to have stashed.

He was a silver freak. The dude was actually weeping. Crying big sobs; the women crowded away from him. I guess they really couldn't feel sorry for him because he was crying about money.

By the time we got to Weequahic Avenue where the spacemen and out-of-town brothers were laying I was tired as a dog. We went in there and wanted to smoke some bush, but these blue dudes had something better. Taste like carrots. It was a cool that took you. You thought something was mildly amusing and everything seemed interesting.

I talked with Pinball and the blue leader about Ben Caldwell's paintings ... the one where the guy is smoking the reefer. We thought about the changing reference of our new world. As it stood already in the old ruins. And we all felt like Bird. The old alto saxophonist ... but the limits opened out into the pure lyric tone of powerful beings. But when the Sun-Ra tape came on this blue dude really opened up. He dug the hell out of it. Perfect harmony these cats had too. Boooooo – Iiiiiiiioooooooooooooo ... daaaaa ahhhhhhhh aaaaahhhhhh ... booooo OOOOOOOOOOOOO oooooooooaaaaaaaaoooaaaaa

Claude McKay I started quoting. Four o'clock in the morning to a blue dude gettin cooled out on carrots. We didn't have no duty until ten o'clock the next day, and me and Lorenzo and Ish had to question a bunch of prisoners and stuff for the TV news. Chazee had a play to put on that next afternoon about the Chicago stuff. Ray talked to him. And the name of the play was Big Fat Fire.

Man I was tired. We had taped the Sigma. They were already infested with Buddhas there, and we spoke very quietly about how we knew it was our turn. I had burned my hand somewhere and this blue cat looked at it hard and cooled it out. White came in with the design for a flag he'd been working on. Black heads, black hearts, and blue fiery space in the background. Love was heavy in the atmosphere. Ball wanted to know what the blue chicks looked like. But I didn't. Cause I knew after tomorrow's duty, I had a day off, and I knew somebody waitin for me at my house, and some kids, and some fried fish, and those carrots, and wow.

That's the way the fifth day ended.

March 1967

JERZY KOSINSKI was born in Poland in 1933 and now lives in New York City. Although he has been widely translated, he writes only in English. Under the pen name of Joseph Novak, he is the author of two books on collective behaviour: *The Future Is Ours, Comrade* and *No Third Path*; and two novels, *The Painted Bird* and *Steps*, which received the National Book Award in 1968 and from which the following extract is taken. A dramatic version of *Steps* was produced by the Vale Repertory Theatre early in 1971.

from steps

JERZY KOSINSKI

If I could become one of them, if I could only part with my language, my manner, my belongings.

I was in a bar in a run-down section of the city beyond the covered bazaar. Without hesitating I walked over to the bartender. As he leaned forward I began my deaf-mute charade, signalling for a glass of water. The barman waved me away impatiently, but I stood my ground and repeated my pantomime. I could feel the stares of the people in the bar. When I jerked my shoulders and flapped my ear like a spastic they scrutinized me closely, and I sensed that to some of them I had suddenly become an object of interest. I knew I had to be very careful of their suspicions, of any attempt to find out who I was or where I had come from.

Two men and a woman edged nearer, and touched me. At first I ignored their overtures, giving the woman, the boldest and most silent, a chance to elbow the others aside.

I continued to motion for water. A man came forward to order a drink for me, but I refused, grimacing my disgust for arrack and gesturing apologies for my refusal. A couple drew closer. They beckoned me to leave with them. I did not understand what they were saying, and making a show of being attracted to the bright jewellery they wore, I turned and slowly looked into their faces. Their gaze bore down on me.

There was a store I entered several times. Nothing distinguished it from the others of the neighbourhood. Most of the shops and bars in the vicinity had some connexion with illegal activities – the black market, stolen goods, or traffic in young country girls. Often I hung around the shop until closing time, and watched the patrons wandering out the back door to the barn in the yard. As a silent, gesturing spastic I was not a threat to the callers – I could be given a task, a few coins, and then be dismissed. Eventually I followed them, but was pushed back into the shop and out into the street. The final time I stayed late and tried to join the men. No one stopped me, but at the barn door a woman motioned me to stand guard.

From my vantage point I peered into the barn. I saw a great circle of naked men lying on their backs, their feet joined at the centre like the spokes of a wheel. A woman was standing at their feet, pulling off her ragged dress. She was gross and heavy, her skin moist and hairy. She was splashing water from a wooden bucket over her belly and legs. And as she washed herself and the water spattered on the ground, the men fidgeted, their hands playing at their thighs or their arms shifting behind their heads. It was as though she had become the healer of these broken men, and at the sound of the water a momentary surge went through these petty thieves and weary pimps. She plodded across to one of them, squatting over him. For a moment he grunted, cried out hoarsely, half rose, and then fell heavily back. The woman stepped away from him and passed on to his neighbour, picking her way like a bloated toad over the worn stones of a mudhole. One by one she served them; those she had not yet reached twitched in their efforts to restrain the energy that surged through their loins. One by one they fell back, like corpses laid out in shallow coffins. Now the barn looked as if it had been pressed into service for the dead and the dying from a derailed train. As she rose and walked around the silent men, the woman resembled a nurse checking the victims. She bathed, and again the water splashed. Now there was no answering sound, no movement.

At times my disguise became a hazard. One day, wandering about longer than usual, I decided to have a meal before finding a place to sleep. I went into a place that I knew was usually crowded. The bar itself was almost empty that night. But I spotted several familiar faces – a group of manual workers in the front of the room and two or three of the local bosses, their heads together, at the private tables in the back.

A surly peasant stood at the counter, mumbling as he drank. Away by the wall, half lost in the shadows, a man was slumped over his glass.

Suddenly the street door blew open and a dozen policemen rushed in. Some stationed themselves between the door and the crowd; others followed a kitchen boy to the man drooping at the bar.

The police first sat the man up, then pulled him off the stool. As his body swung around I caught sight of the knife that stuck out from his ribs. There was a bloodstain on the wall. The crowd broke into a frenzy of talk. Only then did I realize that I was the likeliest suspect of them all. There could be no explanation for my dress, my acts, or my presence.

If I continued to be a deaf-mute, I would be accused of this crime, the senseless act of a defective. My mask would trap me further. But if I were to bolt through the police cordon, I would risk a bullet. I realized that within a few seconds I would be led away with the others. Turning towards the bar I picked up the bartender's rag, and seizing a tray of dirty coffee cups, trotted into the kitchen.

Occasionally I would attempt to get part-time jobs. One night, employed as a handyman in a neighbourhood restaurant, I noticed the proprietor sitting and talking with the last customers – three men and a woman.

There had been a short circuit downstairs; I approached the table, motioning to the proprietor. I met the woman's startled, uncertain glance and instantly exaggerated my role: I slapped my right ear several times as the men guffawed. She blushed, as if ashamed of her companions, but she continued to watch me.

The woman returned several days later accompanied by a man I had not seen before. It was late and most of the tables were empty. Since the proprietor was away, I went to the two as soon as they were seated. The woman's left hand lay palm down on the tablecloth, and she was attentively rubbing her cuticles with her right forefinger. I emptied the ashtray and adjusted the napkins and cutlery. The man asked for something, and when I shrugged meekly, the woman spoke, perhaps explaining that she had seen me before and that I could neither hear nor speak. The man scrutinized me coldly, then relaxed as I brushed an invisible speck of dust from the tablecloth. The woman nervously crumpled her handkerchief, obviously conscious of my proximity. I withdrew without turning around and again slapped my ears.

Next day I was summoned by the proprietor, who explained in gestures that I had to do a different job. An hour later one of the waiters led me to a tall apartment house, where we took an elevator to the top floor. The door was opened by the woman I had seen in the restaurant.

I was hired to clean her apartment after the large parties she regularly gave. The parties, catered by the restaurant where I had worked, were often attended by the underworld. I was careful not to wander too close to the rooms with locked doors. I knew of too many people who had vanished from that quarter of the city because of their curiosity. After several days my presence and the hum of my vacuum cleaner went as unnoticed as the familiar creaking of the floorboards or the intermittent rattle of the steam pipes.

While dusting the furniture I covertly watched the woman's face reflected in mirrors: her image split into fragments as she rearranged her hair. I would smile politely when I caught her hesitant glance.

I worked undisturbed because my duties were simple and I needed no instruction. I noticed that when my new employer wanted to tell me something she became selfconscious and was upset by my violent ear-slappings.

Several times she tested me. Once when I was dusting, she silently approached the piano and struck a chord. Another time, as I was putting away the wineglasses, she came from behind and suddenly shouted. I managed to restrain even the smallest twitch. One evening, without looking at me, she motioned for me to follow her.

She forgot herself completely as she stretched under me, her eyes straining towards the headboard. Her whole body became involved in drawing breath, driven by tides and currents flowing and ebbing in rapid surges. Swaying like a clump of weed in the sea, she quivered, a rushing stream of words broke over her lips like foam. It was as if I were the master of all this fluid passion, and her tumbling words its final wave.

In her last outpouring she broke into a language I could understand, and spoke of herself as a zealot entering a church built long ago from the ruins of pagan temples, a novice in the inner sanctum of the church, not knowing at whose altar she knelt, to which god she prayed.

Her voice grew rough and hoarse as she writhed on the bed, thrashing from side to side. I held her arms and shook her, diving into her with all my weight. Like a joyous mare in its solitary stall, she cried out again and again, as though trying to detach into speech what had been fused with her flesh. She whispered that she veered towards the sun, which would melt her with its heat. Her sentences poured and broke, and she muttered that the sun left only the glow of stars brushing close to each other. Slowly her lips grew parched – she slept.

*   *   *

There were rumours that a revolution was about to break out in another country. Its central government was falling apart. The country was divided into two camps: on one side the students and the farmers who opposed the President; on the other, the workers who felt the time was ripe for their party to stage a coup. The President, rumours had it, sided with the party, convinced that it would receive aid from a neighbouring country where it had held power for almost two decades.

For me this was an opportunity. I had never seen or been involved in a revolution; all I had ever done was read about them or watch them on television newsreels.

I left my job and the next day was on a plane. After landing at the palm-fringed airport, I deposited my suitcase in a small hotel and mingled with the large groups of men who roamed the city. More and more of them now carried arms and banners. As I did not understand their language, I played a deaf-mute, and I played my part well.

Each group I joined claimed me as its own, handing me weapons and insignia as if convinced that it was the most natural thing in the world for a spastic to fight for the future they envisioned for their country.

Early one evening a series of explosions shook the capital. When I was ordered to a large truck loaded with assorted weapons, I knew the coup had begun. As we drove through the darkened city, our headlights outlined other armed units crossing our path and entrenching themselves behind overturned buses and makeshift barricades. Soon we saw the dead lying in pools of blood on the sidewalks, like abandoned sacks of wheat. Other bands of armed men joined us, and we raced towards the outskirts of the city. The trucks stopped and we jumped down, carrying our rifles and long knives. In a few moments we had surrounded a group of buildings. The men entered the houses; the rest of us stood expectantly in the background.

The captives were brought out one after another, many of them half naked. Not knowing what had happened, some of them tried to ask questions or say something, but were quickly silenced. Inside the buildings women screamed and children cried. The number of prisoners in front of us kept increasing, and soon there were dozens.

The commander of our group ordered the prisoners to turn and face the wall. I was certain that they were about to be shot. Not wanting to participate in the execution, I gestured to the man next to me, offering to exchange my rifle for his long knife. The man agreed. I was just about to hide behind one of the trucks when I was roughly pushed forward by men also armed with knives. Each of us was ordered to stand directly behind one of the prisoners.

I glanced around me: the armed men, tense and ready, stood at my sides and behind me. Only then did I realize that the prisoners were

about to be beheaded. My refusal to obey orders would mean my being
executed with those who stood in front of me. I could no longer see
their faces, but their shirts were only a few inches from the blade of my
knife.

It was inconceivable, I thought, that I would have to slash the neck of
another man simply because events had placed me behind his back.
What I was about to do was inescapable, yet so unreal that it became
senseless: I had to believe I was not myself any more and that whatever
happened would be imaginary. I saw myself as someone else who felt
nothing, who stood calm and composed, determined enough to stiffen
his arms, to grasp and raise the weapon, to cut down the obstacle in his
path. I knew I was strong enough to do it. I could recall the precision
with which I had felled young trees: I could hear their moaning and
creaking, and see their trembling, and I knew I could jump aside as they
cracked and fell, their leaves brushing my feet.

LEONARD MICHAELS was born in 1933 and is a native New Yorker. His short stories, which have appeared in numerous quarterlies and reviews, were collected in 1969 under the title *Going Places*. He is now attached to the Institute for Creative Arts at the University of California.

mildred

LEONARD MICHAELS

Mildred was at the mirror all morning, cutting and shaping her hair. Then, every hour or so, she came up to me with her head tipped like this, like that, cheeks sucked in, a shine licked across her lips. I said, 'Very nice,' and finally I said, 'Very, very nice.'

'I'm not pretty.'

'Yes; you're pretty.'

'I know I'm attractive in a way, but basically I'm ugly.'

'Your hair is very nice.'

'Basically, I hate my type. When I was little I used to wish my name were Terry. Do you like my hair?'

'Your hair is very nice.'

'I think you're stupid-looking.'

'That's life.'

'You're the only stupid-looking boyfriend I ever had. I've had stupid boyfriends, but none of them looked stupid. You look stupid.'

'I like your looks.'

'You're also incompetent, indifferent, a liar, a crook, and a coward.'

'I like your looks.'

'I was told that except for my nose my face is perfect. It's true.'

'What's wrong with your nose?'

'I don't have to say it, Miller.'

'What's wrong with it?'

'My nose, I've been told, is a millimetre too long. Isn't it?'

'I like your nose.'

'Coward. I can forgive you for some things, but cowardice is unforgivable. And I'll get you for this, Miller. I'll make you cry.'

'I like your legs.'

'You're the only boyfriend I've ever had who was a coward. It's easy to like my legs.'

'They're beautiful. I like both of them.'

'Ha. Ha. What about my nose?'

'I'm crazy about your big nose.'

'You dirty, fuck'n aardvark. What about yours, Miller? Tell me . . .'

The phone rang.

'His master's voice,' she said and snatched it away from me. 'Me, this time. Hello.' She smacked it down.

'What was that about?'

'A man.'

'What did he say?'

'Disgusting.'

'What did he say?'

'He asked how much I charged . . . I don't care to talk about it.'

'To what?'

'It was disgusting. I don't care to talk about it, understand. Answer the fuck'n phone yourself next time.'

She dropped on to the bed. 'Hideous.'

'Did you recognize the voice?'

'I was humiliated.'

'Tell me what he said.'

'It must have been one of your stinking friends. I'm going to rip that phone out of the wall. Just hideous, hideous.'

I lay down beside her.

'He asked how much I charged to suck assholes.'

I shut my eyes.

'Did you hear what I said, Miller?'

'Big deal.'

'I was humiliated.'

'You can't stand intimacy.'

'I'll rip out the phone if it happens once more. You can make your calls across the street in the bar.'

'He was trying to say he loves you.'

She thrashed into one position, then another, then another. I opened my eyes and said, 'Let's play our game.'

'No; I want to sleep.'

'All right, lie still. I want to sleep too.'

'Then sleep.'

I shut my eyes.

'I'll play once. You send.'

'Never mind. Let me sleep.'

'You suggested it.'

'I've changed my mind.'

'Son of a bitch. Always the same damn shit.'

'I'm sending. Go on.'

'Do you see it clearly?'

'Yes.'

'I see a triangle.'

I didn't say anything.

'A triangle, that's all. I see a triangle, Miller. What are you sending?'

'Jesus Christ. Jee-zuss Chrice. I've got chills everywhere.'

'Tell me what you were sending.'

'A diamond. First a sailboat with a white triangular sail, then a diamond. I sent the diamond.'

I turned. Her eyes were waiting for me.

'You and me,' I whispered.

'We're the same, Miller. Aren't we?'

I kissed her on the mouth. 'If you want to change your mind, say so.'

'I am you,' she whispered, kissing me. 'Let's play more.'

'I'll call Max and tell him not to come.'

'He isn't coming, anyway. Let's play more.'

'I'm sleepy.'

'It's my turn to send.'

'I'm very sleepy.'

'You are a son of a bitch.'

'Enough. I haven't slept for days.'

'What about me? Don't you ever think about me? I warn you, Miller, don't go to sleep. I'll do something.'

'I want to sleep.'

'Miller, I see something. Quick. Please.'

'A flower.'

'You see a flower?'

'It's red.'

'What kind of flower? I was sending a parachute.'

'That's it, Mildred. A parachute flower.'

'Fuck you, Miller.'

'You, too. Let me sleep.'

'Miller, I still see something. Hurry. Try again.'

I lay still, eyes shut. Nothing came to me except a knock at the door, so quiet I imagined I hadn't heard it. She said, 'Was that a knock?'

I sat up and listened, then got out of bed and went to the door. It was Max and Sleek. Max nodded hello. Sleek stepped backwards, but a smile moved in his pallor. I said, 'Hi.' I heard Mildred rushing to the kitchen sink and held them at the door. 'Only one room and a kitchen,' I said. Max nodded again. The smile faded slowly in Sleek's pale, flat face. Water crashed, then she was shooting to the closet, jamming into heels, scrambling a blouse on her back. A light went on. She slashed her mouth with lipstick. 'Come in, come in.'

They came in.

'Please sit down.'

Max sat down in his coat, looked into the folds across his lap, and began to roll a cigarette. Sleek sat down in his coat, too, watching Max. Both of them glanced once at Mildred, then at each other. I said, then Max said. Sleek laughed feebly as if suppressing a cough. Then they both stared at her, Max offered her the first drag on the cigarette. She said quickly, but in a soft voice, cool, shy. They looked at one another, Max and Sleek, and agreed with their eyes: she was a smart little girl. I sat down. I told them she might be pregnant. We were thinking about getting married, I said. I was going to look for a new job. Everyone laughed at something. Max said, Sleek said. They took off their coats. She was now shining awake, feeling herself, being looked at.

'Do you want some coffee?' She tossed her hair slightly with the question.

Max said, 'Do you have milk?'

Sleek said, 'Coffee.'

She curled tightly in her chair, legs underneath, making knees, shins, ankles to look at. They looked. I stood up and went into the kitchen for the coffee and milk. Max was saying and Sleek added. She was quick again, laughing, doing all right for herself. I took my time, then came back in with the coffee and milk. I asked what they were into lately, imports, exports, hustlers, what. Sleek sucked the cigarette. Max rolled another and was looking at Mildred. He asked if she had considered an abortion. She smiled. Sleek said I was an old friend. He would get us a discount. They wouldn't take their cut until I had a new job. They shook their heads. No cut. Max mentioned a doctor in Jersey, a chiropractor on Seventy-second Street. He said his own girl had had an abortion and died. Almost drove him nuts. He drank like a pleeb. You have to get a clean doctor. Otherwise it can be discouraging. His stable was clean. Sleek nodded shrewdly, something tight in his face, as if he knew. 'Of course,' he said. 'Of course.' He opened his hand and showed Mildred some pills. She raised an eyebrow, shrugged, looked at me. I was grinning, almost blind.

'Do what you like.'

She took a pill. I took a pill, too. Max talked about the eggbeater they used and what comes out, little fingers, little feet. Mildred squirmed, showed a line of thigh, feel of hip, ankles shaped like fire.

'Abortions are safe,' I said and waved a hand.

'Right,' said Max. He tossed a pill into his mouth.

Sleek said he had a new kind of pill. Mildred asked shyly with her eyes. He offered immediately. She took it. 'The whole country shoves pills up itself,' he said. 'My mother takes stoppies at night and goies in the morning.' He gleamed, sucked the cigarette, and sat back as if something had been achieved.

Max frowned, mentioned his dead girl, and said it hadn't been his baby. He shook his head, grinding pity, and said, 'Discouraging.'

'Your mother?' asked Mildred.

Sleek said she lived in Brooklyn. I nodded as if to confirm that he had a mother. He whispered, 'The womb is resilient. Always recovers.' Max said, 'Made of steel.' 'Of course,' said Sleek, 'chicks are tough.' Mildred agreed, sat up, showed us her womb. Max took it, squeezed, passed it to Sleek. He suppressed a laugh, then glanced at me.

'Squeeze, squeeze,' I said.

He said, 'Tough number. Like steel.'

I said it looked edible. Sleek stared at Mildred. She got up and took her womb to the stove. I had a bite. Max munched and let his eyelids fall to show his pleasure. Sleek took a sharp little bite and made a smacking noise in his mouth. I felt embarrassed, happy. Mildred seemed happy, seeing us eat. I noticed her grope furtively for something else to eat. But it was late now. Rain banged like hammers, no traffic moved in the street. They waited for a few more minutes, then Max yawned, belched, stood up. 'We'll get a cab on Sixth Avenue,' he said to Sleek. I said we would decide, then get in touch with him right away. We thanked them for the visit. I apologized for not being more definite. Max shrugged. They were in the neighbourhood, anyway. Sleek said take a couple of days to think about it. Gay things were said at the door. Max said, Sleek said, Mildred laughed goodbye. Their voices and feet went down the stairs.

Mildred kicked off her shoes. I turned out the light. We kissed. I put my hand between her legs. She began to cry.

'You may not love me, Miller, but you'll cry when I'm gone.'

'Stop it,' I said.

She cried. I made fists and pummelled my head. She cried. I pummelled until my head slipped into my neck. She stopped crying. I smashed my mouth with my knee. She smiled a little.

'Do it again.'

I started eating my face. She watched, then her eyes grew lazy, lids like gulls, sailing down. She lay back and spread underneath like a parachute. I lay beside her and looked at the window. It was black and shining with rain. I said, 'I like your hair, Mildred, your eyes, your nose, your legs. I love your voice.' She breathed plateaux and shallow, ragged gullies. She slept on her back, mouth open, hands at her sides, turned up. Rain drilled the window. Thunder burdened the air.

H. L. MOUNTZOURES was born in 1934 on Fishers Island in New York and now lives in New London, Connecticut. Several of his stories have appeared in *The Atlantic, Redbook,* and *The New Yorker,* and a collection was published in 1968 under the title *The Empire of Things and Other Stories.*

the empire of things

H. L. MOUNTZOURES

We walked through the vast Tudor building. There were many of us registering. I was surprised and happy to see college friends from ten years ago whom I had not seen since graduation. Don Fielding came in. His face was red and shiny, and he had all of his hair; he looked exactly as he had in first-year French; only a class beanie was lacking. 'What are you doing here?' I asked him. Shyly, he pulled at his crew-neck sweater and said, 'The same thing you are.'

We shuffled through a long line. Trembling little old women gave us our clothes and gear. At the end of the first line, a fat woman handed me a folded green entrenching tool. 'You must be careful of colour and concealment,' she said. I looked at her closely. She was my elementary-school physical-education teacher — Miss Holstein. Her face was very tan. There was no lipstick on her mouth. She had short, fuzzy brown hair and bowling-pin legs, and she wore a plain mauve suit and pale calfskin flat shoes with thick soles. She held a big brown rubber dodge ball in her left hand.

I started to acknowledge her. She raised a finger and frowned. I moved on to another line. One of my best friends from college, Tim O'Connell, came in through a dark-stained door full of tiny glittering window-panes. We embraced and shook hands. He, too, had not changed. He was huge and burly as always, and his laughter was exactly as I remembered it – deep, throaty, almost mournful. He had a large mouth.

I said, 'You look the same after all this time.'

'So do you,' he said. 'You haven't changed a bit.'

'But I'd have thought everyone would look older.'

He shrugged. 'How's your family?'

'Great. I miss them. Especially my son. He's seven. The last time I saw him, he was boarding a big yellow school bus on the hill in front of our house. I'd just turned to get into my car when I saw the red signals of the bus flashing. It was raining, and Charlie – that's my son – was the last one on, because he was having trouble closing his umbrella. It was a red umbrella. He's so little I wondered if he was ever going to get it down, but he finally did. I waved with my briefcase, he waved back, and the bus shut off its signals and chugged up the hill. That's the last I saw of him. The rascal.'

The huge room, nostalgically like my college dining-hall, bustled with men getting their packs together. Someone blew a whistle. Milling and chatting, we settled on the floor. How odd. Now it was kindergarten, with narrow planks beneath us, shiny oak, and we were very close to earth, to the bottom. Would there be a piano and singing? Or cut-out time, and furtive eating of paste that tasted of wintergreen.

Miss Holstein came to the front. We stood. She pulled down a silvery granulated screen. There was a flag behind her. We pledged allegiance, sang God Bless America, and sat down again. With pointer in hand, she said softly, 'I am going to give a very brief orientation. Then we will go into the warehouse.'

As she talked slowly on and on, the sun shone on her tan, fuzzy face. How much it was like the sun of childhood autumns, early Septembers, when school started. '. . . here to help the troops,' she was saying. 'We are brave little soldiers in our own way.' There was a squirming around me. 'Soldiers of mercy. Soldiers of peace, dealing with things. We are going to help our fighting men not with prayer, not with entertainment, not even with coffee and doughnuts, but with concrete things that will remind them of home, and civilization, and history, and meaning. Things that will boost our men's morale and help them see it through. Do you understand?'

We all droned peacefully.

'Pull the shades. First slide, please.' The windows became deep, warm yellow, the room pleasantly dark. Several maps flashed onto the screen. They showed crude road lines, supply lines, chow areas, latrine areas, the combat zone. Company headquarters – our location – lay on the west. From it three fat black arrows flared north, east, and south. Miss Holstein swept the pointer over the arrows. She said, 'This part of the jungle is your working radius. You will use compasses. Next slide, please. Ah. Here are some of the things.' Slides flashed in rapid succession. They showed small articles of furniture, glassware, china, toys, linen. The slides ended.

We were taken to an adjoining room, the warehouse. It turned out to be an immaculate museum, with much the same kind of things we had seen on the screen. Each was encased in glass and labelled. 'Chippendale chair.' 'Porringer, 1784.' 'Hand mirror of Mme Pompadour.' 'Earrings from Knossos, 1600 BC.' Stuff like that. We were all impressed.

Miss Holstein gathered us around like a large group of tourists. Pointing, she said, 'When you go through that door, you'll be on your own. Remember to gather your things compactly in a container you'll find, such as a chest or a bureau. And don't take more than you can carry alone. By the time you fill your containers, you should be near enough the combat zone to deliver them personally to our fighting men. Then your mission is done. You will return here. It'll be cookies and milk and a long rest. You'll have earned it. Good luck.'

We applauded respectfully. She marched to the door and opened it. Everyone filed through.

The jungle was like home – the woods in New Hampshire. I did not understand. Maple trees, birch, oak, beech, pines. Some swamp. Rocks. But no open fields.

We spread out to find containers for our things. It was fun – like a large Easter-egg hunt. We discovered dust-covered chests; spider-webbed bathtubs with claw feet; old, discarded refrigerators with no doors; abandoned automobiles, upholstery coming out of the seats; huge Victorian trunks. Everything was hidden among bushes, under trees, behind boulders. My colleagues cheered as they found suitable containers. Tim O'Connell was using a baby-blue Volkswagen with no wheels and no engine.

I am not a big man. I chose a strange combination of small bureau and chest. I had never seen such a piece of furniture, so I did not know the name of it. I called it a trunk. It had six big brass handles – three on each long side. Drawers with cut-glass knobs pulled magically out of the narrow ends. Yet the top opened like a lid, and inside there was no sign of the drawers. It was roomy, and you could store a lot in it if you were eclectic and not greedy for large, ostentatious things.

All the men had chosen containers. One picked a 1940-vintage washing machine. It had a small black rubber knob that you turned to let out the water. A stick to stop the agitator. No hose. As I walked by, I peeked in; the large, propeller-like agitator was still in place. I wondered how he expected to fit much in it at all.

Everyone moved out smartly with his empty container. I dragged mine for a while, then shouldered it. It got heavier and heavier. How rapidly we tire, I thought. How frail we are.

When we reached the first large cache, we shouted, 'Hurrah!' Men put down their containers and began to scoop up things. We gathered glittering identification necklaces from the green-leaved trees. Sunlight made the quick-moving men shimmer. I stopped. Was it innocence I saw on their faces? The jungle was filled with a shadowy, dappled glow and the sneaky, lithe movements of small boys. Who were the Indians, I wondered. The cowboys. Who were the bad guys and who were the good? I plucked two splendid ruby earrings from a bush where they were hanging and laid them carefully in the flowered fabric bottom of my trunk. No. They would be lost there. They were too small. I put them in one of the small end drawers instead. The drawer was lined with maroon-and-ecru striped silk. It smelled of old perfume, talcum powder. Ephemera. Death. I shook my head.

I found a tortoiseshell comb, a satinwood natural-bristle brush. I wondered whose they had been as I laid them gently in the drawer. A bag of marbles, with 'Joe – 1876' embroidered on it. A First World War lead soldier. He had a pink painted face and a brilliant red dot of a mouth.

I spotted a large, beautiful white porcelain Cheshire cat. I must have dragged the trunk a mile farther before I found some burlap, wrapped the cat up, and put him in the bottom of the sweet-sour trunk. Next to a tree stump, I found a long leather change purse divided into two compartments, with two snap prongs to open and close it. It smelled wonderfully of leather, slightly mouldy. Someone could use it. I put it in one of the drawers. This drawer was lined with an old yellowed news-paper. The visible headlines were about a Senate debate, a stock-market decline, and an accidental drowning. I came on two hurricane lamps tangled in brambles. They would do to light a soldier's reading and correspondence. I wrapped the lamps in many green leaves and placed them gently in the trunk.

I heard a bullet zing. Must be getting near the front line. Act fast, I told myself, but choose. Here was a hobby-horse with one of its madly staring agate eyes missing. Painted spots on its rippling body were fading, gone. I wanted to take that, but I had to be selective. Beside it stood a squat black iron play stove. Charming but useless. A pair of opera glasses. Perfect for reconnaissance. Into the trunk with them. Seven home-knitted brown woollen mufflers. Four sealed pints of brown, coagulated Red Cross blood dated January, 1944. Good.

T—I

The mosquitoes were intolerable. It was getting hotter. Creatures were screaming and moving in the brush. I found a toy drum. That would do. For signals, maybe. But it dissolved when I picked it up – rust. Suddenly Tim O'Connell was in front of me. He had taken off all his clothes. He was hairy and laughable, his beer belly hanging out. With palette in one hand and brush in the other, he was painting his baby-blue Volkswagen khaki and brown, green and black, beige and grey, in patches like pieces of a jigsaw puzzle.

'Miss Holstein,' he said. 'Concealment.'

I went on, dragging my trunk. As I passed, I looked at what he had in his Volkswagen. An enormous clear-plastic bag of popcorn. An elaborate Telefunken radio. Several red-and-black plaid blankets. An embalming kit. An old, mineral-stained porcelain toilet bowl. About ten pairs of ladies' high-heel pumps, an ostrich boa, and a large goldfish bowl full of packs of prophylactics. A sawhorse, and two stuffed baby alligators. Not very selective, I thought. Yet I must not judge. 'I'll see you later,' I said. 'That's quite a fine collection of things.'

'Thanks.'

I heaved my trunk on to my back. The terrain was changing. There were vines. Huge tropical flowers. Sweet-smelling, rotting fruit underfoot, and elephant droppings. Monkeys swinging, screeching. Screaming parrots, birds of paradise. Sweat. Flies. The roar of a tiger? You could not be certain. I was groaning under the load of my trunk. God help us, I thought. I heard someone thrashing nearby (cutting with machetes?), and voices. 'A thirteenth-century triptych!' 'Gramophones!' Spanish armour!' Squeals of delight.

I wandered frantically. For a while, I could find no things. I was lost. The needle of my compass spun and spun. I just missed a quicksand pit. A nearly endless python slithered past. I walked for a long time.

All at once I was in a dark, misty paradise of things. I could hear no one. The others had gone. I began to gather the things as swiftly as I could, shoving them into drawers, into the trunk. It became a hungry mouth. Rain was threatening. I worked fast. I put in a dozen candlewick cutters and snuffers – silver. Sixteen morning suits, complete with striped cravats. Two beautiful heavy green-and-white croquet mallets, six croquet balls. From a tree, a large, delicate, empty gilded bird-cage. Three small crystal chandeliers. A satin wedding gown. The Regent diamond. A music box, a pillbox, and a snuffbox, all carved and jewelled. A complete moroccan-leather-bound and gold-edged set of Shakespeare. An enormous string of black pearls. A silver carving set, with jade handles. Four sets of diamond-studded andirons and pokers. An Indian inlaid-ivory jewel box.

Not bad duty, I thought. Not a bad way to serve your country. Some poor soldier will be very happy with these. I kept stuffing things into the trunk. I wanted to make someone happy. To do my part.

The heat; my khaki shirt was dripping wet. Thunder. Hurry. I found a large cut-class fruit bowl and placed it carefully in the trunk. A great pile of stage costumes with 'Traviata, Act I' labels attached to them with rusty common pins. Four cylinder Edison records, a dozen thick 78s. One was *Annie Laurie*, sung by John McCormack. I didn't read the others. What treasures. A thick velvet-covered foot-stool. A Louis XV commode. The throne with the Stone of Scone. Two American Colonial corner cupboards. All of Bach's original music scores in seventy-three huge bundles. A forty-room English castle, furnished. The trunk took everything. An old, ornate wood-and-glass hearse. Napoleon's and Josephine's bed. Three stuffed owls, a Victorian coach. The Venus de Milo. She was sticking out of the dirt, and I spent a long time carefully digging her up with my entrenching tool. She excited me as I uncovered her, but I had no time. 'La Gioconda.' I discarded it. Must choose with care. Michelangelo's 'Pietà'. The original puppet Pinocchio. All the drapes and mirrors from Versailles. And sixty-seven issues of the *Saturday Evening Post* from 1928 and 1929. Riches. I was a conquistador. Ah, a jewelled dagger. I put it in my belt. A sword. I hung that beside the dagger, swashbuckling at my side. A pirate's pistol, loaded. Three rifles, a flamethrower, four hand grenades, two bazookas, a tank, seven napalm bombs.

Let them come, the bastards. I was ready. My things were heaped high, spilling out of the trunk. I could get anyone – pick them off one by one – anyone who tried to take my things. Mosquitoes buzzed and bit me. Men's shouts in my ears; anguish. *My* stuff. I found it. Natural rights – stake a claim. Noise. Scuffles. Machine-gun fire. Snipers? I took out my weapons. I flung hand grenades. Fired the bazookas. Used the flamethrower. Scores of the enemy screamed and fell at my feet. I looked. Tim O'Connell lay there, dead, his face grinning.

It began to rain, making the flamethrower useless. A red thing was coming at me. Fast. The rain was thick and hot, steaming. The red thing ran. I could not see. I took out the pirate's pistol, aimed as best I could, and fired. It went off with a tremendous boom. There were blood flecks on my hand from the powder. The red thing quivered and fell. I looked to my side. My treasure was safe. I eased forward a few steps. The rain was pouring down like hot silver coins, and I slogged ahead in the mud and vines. The form was still. I turned it over quickly with my foot.

It was my son, Charlie, the red thing his umbrella. It stood bottom side up, filling fast with water. Charlie's tiny red mouth was open slightly. I snatched him to me. I was crying, and the rain kept coming. I kissed his limp and weightless body again and again. I carried him to the trunk. I flung out all the stuff. It took me hours. I put Charlie in gently among the cloth flowers, got the umbrella, put that in beside him. I closed the trunk. Slowly, dragging my treasure, in the stupendous jungle rain, I began to try to find my way back.

SYLVIA PLATH was born in Boston. She is best known as a poet, especially for her volumes called *Colossus* and *Ariel*; but since her suicide in 1963, at the age of thirty, a good deal of fiction has turned up in the papers she left behind. Now, less than a decade after her death, a cult is growing around her name which calls her work in both forms prophetic.

johnny panic and the bible of dreams

SYLVIA PLATH

Every day from nine to five I sit at my desk facing the door of the office and type up other people's dreams. Not just dreams. That wouldn't be practical enough for my bosses. I type up also people's daytime complaints: trouble with mother, trouble with father, trouble with the bottle, the bed, the headache that bangs home and blacks out the sweet world for no known reason. Nobody comes to our office unless they have troubles. Troubles that can't be pinpointed by Wassermanns or Wechsler-Bellevues alone.

Maybe a mouse gets to thinking pretty early on how the whole world is run by these enormous feet. Well, from where I sit I figure the world is run by one thing and this one thing only. Panic with a dog-face, devil-face, hag-face, whore-face, panic in capital letters with no face at all — it's the same Johnny Panic, awake or asleep.

When people ask me where I work, I tell them I'm assistant to the secretary in one of the outpatient departments of the Clinics Building of the City Hospital. This sounds so be-all, end-all they seldom get around to asking me more than what I do, and what I do is mainly type up records. On my own hook though, and completely under cover, I am pursuing a vocation that would set these doctors on their ears. In the privacy of my one-room apartment I call myself secretary to none other than Johnny Panic himself.

Dream by dream I am educating myself to become that rare character, rarer, in truth, than any member of the Psychoanalytic Institute: a dream connoisseur. Not a dream stopper, a dream explainer, an exploiter of dreams for the crass practical ends of health and happiness, but an unsordid collector of dreams for themselves alone. A lover of dreams for Johnny Panic's sake, the Maker of them all.

There isn't a dream I've typed up in our record books that I don't know by heart. There isn't a dream I haven't copied out at home into Johnny Panic's Bible of Dreams.

This is my real calling.

Some nights I take the elevator up to the roof of my apartment building. Some nights, about 3 A.M. Over the trees at the far side of the Common the United Fund torch flare flattens and recovers under some witchy invisible push, and here and there in the hunks of stone and brick I see a light. Most of all, though, I feel the city sleeping. Sleeping from the river on the west to the ocean on the east, like some rootless island rockabying itself on nothing at all.

I can be tight and nervy as the top string on a violin, and yet by the time the sky begins to blue I'm ready for sleep. It's the thought of all those dreamers and what they're dreaming wears me down till I sleep the sleep of fever. Monday to Friday what do I do but type up those same dreams. Sure, I don't touch a fraction of them the city over, but page by page, dream by dream, my Intake books fatten and weigh down the bookshelves of the cabinet in the narrow passage running parallel to the main hall, off which passage the doors to all the doctors' little interviewing cubicles open.

I've got a funny habit of identifying the people who come in by their dreams. As far as I'm concerned, the dreams single them out more than any Christian name. This one guy, for example, who works for a ball-bearing company in town, dreams every night how he's lying on his back with a grain of sand on his chest. Bit by bit this grain of sand grows bigger and bigger till it's big as a fair-sized house and he can't draw breath. Another fellow I know of has had a certain dream ever since they gave him ether and cut out his tonsils and adenoids when he was a kid. In this dream he's caught in the rollers of a cotton mill, fighting for his life. Oh, he's not alone, although he thinks he is. A lot of people these days dream they're being run over or eaten by machines. They're the cagey ones who won't go on the subway or the elevators. Coming back from my lunch hour in the hospital cafeteria I often pass them, puffing up the unswept stone stairs to our office on the fourth floor. I wonder, now and then, what dreams people had before ball-bearings and cotton mills were invented.

I've got a dream of my own. My one dream. A dream of dreams.

In this dream there's a great half-transparent lake stretching away in every direction, too big for me to see the shores of it, if there are any shores, and I'm hanging over it looking down from the glass belly of some helicopter. At the bottom of the lake – so deep I can only guess at the dark masses moving and heaving – are the real dragons. The ones that were around before men started living in caves and cooking meat over fires and figuring out the wheel and the alphabet. Enormous isn't the word for them; they've got more wrinkles than Johnny Panic himself. Dream about these long enough, and your feet and hands shrivel away when you look at them too closely; the sun shrinks to the size of an orange, only chillier, and you've been living in Roxbury since the last Ice Age. No place for you but a room padded soft as the first room you knew of, where you can dream and float, float and dream, till at last you actually are back among those great originals and there's no point in any dreams at all.

It's into this lake people's minds run at night, brooks and gutter-trickles to one borderless common reservoir. It bears no resemblance to those pure sparkling blue sources of drinking water the suburbs guard more jealously than the Hope diamond in the middle of pinewoods and barbed fences.

It's the sewage farm of the ages, transparence aside.

Now the water in this lake naturally stinks and smokes from what dreams have been left sogging around in it over the centuries. When you think how much room one night of dream props would take up for one person in one city, and that city a mere pinprick on a map of the world, and when you start multiplying this space by the population of the world, and that space by the number of nights there have been since the apes took to chipping axes out of stone and losing their hair, you have some idea what I mean. I'm not the mathematical type: my head starts splitting when I get only as far as the number of dreams going on during one night in the state of Massachusetts.

By this time, I already see the surface of the lake swarming with snakes, dead bodies puffed as blowfish, human embryos bobbing around in laboratory bottles like so many unfinished messages from the great I Am. I see whole storehouses of hardware: knives, paper cutters, pistons and cogs and nutcrackers; the shiny fronts of cars looming up, glass-eyed and evil-toothed. Then there's the spider-man and the web-footed man from Mars, and the simple, lugubrious vision of a human face turning aside forever, in spite of rings and vows, to the last lover of all.

One of the most frequent shapes in this large stew is so commonplace it seems silly to mention it. It's a grain of dirt. The water is thick with these grains. They seep in among everything else and revolve under some queer power of their own, opaque, ubiquitous. Call the water what you will, Lake Nightmare, Bog of Madness, it's here the sleeping people lie and toss together among the props of their worst dreams, one great brotherhood, though each of them, waking, thinks himself singular, utterly apart.

This is my dream. You won't find it written up in any casebook.

Now the routine in our office is very different from the routine in Skin Clinic, for example, or in Tumour. The other clinics have strong similarities to each other; none are like ours. In our clinic, treatment doesn't get prescribed. It is invisible. It goes right on in those little cubicles, each with its desk, its two chairs, its window, and its door with the opaque glass rectangle set in the wood. There is a certain spiritual purity about this kind of doctoring. I can't help feeling the special privilege of my position as assistant secretary in the Adult Psychiatric Clinic. My sense of pride is borne out by the rude invasions of other clinics into our cubicles on certain days of the week for lack of space elsewhere: our building is a very old one, and the facilities have not expanded with the expanding needs of the time. On these days of overlap the contrast between us and the other clinics is marked.

On Tuesdays and Thursdays, for instance, we have lumbar punctures in one of our offices in the morning. If the practical nurse chances to leave the door of the cubicle open, as she usually does, I can glimpse the end of the white cot and the dirty yellow-soled bare feet of the patient sticking out from under the sheet. In spite of my distaste at this sight, I can't keep my eyes away from the bare feet, and I find myself glancing back from my typing every few minutes to see if they are still there, if they have changed their position at all. You can understand what a distraction this is in the middle of my work. I often have to reread what I have typed several times, under the pretence of careful proof-reading, in order to memorize the dreams I have copied down from the doctor's voice over the audiograph.

Nerve Clinic next door, which tends to the grosser, more unimaginative end of our business, also disturbs us in the mornings. We use their offices for therapy in the afternoon, as they are only a morning clinic, but to have their people crying, or singing, or chattering loudly in Italian or Chinese, as they often do, without break for four hours at a stretch every morning is distracting to say the least. The patients down there are often referred to us if their troubles have no ostensible basis in the body.

In spite of such interruptions by other clinics, my own work is advancing at a great rate. By now I am far beyond copying only what comes after the patient's saying: 'I have this dream, Doctor.' I am at the point of recreating dreams that are not even written down at all. Dreams that shadow themselves forth in the vaguest way, but are themselves hid, like a statue under red velvet before the grand unveiling.

To illustrate. This woman came in with her tongue swollen and stuck out so far she had to leave a party she was giving for twenty friends of her French-Canadian mother-in-law and be rushed to our emergency ward. She thought she didn't want her tongue to stick out, and to tell the truth, it was an exceedingly embarrassing affair for her, but she hated that French-Canadian mother-in-law worse than pigs, and her tongue was true to her opinion, even if the rest of her wasn't. Now she didn't lay claim to any dreams. I have only the bare facts above to begin with, yet behind them I detect the bulge and promise of a dream.

So I set myself to uprooting this dream from its comfortable purchase under her tongue.

Whatever the dream I unearth, by work, taxing work, and even by a kind of prayer, I am sure to find a thumbprint in the corner, a bodiless mid-air Cheshire cat grin, which shows the whole work to be gotten up by the genius of Johnny Panic, and him alone. He's sly, he's subtle, he's sudden as thunder, but he gives himself away only too often. He simply can't resist melodrama. Melodrama of the oldest, most obvious variety.

I remember one guy, a stocky fellow in a nail-studded black leather jacket, running straight into us from a boxing match at Mechanics Hall, Johnny Panic hot at his heels. This guy, good Catholic though he was, young and upright and all, had one mean fear of death. He was actually scared blue he'd go to hell. He was a pieceworker at a fluorescent light plant. I remember this detail because I thought it funny he should work there, him being so afraid of the dark as it turned out. Johnny Panic injects a poetic element in this business you don't often find elsewhere. And for that he has my eternal gratitude.

I also remember quite clearly the scenario of the dream I had worked out for this guy: a Gothic interior in some monastery cellar, going on and on as far as you could see, one of those endless perspectives between two mirrors, and the pillars and walls were made of nothing but human skulls and bones, and in every niche there was a body laid out, and it was the Hall of Time, with the bodies in the foreground still warm, discolouring and starting to rot in the middle distance, and the bones emerging, clean as a whistle, in a kind of white futuristic glow at the end of the line. As I recall, I had the whole scene lighted, for the sake of accuracy, not with candles, but with the ice-bright fluorescence that makes the skin look green and all the pink and red flushes dead black-purple.

You ask, how do I know this was the dream of the guy in the black leather jacket? I don't know. I only believe this was his dream, and I work at belief with more energy and tears and entreaties than I work at recreating the dream itself.

My office, of course, has its limitations. The lady with her tongue stuck out, the guy from Mechanics Hall — these are our wildest ones. The people who have really gone floating down towards the bottom of that boggy lake come in only once, and are then referred to a place more permanent than our office, which receives the public from nine to five, five days a week only. Even those people who are barely able to walk about the streets and keep working, who aren't yet halfway down in the lake, get sent to the out-patient department at another hospital specializing in severer cases. Or they may stay a month or so in our own observation ward in the central hospital, which I've never seen.

I've seen the secretary of that ward, though. Something about her merely smoking and drinking her coffee in the cafeteria at the ten o'clock break put me off so I never went to sit next to her again. She has a funny name I don't ever quite remember correctly, something really odd, like Miss Milleravage. One of those names that seem more like a pun mixing up Milltown and Ravage than anything in the city phone directory. But not so odd a name, after all, if you've ever read through the phone directory, with its Hyman Diddlebockers and Sasparilla Greenleafs. I read through the phone book, once, never mind when, and it satisfied a deep need in me to realize how many people aren't called Smith.

Anyhow, this Miss Milleravage is a large woman, not fat, but all sturdy muscle and tall on top of it. She wears a grey suit over her hard bulk that reminds me vaguely of some kind of uniform, without the details of cut having anything strikingly military about them. Her face, hefty as a bullock's, is covered with a remarkable number of tiny maculae, as if she'd been lying under water for some time and little algae had latched on to her skin, smutching it over with tobacco-browns and greens. These moles are noticeable mainly because the skin around them is so pallid. I sometimes wonder if Miss Milleravage has ever seen the wholesome light of day. I wouldn't be a bit surprised if she'd been brought up from the cradle with the sole benefit of artificial lighting.

Byrna, the secretary in Alcoholic Clinic just across the hall from us, introduced me to Miss Milleravage with the gambit that I'd 'been in England too'.

Miss Milleravage, it turned out, had spent the best years of her life in London hospitals.

'Had a friend,' she boomed in her queer, doggish basso, not favouring me with a direct look, 'a nurse at St Bart's. Tried to get in touch with her after the war, but the head of the nurses had changed, everybody'd changed, nobody'd heard of her. She must've gone down with the old head nurse, rubbish and all, in the bombings.' She followed this with a large grin.

Now I've seen medical students cutting up cadavers, four stiffs to a classroom about as recognizably human as Moby Dick, and the students playing catch with the dead men's livers. I've heard guys joke about sewing a woman up wrong after a delivery at the charity ward of the Lying-In. But I wouldn't want to see what Miss Milleravage would write off as the biggest laugh of all time. No thanks and then some. You could scratch her eyes with a pin and swear you'd struck solid quartz.

My boss has a sense of humour too, only it's gentle. Generous as Santa on Christmas Eve.

I work for a middle-aged lady named Miss Taylor who is the head secretary of the clinic and has been since the clinic started thirty-three years ago – the year of my birth, oddly enough. Miss Taylor knows every doctor, every patient, every outmoded appointment slip, referral slip, and billing procedure the hospital has ever used or thought of using. She plans to stick with the clinic until she's farmed out in the green pastures of social security cheques. A woman more dedicated to her work I never saw. She's the same way about statistics as I am about dreams: if the building caught fire she would throw every last one of those books of statistics to the firemen below at the serious risk of her own skin.

I get along extremely well with Miss Taylor. The one thing I never let her catch me doing is reading the old record books. I have actually very little time for this. Our office is busier than the stock exchange with the staff of twenty-five doctors in and out, medical students in training, patients, patients' relatives, and visiting officials from other clinics referring patients to us, so even when I'm covering the office alone, during Miss Taylor's coffee break and lunch hour, I seldom get to dash down more than a note or two.

This kind of catch-as-catch-can is nerve-racking, to say the least. A lot of the best dreamers are in the old books, the dreamers that come in to us only once or twice for evaluation before they're sent elsewhere. For copying out these dreams I need time, a lot of time. My circumstances are hardly ideal for the unhurried pursuit of my art. There is, of course, a certain derring-do in working under such hazards, but I long for the rich leisure of the true connoisseur who indulges his nostrils above the brandy snifter for an hour before his tongue reaches out for the first taste.

I find myself all too often lately imagining what a relief it would be to bring a briefcase into work, big enough to hold one of those thick, blue, cloth-bound record books full of dreams. At Miss Taylor's lunchtime, in the lull before the doctors and students crowd in to take their afternoon patients, I could simply slip one of the books, dated ten or fifteen years back, into my briefcase, and leave the briefcase under my desk till five o'clock struck. Of course, odd-looking bundles are inspected by the doorman of the Clinics Building, and the hospital has its own staff of flatfeet to check up on the multiple varieties of thievery that go on, but for heaven's sake, I'm not thinking of making off with typewriters or heroin. I'd only borrow the book overnight and slip it back on the shelf first thing the next day before anybody else came in. Still, being caught taking a book out of the hospital would probably mean losing my job and all my source material with it.

This idea of mulling over a record book in the privacy and comfort of my own apartment, even if I have to stay up night after night for this purpose, attracts me so much I become more and more impatient with my usual method of snatching minutes to look up dreams in Miss Taylor's half-hours out of the office.

The trouble is, I can never tell exactly when Miss Taylor will come back to the office. She is so conscientious about her job she'd be likely to cut her half-hour at lunch short and her twenty minutes at coffee shorter if it weren't for her lame left leg. The distinct sound of this lame leg in the corridor warns me of her approach in time for me to whip the record book I'm reading into my drawer out of sight and pretend to be putting down the final flourishes on a phone message, or some such alibi. The only catch, as far as my nerves are concerned, is that Amputee Clinic is around the corner from us in the opposite direction from Nerve Clinic, and I've gotten really jumpy due to a lot of false alarms where I've mistaken some pegleg's hitching step for the step of Miss Taylor herself returning early to the office.

On the blackest days when I've scarcely time to squeeze one dream out of the old books and my copy work is nothing but weepy college sophomores who can't get a lead in *Camino Real*, I feel Johnny Panic turn his back, stony as Everest, higher than Orion, and the motto of the great Bible of Dreams, 'Perfect fear casteth out all else', is ash and lemon water on my lips. I'm a wormy hermit in a country of prize pigs so corn-happy they can't see the slaughterhouse at the end of the track. I'm Jeremiah vision-bitten in the Land of Cockaigne.

What's worse: day by day I see these psyche doctors studying to win Johnny Panic's converts from him by hook, crook, and talk, talk, talk. These deep-eyed, bush-bearded dream-collectors who preceded me in history, and their contemporary inheritors with their white jackets and knotty-pine-panelled offices and leather couches, practised and still practise their dream gathering for worldly ends: health and money, money and health. To be a true member of Johnny Panic's congregation one must forget the dreamer and remember the dream: the dreamer is merely a flimsy vehicle for the great Dream Maker himself. This they will not do. Johnny Panic is gold in the bowels, and they try to root him out by spiritual stomach pumps.

Take what happened to Harry Bilbo. Mr Bilbo came into our office with the hand of Johnny Panic heavy as a lead coffin on his shoulder. He had an interesting notion about the filth in this world. I figured him for a prominent part in Johnny Panic's Bible of Dreams, Third Book of Fear, Chapter Nine on Dirt, Disease, and General Decay. A friend of Harry's blew a trumpet in the Boy Scout band when they were kids. Harry Bilbo'd also blown on this friend's trumpet. Years later the friend got cancer and died. Then, one day not so long ago, a cancer doctor came into Harry's house, sat down in a chair, passed the top of the morning with Harry's mother, and on leaving, shook her hand and opened the door for himself. Suddenly Harry Bilbo wouldn't blow trumpets or sit down on chairs or shake hands if all the cardinals of Rome took to blessing him twenty-four hours around the clock for fear of catching cancer. His mother had to go turning the TV knobs and water faucets on and off and opening doors for him. Pretty soon Harry stopped going to work because of the spit and dog droppings in the street. First that stuff gets on your shoes, and then when you take your shoes off it gets on your hands, and then at dinner it's a quick trip into your mouth and not a hundred Hail Marys can keep you from the chain reaction. The last straw was, Harry quit weight-lifting at the public gym when he saw this cripple exercising with the dumb-bells. You can never tell what germs cripples carry behind their ears and under their fingernails. Day and night Harry Bilbo lived in holy worship of Johnny Panic, devout as any priest among censers and sacraments. He had a beauty all his own.

Well, these white-coated tinkerers managed, the lot of them, to talk Harry into turning on the TV himself, and the water faucets, and to opening closet doors, front doors, bar doors. Before they were through with him, he was sitting down on movie-house chairs, and benches all over the Public Garden, and weight-lifting every day of the week at the gym in spite of the fact another cripple took to using the rowing machine. At the end of his treatment he came in to shake hands with the clinic director. In Harry Bilbo's own words, he was 'a changed man'. The pure Panic-light had left his face; he went out of the office doomed to the crass fate these doctors call health and happiness.

About the time of Harry Bilbo's cure a new idea starts nudging at the bottom of my brain. I find it as hard to ignore as those bare feet sticking out of the lumbar puncture room. If I don't want to risk carrying a record book out of the hospital in case I get discovered and fired and have to end my research forever, I can really speed up work by staying in the Clinics Building overnight. I am nowhere near exhausting the clinic's resources, and the piddling amount of cases I am able to read in Miss Taylor's brief absences during the day are nothing to what I could get through in a few nights of steady copying. I need to accelerate my work if only to counteract those doctors.

Before I know it I am putting on my coat at five and saying goodnight to Miss Taylor, who usually stays a few minutes overtime to clear up the day's statistics, and sneaking around the corner into the ladies' room. It is empty. I slip into the patients' john, lock the door from the inside, and wait. For all I know, one of the clinic cleaning ladies may try to knock the door down, thinking some patient's passed out on the seat. My fingers are crossed. About twenty minutes later the door of the lavatory opens and someone limps over the threshold like a chicken favouring a bad leg. It is Miss Taylor. I can tell by the resigned sigh as she meets the jaundiced eye of the lavatory mirror. I hear the click-cluck of various touch-up equipment on the bowl, water sloshing, the scritch of a comb in frizzed hair, and then the door is closing with a slow-hinged wheeze behind her.

I am lucky. When I come out of the ladies' room at six o'clock the corridor lights are off and the fourth-floor hall is empty as church on Monday. I have my own key to our office; I come in first every morning, so that's no trouble. The typewriters are folded back into the desks, the locks are on the dial phones, all's right with the world.

Outside the window the last of the winter light is fading. Yet I do not forget myself and turn on the overhead bulb. I don't want to be spotted by any hawk-eyed doctor or janitor in the hospital building across the little courtyard. The cabinet with the record books is in the windowless passage opening on to the doctors' cubicles, which have windows overlooking the courtyard. I make sure the doors to all the cubicles are shut. Then I switch on the passage light, a sallow twenty-five-watt affair blackening at the top. Better than an altarful of candles to me at this point, though. I didn't think to bring a sandwich. There is an apple in my desk drawer left over from lunch, so I reserve that for whatever pangs I may feel about one o'clock in the morning, and get out my pocket notebook. At home every evening it is my habit to tear out the notebook pages I've written on at the office during the day and pile them up to be copied in my manuscript. In this way I cover my tracks so no one idly picking up my notebook at the office could ever guess the type or scope of my work.

I begin systematically by opening the oldest book on the bottom shelf. The once-blue cover is no-colour now, the pages are thumbed and blurry carbons, but I'm humming from foot to topknot: this dream book was spanking new the day I was born. When I really get organized I'll have hot soup in a thermos for the dead-of-winter nights, turkey pies, and chocolate eclairs. I'll bring hair curlers and four changes of blouse to work in my biggest handbag Monday mornings so no one will notice me going downhill in looks and start suspecting unhappy love affairs or pink affiliations or my working on dream books in the clinic four nights a week.

Eleven hours later. I am down to apple core and seeds and in the month of May, 1934, with a private nurse who has just opened a laundry bag in her patient's closet and found five severed heads in it, including her mother's.

A chill air touches the nape of my neck. From where I am sitting cross-legged on the floor in front of the cabinet, the record book heavy on my lap, I notice out of the corner of my eye that the door of the cubicle beside me is letting in a little crack of blue light. Not only along the floor, but up the side of the door too. This is odd since I made sure from the first that all the doors were shut tight. The crack of blue light is widening and my eyes are fastened to two motionless shoes in the doorway, toes pointing towards me.

They are brown leather shoes of a foreign make, with thick elevator soles. Above the shoes are black silk socks through which shows a pallor of flesh. I get as far as the grey pinstripe trouser cuffs.

'Tch, tch,' chides an infinitely gentle voice from the cloudy regions above my head. 'Such an uncomfortable position! Your legs must be asleep by now. Let me help you up. The sun will be rising shortly.'

Two hands slip under my arms from behind, and I am raised, wobbly as an unset custard, to my feet, which I cannot feel because my legs are, in fact, asleep. The record book slumps to the floor, pages splayed.

'Stand still a minute.' The clinic director's voice fans the lobe of my right ear. 'Then the circulation will revive.'

The blood in my not-there legs starts pinging under a million sewing-machine needles, and a vision of the clinic director acid-etches itself on my brain. I don't even need to look around: the fat pot-belly buttoned into his grey pinstripe waistcoat, woodchuck teeth yellow and buck, every-colour eyes behind the thick-lensed glasses quick as minnows.

I clutch my notebook. The last floating timber of the *Titanic*.

What does he know, what does he know?

Everything.

'I know where there is a nice hot bowl of chicken noodle soup.' His voice rustles, dust under the bed, mice in the straw. His hand welds on to my left upper arm in fatherly love. The record book of all the dreams going on in the city of my birth at my first yawp in this world's air he nudges under the bookcase with a polished toe.

We meet nobody in the dawn-dark hall. Nobody on the chill stone stair down to the basement corridors where Jerry the Record Room boy cracked his head skipping steps one night on a rush errand.

I begin to double-quick-step so he won't think it's me he's hustling. 'You can't fire me,' I say calmly. 'I quit.'

The clinic director's laugh wheezes up from his accordion-pleated bottom gut. 'We mustn't lose you so soon.' His whisper snakes off down the whitewashed basement passages, echoing among the elbow pipes, the wheelchairs and stretchers beached for the night along the steam-stained walls. 'Why, we need you more than you know.'

We wind and double, and my legs keep time with his until we come, somewhere in those barren rat tunnels, to an all-night elevator run by a one-armed Negro. We get on and the door grinds shut like the door on a cattle car and we go up and up. It is a freight elevator, crude and clanky, a far cry from the plush one in the Clinics Building.

We get off at an indeterminate floor. The clinic director leads me down a bare corridor lit at intervals by socketed bulbs in little wire cages on the ceiling. Locked doors set with screened windows line the hall on either hand. I plan to part company with the clinic director at the first red exit sign, but on our journey there are none. I am in alien territory, coat on the hanger in the office, handbag and money in my top desk drawer, notebook in my hand, and only Johnny Panic to warm me against the Ice Age outside.

Ahead a light gathers, brightens. The clinic director, puffing slightly at the walk, brisk and long, to which he is obviously unaccustomed, propels me around a bend and into a square, brilliantly lit room.

'Here she is.'

'The little witch!'

Miss Milleravage hoists her tonnage up from behind the steel desk facing the door.

The walls and the ceiling of the room are riveted metal battleship plates. There are no windows.

From small, barred cells lining the sides and back of the room I see Johnny Panic's top priests staring out at me, arms swaddled behind their backs in the white ward nightshirts, eyes redder than coals and hungry-hot.

They welcome me with queer croaks and grunts as if their tongues were locked in their jaws. They have no doubt heard of my work by way of Johnny Panic's grapevine and want to know how his apostles thrive in the world.

I lift my hands to reassure them, holding up my notebook, my voice loud as Johnny Panic's organ with all stops out.

'Peace! I bring to you ...'

The Book.

'None of that old stuff, sweetie,' Miss Milleravage is dancing out at me from behind her desk like a trick elephant.

The clinic director closes the door to the room.

The minute Miss Milleravage moves I notice what her hulk has been hiding from view behind the desk – a white cot high as a man's waist with a single sheet stretched over the mattress, spotless and drumskin tight. At the head of the cot is a table on which sits a metal box covered with dials and gauges. The box seems to be eyeing me, copperhead-ugly, from its coil of electric wires, the latest model in Johnny-Panic-Killers.

I get ready to dodge to one side. When Miss Milleravage grabs, her fat hand comes away a fist full of nothing. She starts for me again, her smile heavy as dogdays in August.

'None of that. None of that. I'll have that little black book.'

Fast as I run around the high white cot, Miss Milleravage is so fast you'd think she wore roller skates. She grabs and gets. Against her great bulk I beat my fists, and against her whopping milkless breasts, until her hands on my wrists are iron hoops and her breath hushabys me with a love-stink fouler than Undertaker's Basement.

'My baby, my own baby's come back to me ...'

'She,' the clinic director says, sad and stern, 'has been making time with Johnny Panic again.'

'Naughty naughty.'

The white cot is ready. With a terrible gentleness Miss Milleravage takes the watch from my wrist, the rings from my fingers, the hairpins from my hair. She begins to undress me. When I am bare, I am anointed on the temples and robed in sheets virginal as the first snow. Then, from the four corners of the room and from the door behind me come five false priests in white surgical gowns and masks whose one lifework is to unseat Johnny Panic from his own throne. They extend me full-length on my back on the cot. The crown of wire is placed on my head, the wafer of forgetfulness on my tongue. The masked priests move to their posts and take hold: one of my left leg, one of my right, one of my right arm, one of my left. One behind my head at the metal box where I can't see.

From their cramped niches along the wall, the votaries raise their voices in protest. They begin the devotional chant:

The only thing to love is Fear itself.
Love of Fear is the beginning of wisdom.
The only thing to love is Fear itself.
May Fear and Fear and Fear be everywhere.

There is no time for Miss Milleravage or the clinic director or the priests to muzzle them.

The signal is given.

The machine betrays them.

At the moment when I think I am most lost the face of Johnny Panic appears in a nimbus of arc lights on the ceiling overhead. I am shaken like a leaf in the teeth of glory. His beard is lightning. Lightning is in his eye. His Word charges and illumes the universe.

The air crackles with the blue-tongued, lightning-haloed angels.

His love is the twenty-storey leap, the rope at the throat, the knife at the heart.

He forgets not his own.

JAMES PURDY was born in rural Ohio in 1923 and at present lives in Brooklyn. His growing reputation is based on the novels *Malcolm, the Nephew, Cabot Wright Begins*, and *Eustace Chisolm and the Works*; and on collections of short fiction called *Colour of Darkness* and *Children Is All*. A recent work is the novel *Jeremy's Version*.

goodnight, sweetheart

JAMES PURDY

Pearl Miranda walked stark naked from her classroom in the George Washington School where she taught the eighth grade, down Locust Street, where she waited until some of the cars which had stopped for a red traffic light had driven on, then hurried as fast as her weight could allow her down Smith Avenue.

She waited under a catalpa tree, not yet in leaf, for some men to pass by on the other side of the street. It was fairly dark, but she could not be sure if they would see her.

Hurrying on down Smith Avenue then, she passed a little girl, who called out to her, though the child did not recognize her.

The house she at last turned into was that of Winston Cramer, who gave piano lessons to beginners, and whom she herself had taught in the eighth grade nearly twenty years before.

She rang the doorbell.

She could see Winston beyond the picture window sitting in an easy chair engaged in manicuring his nails.

She rang and rang, but he did not move from his sitting position.

A woman from across the street came out on the porch and stood there watching.

Pearl rapped now on the door, and called Winston's name softly. Then she saw him get up. He looked angry.

'I discontinued the subscription,' she heard his cross high voice. 'I don't want the *News*—' and he caught sight of her.

He stood looking at her, immobile behind the glass of the door. Then he opened the door cautiously.

'Miss Miranda?'

'Let me in, for pity's sake,' she answered him. 'It's all right to open the door.'

The woman across the street went on standing on her porch looking over at the Cramer house.

'Miss Miranda,' Winston could only go on repeating when she was inside.

'Go and get me a bathrobe or something, Winston. For pity's sake.' She scolded with her eyes.

Winston stood on for a minute more, trying to keep his gaze only on her face.

She could hear him mumbling and making other silly sounds as he went upstairs.

Pearl Miranda lowered the shade for the picture window, and then seeing the shade up on a smaller side window, she lowered it also. She picked up a music album and held this over her.

'For God Almighty's sake,' Winston said when he handed her a bathrobe.

She put it on with some difficulty, and Winston did not help her. She sat down.

'What can I get for you?' he wondered.

'Usually they give people brandy in such cases,' Miss Miranda said. 'Cases of exposure,' she spoke with her usual precise culture and refinement. 'But I think you remember my views on drinking.'

'I don't drink either, Miss Miranda,' Winston told her.

'Some hot milk might be all right.' She seemed to speak condescendingly now. 'In case of a chill coming on.' Looking down at her bare feet, she inquired. 'Do you have any house slippers, by chance?'

'I have some that were my mother's,' Winston told her.

That will be fine she was about to say, but he was already racing up the steps.

When he came back, he acted a bit more like himself, and he helped her on with the tickly, rabbit-lined house slippers.

'What happened to you?' he asked, looking up at her from his kneeling posture before her.

'Get me the hot milk first,' she told him.

He turned to go out into the kitchen, then wheeling around he said: 'Miss Miranda, are you really all right?'

She nodded.

'Shouldn't I call the doctor?'

She shook her head vigorously.

He came back into the room, his left hand slowly stealing up to his throat. 'You were assaulted, weren't you?' he asked.

'No, Winston, I was not,' she replied. 'Now please fix me my milk.' She spoke to him much as she would have twenty years ago in her classroom.

Miss Miranda sank back into the warmth and mild comfort of the bathrobe and slippers while he was in the kitchen. She could hear him muttering to himself out there as he went about the task of warming the milk. She supposed all lonely people muttered to themselves, and it was one of the regrettable habits she could never break in herself.

Waiting, she looked at his Baldwin piano loaded with Czerny practice books. Another stack of music books sat on his piano stool.

She felt depressed thinking of Winston earning his living sitting all day and part of the evening hearing ungifted children play scales. It was not a job for a man.

Then she thought of how her own sister had felt sorry for her having to teach the eighth grade.

'I'm shaking more now than when you walked in,' Winston mumbled inaudibly, bringing in a little Mexican tray with a steaming pot of milk and a cup.

'Doesn't that look nice,' Miss Miranda said.

'I'll get you a napkin, too.' And he left the room again.

'Don't bother,' Miss Miranda called out after him, but not vigorously, for she wanted a napkin.

She hiccuped a bit drinking the hot milk.

Winston cleared the exercise books from the piano stool, sat down, and watched her drink the milk.

'Just a touch of cinnamon maybe?' He pointed to her cup.

She shook her head.

'I just took a pie out of the oven a couple of hours ago,' he informed her. 'Would you like a piece?'

'What flavour is it, Winston?' Miss Miranda wondered.

'Red raspberry,' he told her. 'Fresh ones.'

She studied his face a second. 'I might at that,' she spoke as if consulting with a third party. 'Do you do all your own cooking, Winston?'

'Since Mother died, yes,' he said. 'But even in her day I did quite a bit, you know.'

'I bet you're a good cook, Winston. You were always a capable boy.' Her voice lowered as she said the second sentence.

'I haven't really talked to you since the eighth grade,' Winston reminded her in a rather loud voice.

'I expect not.' Miss Miranda drank some more of the milk. 'My, that hits the spot.'

'Wouldn't you like another hot cup?'

'Yes, I think I would,' she replied.

He took the tray and all and went out into the kitchen.

Miss Miranda muttered when he had gone, and held her head in her hands, and then suddenly, as if in pain, she cried out, 'God!'

Then she straightened out her face and got calm, her hands folded on her bathrobe, for Winston's return.

He handed her a new cup of milk, and she thanked him.

'You're not hurt now, Miss Miranda,' he ventured again. He looked very scared.

'I've had a trick played on me is all, Winston.' She opened her eyes at him wide.

Somehow, however, she did not seem to be telling the truth, and as she did not look away, Winston looked down at the floor, an expression of sorrow and disappointment about his mouth and eyes. Then he got up from the piano stool and went over to an easy chair and plumped himself down.

'You gave me a start.' He put his hand across his chest.

'Now don't you give out on me,' she said.

'You don't want me to call the police or anybody?' he asked, and she could see how upset he was getting.

'Just calm down, now. Of course I don't want the police. We'll handle this our own way.'

'You said it was a joke, Miss Miranda.'

She nodded.

There was a long silence.

'Ready for your raspberry pie?' he asked weakly.

She wiped her hands carefully on the linen napkin. 'You could have just given me a paper napkin, Winston,' she told him. 'Do you have to do your own laundry, too?'

He mumbled something which sounded like *I'm afraid I do*. 'I'll get you that pie.' He went out of the room.

He came back, after rather a lengthy absence, with a generous piece of red raspberry pie on a hand-painted plate.

'A pretty, pretty sight,' Miss Miranda said.

She bit into her piece of pie and said *Mmm*.

'I wish you would let me do something for you,' he almost whined.

'Now sit down, Winston, and be quiet. Better do nothing than do the wrong thing,' she admonished.

'I know you haven't done anything wrong, of course,' Winston said, and his voice sounded prophetic of weeping.

'Now, I'll explain everything just as soon as I have eaten your pie here,' she told him. 'But it's all nothing to be concerned about.'

'Did anybody see you come in here?' he wondered.

She chewed on for a few seconds. 'I suspect they may have. Who lives across the street from you there?' She pointed with her fork in the direction of the house in question.

'Not Bertha Wilson!' Winston exclaimed.

'A woman came out on that porch. I think she saw me. Of course I know Bertha Wilson,' Miss Miranda said.

'Oh, gosh.' Winston raised his voice. He looked at her now almost accusingly. 'It's all so unusual,' he cried, thinking something much more extreme than his words gave inkling of.

'Winston, you've got to keep calm,' Miss Miranda told him. 'I *had* to come in here tonight. You know that.'

'I don't begrudge you coming in here,' he said, and he was more in possession of himself.

'Then let's both be calm and collected.' She handed him the empty pie plate. 'What beautiful work people did when they painted their own china.' She nodded at the plate.

'My Aunt Lois hand-painted all of Mother's china.'

He left the room with the plate, and there was complete silence everywhere for a few minutes. Then she heard the water running in the kitchen, and she realized he was doing the dishes.

'He's a neat one,' she said out loud.

She shook her head then, though she did this about something else than his neatness, and she cried, 'God!' again.

In about a quarter of an hour he came on back into the living-room, sat down, crossed his legs, and said, 'Now.'

'I don't think I'm even going to have a chill.' She smiled at him.

Winston was looking at her narrowly, and she thought he was less sympathetic. There was a look of irritability on his face. His mouth had set.

'How long has it been since you lost your mother?' Miss Miranda said.

'Two years this April,' he replied without expression.

Miss Miranda shook her head. She opened the linen napkin out and put it over the lap of the bathrobe.

'What happened tonight was a joke,' she said, and stopped.

'Did many people see you cross over the school playground?' he wondered.

'The school playground?'

'There are the fewest trees there to hide under,' he explained.

'I couldn't tell if anybody saw me or not,' she said.

'Miss Miranda, if you were . . . *harmed*, you must have me call the doctor.'

'You want me to leave?' she inquired. 'I will—'

'I didn't mean leave,' he protested.

'Please be calm, Winston,' she asked him.

'I am calm, Miss Miranda . . . But gosh almighty, nobody can just sit here and act like nothing happened to you . . . I never heard of such a thing as tonight!'

She sat thinking how it all must seem to him. At the height of her predicament she had not had time to think.

'I'm unhurt, Winston, except for the exposure, and I told you I can see I'm not going to have a chill.'

'I can go over to your house and get your clothes.'

She nodded pleasantly. 'Tomorrow,' she said.

'Tonight!' He was emphatic.

'This young man who looked like one of my own former students came into my classroom at six o'clock tonight,' she began her story. 'I was cleaning the blackboard.'

Winston watched her, his face drained of blood.

'He asked me if I remembered him, and I said I didn't, though his face was familiar . . . He then asked if I remembered Alice Rodgers. Of course, I remembered her. We just expelled her last term, you know. She had gotten herself and nearly every boy in the eighth grade in all that trouble. You remember reading about it all in the paper . . . Do you remember all that about Alice Rodgers?' Miss Miranda asked him.

Winston half-nodded.

'This young man, oh, he couldn't have been more than twenty . . . certainly not more than your age at the most, Winston . . . he said, "I think you ought to have to pay for what you did to Alice Rodgers, ruining her name and reputation."

' "I only wanted to make a real future for Alice Rodgers," I told him.

' "In the reformatory?" he asked with an ugly grin.'

Miss Miranda stopped, perhaps expecting Winston to help her on, but he did nothing.

'Then,' Miss Miranda said, 'he asked me to take off my clothes. He had a gun, you see.'

Winston got up and walked in the direction of the next room.

'Where are you going?' Miss Miranda cried.

He looked back at her, asked her to excuse him, and then came back and sat down.

'He said he would use the gun if I didn't do exactly as he said,' she spoke in a matter-of-fact-tone.

Miss Miranda was looking at Winston, for she was certain that he was not listening to what she said.

'He took all my clothes away from me, including my shoes and keys, and then, saying he hoped I would remember Alice Rodgers for the rest of all our lives, he walked out, leaving me to my plight . . .'

Winston was looking down at the carpet again.

Miss Miranda's voice continued: 'I called out to him from the banister to come back. "How will I get home?" I called after him.'

Her voice now trailed off. Suddenly she held her head in her hands and cried, 'Oh, God! God!'

'Are you in pain?' Winston looked up sleepily from the carpet.

'No,' Miss Miranda replied quickly.

'My head's in a whirl,' Winston told her.

'I don't remember that young man at all,' Miss Miranda went on. 'But you know, Winston, after you've taught so many years, and when you're as old as I am, all young people, all old people, too, look so much alike.'

'Miss Miranda, let me call somebody! We should inform—'

'No,' she told him. 'I won't hear of it. Now, please be calm and don't let what has happened upset you. I want to stay here tonight.'

'This young man you describe. He didn't harm you in any way?'

'He did not,' Miss Miranda said in the voice of one who defends. She looked at Winston.

Without warning, he began to gag. He rushed out of the parlour to a small room near the kitchen.

He evidently did not have time to close the door behind him. She could hear him vomiting.

'Oh, dear,' Miss Miranda said.

She came into the bathroom and watched him. He was straining very hard over the toilet bowl.

'Winston, I am going to hold your head,' she advised him. He made no motion.

She held his head while he vomited some more.

When he had stopped, she took a fresh washcloth off the rack, and wiped his mouth.

'I've had the virus,' he explained.

Suddenly he turned to the bowl again and vomited.

'Poor lad,' she said, wiping his mouth again with the cloth.

'You must lie down now,' she admonished him.

He walked towards an adjoining room where there was a double bed, and lay down on it.

She helped him off with his shoes, and put the covers partly over him.

'I'm afraid it was me who upset you,' she apologized.

'No, Miss Miranda, it's the virus. Can't seem to shake it off. I catch it off and on from my pupils. First from one, then the other.'

'Just rest quietly,' she said.

When he had dozed off, she exclaimed again, 'God! God!'

She must have dozed off, too, in her chair by the double bed, for some time later she awoke with a start and heard him vomiting again in the bathroom, and she hurried in to hold his head.

'Winston, poor lad,' she said, feeling his hair wet with sweat.

'How could you stand to watch me be sick like that?' he wondered later when they were back in the bedroom.

'I've taught public school for thirty years,' she reminded him.

'Miss Miranda,' he said suddenly, 'you were raped tonight, weren't you?'

She stared at him.

'You've got to let me call the doctor.' He wiped his mouth.

'I was not . . . raped,' she denied his statement.

He watched her.

'That fellow just asked you to take off your clothes?'

She nodded.

'On account of Alice Rodgers.' He echoed her story.

'I had testified against Alice in court,' she added, 'and they sent her to the reformatory.'

'Well, if it's your story,' he said.

'I wouldn't lie to you,' Miss Miranda said.

'Nobody will believe you,' he told her.

'Aren't you talking too much, Winston?' Miss Miranda showed concern for his health.

He did not answer.

'Bertha Wilson saw you across the street,' he said sleepily.

'She was looking in my direction all right,' Miss Miranda admitted.

'She must have seen you then.'

'Oh, it was quite dark, Winston, after all.'

'Bertha's got real X-ray eyes.'

'Well, so she saw me,' Miss Miranda said. 'I had to come in some-where.'

'Oh, it's all right,' Winston said. 'Nobody will think anything about *us*.'

'Oh God!' Miss Miranda cried suddenly.

Winston raised himself on his elbows.

'You in pain, Miss Miranda? Physical pain?'

She stifled back her sobs.

'Miss Miranda,' Winston began. 'That young man that came into your classroom tonight ... are you listening to me ... that young man was Fred Rodgers. Alice Rodgers' older brother.'

Miss Miranda went on making the stifling sounds.

'Did you hear what I said, Miss Miranda?'

She nodded.

'Alice Rodgers' older brother,' he repeated. 'I know him. Listen, Miss Miranda, I know he wouldn't stop at just taking away your clothes. Don't you think I have any sense at all?'

He looked away from the look she gave him then.

'Knowing Fred Rodgers the way I do, Miss Miranda, I know he wouldn't stop at what you said he did. He had it in for you for sending his sister to the reform school.'

'I'm nearly sixty years old, Winston,' Miss Miranda said in the pool of darkness that was her chair. 'I'd rather we didn't talk about it, if you don't mind.'

'You've got to call the doctor,' he said.

Miss Miranda looked down at the long lapel of her bathrobe.

'You had blood on you, too,' Winston told her.

A moment later, he screamed and doubled up with pain in the bed.

'Winston, for pity's sake.'

'I think I got an attack of appendicitis,' he groaned. 'Ouch, ouch, ouch.' He touched his stomach.

'Do you want a doctor then?' she cried, as it he had betrayed her.

He lay back in the bed and groaned. His face went a kind of green, then yellow, as it suddenly illuminated by a searchlight.

'Dear God. God!' Miss Miranda cried.

'I may get all right,' Winston told her, and he smiled encouragement at her from out of his own distress.

'Oh, what shall I do? What *shall* I do?' she cried.

'I guess we both will have to have the doctor,' Winston told her.

'I can't tell him, Winston ... I'm sixty years old.'

'Well, you let *him* do the worrying now, Miss Miranda.'

'You knew this Fred Rodgers?' She cried a little now.

Winston nodded.

'I never taught him, though.' She sighed. Suddenly she cried again, 'Dear God. God!'

'You try to be calm, Miss Miranda,' he comforted her.

He seemed almost calm now himself.

'Why don't you lay your head down on the bed, you look so bad,' he told her.

'Oh, aren't we in the worst situation, Winston,' she said.

She cried a little.

She laid her head down on the bed, and he patted her hair a moment.

'I don't know how many people saw me,' she said.

Winston lay back, easier now. His pain had quit.

Miss Miranda, suddenly, as if in response to his pain's easing, began to tremble violently.

'Get into bed,' he told her. 'You've got a chill coming on.'

He helped her under the covers.

She screamed suddenly as he put her head down on the pillow.

'Just try to get as quiet as possible, Miss Miranda.' He helped her cover up.

She was trembling now all over, crying, 'Oh, God! At sixty!'

'If you can just get a good night's rest,' he comforted her.

'Dear God. Oh, God!'

'In the morning the doctor will fix you up.'

'I can never go back and teach those children,' she said.

Winston patted her hand. His nausea had left him, but he had a severe headache that throbbed over his temples.

'What is that woman's name across the street again?' Miss Miranda questioned him.

'You mean Bertha Wilson.'

Miss Miranda nodded.

'I taught her in the eighth grade. Way back in 1930, just think.'

'I wouldn't think about it, Miss Miranda.'

'Wouldn't think about what?'

'Anything.'

'I can't believe this has happened,' she told Winston.

'The doctor will come and fix us both up.'

'I don't see how I can have the doctor or go back to school or anything,' she wept.

She began crying hard now, and then after a while she got quiet.

'Go to sleep,' he said.

He had thought to go upstairs and sleep in the bedroom that had been his mother's, but he didn't know whether he had the strength to get up there, and in the end he had crawled back under the covers next to Miss Miranda, and they both lay there close to one another, and they both muttered to themselves in the darkness as if they were separated by different rooms from one another.

'Goodnight,' he said to her.

She looked up from her pillow for a moment.

'Goodnight, sweetheart,' he said again, in a much lower voice.

She looked at the wall against which he had said the last words. There was a picture of his mother there, pretty much as Miss Miranda remembered her.

'God,' Miss Miranda whispered. 'Dear God.'

JAN GERHARD TOONDER, a native Dutchman, currently lives in Amsterdam. He has published nine novels in Dutch and several stories in English, which he has himself helped to translate, in the *Paris Review*.

the spider

JAN GERHARD TOONDER

Victor had just opened the door and taken his young wife in his arms to carry her over the threshold, when the agent, Judgeworth, stepped out of the bushes and asked him if he did not think this the right moment to buy a good, solid insurance policy. Marietta laughed and Victor said, 'Certainly not!'

'It is very important,' claimed the agent, Judgeworth. 'I'll give you my card.'

But Victor's hands were not free so the agent had to slip the card into his coat pocket. After that, the agent Judgeworth watched Victor carry his bride inside, into the cool silence of the country house, and kiss her before he kicked the door shut behind him.

They listened to the agent's footsteps disappear down the gravelled walk. There was no other sound, except that of some birds outside. Victor felt embarrassed for a moment. As long as he carried her in his arms, he could be nothing but clumsy, and the worst of it was that suddenly there was nothing more to talk about. I wish my dog were here, he thought. A dog always provides diversion. In his embarrassment he hugged her somewhat closer and felt how slender and warm she was; then, finally, he carried her to the bedroom.

Luckily, the family had seen to it that there were several surprises.

Looking at the flowers and the embroidered tablecloths, at the home-made cushions and the vases, they could talk and laugh again. Marietta was moved by the bowl of fruit her mother had put beside the bed and he pointed out to her the little silver fruit knife his practical father had placed next to it. It looked so inviting that she sat down on the edge of the bed to peel an apple. When she put a second little slice in his mouth he took her in his arms and eased her down into the cushions. Marietta was beautiful and glowing. The soft light of the afternoon became dusk and the dusk became night and soon afterwards another day went by. They loved each other and they had been married before the law.

Victor was awakened by a sound. There was a half-darkness in the room; he did not know if it was morning or evening. Her head rested on his shoulder and the small face with smiling mouth, ever-so-slightly opened, looked so childlike that he felt a deep tenderness for her as he softly stroked the smooth skin of her breast and hip.

But the sound that woke him was repeated – a shrill, silly sound like a child's trumpet, coming, probably, from an instrument with which a street vendor was trying to attract attention. The piping drew nearer until it sounded beneath the window; at first he smiled, but when it kept up he became afraid that it would wake Marietta and so he slipped softly out of the bed and went to the door.

'Who's there?' he asked, through the door slot.

Outside a full voice answered, sounding jubilant, as though belonging to someone who knows himself to be a long-expected guest, 'The fishmonger!'

'Oh – go on!' shouted Victor. The piping became softer and softer and then vanished down the street.

Nevertheless, Marietta had been awakened. When he entered the room she was sitting upright and asked, 'What was that?'

'The fishmonger,' he said.

She laughed. 'Did you buy anything?'

'I don't like fish.'

He thought her irresistibly attractive as she lay there between the back-flung sheets, but the coming of the fishmonger had called them back to reality. He wound his watch. They looked outside and took in their surroundings and after that the days and nights were paid out to them regularly, as to all other people.

After a few days he felt that his work needed him again.

'But there is no real necessity,' said Marietta.

'Let's not talk about that again,' he answered curtly. Marietta had an income on which they could live, but he liked his work and it required his presence, and he had arranged before their wedding to carry on with it.

'I'm jealous of your work,' she said. Because he had been short with her, he embraced her that night with a still greater tenderness. When he left the house the next morning, she waved to him, laughing.

Victor was happy and since happiness is still more blinding than love, it took him quite a long time to notice that she had become pale and laughed less easily, and that there was something forced in her caresses.

'Is there something bothering you?' he asked at last.

'No,' she said. 'Or . . . yes.' She looked at him as though he were a stranger she wanted to know, and then she looked away again. 'No, of course there's nothing.'

He paid more attention to her now and a few days later he asked, 'Shall I have the dog brought here after all? You'd be less lonely then.'

'Please, no,' she said. She did not like the dog; she was afraid of him.

'I feel there is something. Perhaps it is being alone,' he pressed her. 'You'd get used to the dog quickly enough.'

She said hurriedly, 'That isn't it. It's just a very small thing.'

'What?'

'Promise you won't laugh at me?'

'Promise.'

'There is a spider in the house.'

Because he remembered his promise in time he did not laugh, but said, 'There will be more than one. That's country life for you.'

'Yes – but this is no ordinary spider. It races through the room now and then and it's this big.' She indicated the size of a large marble.

In that moment he did not love her. The fear of a spider seemed unnatural to him and apart from that, she had no right really to deny him the dog. It was a kind, true dog, so attached to him that it always carried his newspaper and his pipe and other little things after him.

At night he wanted to make up for this moment of estrangement, but he felt too tired.

Then for a time nothing much happened. They had a small quarrel once when she gave him fish for dinner though she knew he did not like it, but then she told him how the fishmonger had insisted upon her buying something, and after that they both considered the subject too unimportant. But again he regretted his shortness and that only made him look at her with more curiosity until at last he asked, 'And is it really only the spider that's bothering you?' – for he missed her former gaiety.

'Yes – it's this big,' she said, and this time indicated something the size of a dove's egg. 'It has long, hairy legs. It comes suddenly and races through the room. I never see where it comes from or where it goes.'

Always, when she spoke of the spider he felt a chill disgust for her. Of course, he let no outward sign of this escape. Nevertheless he covered the house from top to bottom with a powerful insecticide. A few days later he found her crying on the doorstep of the house without the courage to enter it again.

'I've seen him again,' she whispered, 'and he's growing; he's getting bigger all the time.'

'Nonsense,' he said.

'Don't go inside. Come with me – away!' She clung to him desperately. 'Please let's go somewhere, together. Please, I beg you. That thing is bad luck.'

'Will you finish with that nonsense?' he demanded. He entered the house; he inspected it from cellar to attic but could find no opening where an insect of that size could hide. Of course, he had never seen the animal himself.

When at last she overcame her fear and followed him, shivering, he said, 'This has been enough. I'll send for the dog. You'll get to like him after a while and you won't be so alone. He's a fast dog and if there is a spider here, he'll catch it soon enough.'

He would have preferred to fetch the dog himself but since his work obliged him to take a trip for several days, he ordered the kennel to bring the animal to his house.

Returning from the trip he found Marietta more silent and pale than ever. A fish dinner was awaiting him; the whole house smelled of cooked fish. It nauseated him.

'Where's the dog?' he asked.

She divided the fish and answered without looking up, 'It was terrible.'

'Where is he?'

'He hated me. I was frightened. I thought I'd go crazy.'

'What did you do?' Victor asked, menacingly.

'Then the fishmonger came. He has taken him with him for the time being.'

Victor cursed.

'He'll bring him back,' she said, hurriedly. 'Now that you're home he'll bring him back; he promised – but I couldn't bear being alone with that dog any longer.'

'I suppose you would rather be alone with your spider,' Victor said angrily.

She shook her head. 'The spider has gone,' she said.

In the next few days Victor tried to find the fishmonger. He asked after him everywhere. He searched the entire neighbourhood, but in vain. Marietta. too, said that she knew nothing about him and never saw him any more.

It was a time of silence between the two. Victor longed for what had once made him happy but knew that it was over. She grew thin and pale – but he was incapable of worrying about her any more and she did not complain. The tenderness between them had gone, but neither were there reproaches – until one morning, getting up, he said rather sharply, 'You could do a better job of cleaning the place. There are fleas.'

'Impossible,' she said.

'I've been bitten tonight. I felt it.'

'Show me.'

He bared his chest. In his sleep he had distinctly felt the sharp bite, but there was nothing to be seen. She shrugged her shoulders. 'You are just nagging,' she said.

But in the nights following, he felt again that he was being bitten. So there were vermin in the house and it was her fault. It was the only thing he could rightly hold against her; but he never mentioned it because the mark of the bites could not be found. After a week he resolved to stay awake one night; if he could catch something he would then have proof.

For a few hours he lay staring. It was a moonlit night and enough light filtered in to outline the furniture and also the face of the sleeping woman beside him There had been a time when he had been moved because she slept with her mouth so slightly opened; now it merely irritated him and he avoided looking at her. At last his tiredness overcame him and he sank into sleep – so lightly, however, that he was immediately wide awake upon feeling the bite. He bolted up and was just in time to see something dark scurrying away; but he could do nothing more and sat there paralysed from the shock. The dark thing had been as big as an egg. It was too big to hide unnoticed in the bed, bigger than any insect could be.

When he calmed down he was forced to blame it upon his imagination. Such things do not exist. He was overstrung; perhaps he had had too much to drink – and he had reproached Marietta unjustly.

Despite his reasoning, he spent the next day chilled with shock and he understood that at any cost he had to conquer this twisted fantasy. The only way to succeed, he knew, was to force himself to stay awake through the night and thus convince himself that nothing had actually happened.

Had he wanted it, he would have found sleep impossible that

following night – the frightful fantasy had struck so deep that merely lying in the same bed filled him with horror. So he was grateful for the moonlight gliding in. Darkness would have been unbearable and he did not want to light a lamp for fear of awakening Marietta.

The hours passed. It was a still night and nothing could be heard but the occasional distant howling of a dog. Nothing moved; only the moonlight, creeping with time along the ceiling and the furniture, and over the bed. There was so little to distract him that Victor was forced to become ever more conscious of the sleeping woman beside him, of her breathing, of her face on the pillow.

At first it appeared as a dark spot. This is reality, he thought, this is no imagination, this cannot be escaped. Then the moonlight came creeping slowly, slowly over her loose, fanned hair and finally to her face.

That face had become thin and pale and she slept with her mouth open; it was no mere dark spot now, but everything loved and lost and fiendish that Victor knew. He tried to divert his eyes but could not, for there was, after all, nothing to be seen but this.

She looked a corpse, he thought. He wished that something in that face would stir – he did not want to wake her but he longed for some movement, some small sign of life.

And at last he saw something. Something moved along the edge of her teeth – the lips pursed forward as though she intended to stick out her tongue, but it was not her tongue that emerged.

It was a thick black thread, moving hesitantly, feeling about her underlip. A moment later a second thread appeared, then a third; then something moved inside her mouth and a dark mass crawled forward.

Victor shouted and before the weird thing could escape, his hand swept with a blind instinct in a swift arc and dealt her a crushing blow on the mouth.

She awoke terrified and the imprint of his open hand showed white on her skin. She cried in pain and asked why he had done it, what was the matter; but he only mumbled incoherently – something about a mishap in his sleep. He had had a nightmare, he said.

To escape the fear that pursued him, there was no recourse but sleeping pills; and the night passed unconscious. He did not even experience the feeling of being bitten. And when day came he was able to adjust himself to think clearly. The memory of the blow he had dealt her filled him with remorse and pity and he forced a solicitousness and even a display of love for her which in his heart had no real place, but she responded to this unexpected warmth in a vague, distraught way. However, she took painstaking care of the house and of his things.

Once she gave him some slips of paper and odds and ends she had taken from the pockets of an old coat; they were forgotten, unimportant things and he threw them away, except the card from the agent Judgeworth.

That remained on his desk for some time and he only tore it up after writing Judgeworth a letter, inviting him to call the following evening to arrange an insurance policy on Marietta's life.

Only that night, having written the letter, did the thought dawn upon him that by taking out a policy he might make his wife's poor health profitable to himself, and this thought would not leave him alone; despite the sleeping pills he could do no more than doze off into a fitful slumber wracked with restless dreams that brought him time and again to the edge of consciousness.

Because he was not benumbed as on previous nights, he felt the bite again; but when the small, sharp pain woke him he resolved not to move, only to look, and verify the fact at last. Very slowly he opened his eyes. In the pale stripe of moonlight he saw the spider standing on his chest.

The beast with the eight hairy threadlike legs was the size of a fist. The hollow, lustreless eyes stared straight into his. It had grown much bigger, Victor thought calmly. He understood that he had already known about this for some time.

The spider retreated crabwise; he could scarcely feel the wriggling legs on his skin, and the monster moved in such a way that the expressionless eyes fixed themselves unwaveringly upon his as it crept to his shoulder and then crossed to the breast of the sleeping woman. Still staring, it moved backwards along her throat, stood waiting a moment upon her chin until her mouth opened wider, and it slipped inside.

She slept undisturbed; she did not stir; he only saw that she swallowed and that something moved in her throat. By then his groping hand had clutched the silver fruit knife from the night table and with all his force he stabbed it into that moving spot.

He knew that something terrible had happened; but it seemed as though it had happened to someone else; as if it had been one of those twisted dreams which kept him fitfully awake until the sleeping pills took effect. They did now. Sleep came to him like a coma.

Waking late the next day he was still groggy. He got up, went to wash and shave, dressed, and only then went back to the bed to look. Her eyes and mouth were half opened. The knife protruded from her throat, the source of the coagulated trail of blood. She must have stayed alive a long time, he thought, otherwise it wouldn't have bled so much. The blood had dripped over the bed and had formed a pool under the window. He went downstairs and found that it had leaked through the ceiling; a second pool had formed behind the front door and a thin stream had even trickled outside, beyond the threshold. A great deal of blood, he thought.

He wanted to begin cleaning it up from its source so he went back to the bed and drew the knife from her throat. He looked at it, washed it in the basin and put it down next to the fruitbowl. At that moment he heard her say, 'Thank you. Thank you very much.'

He felt the instinctive impulse to answer, but then saw all too clearly that she was dead. Her eyes had gone glassy, her mouth had stiffened, her skin showed green. Still more important than cleaning up the blood, he had to bury her before she would be discovered, but when he lifted her he again heard her voice, coming clear and lifelike from her throat, 'I thank you. Thank you. Thank you.'

He laid her down and stood rooted there, looking at her and making no movement; and the time passed. Dusk came, darkness came, but he could not move.

At the appointed hour, the agent Judgeworth rang the bell. He rang the bell again and waited for some time, but then apparently he noticed the blood-trail that had trickled past the threshold. The sound of his rapidly retreating footsteps over the gravelled walk brought Victor back to reality. He was given away now, he thought. He would have to act quickly before the chase was on, and so he picked up the corpse, carried it down the stairs and outside into the garden.

'Thank you,' she said.

'Shut up!' he ordered. He had to dig a hole to make her disappear, to smother her voice forever under two heavy cubic yards of earth, and he had to be quick about it. A sound approached already; and panic gripped his mind.

'Shut up! Shut up!' he hissed once more, looking about for a spade and suitable spot. The sound came nearer.

'Oh – thank you,' her voice said.

He hit her on the mouth again, as he had done once before, but the voice went on, 'Because now you will always be with me.'

'No,' he said. 'No. That's what you wanted but it will not be. I'll not allow it to . . .' He shoved her into the shrubbery. She remained silent and his hands were free, but the sound drew level with the corner of the garden path, a bleating noise like that of a cardboard trumpet. It ceased only when Victor went to it. In the bend of the path he found a large cart, a little house on wheels almost, with a thin, pale man standing next to it.

'The fishmonger,' said the man.

In each hand he held a small fish and he said in a seductive voice, 'Tender and soft, the healthiest food.'

'You haven't come for that – at this time of night,' said Victor.

The fishmonger took a step forward to whisper, 'No, I have not come to peddle but to help.'

'To help – with what?'

'The law is on its way,' said the fishmonger. 'The law knows all and exacts its punishment. Only I can help you.'

'Why do you do that?'

'I have been given your dog.'

The fishmonger preceded him to the hole in the shrubbery where he had pushed the corpse, bowed down, and picked it up. 'Let me carry it,' he said. 'You are tired. Come with me. You can rest and then hide from the law.'

He laid the body on the bottom of the cart and made Victor understand that he had to lie down next to it. 'No,' said Victor, 'that is impossible. I'll do anything. Push the cart – anything but not that.'

'Only there will you remain undetected,' replied the fishmonger, lifting him with irresistible strength and forcing him to the bottom of the cart. 'You needn't do anything. I'll bring you to safety. I'll take care of everything for you. Obey me and you shall escape the law.'

Victor lay in the darkness of the heavy, shuddering cart which seemed too ponderous a thing to be moved by any single person; but the wheels clattered over the cobblestones and beside them he heard the tireless and regular footsteps leading through the night. The hard cart bottom went up and down. There was a warm smell of rotting fish and the dead body lay so near that he was forced to touch it at every bump and lurch – but she said nothing and this silence made the black ride bearable.

When the cart stopped and Victor was permitted to step out, he saw that they were in a high, cold, vault-like room, a place he had never seen before. Besides the cart, there were only a few crates and benches and a refectory table. A few passages led into the room, looking like dark and gaping mouths.

The fishmonger lit two candles. He took the corpse from the cart and laid it on the table, near the edge and leaving some room.

'Here you are well hidden,' he said. 'Here you are safe forever.'

'What should I do?' asked Victor.

'Nothing,' replied the fishmonger, pressing him on to one of the benches by the table with his immense strength. 'Nothing. Please relax. I do everything.'

Victor sat very close to the dead face and had to look past it to see the fishmonger spread fish over the unoccupied part of the table and how with rapid, deft movements he slit out their entrails.

'I'll be sick. I have to vomit,' Victor whispered.

The fishmonger glanced up and said, shaking his head, 'Fight it down. Better think of something else – nothing can happen, after all.'

He tried not to watch the quick, pale hands and the disembowelled fish but in the dark room there was nothing else to attract his attention – except the face of the dead. When, despite his will, his eyes came to rest upon her, a voice spoke very softly, 'Thank you. Now you shall always stay with me.'

'It's the spider,' Victor said, with horror. 'The spider is alive.'

The fishmonger nodded. 'That is your fault.'

'No – not my fault. Yours . . . You didn't bring back the dog.'

The other stood up and came towards him from behind the table. 'I needed him. He drew my cart.' They looked at each other a moment and in the silence only the whispering of the dead could be heard, until Victor summoned all his strength to shout out the name of the dog; and before the echo had died in the hollow room he was answered by a wild, delirious barking, sounding from one of the passages.

Alarmed, the fishmonger stepped back.

From the passage came the sound of wood creaking under a barrage of blows, then a new burst of barking, then a rending and splintering. But Victor could not wait. The fishmonger had turned to the corpse and he saw that now, as though it had been conjured forth, something began to move in the stiff mouth.

He fled into another passage and behind him heard the grateful voice thanking him loudly and the rushing approach of the dog – then suddenly there was silence and though he groped his way blindly through darkness he dared not run back. Silence accompanied him, the silence of the three beings he left behind, who must have encountered each other back there but who gave no indication as to whether they would fight or only wait; of whom he knew nothing now but that they were silent.

Then he stood in an early dawn by the bank of a river, at a spot he has never been able to find since.

'It's morning. I'll hear the birds again soon,' he thought. But it remained silent.

nonfiction

NORMAN O. BROWN was born in 1913 in El Oro, Mexico, where his father was a mining engineer, and at present is teaching at Santa Cruz, California. He is the author of *Life Against Death*, a psychoanalytic view of history and the historical process, and *Love's Body*. The selection 'Boundary!' is Chapter VIII of *Love's Body*.

from love's body

NORMAN O. BROWN

Originally everything was body, ONE BODY (Novalis); or Freud: 'Originally the ego includes everything, later it detaches from itself the external world. The ego-feeling we are aware of now is thus only a shrunken vestige of a far more extensive feeling – a feeling which embraced the universe and expressed an inseparable connexion of the ego with the external world.' The possibilities adumbrated in infancy are to be taken as normative: as in Wordsworth's 'Ode': before shades of the prison house close in; before we shrink up into the fallen condition which is normal adulthood.

Novalis, *Hymne*, 'Wenigewissen das Geheimniss der Liebe', *Geistliche Lieder*. Freud, *Civilization and Its Discontents*, 13.

Man is the dwarf of himself. Once he was permeated and dissolved by spirit. He filled nature with the overflowing currents. Out from him sprang the sun and moon; from man, the sun; from woman, the moon. The laws of his mind, the periods of his actions externized themselves into day and night, into the year and the seasons. But, having made for himself this huge shell, his waters retired; he no longer fills the veins and veinlets; he is shrunk to a drop. He sees, that the structure still fits him, but fits him colossally. Say, rather, once it fitted him, now it corresponds to him from far and on high.

Emerson, *Nature*, ch. VIII.

Psychoanalysis can be used to uncover the principle of union, or communion, buried beneath the surface separations, the surface declarations of independence, the surface signs of private property. Psychoanalysis also discloses the pathology of the process whereby the normal sense of being a self separate from the external world was constructed. Contrary to what is taken for granted the lunatic state called normalcy or common sense, the distinction between self and external world is not an immutable fact, but an artificial construction. It is a boundary line; like all boundaries not natural but conventional; like all boundaries, based on love and hate.

The distinction between self and not-self is made by the childish decision to claim all that the ego likes as 'mine', and to repudiate all that the ego dislikes as 'not-mine'. It is as simple as that; but here is Freud's more formal description: 'The objects presenting themselves, in so far as they are sources of pleasure, are absorbed by the ego into itself, "introjected" (according to an expression coined by Ferenczi); while, on the other hand, the ego thrusts forth upon the external world whatever within itself gives rise to pain (the mechanism of projection).' 'Thus at the very beginning, the external world, objects, and that which was hated were one and the same thing. When later on an object manifests itself as a source of pleasure, it becomes loved, but also incorporated into the ego.'

Freud, 'Instincts and their Vicissitudes', 78, 79; cf 'Negation', 183; *Civilization and Its Discontents*, 12.

Here is the fall: the distinction between 'good' and 'bad', between 'mine' and 'thine', between 'me' and 'thee' (or 'it'), come all together – boundaries between persons; boundaries between properties; and the polarity of love and hate.

The boundary line between self and external world bears no relation to reality; the distinction between ego and world is made by spitting out part of the inside, and swallowing in part of the outside. On this Freudian insight Melanie Klein and her followers have built. 'Owing to these mechanisms [of introjection and projection] the infant's object can be

defined as what is inside or outside his own body, but even while outside, it is still part of himself and refers to himself, since "outside"
results from being ejected, "spat out": thus the body boundaries are
blurred. This might also be put the other way round: because the object
outside the body is "spat out", and still relates to the infant's body,
there is no sharp distinction between his body and what is outside.'

Heimann, 'Certain Functions of Introjection and Projection in Early Infancy', 143.

The net effect of the establishment of the boundary between self and
external world is inside-out and outside-in; confusion. The erection of
the boundary does not alter the fact that there is, in reality, no boundary. The net effect is illusion, self-deception; the big lie. Or alienation.
'Le premier mythe du dehors et du dedans: l'aliénation se fond sur ces
deux termes.' Where Freud and Marx meet.

Hyppolite, 'Commentaire parlé sur la Verneinung de Freud', 35.
Cf Bachelard, La Poétique de l'espace, 192.

The soul (self) we call our own is an illusion. The real psycho-
analytical contribution to 'ego-psychology' is the revelation that the ego
is a bit of the outside world swallowed, introjected; or rather a bit of
the outside world that we insist on pretending we have swallowed. The
nucleus of one's own self is the incorporated other.

The superego is your father in you; your father introjected; your
father swallowed. In his most sophisticated description of superego
formation Freud says: 'A portion of the external world has, at least
partially, been given up as an object and instead, by means of
identification, taken into the ego – that is, has become an integral part
of the internal world.'

Freud, Outline, 77.

Melanie Klein has shown the same kind of origin for the ego. The ego
'is based on object libido reinvested in the body'; the self is a substitute
for the lost other, a substitute which pretends to be the lost other; so
that we may embrace ourselves thinking we embrace our mother. Our
identity is always a case of mistaken identity. The ego is our mother in
us. It originally 'embraced the universe and expressed an inseparable
connexion of the ego with the external world', because originally the
whole world is the mother and the mother is the whole world. It originates in the dual unity of mother and child; mother and child, these
two, as one. Its present structure, its illusory separate and substantial
identity results from the desire to perpetuate that original union with
the mother, by the device of pretending to have swallowed her, ie, to

have incorporated her into oneself. The shadow of the lost object becomes the nucleus of the ego; a shade, a spectre.

Roheim, *War, Crime and the Covenant*, 142.

Possessive introjection is the basis of the ego; the soul is something that we can call our own. 'The ambitions of the id, while that was the sole governing force, were towards *being* the thing at the other side of whatever relationship it established. When the ego takes control of the id's impulses, it directs them towards *having*.' The possessive orientation originates in what Freud calls instinctual ambivalence, ie, the split between 'good' and 'bad', love and hatred, Eros and Thanatos. The aim of the possessive orientation is to keep the loved object entire and intact: to separate and keep the good, to separate and expel the bad. An either/or or undialectical attitude. What we desire to possess we fear to lose; it is a source of anxiety and we are ambivalent towards it, hate as well as love.

Brophy, *Black Ship to Hell*, 56.
Cf Klein and Riviere, *Love, Hate and Reparation*, 96–8.

I am what is mine. Personality is the original personal property. As the great philosopher of private property says, 'By property I must be understood here, as in other places, to mean that property which men have in their persons as well as goods.' Here is the psychological root of private property. Every man has a 'property' in his own person. 'Man (by being master of himself, and proprietor of his own person, and the actions or labour of it) had still in himself the great foundation of property.' The boundaries of our property are extended by mixing our persons with things, and this is the essence of the labour process: 'Whatsoever, then, he removes out of the state that Nature hath provided and left it in, he hath mixed his labour with it, and joined to it something that is his own, and thereby makes it his property.'

Locke, *Two Treatises of Civil Government*, 130, 138, 206.

'Cain means "ownership". Ownership was the originator of the earthly city.' The crucial bit of property is neither nature (land) nor natural produce, nor factories nor manufactured products, but persons, our own persons. Free persons, whether in the state of nature or in civil society, are those who own their own persons. It is because we own our own persons that we are entitled to appropriate things that, through labour, become part of our personality or personalty. The defence of personal liberty is identical with the defence of property. There is a part of Karl Marx which attempts to base communism on Lockean premises. The Marxian proletariat is propertyless; they do not own themselves;

they sell their labour (themselves) and are therefore not free, but wage slaves; they are not persons. The case against the notion of private property is based on the notion of person: but they are the same notion. Hobbes says a person is either his own or another's. This dilemma is escaped only by those willing to discard personality.

Augustine, *De Civitate Dei*, XV, 17.
Cf Hobbes, *Leviathan*, 133.

The existence of the 'let's pretend' boundary does not prevent the continuance of the real traffic across it. Projection and introjection, the process whereby the self as distinct from the other is constituted, is not past history, an event in childhood, but a present process of continuous creation. The dualism of self and external world is built up by a constant process of reciprocal exchange between the two. The self as a stable substance enduring through time, an identity, is maintained by constantly absorbing good parts (or people) from the outside world and expelling bad parts from the inner world. 'There is a continual "unconscious" wandering of other personalities into ourselves.'

Schilder, *The Image and Appearance of the Human Body*, 252.
Cf Klein, *Psychoanalysis of Children*, 203–204, 217, 246–9. Money-Kryle, *Psychoanalysis and Politics*, 51.

Every person, then, is many persons; a multitude made into one person; a corporate body; incorporated, a corporation. A 'corporation sole'; everyman a parson-person. The unity of the person is as real, or unreal, as the unity of the corporation.   .

We tend to think of any one individual in isolation; it is a convenient fiction. We may isolate him physically, as in the analytic room; in two minutes we find that he has brought his world in with him, and that even before he set eyes on the analyst, he had developed inside himself an elaborate relation with him. There is no such thing as a single human being, pure and simple, unmixed with other human beings. Each personality is a world in himself, a company of many. That self, that life of one's own, which is in fact so precious though so casually taken for granted, is a composite structure which has been and is being formed and built up since the day of our birth out of countless never-ending influences and exchanges between ourselves and others ... These other persons are in fact therefore parts of ourselves. And we ourselves similarly have and have had effects and influences, intended or not, on all others who have an emotional relation to us, have loved or hated us. We are members one of another.

Riviere, 'The Unconscious Phantasy of an Inner World', 358–9.
Cf Maitland, 'Corporation Sole', 214.

Separation (on the outside) is repression (on the inside): 'The ego is incapable of splitting the object [or splitting with the object] without a corresponding split taking place within the ego.' The declaration of independence from the mother (country) is a claim to be one's own mother; it splits the self into mother and child.

Klein, 'Notes on Some Schizoid Mechanisms', 298.

Separation (on the outside) is repression (on the inside). The boundary between the self and the external world is the model for the boundary between the ego and the id. The essence of repression, says Freud, is to treat an inner stimulus as if it were an outer one; casting it out (projection). The external world and inner id are both foreign territory – the same foreign territory.

Cf Freud, 'The Two Principles in Mental Functioning', 15n.

And all the boundaries, the false fronts or frontiers – between ego and external world, between ego and superego, between ego and id – are fortified. The walls are fortified, with 'defence mechanisms', and 'character armour'. 'The natural man is self-centred, or ego-centric; everything he regards as real he also regards as outside himself; everything he takes "in" immediately becomes unreal and "spectral". He tries to become an armoured crustacean alert for attack or defence; the price of selfishness is eternal vigilance. This kind of Argus-eyed tenseness proceeds from the sealed prison of consciousness which Blake calls "opaque".'

Frye, *Fearful Symmetry*, 348–9.

Separateness, then, is the fall – the fall into division, the original lie. Separation is secrecy, hiding from one another, the private parts or property. Ownership is hiding; separation is repression. It is a private corporation. The right to privacy: something secret and shameful, which is one's own. 'We hide in secret. I will build thee a Labyrinth where we may remain for ever alone.' 'The striving for the right to have secrets from which the parents are excluded is one of the most powerful factors in the formation of the ego.' The plague of darkness is a symbol of the opaque Selfhood: 'For while they thought they were unseen in their secret sins, they were sundered one from another by a dark curtain of forgetfulness, stricken with terrible awe, and sore troubled by spectral forms.'

Blake, *Night* I, 28; cf 21–27. Tausk, 'The "Influencing Machine" in Schizophrenia,' 535. Wisdom of Solomon XVII, 3.
Cf Roheim, *Riddle of the Sphinx*, 153. Frye, *Fearful Symmetry*, 133–4.

The self being made by projection and introjection, to have a self is to have enemies, and to be a self is to be at war (the war of every man against every man). To abolish war, therefore, is to abolish the self; and the war to end war is total war; to have no more enemies, or self.

The conclusion of the whole matter is, break down the boundaries, the walls. Down with defence mechanisms, character armour; disarmament. Ephesians II, 14: 'For he is our peace, who hath made both one, and hath broken down the middle wall of partition between us.'

To give up boundaries is to give up the reality principle. The reality principle, the light by which psychoanalysis has set its course, is a false boundary drawn between inside and outside; subject and object; real and imaginary; physical and mental. It gives us the divided world, the split or schizoid world – the 'two principles of mental functioning' – in which psychoanalysis is stuck. Psychoanalysis begins on the side of imperialism, or enlightenment, invading the heart of darkness, carrying bright shafts of daylight (*lucida tele diei*), carrying the Bible and flag of the reality principle. Psychoanalysis ends in the recognition of the reality principle as Lucifer, the prince of darkness, the prince of this world, the governing principle, the ruler of the darkness of this world. The reality principle is the prince of darkness; its function is to *scotomize*, to spread darkness; to make walls of thick darkness, walls of separation and concealment. Psychoanalysis ends here: Freud remained officially faithful to the principle whose pretensions he finally exposed. Really to go beyond Freud means to go beyond the reality principle. And really to go beyond the pleasure principle is to go beyond the reality principle; for Freud himself showed that these two are one.

The reality principle is an unreal boundary drawn between real and imaginary. Psychoanalysis itself has shown that 'There is a most surprising characteristic of unconscious (repressed) processes to which every investigator accustoms himself only by exercising great control; it results from their entire disregard of the reality-test; thought-reality is placed on an equality with external reality, wishes with fulfilment and occurrence.' 'What determines the symptoms is the reality not of experience but of thought.'
Freud, 'The Two Principles in Mental Functioning', 20; *Totem and Taboo*, 86.

'Animism, magic and omnipotence of thought' – the child, the savage, and the neurotic are right. 'The omnipotence of thoughts, the overvaluation of mental processes as compared with reality, is seen to have unrestricted play in the emotional life of neurotic patients ... This behaviour as well as the superstitions which he practises in ordinary life, reveals his resemblance to the savages, who believe they can alter the external world by mere thinking.' But the lesson of psychoanalysis is that 'we have to give up that prejudice in favour of external reality, that underestimation of internal reality, which is the attitude of the ego in ordinary civilized life today'. That 'advance', that 'adaptation to reality', which consists in the child's learning to distinguish between the wish and the deed, between external facts and his feelings about them has to be undone, or overcome. 'Mental Things are alone Real.'

Freud, *Totem and Taboo*, 87. Isaacs, 'The Nature and Function of Phantasy', 82. Blake, *A Vision of the Last Judgement*, 617.

The real world, which is not the world of the reality principle, is the world where thoughts are omnipotent, where no distinction is drawn between wish and deed. As in the New Testament: 'Ye have heard that it was said by them of old time, Thou shalt not commit adultery: But I say unto you, That whosoever looketh on a woman to lust after her hath committed adultery with her already in his heart.' Or Freud: 'It is a matter of indifference who actually committed the crime; psychology is only concerned to know who desired it emotionally and who welcomed it when it was done. And for that reason all of the brothers [of the family Karamazov; or of the human family] are equally guilty.'

Matthew V, 27–28. Freud, 'Dostoevsky and Parricide', 236.

The outcome, then, of Freud or of Dostoevsky, is a radical rejection of government of the reality principle. Freud sees the collision between psychoanalysis and our penal institutions: 'It is not psychology that deserves to be laughed at, but the procedure of judicial inquiry.' Reik, in a moment of apocalyptic optimism, declares that 'The enormous importance attached by criminal justice to the deed as such derives from a cultural phase which is approaching its end.' A social order based on the reality principle, a social order which draws a distinction between the wish and the deed, between the criminal and the righteous, is still a kingdom of darkness. It is only as long as a distinction is made between real and imaginary murders that real murders are worth committing; as long as the universal guilt is denied, there is a need to resort to individual crime, as a form of confession, and a request for punishment. The strength of sin is the law. Heraclitus said, the law is a wall.

Freud, 'Dostoevsky and Parricide', 236. Reik, *The Compulsion to Confess*, 155. I Corinthians XV, 56.

Psychoanalysis manages to salvage its allegiance to the (false) reality principle by its use of the word *fantasy* to describe the contents of the unconscious ('unconscious fantasies'). It is in the unconscious that 'we are members one of another', 'we incorporate each other'. As long as we accept the reality principle, the reality of the boundary between inside and outside, we do not 'really' incorporate each other. It is then in fantasy that we 'project' or 'introject'; it is then purely mental, and mental means not real; the unconscious then contains not the hidden reality of human nature but some (aberrant) fancies, or fantasies. But the unconscious is the true psychic reality. The language of psychoanalysis becomes self-contradictory: 'Fantasy has real effects, not only on the inner world of the mind, but also on the external world of the subject's bodily development and behaviour.' 'When contrasted with external bodily realities, the fantasy, like other mental activities, is a figment since it cannot be touched or handled or seen; yet it is real in the experience of the subject.'

Isaacs, 'The Nature and Function of Phantasy', 99.
Cf Klein, 'Notes on Some Schizoid Mechanisms', 298.

'Fantasy' is not real; is mental; is inside. The psychoanalytic model of two principles of mental functioning still adheres to the Lockean and Cartesian notion of human experience as consisting of mental events, inside the mind, and distinct from external, material, reality. Freud says, 'With the introduction of the reality principle one mode of thought-activity was split off; it was kept free from reality-testing and remained subordinated to the pleasure principle alone. This is the act of fantasy-making.' Reality-testing grows out of fantasy-making — 'it is now a question whether something which is present in the ego as an image can also be rediscovered in reality'. And in the final 'reality-ego' — that is to say, the separate self of private property 'Once more it will be seen, the question is one of *external* and *internal*. What is not real, what is merely imagined or subjective, is only *internal*; while on the other hand what is real is also present externally.' Then the basic stock-in-trade of the mind is images, fantasies, obtained by the power of the mind to revive the image of former perceptions, ie, to hallucinate, as in dreams. The nucleus of mental life is then a spectral double of the external world, on the model of the dream; a world of images; a mental, an imaginary internal subjective unreal world, which may or may not reflect (correspond to) the bodily real external and material world.

Freud, 'The Two Principles in Mental Functioning', 16–17; 'Negation', 183.

In rejecting the split world of the reality principle — 'Two Horn'd Reasoning, Cloven Fiction' — Blake said, 'Mental Things are alone Real; what is call'd Corporeal, Nobody Knows of its Dwelling Place.' There is, then, after all a sense in which the body is not real; but the body that is not real is the false body of the separate self, the reality-ego. That false body we must cast off; in order to begin the Odyssey of consciousness in quest of its own true body.

Blake, *The Gates of Paradise*, 770; *A Vision of the Last Judgement*, 617.

The fallacy in the false body is Whitehead's Fallacy of Simple Location; which is the notion that 'material can be said to be *here* in space and *here* in time, or *here* in space-time, in a perfectly definite sense which does not require for its explanation any reference to other regions of space-time'. The fallacy of Simple Location is to accept the boundary as real: to accept as real that separateness which the reality principle takes to be the essence of a body or a thing, the essence of the body as thing.

Whitehead, *Science and the Modern World*, 62; cf 72.

The reality principle says, if *here* then not *there*; if inside, then not outside. The alternative to dualism is dialectics; that is to say, love—

> Two distincts, division none:
> Number there in love was slain.

Whitehead says that reality is unification: reality is events (not things), which are prehensive unifications; gathering diversities together in a unity; not simply *here*, or *there*, but a gathering of here and there (subject and object) into a unity.

Shakespeare, 'The Phoenix and the Turtle.'
Cf Whitehead, *Science and the Modern World*, 86–92.

Reality is not things (dead matter, or heavy stuff), in simple location. Reality is energy, or instinct; Eros and Thanatos, 'the "prehensive" and "separative" characters of space time'; one sea of energy: 'In the analogy with Spinoza, his one substance is for me the one underlying activity of realization individualizing itself in an interlocking plurality of modes.' One substance, the id or It.

Whitehead, *Science and the Modern World*, 80, 87.

The human body is not a thing or substance, given, but a continuous creation (Nietzsche: *beständige Schöpfung*). The human body is an energy system, Schilder's postural model, which is never a complete structure: never static; is in perpetual inner self-construction and self-destruction; we destroy in order to make it new. Destroy this temple, and in three days I will raise it up.

Cf Schilder, *The Image and Appearance of the Human Body*, 15–16, 193, 241, 287, 166. John II, 19.

Reality does not consist of substances, solidly and stolidly each in its own place; but in events, activity; activity which crosses the boundary; action at a distance. Whitehead finds his paradigm in a text from Francis Bacon: 'It is certain that all bodies whatsoever, though they have no sense, yet they have perception . . . And this perception is sometimes at a distance, as well as upon the touch; as when the loadstone draweth iron: or flame naphtha of Babylon, a great distance off.' Compare Nietzsche: 'Man kann Druck und Stoss selber nicht "erklären", man wird die *actio in distans* nicht los.'

Whitehead, *Science and the Modern World*, 52, 86. Nietzsche, *Aus dem Nachlass*, 455.

The 'postural model' of the body consists of 'lines of energy', 'psychic streams', Freud's 'libidinal cathexes', which are, like electricity, action at a distance; flux, influx, reflux; connecting different erogenous points in the body (the psychosexual organizations); and connecting one body with other bodies. 'The space in and around the postural model is not the space of physics. The body-image incorporates objects or spreads itself in space.' 'In an individual's own postural image many postural images of others are melted together.' 'We could describe the relation between the body-images of different persons under the metaphor of a magnetic field with stream-lines going in all directions.' A magnetic field, of action at a distance; or a magical field; 'magic action is an action which influences the body-image irrespective of the actual distance in space'. In magic action there is a space connexion between the most distant things –

> For head with foot hath private amity,
> And both with moons and tides.

Herbert, 'Man.' Schilder, *Image and Appearance of the Human Body*, 213, 216, 234, 236; cf 16, 137, 241, 252.

The processes of identification and incorporation known to psychoanalysis conform to Lévy-Bruhl's pattern of mystical (magical) participation in primitive mentality; 'The opposition between the one and the many, the same and another, etc, does not impose upon this mentality the necessity of affirming one of these terms if the other be denied.' 'Identification' is participation; self and not-self identified; an extra-sensory link between self and not-self. Identification is action at a distance; or *telepathy*; the centre of Freud's interest in the 'Occult'. If body, corporeal substance, is taken to be in Simple Location (as Freud took it to be) then the question of telepathy is whether thoughts or spiritual beings can exist with no ascertainable connexion with a corporeal body. But Freud himself said, that 'by inserting the unconscious between the physical and what has been regarded as the mental, psychoanalysis has prepared the way for the acceptance of such processes as telepathy.' The question is not the existence of disembodied spirit, but the modalities of bodily action at a distance.

Lévy-Bruhl cited in Schilder, *Image and Appearance of the Human Body*, 274. Freud, *New Introductory Lectures*, 75–76.
Cf Jones, *Sigmund Freud*, III, 402. Barfield, *Saving the Appearances*, 32–34.

The hidden psychic reality contained in the unconscious does not consist of fantasies, but of action at a distance, psychic streams, projects, in a direction: germs of movement; seeds of living thought. These seeds are Freud's 'unconscious ideas', which are concrete ideas; that is to say ideas of things, and not simply of the words, or images inside the mind corresponding to the things outside. Concrete ideas are cathexes of things: 'The Unconscious contains the thing-cathexes of objects, the first and true object-cathexes'; the original telepathy.

Freud, 'The Unconscious', 134.

The 'thing-cathexes of the objects, the first and true object-cathexes'; 'a proto-mental system in which physical and mental activity is undifferentiated'. A kind of body-thinking, 'at first without visual or other plastic images'; 'unconscious knowledge', carried in deeper centres of the body than head or eye; a knowledge not derived from the senses, extra-sensory; sub-sensible or super-sensible. For example, that unconscious knowledge about sexual intercourse between parents attributed by psychoanalysis to babes in arms. 'The world of thought at those levels is quite alien to our own, so that it is quite impossible to reproduce them in words as one seems to perceive them in analysis. Let us consider, for instance, what a demand we are making on anyone who has not been able to convince himself of the fact in an analysis, if we ask him to believe that a small child becomes like his mother because he thinks he has eaten her up, and that, if he thinks he is being tormented or "poisoned" by this internal mother, he can in some circumstances spit her out again. The details of this kind of "body-thinking" of which we have a glimpse in analysis and which is bound up with ideas of incorporation must perpetually evade any exact comprehension.'

Isaacs, 'The Nature and Function of Phantasy', 92.
Cf Klein, 'Criminal Tendencies in Normal Children', 188. Fenichel, 'Pre-oedipal Phase in Girls', 242. Bion, 'Group Dynamics: a review', 449. Klein, *Psychoanalysis of Children*, 188–9, 296–7.

In the deepest level of the unconscious we find not fantasies, but telepathy. That is to say, the deepest and still-unconscious level of our being is not modelled on the dream; in which fission, duplication, is the basic mechanism; in which we withdraw from the world into a second world of (visual) images, projected.

> Reuben slept on Penmaenmawr and Levi slept on Snowdon.
> Their eyes, their ears, nostrils and tongues roll outward, they behold
> What is within now seen without.

To overcome the dualism would be to awake out of sleep; to arise from the dead.

Blake, *Night* II, 52–4.
Cf Schilder, *Image and Appearance of the Human Body*, 51–2, 60. Roheim, *Gates of the Dream*, 20, 58, 116. Ephesians V, 14; Romans XIII, 11.

It is not schizophrenia but normality that is split-minded; in schizophrenia the false boundaries are disintegrating. 'From pathology we have come to know a large number of states in which the boundary lines between ego and outside world become uncertain.' Schizophrenics are suffering from the truth. ' "Everyone knows" the patient's thoughts: a regression to a stage before the first lie.' Schizophrenia testifies to 'experiences in which the discrimination between the consciousness of self and the consciousness of the object was entirely suspended, the ego being no longer distinct from the object; the subject no longer distinct from the object; the self and the world were fused in an inseparable total complex'. Schizophrenic thought is 'adualistic'; lack of ego boundaries makes it impossible to set limits to the process of identification with the environment. The schizophrenic world is one of mystical participation; an 'indescribable extension of inner sense'; 'uncanny feelings of reference'; occult psychosomatic influences and powers; currents of electricity, or sexual attraction – action at a distance.

Freud, *Civilization and Its Discontents*, 11. Tausk, 'The "Influencing Machine" in Schizophrenia', 535. Storch, *Primitive Archaic Forms*, 31, 61, 62.
Cf Sèchehaye, *A New Psychotherapy in Schizophrenia*, 134. Roheim, *Magic and Schizophrenia*, 101.

'The patient connects herself with everybody.' 'You and I, are we not the same? ... Sometimes I cannot tell myself from other people ... It seemed to me as though I no longer existed in my own person alone, as though I were one with the all.' In a patient called Julie, 'all perception seemed to threaten confusion with the object. "That's the rain. I could be the rain." "That chair – that wall. I could be that wall. It's a terrible thing for a girl to be a wall." '

Storch, *Primitive Archaic Forms*, 27–8. Laing, *Divided Self*, 217.
Cf Schilder, *Image and Appearance of the Human Body*, 215. Roheim, *Magic and Schizophrenia*, 101, 115.

Definitions are boundaries; schizophrenics pass beyond the reality principle into a world of symbolic connexions: 'all things lost their definite boundaries, became iridescent with many-coloured significances.' Schizophrenics pass beyond ordinary language (the language of the reality principle) into a truer, more symbolic language: 'I'm thousands. I'm an in-divide-you-all. I'm a no un (ie, nun, no-un, no one).' The language of *Finnegans Wake*. James Joyce and his daughter, crazy Lucia, these two are one. The god is Dionysus, the mad truth.

Storch, *Primitive Archaic Forms*, 62. Laing, *Divided Self*, 223.
Cf Sèchehaye, *A New Psychotherapy for Schizophrenia*, 135–150. Ellmann, *James Joyce*, 692, 692n. Roheim, *Magic and Schizophrenia*, 94, 108.

The mad truth: the boundary between sanity and insanity is a false one. The proper outcome of psychoanalysis is the abolition of the boundary, the healing of the split, the integration of the human race. The proper posture is to listen to and learn from lunatics, as in former times— 'We cannot deny them a measure of that awe with which madmen were regarded by people of ancient times.' The insane do not share 'the normal prejudice in favour of external reality'. The 'normal prejudice in favour of external reality' can be sustained only by ejecting (projecting) these dissidents from the human race; scotomizing them, keeping them out of sight, in asylums; insulating the so-called reality principle from all evidence to the contrary.

Freud, *New Introductory Lectures*, 80.
Cf Storch, *Primitive Archaic Forms*, 97.

Dionysus, the mad god, breaks down the boundaries; releases the prisoners; abolishes repression; and abolishes the *principium individuationis*, substituting for it the unity of man and the unity of man with nature. In this age of schizophrenia, with the atom, the individual self, the boundaries disintegrating, there is, for those who would save our souls, the ego-psychologists, 'the Problem of Identity'. But the breakdown is to be made into a breakthrough; as Conrad said, in the destructive element immerse. The soul that we can call our own is not a real one. The solution to the problem of identity is, get lost. Or as it says in the New Testament: 'He that findeth his own psyche shall lose it, and he that loseth his psyche for my sake shall find it.'

Matthew X, 39.

KEN KESEY was born in La Junta, Colorado, in 1935 and has lived on the West Coast most of his life. Author of two well-received novels, *One Flew Over the Cuckoo's Nest* and *Sometimes a Great Notion*, Kesey organized a group, called The Merry Pranksters, who toured the United States for three years filming the country and the people as they went. Accused and later convicted of possessing marijuana, Kesey hid out in Mexico until the autumn of 1966.

letters from mexico

KEN KESEY

Larry:

Phone calls to the state min. 8 bucks a piece besides was ever a good board to bounce my favourite ball of bullshit offen, it was you. And with the light steady enough to instruct where the end of the breakwater is out across the bay, ocean calm and warm fifty feet from mine here in outside under tarp beside that cursed bus and kids asleep inside, first time in some moons I feel like bouncing a jubilant ball.

I feel good. Healthy, tanned, standing happily tall again after too many stooped hours ambling stiffly about fink ridden Mexico as the white-haired, bespecticled and of course mild-mannered reporter, Steve Lamb, I am chancing here a stretch or two in full daylight as Sol Almande, Prankster Extraordinaire.

Is relatively now. In between here and whatever furthest time back my pen touches lies many an experience, no small amount of achievements and a tidy sum of insights. I was never one to happen through the market place *any* place on this world without grabbing on to whatever my fancy and my resourcefulness could compromise upon.

cut to

(longshot right down on rooftop of San Francisco North Beach – levels, ladders, asphalt squares. At first glance almost a set – semi-symbolic University theatre clever Jewish director type of stage set – then a man and a young woman interrupt the parallel arrangement of horizontal surfaces. On a thin and rather ragged mattress, 1½ inch foam in blue cover, shape indicates it was a pad for the back of station wagon. The man has all the usual stigmata of the bohemian in vogue at that period ... a bohemian crowding that age when 'its time the goddam ninny stopped actin like them snotty Vietniks and dope fiends and acted his age'. No longer even the argument of ideals and escape, just pure social outrage, voiced by the fleecy image of daddy-mama-and-other-dear-but-square-ones.

(He has partially balded and has been sick long enough it is difficult to know if he is 25 or 35. Hair boils wildly from his head in thick kinky blond locks. His neck and torso are thick and muscular though he is not short as those built thus usually are. His face is excited but tired, lop-sided with the strain faces show after too long forced to smile diplomat-ically. The girl almost as big as her companion, matching his six feet in height but not his weight. Her hair is long and reddish brown; dark appearing cool black except where the light occasionally sets off the reddish lustre. Her eyes almost identical hue, and quite large. Rather like the eyes of an Irish setter pup just turning from awkward carefree frolic to the task of devotion. Her face is young and pretty despite a too broadness and her manner is ornery and fun-loving as she and her companion banter over the plans for the forthcoming Trips Festival. Their talk concerns personalities and wiring problems.)

'With that big new speaker' – the girl is on the optimistic side of the banter – 'we'll be able to wire that place so you can hear a *flea* fart!'

'Hasn't happened yet,' the man says. Pessimism nowhere near the strength of her mood.

'With this many days to get it set up? Always before we were in the hall that night and maybe set up before we finished in the morning. We got almost a week till Friday.'

'I hope Stewart gets that Albright business straight. Fillmore was enough of us getting booted out at two.'

'Just when we got this system working good,' she agreed, a bit too unanimously.

'Just when we got everything to where we could quit playing with wires and start playing. No more of that shit. Stewart's got to have the cops, managers, everybody cooled completely before we get so deep into it that it'll be obvious we don't plan to pull out.'

'Because without the Pranksters the Festival will be just another rock and roll dance.'

'Just another Family Dog.'

'Right!' the girl agrees this time her tone shrewd and curt as well as confident.

The pair lie on their stomachs chins on hands looking down 4 storeys to the alley below. As they talk they each occasionally scrape from the asphalt rooftop large gravels to toss down (and see?

Cut back now

See? Just as the pair see a police car pull in, park in the alley, and red light in the hillside drive 50 yards to my left blinks in the dawn – do I learn *anything?* Or once again lie loaded and disbelieving as two cops climb 5 storeys to drag me to cooler?

Oh well; a man could get piles sit too long one spot.

Stay tuned,
Kesey

Larry: This at Puerto Vallarta not long after news leak set me scrambling.

For a long time now he had been sitting watching a fruitless surf, sitting sadly staring out with a swarm of situations and the fact that he could illiterate up a f—ing storm in the flush, flush, lush lush lush of Mexico.

He had seen a fish, yellow tail tuna's broken leap. Two times now. Both times had been good. And he hoped that he could see it leap again without turning into Hemmingway. But his hopes proved vain. For he went back and rewrote rearranged picked and changed for a full half-hour when it lept the third.

And after that he was compelled to spend another ten until clang! Somebody! not just humble hermit crabs any more but a tourist a noise a *federale?* sound of jeep. Clang Clang Clang sudden reappearance of hatted American followed by mex! roar again of jeep – then – ah – the two turn, leave. WHOP! of surf again into that crack left by the fear change of their leaving. Still around though, close. What if they should connect his sitting alone writing with the KESEY CAVORTS IN PUERTO VALLARTA headline? He opened his other pad, let the coloured part show; always do a quick sketch pass off image as artist.

And beneath these everlasting the call I hear. Grit and take it. Maybe

I gotta kind of grit-your-teeth-and-grin-John-Wayney sorta zen. And sometimes the third 'It's all shit' followed by, slower, slyer, 'but it's all goood shit'.

Until he achieved a levelling with a three-sided palm hut housing empty bottles an empty cot and doodlebug holes thick and heavy about in the dust indicating a bad year for ants. Also some of those scrawny trees with those greeny things – not coconuts but mangoes or papas or one of those tropical gizmos he hadn't got to know because he hadn't really come to believing in them yet.

'Wellsir, this place might just hold me a spell,' he drawled and took off his shirt. Ten minutes later he was smoking the 3 roaches rolled together in a cone and examining with his knife one of the green gizmos as it bled meekly white in his lap. The innards were white and meek and full of pale little rabbit pills. A papaya, he surmised, and mighty young papaya to be put to the sword, let alone the tooth. He hid its remains lest some Mex uncle tom hermit come back up to his shack and see his prize papaya caught redhanded dead before its prime, unzipped his fly to let his sweating nuts air out, and leaned back into twilighting crickets to ring his planetarium, see what the next moment was going to bring.

And was suddenly alert to a rare alarm – 'Ritual, Ritual,' it whispered, faint. The alarm starts and startles beat an even bigger fear. That he wasn't taking care of his job. Mex returns shorts swims suspicious – maybe sketch now? And had they put out a reward for Chrissakes every f—ing peon in the *state* after his ass and 75 pesos? Okay. If this is them straight out the surf over the rocks he'd checked out earlier go under turn sharp left far under as he could swim *voices!* clang clang again this could be the show un-f—ing believable as it seemed but by god it was keep loose or get busted maybe five years five years even staying outside bars playing stacked low game as pawn not even player, five years against possibility of getting snuffed while staying loose. That pat. All the time. And he knew why. He was at last being forced to the brink of his professed beliefs. Of all that he had babbled about for years now being brought up continually for actual down-to-the-wire testing!

'OOO OOOO!' God almighty! Now some fool over the rocks there wailing like a ghost! 'OOO OOO!' A signal? Door slams. Man is hot again. Shows up again take out pen and draw the f—er fast. Only possibility against true foe as well as 3rd level foe like american fink. *Draw* him. *Write* him. *Imagine* him into plot always and then believe all that crap you've been claiming about altering by accepting. Believe it! Or you are a goner, m'boy, a walking dead man for evermore fading finally inaudible like the voices mumbling litanies in the cathedral!

So having vowed thus – and having checked to find the Mex working on the road above – he resolutely dug up his stash, lit up the next to last joint in all of Mexico, and just leaning back to embark once again upon the will of God – Ka-BOOOM! – up the hill dynamiting? Now that's a ka-boom of a different colour. I'd go watch them do a little blasting. 'And have every Gringo driving past' another voice interrupted 'pointing at you gawking there's Ken *Kee-zee*, Mabel!'

In short, this young, handsome, successful, happily-married-three-lovely-children father, was a fear-crazed dope fiend in flight to avoid prosecution on 3 felonies god knows how many misdemeanours and seeking at the same time to sculpt a new satori from an old surf and – in even shorter – mad as a hatter.

Once an athlete so valued he had been given the job of calling signals from the line and risen into contention for nationwide amature wrestling crown, now he didn't know if he could do a dozen push-ups. Once possessor of phenominal bank account and money waving from every hand now it was all his poor wife could do to scrape together 8.00 dollars to send as gettaway money to Mexico. But a few years previous he had been listed in *Who's Who* and asked to speak to such auspacous gatherings as the Wellsley Club in Dahlahs and now they wouldn't even allow him to speak at a VDC gathering. What was it that had brought a man so high of promise to so low a state in so short a time? Well the answer can be found in just one short word, my friends, in just one all-welused sylable.

Dope!

And while it may be claimed by some of the addled advocates of these chemicals that our hero is known to have indulged in drugs *before* his literary success we must point out that there was evidence of his literary prowess *well before* the advent of the so called psychedelic into his life but *no evidence at all* of any of the lunitic thinking that we find thereafter!

> (Oh yeah, the wind hums
> time ago – time ago—
> the rafter drums and the walls see
> ... and there's a door to that bird
> in the sa-a-a-apling sky
> time ago by—
>
> Oh yeah the surf giggles
> time ago time ago
> of under things killed when
> bad was banished and all the
> doors to the birds vanished
> time ago then.)

And thought then 'Let my winds of whatever thru and out of this
man-place paranoia be damned and into the jungle—
  'Where its *really* scary.'
  The road he'd reached was a Mexican fantasy that had petered out for
the same reason his heart and lungs were working so hard now – too
steep. He sat down in the road looking out at the sea. No cars had been
along the road – what reason? it petered out right there? when? time
ago? – since the last rainfall.
  The sky had clouded. The sun, nearing its setting, vanished through
the clouds into the sea thump! a car on the road above. Stops. Starts.
Probably the workers but – he stands, effecting a satori smile—

> If you gonna ride the
> wind
> Ride the fat and ride the thin
> Ride the soft and ride the boney
> time ago——time ago
> because there ain't no other
>   poney
> time ago agin.

. . . Someone approaching!
  He waits. Long time. It creaks closer and comes out in the very last of
the jungles fading light. A little honeybear of a thing. He is delighted
and tries to whistle it over but it turns as soon as it senses his presence
and sckuffles back. And the mosquitoes get him up and moving
again.

                                                        Kesey

Larry:
  Isn't it a drag? interrupted right in the middle of the past to have to
out into the world and actually *deal* with it. The past don't come The
End Twentieth Century Fox and you can get up walk home and tell
people who it was because it's over.
  Because it isn't over. Up on the same hill I saw red lights. To shit, and
while I'm at it peek over the edge see what the FB Eyes are looking at
this morning. *Plus* 'don't forget the San Mateo Sheriff's office, a lot of
them are taking vacations in Mexico for the specific purpose of bringing
you in.'
  Is some of the news Faye brings from USA.
  By the time I get sit it's full grey dawn. A slate fan of clouds rattle
above the Sierra Madre Occidental. Egrets gulls and grackles rise calling

from the backwater across the highway, flapping overhead to the beach behind mc to early-bird the worm. Bells ring across the bay in town 20 or 30 times – mexican chime code still a complete mystery. Be able to crack it in a few weeks tho, sir; at most one month. 'A *month*! By God, Mister, you think I want information of such stature in time for the *Universal Wake*? Strange vehicles sculking around the rocks not five minutes ago *who knows* they're cops American or Mexican? A manta ray cruzing the beach like a frigging doberman out of the K9 Korp, and out in the bay some brand new contrivance like never before floated water before – great rustproof triangle would cover a *city block* with all three points of the vessle running black and yellow steel pools big around as these tugs that went out to nose around and were waved off *sticking straight into the sky 3 times as high as the hotel over in town yonder —* and you tell me *a month*? Well, mister, you figure that bell code pronto. I need to know the time within the frigging hour or you'll be playing with those slide rules and charts up in *Ancorage*!'

The old captain pivots smartly and stalks off, returning the frightened salute of the younger officer who was stammering at the departure.

The horizon was colouring now in the east; it reminded the officer of paintings speed painters at Bakersfield County Fair splashed onto white fibreboard in one minute flat – 3 dollars apiece 2 for five bucks – still hanging when he enlisted; a rectangular sunrise, one on each side of FDR.

The bells chimed again. Barely moments since the last ringing. No ryme or reason, pattern or possibility. 'In an *hour*?' In fact, for all anybody knew, it might be the Police Chiefs Idiot daughter at the rope again. He shivered. To have to check *that* out again. And find an armless and legless unfortunate – result of food poisoning; the mother 2 months after conception nearly dieing from a can of bad green beans paralysing development of the embryonic limbs and producing a, well, child with an alarmingly lovely face – features that might have posed for Leonardo's *Pietà* despite the fact that closer examination revealed the mouth to be but two beautiful lips sealed forever over a skull that showed no evidence of an oral opening whatsoever. Below the cute nose the bone ran in a solid fortress to the chin. A quick tracheotomy by a clever intern was all that saved the poor creature from asphyxiation moments after birth. X-rays and a 3/16 in carpenter's auger finally afforded the infant the luxury of breathing from her nostrils instead of a hole between her collar-bones, but a mouth the doctors were unable to provide. X-rays showed a complete absence of tongue, glottis, throat, or any cavity whatsoever where the mouth might be jenny-rigged.

'We're feeding the little darling through her nose,' the doctors infor-med the grief-crazed mother (the father, so claimed those of the sisters at the cathedral, unfortunately unhampered by any oral malfunction, who just happened to be the one who had purchased the evil can of beans, expired not many weeks after the birth as a result of botulism – rumour had it he left the hospital immediately after his legless, armless, and mouthless offspring, to buy all the canned green beans the market-place could provide, take out a large life insurance policy (which proved worthless owing to a ridiculously small mistake made in the forms by the distraught father) and lock himself in a secret out-of-town hotel hide-away eating beans, letting them set, opened, adding houseflies and horned toads, recapping them, recapping and days later eating until he either successfully bred and consumed the proper poison, or until his system surrendered under the constant onslaught of beans and flies).

'But if you disregard the child's ah deficiencies,' the doctors consoled the grief-freaked mother when they decided she might try to follow her husband's lead, 'she is a very *very* lovely child.'

'*Already* she has the most expressive eyes I've *ever* in all my *years* witnessed,' a kind old nurse added. 'She'll be a beautiful girl! The two of you will do fine. God will see to it.'

This was adequate to drive mother and infant from the canned goods into the nunnery, where the mother found St Teresa and crocheting, and the child did grow into a very *very* lovely girl. The medical men in their haste to get a potential suicide and/or mercy killing off the hospital grounds had benevolently neglected to inform the mother that the X-rays indicated very little more space for brain than mouth, and the girl had exhausted this area by the time she was 3 or 4. After that the mother or one of the other sisters could frequently be seen pulling a wagon about the cathedral in which was propped a face that grew yearly more and more strikingly beautiful.

'Who gives a snap how *pretty* the girl is,' the young officer grumbled, returning to his office in the decoding department, 'when you climb ten miles of treacherous ol ladder to find her swinging on the bell-rope *like that*.' He shivered again. 'I mean who cares if she's *Hayley Mills*?'

Though bulging from the simple mock-habit sewn for the girl and torn (just like last time, by god . . .) from neck to belly button, were two of the most inviting prizes ever to quiver at the end of a bell-rope.

'But who cares if she's Jayne Mansfield or even June *Wilkinson*? C'mere you—' Again he had to carry the creature over one shoulder as he descended the precarious ladder. And just as before her lewd buzom was forced against his cheek or – when he tried to hold her away from his sweat-soaked face – that tongueless mouth, and those large elo-quent eyes smiled at him so suggestively he was forced to confess some grave doubts concerning the girl's reputed imbecility.

'But what I can't phathom,' he panted, 'is how you get up that ladder and get *out* on that bell-rope that way.'

A rung broke like a dry pistol crack; half-falling he grasped the ladder pole with one hand and lurching snatched out to secure a better purchase on his load with the other hand. Which fell full over one of the full crimson nippled breasts. As soon as he regained a solid rung once again he quickly resumed his former and more decorous hold on his load.

He made no mention of the incident – it was an accident, a slip! – to the Mother Superior nor to the anonymous ear that listened to the mundane sins he droned into the confessional box. Nor even thought of it again himself the rest of the day as he prepared his report for the captain.

But in bed that evening, locked alone in his quarters, the discovery finally burst loudly into his consciousness. 'That – her – *it* felt *back*!'

And barely slept at all that night for the listening out the window across the bay.

Little love story just for variety.

I've still heard nothing from Estrella. Plan was he'd contact me through alias at Telegrafo in Manzanillo. Don't know *what's* happening (fear Rohan didn't send cash. Lawyers someway always suspect other lawyers being crooks. Wonder why.) But I like Estrella. He's pompous and prideful and *just* right.

Did I ever thank you?

Kesey